Tim Jordan

GLOW

**ANGRY
ROBOT**

ANGRY ROBOT
An imprint of Watkins Media Ltd

Unit 11, Shepperton House
89–93 Shepperton Road
London N1 3DF
UK

angryrobotbooks.com
twitter.com/angryrobotbooks
Glowworms grow worms

An Angry Robot paperback original, 2021

Edited by Paul Simpson and Gemma Creffield
Cover by Glen Wilkins

ISBN 978 0 85766 843 1
Ebook ISBN 978 0 85766 887 5

Printed and bound in the United Kingdom by TJ Books Limited

9 8 7 6 5 4 3 2 1

MIX
Paper from
responsible sources
FSC
www.fsc.org   FSC® C013056

For Mum and Dad, and for Joanna

CHAPTER 1

Rex

Rex woke and looked straight into the eyes of a dead man.

He screamed through clenched teeth, swallowing the sound, muffling it with his tongue so it exploded safe and silent inside the barrel of his chest. The mantra he'd lived by for years clattered through his skull: *Act dead, act crazy, run like hell... fight!*

He ran.

Peeling his head off the pavement, Rex rolled and stumbled upright, but something held him down. The corpse! It loomed from the gutter, hand clamped to Rex's elbow, head slapping against his ankles as if devouring him feet-first. His scream came louder, harder, seeping through his conditioned restraint like steam from a blown engine.

His feet found traction in the mud and suddenly he was running, the corpse grinding along on its knees as they blundered from wall to wall like drunks in a storm, until his foot caught on a downpipe and he tumbled backwards into the mud, hauling the corpse across his chest.

Act dead.

He lay still, reading the sounds of rain and flowing water, heart pounding, eyes scanning the starlit alleyway, brick walls and barred windows, the slick, wet pavement of vitrified-pumice tiles that cobbled the streets of Coriolis City.

In that sodden stillness, he glanced down at the dead man's head. *Who are you?* He asked using one of his inner voices. The man looked familiar, but death did strange things to people, stripping away identity leaving just bones, fur and meat.

The dead hand remained attached to Rex's elbow with the ratchet-grip of rigor mortis. Plastic zip-ties wound around the hand, looping through the fingers securing it to the crook of Rex's elbow. *Right in the dead area... where the needles go.*

His free hand took on its own life, caressing his head, tracing jutting cheekbones through days of stubble growth. Scar lines splintered out from his eye sockets. The same lines he saw reflected on that dead face: the lines of an addict, a user, a junkie, a man whose good times and luck had all been washed away. His hand touched his ear and he jumped – larger than expected.

"Stop that!" he yelled. The hand dropped away, limp by his side.

He remembered sleeping, probably for days judging by the weight of his headache. He never slept until he had to, until he was dead on his feet. Sleeping was terrible: a single long nightmare of falling through concentric rings of darkness as things grabbed at him. Fingers and spikes and words like barbs ripped away at his flesh as he fell until there was nothing left. But something always kept falling, some essence remained after everything was shredded and gone.

No, he never slept unless he had to, or something made him. He checked his head for unfamiliar bumps. Nothing; just raging pain like a hangover of a hundred days. He cupped his hand and sniffed his breath: vomit and some toxic mixture of flammable spirits. He spat at the dead man. *Drinking buddy?*

He eased up off the wet pavement, kneeling, pushing the corpse off to the side. Rain pattered his head. A gentle sound in the night. He tilted his face up and embraced the cool water as the mud washed from his face.

A knife hilt jutted from the dead man's temple. *My knife!* His heart thudded. *I'm a murderer? No. No. Couldn't be.* He shook his head, imagining his bad thoughts flying away with the clods of mud.

The knife made a sucking noise as he eased it free, wiping the blood on the man's tattered jacket. He frisked the body for something, anything... drugs, booze, money... *nothing*. No one out here had anything. The dead eyes were sunken, wide, and deeply sad. Wisps of beard dotted the cheeks and strands of muddy gray hair slicked the pale scalp. His teeth were stumps, tombstones in a fetid swamp.

A dog howled in the distance. A tremble passed up Rex's spine, meeting the warm trickle of rain running down it. He rapped his knuckles on his skull. *How did I get here?* His head felt like a bottle, drunk dry and smashed against a wall. His memories were just hopeful fragments, impossible to make whole.

He gripped the knife and jabbed at the zip-ties, pricking his wrist and drawing blood. *Shit!* Even tiny wounds killed out here.

A flash of movement dropped him flat next to the body. A cloaked figure moved into the alley and stood silhouetted against the dull light of encroaching dawn.

Everyone inside his head knew that look: *A stinking lich.* A drug-crazed cyborg that drained bodies dry, living or dead, harvesting whatever blood and drugs were available, then leaving the husks lined along the gutters like sacks of bones awaiting the militia's trash collection trucks.

Act dead, act crazy, run like hell, fight!

He eyed the zip-ties and the dead body. He assessed its weight and the distance down the alley to what he hoped was a main street. He didn't even know where he was... Coriolis City somewhere, Welkin District? That warren of nasty side streets that ringed the center of downtown.

The lich paused, its hooded head segueing sideways as if triangulating Rex's range. *It's seen me. Fuck. Acting dead, crazy or fighting aren't going to work here.*

The lich stepped forward, throwing out an arm that might have held a gun.

Run like hell!

Everyone in his head ran with him, running by consensus, as no one remembered exactly how running worked. Like a sack of offal on legs, sloshing and twisting, defying all attempts to move in a straight line. The corpse dragged behind like an anchor, catching on curbs, downpipes and doorways.

The lich closed in. Rex felt its headwind.

"I got nothing!" he yelled, lurching down another side alley hauling the dead body, wondering whose arm would snap off first.

Fearing the gunsight lining up on his back, he turned again, weaving a winding course through the maze of alleys. He stopped, chest heaving, and retched air and bile into a corner. He eyed the knife in his hand and his reed-thin arm; a cut here, a slash there? *No time. Just run.*

Another turn, and another, dogs still howling, some of them inside of his head. The rain grew stronger, beating his face, blinding his eyes. Lightning flashed and the lich was only meters behind, hands outstretched, reaching, reaching. *Should have played dead... should have–*

He skidded to a halt as something unfolded from the wall in front, dropping its brickwork camouflage and unfurling its hidden layers of plastic and metal, shimmering with dangerous energy. It came straight toward him, long, spindly legs grazing the ground as a huge fan whirled on top where its head should have been. The thing lifted off the ground and hovered down the alley like a child's balloon.

Lich behind him, machine in front, Rex flailed wildly against doors and barred windows, ripping at boards and grilles. A barricade of coiled wire and wooden planks blocked the only side street. With his single, useable hand, he dug out a hole and dove in, jerking the corpse desperately behind him until it jammed, halting his escape.

He could see the lich through the gaps in the barricade as the machine lifted higher on its fan, coasting over the lich's head. His twin foes ignored each other, both solely focused on reaching him. He pushed his feet further into the barricade, finding a stout point of resistance and heaved, twisting and rolling until the corpse's arm finally snapped through, then a shoulder, and the neck. But the head locked everything in place.

"Come on, come on!" he bellowed, rain still pelting, slime and muck robbing his valuable traction.

Something slipped, something in the mess of wreckage gave a few precious inches. He pulled harder still, free hand slashing at the dead arm with the knife, hoping something would sever. The bonds slipped, rain and mud easing the zip-ties down from his elbow to his wrist and mercifully onto his hand. Suddenly his fingers were wiggling free as the lich clambered over the barricade, its face a luminous, ghostly white.

It reached out its skeletal fingers and Rex heard an arthritic crack as his hand finally jerked free. He rolled backwards turning onto his feet only to find himself staring at a brick wall.

A dead end.

A doorway hung halfway up the wall, way above his head. He leapt at the sill, fingers squeezing into rotten wood, curling over the rim. But he didn't have the grip, didn't have the strength. He crashed back into the alley, spinning and slashing his knife in one last desperate act.

Fight!

A buzzing sound came from overhead and the machine dropped down between himself and the lich that eased down from the barricade to face him.

The bot advanced and Rex instinctively cowered behind his hands awaiting the dart, bullet or whatever this machine would use to kill him. The bot paused just inches from his face. A screen flipped outward. Words danced across the display, unreadable in Rex's addled mind. A metallic voice issued from the robot.

"Are you tired of fear and repression? Do you crave an end to militia rule? The Breakout Alliance is a benevolent, global superpower seeking to take governing control of Coriolis Island. We will revive the economy, bring back security, jobs and prosperity, and make Coriolis Island the hub of ground-to-Earth-halo space travel once again. If you wish to live in a

better, safer society, then please register your DNA and facial profile as a vote of consent."

Rex stared, uncomprehending. Behind the robot, the lich edged closer, poised for ambush, bone-white face peering around the bot, black-hole eyes fixed on its prey.

Repression… that word sounded right. Yes, at this moment Rex definitely felt repressed.

"Ignoring this message will be registered as a no-vote." The bot chimed. An outline of a hand appeared on the display and it edged nearer.

Maybe it was instinct, or just terror, but it seemed this machine was Rex's only hope of not becoming a murdered husk. He reached out and pressed his palm to the outline. A camera on the robot flashed and Rex jolted backwards.

"Your vote has been registered along with your DNA profile and facial scan. Do you wish to register a name with this profile?"

"Err… Rex?" he said, eyes glued to the lich.

The bot shuffled on the spot absorbing the information. *"Any other names?"*

"N-no, just Rex."

"Thank you, Rex-Nojustrex, for your time and vote." The bot turned and with a gust of hot air from its fan, moved back down the alley past the lich as if it wasn't there.

"Wait!" Rex cried, clawing after the bot. "Help me!"

"If you have further questions please visit channel 207 on the Global Broadcast Network or seek out your local Breakout Alliance representative." The bot wafted over the barricade and vanished around the corner leaving Rex staring down his enemy, knife in hand.

The lich surged forward, and Rex's back hit the wall.

"I can help you, Rex." The voice was soft and easy. Wrapped in a black hood, the face hovered only inches from Rex's knife tip. He paused. The face was more like that of a nun than any lich he'd ever seen. Black lines formed childishly simple features drawn on its porcelain-white plastic face.

"What – who are you?" Rex struggled to breathe, his heart pushing at his lungs as if trying to burst out of his throat.

"Call me Sister-Eleven." The black lines curled into a smile and the eye-circles grew wider as if luring him inside.

Rex let the knife drop. "I'm – I'm sorry, Sister. I thought – I thought you were a lich. Life's… pretty hard out here." He glanced past her to the corpse spilling out from the barricade. He felt it needed an explanation but had nothing.

"Things will be easier now, Rex. Come, follow me." She turned away from him, gliding back along the alley. A soft, electrical whirring accompanied her motions as she swept aside the barricade with a swish of her arm.

"You know my name?" he said, struggling to his feet, scared but wanting to follow.

"I heard you talking to that voting machine." She glanced briefly at the corpse, mangled inside the mess of planks and wire, and carried on past.

For a second, Rex was falling again, back into the yammering void full of sharp points and demons. He could run, flee this machine and whatever it promised, back onto the streets, hiding and starving, awaiting the next lich or the next group of thugs or drunken militiamen looking for an amusing kill. He'd done that for so long now, longer than his memories could say. Life on the street was just one long series of "act dead, act crazy, run like hell, fight."

In the end, his legs decided for him, trudging off down the alley as if tugged along in the Sister's slipstream. He walked and turned, walked and turned, until they emerged onto a wide street; oily rainwater sloshed along filth-clogged gullies. An old-fashioned gasoline car sat parked on the sidewalk. Its original paint scoured away to rust.

Sister-Eleven opened the rear door and Rex climbed inside–

Into a cage.

He fought back, but tooth and nail ferocity were no match for machine strength, and she flung him back onto the bench seat and slammed the door. With the machine-faced Sister in the front cab, the car drove itself through the deserted streets and crumbling buildings. She looked back, head turning like a gun turret, shoulders and body pointing straight ahead. Her plastic face was blank now. As he stared, the lines reappeared, flickering through micro-expressions as if testing his responses.

He thrashed and squirmed, jamming his head into the seats, trying to break his neck. A slot opened on the Sister's face where a mouth should have been. A sweet smell filled the air and a chemical calmness washed away his fight.

As the car traversed the matrix of streets through Coriolis City, he began tumbling through the blackness in his mind, shedding the memories and narratives that made him Rex. The fragments whirled away like diamond shards spinning through a void until there was nothing left, nothing but the vaguest sense of ever having existed at all, and that familiar, endless, horrifying feeling... of falling.

CHAPTER 2

Ellayna

35776 kilometers directly above the ragged peak of Coriolis's Transit Mountain, Ellayna Kalishar stalked the deserted corridors of the Cloud9 geostationary orbital.

The low-energy floor lights followed her on and off as she passed. The thump and click of switch relays sounded like footfalls following unseen in the darkness behind.

Ellayna steadied her breath, lengthened her stride, and refused to look behind.

She had grown up alone, just books, games and imaginary friends. When setting up a board game, she'd play all sides. Soloing, she called it. In those days, being alone was fun, alone was safe. But she'd never, ever, expected to be *this* alone. *Soloing for life.* Her bitter laugh reverberated off the metallic walls like a dying cicada.

Once, over a hundred thousand people had lived on Cloud9, part of the all-powerful GFC, Genes and Fullerenes Corporation. But fourteen years ago, the Nova-Insanity had devastated Earth's economy, ripping apart nations, their infrastructure, and even the space-elevator connecting Earth to the GFC orbital halo. Only two of the GFC's ten orbitals remained inhabited now, a handful of people on Cloud8 and barely a thousand on Cloud9. The exact number was hard to tell, even in this highly monitored, post Nova-Insanity age. Her definition of living had become muddied, as bodies existed on life-support while minds inhabited virtual worlds.

She turned a corner, foot hesitating, awaiting the lights, heart pounding a little harder as the darkness ahead vanished and revealed… nothing, just the gym door. The light clicked off behind her, making a different noise, more like a sigh or a gentle death rattle. "Hello?" she said into the blackness. The light popped back on as if telling her there was nothing to worry about. It then flickered as if straining to stay illuminated. Something else failing, a tiny part of the great GFC machine dying of neglect.

She clicked her shoes together, canceling the magnetic pull that kept her attached to the floor. A flick of her toes sent her airborne, gliding through the gym doorway toward the treadmill. She paused and closed the door. *Locked or unlocked?* She rattled the latch, feeling anger at her indecision until finally settling on unlocked. *There's no one here. Just me. Stop being foolish.*

"Gravity to one-g," she said. The walls hummed as hidden motors groaned alive, gently hauling the entire room around the center of a great circle. She dropped slowly to the floor feeling the pain as the acceleration-induced gravity popped her joints, dragging blood and body fluids downward, taxing her heart and muscles the way real gravity would.

A fix of gravity. It really hurt now, but she knew she'd enjoy it soon enough. The mirror in front of the treadmill showed a tall, reed-thin woman whose limbs bowed in odd directions, flexing around overly large elbow and knee joints. The sight of her bald head, however, always shocked. In her mind's eye, she still had that fiery crown of red from her youth, gone now, genetically removed. Hair was too difficult to manage in low-g. Removing it showed commitment to a life in space.

She placed her scent sachet on the shelf: *lavender*, the smell of reality. VR always smelled different and fake. She mounted the treadmill belt, knees protesting under her newly actualized weight. A warning pinged, the belt rolled, and the wall ahead lit up with glorious images of scenery. Her usual choice – hills and mountains, the tantalizing grassy trail weaving a path upward, subliminally posing that eternal question: what's around the next corner?

"They're all waiting for you." The message splashed across her vision, superimposed over reality by her Inner-I – the cluster of nanomachines embedded in her brain.

The message tag showed Martin Haller, her chief of security. She'd like to say *friend*, but Martin was a man with one of those weird, engineering personalities, like one of the early GFC robot humanoids with their uncanny valley looks and mannerisms. She doubted the word *friend* was in Martin's vocabulary, but she was sure the words *loyalty*, *honor* and *commitment* were.

"Give me a minute. I'm busy." The words left her mouth and the Cloud9 communications network routed them back to Martin's Inner-I which pressed them onto his visual cortex.

Let him wait. Let them all wait.

This week's board meeting was not the usual, straightforward affair. For one, Taunau Cho, the self-proclaimed leader of the Protectionist committee, had called for another vote to remove Ellayna's founding director privileges. It wasn't the first time he'd tried this, but each new vote came closer to dethroning her, especially as more of the original five hundred directors vanished into the medical booths, wired themselves into VR and never came to another meeting again.

The problem wasn't the vote. Being pushed off the top of the rotten heap of corporate hierarchy to become an ordinary director wasn't the worst thing that could happen. Her eight billion GFC shares were meaningless in this post-Nova-Insanity world, just numbers on a spreadsheet in a ruined city, far below.

No, the real problem was an older and much simpler enemy: fear.

"Faster!" The belt whined, its sound creeping over the gravity centrifuge noise. The best cure for fear was activity… and anger. "Faster!" Sweat beaded from her body as the orbital's recycling network sucked it away. She felt a twinge of satisfaction knowing her sweat was now pumping through Cloud9's water supply and into the bodies of all those lazy, worthless directors lounging in VR. "Drink my sweat!" she yelled, tilting into a full-on run.

The scenery turned, bending a steep upward path through rocky avalanche scree. The treadmill rolled and bucked, simulating the terrain, and the centrifuge wound a notch faster, working her knees and thighs as the slope steepened. For a second the illusion was complete. The fans blew a cool mountain breeze, an eagle screeched overhead. Just her and nature. Communing, surviving. *Soloing.*

A movement caught her eye near the gym door. *A spider's leg! A gigantic spider's leg easing around the doorframe!* She stumbled, grabbing at the treadmill's handrail as the shiny black appendage groped the air for her.

She gasped in a breath, inhaling the lavender. *Smell the reality! No monsters in reality.* Self-control returned, tears of relief clouded her eyes, and the monstrous leg became just a strand of plastic door insulation flapping wildly in the breeze from the treadmill. *This place really is falling apart!*

"Ellayna?" Martin's voice again. "Meeting?"

"Thirty seconds, Martin." She performed the mental blink that snapped her Inner-I control menu into view, hit the stop, and careened sideways off the belt onto the rest bench. *I might puke.* Bad idea in low-g. She swallowed hard, forcing back the bile. Trying not to relive that moment ten days earlier when her VR relaxation became a life-and-death struggle. A glitch in her Inner-I's ARG, or alternative reality generator, or so Martin had told her. Everything was fine now, a one-in-a-billion error that couldn't possibly happen again. A *"glitch"*. But her world had collapsed inward, a crushing, stifling, claustrophobic coffin filled with giant insects, stingers and mandibles. She could still hear that noise, a million chittering cicadas that stabbed, burrowed and nested inside her pinned and helpless flesh.

She'd mentally grabbed at the exit icon, the reassuring little button in the bottom corner of her vision that would un-paralyze her body and dump her senses back into the real world. But that button wasn't there. She had been trapped in VR.

A pretty significant glitch.

As that life and death struggle unfolded, the real Ellayna had thrashed and writhed around her apartment, tangled in cables and bedsheets, shattering vases and ornaments as her real fingers tried to rip the vile creatures from her mouth and eyeballs.

In the end, her Inner-I life-signs monitor flagged an alert that summoned medics and security. Minutes later they jolted her mind and all its attached technology back into reality with a localized EMP.

Her Simmorta fixed the physical damage quickly enough. She was up and working again the next day. But the biomech body-network technology could do nothing for the mental scars, and VR remained an untouchable terror, off-limits until she could forget that moment and be sure that it really *was* a "glitch".

But they were waiting, now. Waiting in the meeting for Ellayna to come and defend her position, prove she wasn't losing her grip on reality and on the GFC. But where were all meetings held? Inside VR.

She could do it all offline, send an avatar, use a remote link, but they'd know. Someone would notice, and the message would be clear: Ellayna was losing control, slipping, *scared*. More votes would turn, and the little remaining power she had over the failing halo corporation would vanish. And that was the root of her real fear: the loss of control, loss of her "baby", the empire she helped create.

She mentally tweaked her Inner-I controls; menu options scrolled before her eyes sending her virtual vision into the meeting room, while making sure her awareness, her senses, her reality, stayed very much grounded in the gym.

The room swam into vision, suspended somewhere between a powerful thought and a dreamy reality. The directors' avatars were all gathered, twiddling thumbs and staring ahead. Taunau looked relaxed, his faraway gaze rode a smug, knowing smile that said: *she won't be here. Ellayna Kalishar, founder of the greatest, richest corporation ever, was scared to enter VR, scared to chair a meeting… scared!*

Her vision scanned the other members, seeing hope, boredom, frustration, and more smugness. Some faces were blank, the minds behind those avatars were elsewhere. She wondered if they even still existed. Perhaps bugs had eaten their real minds long ago, leaving just machine proxies to continue their routines.

For a second she was a child again, utterly alone in a huge house, setting out the pieces of another battle game, lining-up soldiers, cannons, warships, four different factions, four different colors. She wanted her favorite color, blue, to win. Cupping a handful of dice, she began moving pieces. *My game. My rules.* Blue always won.

She tugged the rest bench's low-g webbing around her body, winding her fingers through mesh, pinning her arms by her sides. Not to prevent her floating away in Cloud9's microgravity, but as protection against her own gouging fingers and shredding fingernails should an attack come again. A mental finger punched the meeting button and her Inner-I blanked her senses, anesthetized her body, and fed her mind solely with the sensory imagery from the virtual meeting room.

The lavender smell was lost, replaced by dusty dry plastic and a mixture of false colognes and perfumes worn by the directors.

And here I am…

Striding out of a side door, taking a very particular path across the room, right through the waiting avatars, a move that was deemed disrespectful, something one just didn't do, she entered. They broke apart into colorful sprays of three-dimensional pixels before reforming into the familiar figures. She was the founder, the only remaining founder. The head of the GFC, of every council and committee, the pivot around which all decisions revolved. Even her avatar outranked theirs, scattering them like dust motes in a gale. She heard the grumbles of protest, but she ignored them.

My rules!

Her eyes commanded the room to silence as she tried not to notice the strips of shiny black insulation flapping around the meeting room doors. She smiled along the row of avatars, mentally tallying each vote from their expression.

"Let's begin, shall we?" she said, in her comfortable, easy voice.

My game.

The count was about even. This would be close.

CHAPTER 3

Jett

Jett was a meteor. He was the mote at the tip of a fiery cone blazing a fifty-kilometer trail across the noon sky. Heat ablated his reentry suit, sowing a trail of chemical lies to fool any observers into believing he was just another incoming rock, part of the glorious Orionids meteor shower that peppered the October sky.

"Your spin vectors are critical." Ursurper Gale's godlike voice was loud and urgent in Jett's mind. It jarred him back from oblivion, from just staring, awestruck, as the world grew larger and more dangerous before him.

"Blink, you fool!" A different voice, one from deep inside his memory. "Stop staring and breathe." But Jett was a voidian, an artificial lifeform. He had no lungs or respiratory system, no eyelids, not even a real face, just the memories of such things.

The fibrous threads covering his skull twitched, imitating what he imagined a blink felt like. The world popped into sharper focus, and he peered through the wildly changing numbers and graphics of his augmented vision. He checked that his Inner-I was set to covert, no transmitting, just receiving, but somehow Ursurper Gale had broken the radio silence – something was wrong.

What should have been a flat, stable reentry vector was a mass of chaotic spins and sheers. His reentry suit had become a centrifuge, spinning his body fibers out to the edges, leaving a hollow void in the center. He bunched his fullerene muscles, tugging his body back together, shoring up the reentry suit with a web of internal struts extruded from his body core. A spray of data splashed across his vision, confirming his worst fears: the suit was disintegrating, its sensors yielding erroneous data that confused his attitude control motors. He flipped a mental switch and the AI flight algorithms dropped offline. Fingers wrestling the manual controls, he visualized torques and angular velocities, sending calibrated puffs of gas from his suit motors to counter the spin.

His AI-tagger system shunted to the front of his vision as it struggled to make sense of the world below, and pasted its labels across his virtual vision.

Earth.

Sky.

Earth. Estimated position: Atlantic coast, equatorial South America.

Altitude: Sixty kilometers.

No longer the hazy ball he knew from geostationary orbit, Earth was up-close and personal. A vast curving plane of textured color tumbling around him. Blue Atlantic changed to the dead brown of the Amazon rainforest as he fought the crazy spin, jarring turbulence, and an erratic wobble that refused to compute.

"Jett?" Gale's voice sounded like a whisper of defeat. "I've detected launches. Incoming GFC drones and an Alliance interceptor. They've seen you."

Jett saw his problem: uneven suit ablation causing chaotic three-dimensional wobble. To the algorithmic part of his mind it was an un-computable mess. Every jolt of reaction mass his engines threw out to counter the problem made things worse as the calculations overshot or mistimed.

Earth. Sky. Earth. Sky. Earth – Quito. Santo Domingo. Jama.

Altitude: Thirty kilometers.

Pacific Ocean.

Out over blue water dotted with towering thunderheads, the shapeless smear of manmade pumice resolved into the unfinished island of New Galapagos smattered with the frail greenery of new life establishing a footing amongst the fissures and crags.

A vicious jolt from an air pocket caused another part of his suit to fall away.

Altitude: Fifteen kilometers

Ahead was his goal: Coriolis Island. A perfect circle of gray and green. At its center, Transit Mountain pierced the sky like a needle, an absurdly disproportionate pile of concentric cylinders, each taller and thinner than the one on which it stood.

Reaction motor failure.

Suit integrity failure.

Disintegration imminent!

Gale's voice crackled through the jarring noise. "Two GFC attack drones from low-orbit and an Alliance interceptor launched from a nearby ice-platform."

Altitude: Ten kilometers.

Jett levelled with Transit Mountain's distant peak. Once, the cable of the space-elevator had connected it to the TwoLunar orbital. The top was now a jagged point, the cable gone. The only way to Earth was to fall and the only way back was by rocket. But Jett wasn't going back. This was a one-way mission, a mission he'd trained for his whole life. All his memories were of training, but that training was failing, and he was dying.

Calculations impossible. Jett switched the computations off, mentally floating free, seeking the calm of a deeper truth, something hidden in the dark uncertainty of his past.

Memories. Waiting like troves of gemstones, buried by his creator. *"In combat a mind shouldn't be clogged with sympathies and emotions,"* Gale had told him. *"Memories will appear when you need them."*

And then a memory surfaced.

He sat atop an animal, its back a fleshy warm carpet over big, heavy bones. A horse. The motion jolted him up, down, sideways, forward and backward, torquing and bucking in impossible chaos.

"Blink, you fool," said the woman riding alongside on another horse. "Stop fighting it, stop staring and just breathe."

Jett relaxed, flesh and muscle sinking into the saddle. No fighting. No analyzing. Easy and natural. Just riding the changes in perfect counter-coordination, so smooth his head barely deviated from its optimal path.

He focused on her, the one galloping alongside. She had a name, gone now, erased, even as their bond remained deep and affectionate. But that didn't matter, all that mattered was riding, not falling. Surviving

Altitude: Five kilometers.

He switched off his image stabilizer and the world jerked and blurred as he focused on a point ahead. The sun reflected off the ocean in a yellow blaze. He rode the air like a horse, feathering and nurturing the remaining reaction motors as if adjusting the muscles of a real flesh-and-bone body. He rode the violence down to the rough, and then the rough down to the smooth, as his spin slowed and his mental spin and torque gauges dropped from red to yellow and down to green.

The GFC drones appeared on Jett's virtual vision, two slim cylinders curving through the atmosphere. The Alliance interceptor was much bigger, bloated with weapon pods and countermeasures, hanging low and close to the water, a machine that could fight a war on its own.

"ETA fifteen seconds for the drones, eighteen for the interceptor," Gale said, his voice battling through the electronic barrage of war. "The interceptor will attack the GFC drones before focusing on you."

Laser beams lanced the sky as the machines exchanged fire. Tiny missiles flooded from the drones' munition pods, winding corkscrew paths around Jett where the interceptor's goalkeeper guns knocked them from the sky.

The equator was now a stable, green line superimposed across Jett's virtual vision. His body flattened to an efficient flight surface taking on air and stress, decelerating him into a controlled glide.

"The GFC thinks you're a defector from an orbital, Jett. A soft human target. The Alliance wants you alive."

Banking sharply, Jett veered toward the interceptor away from his target of Coriolis Island, steepening his dive angle as the triad of war machines opened fire. The air filled with starbursts and shrapnel, as electronic and concussion waves battered his body. Microscopic hyper-velocity beads tore through his fullerene flesh.

Jett felt no pain, bodily damage just made red markers on a combat screen. His biomech body, made of intricately woven hypertubes, scattered and deflected energy weapons, while bullets passed harmlessly between his fibers. And still the number of damage markers grew. At some point his distributed body-architecture would falter, and material loss would become critical.

"Taking heavy fire." Jett broke radio silence and canceled his message encryption so every listener could understand. "Death is imminent." A lie, a distraction to bait the enemy. Ursurper Gale wouldn't be so easily fooled.

He engaged the parachute release and deceleration hauled on his body as the jellyfish-shaped chute ripped open. The drones streaked ahead and circled back past the interceptor. One of them exploded, yielding eighty-kilotons of heat, radiation, and compression energy. The interceptor coiled away in a complex series of evasive maneuvers, hurling heat-deflecting chaff behind it.

"–gone nuclear–" Gale's voice modulated and crackled through the interference "–to kill the Alliance craft. Second blast will target you directly."

Altitude: Three hundred meters.

The second drone pulled a sharp turn veering closer to Jett. Parts of its reactive shell blew away as the interceptor drilled it with all the offensive fire it could muster.

The drone exploded, and a core of searing white light blacked out Jett's sensors.

He hit the release and left the parachute in the air. Heat flashed the ablative coating from his body as the nuclear compression wave flung him sideways. He curled into a ball as the wind blast sheared him across the ocean surface in a superheated soup of gas and steam.

He hit the water at over four hundred kilometers per hour, plunging through seething currents of bubbles into cold, deep darkness. His vision a collage of damage warnings.

Water pressure increased, squashing any air from between his body fibers, compressing him down to the size of a child. Only his head remained unchanged: a solid chunk of fullerene crystal.

The drones were gone, and as far as any watchers could tell he was gone too, vaporized, crushed, drowned. He hung there in the pitch darkness, resembling a charred fetus, gently bouncing off the ocean floor as unperceived days and nights rolled past, and the damage warnings flickered and faded. The micro-cellular fusion reactors powering his metabolism drew hydrogen from the water like leeches, flooding the nanoscale conduits of his body with energy, firing up the biomech repair nodes and shunting reserve materials to damaged regions.

Slowly, like a deeply wounded animal, he healed.

Squid circled cautiously, their huge eyes seeing nothing edible. An ancient deep-sea shark nibbled at an appendage, confused by the flickers of electrical activity inside. Jett's fibers gradually grew strong again, winding into coils of synthetic tendon and muscle; thicker bundles formed bones and structural elements mimicking the shape and size of an adult human. Slowly, he pushed up to the surface, expanding and growing in strength as he rose through bioluminescence toward sunlight.

As he broke the surface, he saw blue sky, calm seas, and felt the gentle pinch of atmospheric pressure on his freshly woven skin. The ocean had long absorbed all signs of violence.

Jett was a creature of the vacuum, designed to inhabit and colonize space. Water was an unfamiliar substance to him and oceans were alien worlds. He rode the waves like he was taming a wild horse, while expanding his skeleton, adjusting density until he floated. His Inner-I showed him Coriolis Island, two hundred and seventy-four kilometers away. Much farther than they'd planned in training. But a flashing green arrow in his mind showed him which way to go.

He looked up into the sky, at the distant metallic specks of orbitals and the battered barrel-shape of TwoLunar from where Ursurper Gale watched. And then, having never swum a stroke in his life, he set out on the long crawl toward Coriolis Island.

CHAPTER 4

Free Fallen

"Four votes, Tomas." Ellayna lay sprawled across her bed inside her Cloud9 apartment watching Tomas Narellion's aging, silver-haired avatar stare off into the distance, as if the corner of her living area was some endlessly fascinating landscape.

"Does it matter, Ellayna? Does the position of director, founder or even shareholder mean anything anymore?"

She shrugged, rolling lazily onto her back. "I like the illusion of security. Power makes me feel safe, gives me options. Other than that, I get to veto, and that turns Taunau beet red and starts him cussing in Korean. Surely that's worth something?"

That teased a chuckle from Tomas, his lips not moving quite in synch with the words in her mind. "I think Taunau forgets his Inner-I translates everything he says."

"He also forgets who's boss around here. Even if it is by only four lousy votes." She wondered if her avatar adorned Tomas's room in a similar, tasteful fashion, or was she sprawled naked across his bed. She forced away those ideas. He'd never been secretive about his feelings for her. Feelings she had never reciprocated.

Stifling a sigh, she used her Inner-I to route a different camera feed to her ceiling display. The starfield vanished, replaced by Earth. The day-night terminator crept imperceptibly across Africa. Thousands of tiny blast circles from the lakes of fusion-glass left behind by the nuclear blasts of the Nova-Insanity caught the sunlight, reflecting it back into space like colored sequins.

Fourteen years ago! Fourteen years she'd been here, lying on this bed. Cloud9 had been a crowded, bustling city of hope until someone released the plans for a microscopic solid-state fusion reactor onto the Internet. *Let everyone have power!* the anonymous message proclaimed, giving every person with a 3D-printer access to the new technology. Only days later, hackers discovered how to cluster the reactors into a ring and create fusion bombs, nova devices, and suddenly every terrorist, teenager and tinpot dictator had a nuclear arsenal. *Insanity!* The world went mad, and she'd watched it all unfold from this bed, on the screen before her. The tiny explosions of war, vengeance and injustice spread across the globe as governments and corporations struggled to shut everything down. *Too late. The Nova-Insanity had begun.*

Back in the present, she spun her index finger and the world rotated up and across Central America and on through North America to Canada. *Such power in my tiny finger.* A reverse-pinch zoomed her in, down through clouds; she knew exactly where she wanted to go, the coordinates imprinted in her mind.

Utopia. The zoom stopped, reaching the limit of her system's image processing capability. To get closer would mean asking for help, for better algorithms and access to higher resolution imaging equipment. Then, they'd know her secret, her Utopia. She couldn't allow that.

Her remote vision hovered over a huge estate, a mansion in the mountains, its grounds nestled in the fork of a river. A hundred square kilometers of land and a state-of-the-art, self-maintaining smart home. It even had its own security force... or so the Breakout Alliance claimed.

The words from their contact message were burned into her mind: "All yours Ellayna. Just say the word."

All mine. All I have to do is defect. Turn my colleges and friends over to the Alliance forces. Abandon them all and flee. Aid the downfall of the GFC, the very thing I helped create... That is all I have to do.

"Something bothering you?" Tomas said, his avatar turning to stare directly at her, eyes maintaining their faraway gaze.

"I guess I did call you, didn't I?" She channeled a double-encrypted feed of her own vision through her Inner-I to Tomas, showing him the aerial view of the mansion. "Wanted your confidential opinion on something." She held her breath.

"Very nice. Trying to bribe me, Ellayna?"

"I call it Utopia." Her fingers twitched trying to bring it closer, to make it just a little more real, but nothing changed.

"So…" he seemed to fish for the right words. The encryption level of his message feed ramped higher. "I see you've been… *approached*, as well."

Her breath escaped in a giant, relieved gasp. "You mean, I'm not alone then?"

"Mmm. Suspect we've all been sent them. The post Nova-Insanity equivalent of spam."

"You think it's even real?"

Tomas shrugged. "Mine's different to yours, small city compound in Paris. Artsy!"

"They know you so well, Tomas." She fought the sinking feeling in her gut, that great let-down. Of course, she'd known it was false, of course everyone was being bribed… of course. But that little hope had been something to hang on to.

Tomas threw up his arms in a wild expansive expression. "Custom made beacons of light to lure these fragile ships onto rocky shores." The super-high encryption level slowed the processing of his image, breaking him briefly into monochrome rectangles. No one could crack that code… in theory. But just talking through super-encrypted channels would raise suspicion in these paranoid times.

The full confession tumbled out of her. "I use an Earth-based proxy account to relay messages to people on the surface. Had it set up years ago to talk with family and friends. Don't really have any of those left now, though. The Alliance just messaged me out of the blue."

Tomas nodded. "I have a similar illegal proxy-account and had the same doubts."

She went quiet, letting her fingers reach out and disrupt Tomas's image. Trying to ignore his emphasis on the word "illegal". It felt good to have a friend, someone who understood, who had the same flaws. "I'm afraid I went a little further than just messaging, Tomas." She whispered the words aloud as if wanting to hear her crime. Daring somebody to catch her.

"Oh?"

"They sent me a simulation of the estate. A detailed, full-immersion sim. It's… it's wonderful. It feeds all my needs. After being stuck up here, alone and vulnerable in this tin can for years… It's got security, nature… gravity."

"I understand."

"By running their sim, I'm worried they might have hacked my Inner-I. You know… software virus or something."

"Thus, the bugs attacking you in VR?"

"Yeah… the bugs."

"Get one of the techs to check you out. Jesh Nameeb is a reliable guy… discreet."

"Then someone else knows I've been poking around in false utopias and colluding with the Alliance." She waved the dream estate away and it turned back into a cold, lifeless starfield, angry that she had shown weakness by confiding in Tomas and even angrier that she'd harbored hopes that it could be real.

"Thinking something shouldn't be a crime, Ellayna. Last I checked, looking at something wasn't either. But then, I suppose, these are unusual times, not like the era of freedom we grew up in."

"I've been foolish, Tomas. I trust you would never fall for such a ruse?"

"Desperate minds cling to the thinnest of ropes." He went quiet and his avatar faded to transparent. "I'm getting an alert coming in."

Ellayna let out a groan. Suddenly she was tired and just wanted to sleep, but message alerts were springing up across her Inner-I too. "What do you see, Tomas?"

"One of our AIs flagged a chemical anomaly on a meteor, thinks it could be a defector."

"I'll talk with security."

"No need. Taunau and his ever-vigilant Protectionists are on duty and following procedure with their usual tenacity. You're off the hook. Get some rest."

Tomas's image vanished from her room and she was left staring at the stars, drowning in silence. Once, this wing of Cloud9 had buzzed with life – thousands of apartments, parks, restaurants. The staging ground for construction of the next big thing: Cloud10, christened TwoLunar, a vast, rotating orbital with cities, factories, farms, and the anchor point for the GFC's space-elevator. And after that... on to the stars. But now, there was just silence. As far as she could tell, she was completely alone.

"Fine," she said to nobody and pulled up her tactical screens. "Defector? We'll see shall we." It wouldn't hurt her to observe Taunau in action, maybe note a weakness or two, some point of leverage she could exploit later. She pinged Taunau, letting him know she was online.

"Permission to carry on?" Taunau asked.

"Do we know who the defector is?"

"No. Might be an empty drone, or a smuggling op."

"Reel him in, Taunau." A quaint, sanitary way of saying: *Kill the bastard.* Defecting in an escape pod was a signature upon one's own death warrant. There was no retrieval system, no way to surrender, and no chance of returning to orbit and facing punishment.

Images unfurled in virtual space around her. Two GFC drones dropped from high orbit storage bunkers. A warning flashed on screen as an Alliance craft – a bulky interceptor unit – took off from one of the ice platforms that the Alliance liked to use as mobile carriers.

She zoomed in on the meteor as it began its burn through the upper atmosphere. "How come it's so low? Why didn't we spot this earlier?"

"It was just an innocent chunk of rock until the AI took a closer look."

Ellayna watched the chase. The ballet of warring drones and the Alliance interceptor. If the Alliance captured a defector alive, then valuable GFC secrets could be lost. Their monopoly on longevity drugs threatened. Without that monopoly, they'd have nothing left to trade and would starve in space.

She bit chunks from her lip, recalling memories of eight years ago: the Great Defection. A mass of dissenters stormed a GFC transporter and fled. All were killed when security hacked the vehicle's AI and vented them into space. A tragic accident, or so they told everyone outside of the security committee: "In their hurry to flee, an error in securing the door occurred..."

But really it was my decision. I killed them.

She recalled the inquest; Taunau roaring and pointing, his face blood red. "Everybody here made a commitment to the GFC. To the future of humanity. The defectors betrayed us all and deserved to die."

Her mind returned to the present as a nuclear blast dazzled her, blanking information screens to white. Seconds later, another blast followed. Somehow, the big Alliance craft survived, but whoever was riding that fake meteor was gone.

"Threat neutralized, Ellayna," Taunau said, like a businessman concluding a trivial transaction.

"Well done," she forced the words out, bitter on her lips. "Get security to find out who the defector was."

She spent the next hour staring at the camera feed showing the Alliance interceptor. She watched as it circled endlessly over the empty sea, *soloing*. They'd annihilated the defector right on the equator. *Where were you heading, Coriolis Island?*

As sleep took her away, the images in her head drifted north, finding the Canadian Rockies. The glorious estate of Utopia was a smudge on her vision, impossibly far away. Flicking back to the Alliance interceptor, a mere dot against the blue, it seemed to speak to her, repeating the words of their contact message: "All yours Ellayna. Just say the word."

* * *

Rex stood at the end of his tiny bed, arms stretched out to the sides, fingertips touching the door and the opposite wall. Then, swinging his arms to the front, he reached over the sink to his double row of checkmarks drawn in red crayon on the off-white wall: fourteen Xs meant two weeks. Two weeks of captivity, or two weeks of salvation in the eyes of the Sisters.

He touched the crayon to his neck, imagining it were a drug dispenser, feeling the flow of tiny machines slip into his bloodstream. He mimicked the gasp of relief, that bluster of new energy. He felt his back straighten, eyes open wider, the pleasure, the warmth, the moment when the inner darkness fled... and all the yammering voices were silenced. Glow. His savior, his tormentor.

"How are you, Rex?" The wall spoke to him each morning and again before he went to bed. Usually it asked the same questions, sometimes it surprised him.

"Good," he said.

"Do I still call you Rex?"

He ignored the question, instead scanned his wall markings, each a miniature masterpiece of encoding. Some hidden part of him enjoyed that, needed it. His private way of documenting his life, secret from the Sisters' spies, and not reliant on his own treacherous memory. The top-left corner of each X encoded what he'd eaten for breakfast that morning. The top-right was lunch and bottom-left dinner. Wavy meant porridge, straight was toast, humps were fake eggs and triangles were waffles. He'd struggled to find symbols for mock-meat stew and fake chicken, contriving various loops, cones and zigzags. The bottom-right corner encoded his daily duties, waves meant cleaning, squares were re-education classes, and gaps in the line indicated those tiny breaks he took to just stare or wonder.

"How does it feel to be clean for this long, Rex?"

"I've been clean much longer than fourteen days," he said, head shaking in disappointment. "The addicts are inside my head. They're not me."

"Glow finds its own way, Rex. It twists minds, making people do things they would never do."

He stared on, guilty as charged. The image of the dead man in the alley appeared vivid in his mind, as his eyes settled on the third X-mark along the top row. He'd circled that one, meaning he'd added it the next day when he was Rex once again. He had no name for that other persona. None of his minds had names. They just came and went, often leaving nothing behind, not even a memory.

The Sister behind the wall seemed to catch his gaze and said, "I think you are Rex today and have been for many days now. This is excellent progress."

He remembered back to his months of madness on the edge of town, just still-frame memories now of roaming like an animal, eating trash and dead things off roads. "These days I'm usually Rex," he said quietly, as if the other walls might overhear.

"Have you remembered anything about who you were before?" She asked that question every day. Stupid really. He was no one before: no memories, no body, nothing. He'd just fallen out of the darkness as if it had birthed him, dumping him into the world, functional and terrified. When he slept, he fell back into that darkness, and sometimes what tumbled out of the bottom was him, but other times it was someone else. The more he emerged as Rex, the more he got to see through the emptiness and witness what the others did with his body while he was away. It was war inside his skull, demons constantly vying for control, and yet, somehow, he was winning.

"Nothing, Sister," he said. "I don't remember anything from before." Tired of her questions, he attacked with his own. "Why the cage? Why drag me here from the alley and put me in this prison?"

"Sister-Eleven follows her own rules. You went with her voluntarily. You needed rehabilitation. The drug in you resists and we are helping you fight it."

"Why do you all have numbers and not names?"

"We have ten distinct functions. Sisters that perform the same function use the same number. Those outside the direct control of the Sisterhood are numbered simply as eleven."

Zip-ties, rusty knives, and dead faces muddled his thoughts. "Did she tell you how she found me?" He swallowed, steeling for the answer he dreaded.

"She found you in Brook Alley, northern Welkin, in a gutter. You and your friend had been attacked. Your friend was dead. Do you remember your friend, Rex?"

So, the Sisters could lie! He swallowed again, unsure if she was baiting him. "I never knew his name. He was just a… a drinking buddy."

There was a long silence and the crayon dropped from his fingers to the floor. Rex felt his body trembles rising and couldn't face looking at the wall with its dots and Xs – eyes and dead eyes. His crumpled bedsheets became bodies folded and tormented in death, drained of life and color. He gasped, grabbing at the sink as his knees caved in under him.

Act dead, act crazy, run like hell… fight!

Decoherence, the Sisters called it. That moment when his mind fell apart and tumbled back into the void.

"You must be hungry, Rex," the wall said. "Go and earn your breakfast." He lunged at the door handle as if the air in the room was gone and he had just seconds to live. "Don't forget your headphones." He snatched them from the hook on the door and wrapped them around his ears. The Sisters made them especially for him: music-canceling headphones. The hostel was full of music, ditties, nursery rhymes and old songs. Music helped fragmented minds cohere because the brain rarely forgot a tune. But Rex was different. No tune or lyric created positive change in him, only decoherence. The Sisters made the headphones to help him, and labeled him as melophobic: terrified of music.

Rex ran through the bland corridors, spiraling past Sisters and slack-faced inmates, hands clattering along the walls for support until the world stopped shearing away in slivers and sheets and grew stable and calm again. The feeling of decoherence subsided and was gone.

Work helped. Work calmed. He enjoyed work. Small tasks, things to get lost in while moving and making little changes to the world, even if that change was as simple as making it cleaner.

He scrubbed kitchen floors before breakfast, bussed dishes, gathered plastic cutlery and plates into huge piles and wiped tables after. The afternoon saw him up ladders, dusting the ornate arches and corners of rooms in the vast building that he was sure must look like a cathedral from the outside.

He'd tried leaving several times, of course. But the Sisters were everywhere, gliding silently like chess pieces blocking his moves, corralling him back to his room or his work. Not that he especially wanted to leave; they fed him, gave him a bed and fresh water. Life was good really, even if it was a kind of prison.

The day passed. Exhausted and fed, he attended the obligatory Future-Lord classes that Sisters-Seven and Eight taught. It seemed like madness to Rex. They believed in a god, but one that didn't yet exist, one they'd eventually create, like an idea, an "Intention" they called it.

Sister-Eight used the same example again and again: "People Intended to go to the Moon. They made the near-impossible happen. We Intend to create a god, a benevolent superbeing. The logical conclusion of cognition and understanding: the Future-Lord will transcend dimension and causality and create Haven for all his followers outside of space and time. As a believer you will learn to sense His influence on your life."

As crazy an idea as this Future-Lord seemed, Rex couldn't help feeling the presence of something echoingly huge inside his mind, something bigger and stronger than all those thin, nameless voices that tried to take him over whenever he slept. Back in his room, Rex sculped another X onto his wall, coding in the toast, the egg, the ticks of fake meat and the dots of vegetables, along with his cleaning and classes.

"Can the Future-Lord be inside my head?" he asked the wall.

"The Future-Lord is everywhere, Rex, like a resonance, an enhancement to a life well lived."

"I'd like a life well lived."

"What would you ask of your future self, Rex?"

He pondered for a few seconds, dismissing images of meaty burgers and Glow dispensers. "I'd ask him to help me work outside more. To see the sun and the sky and breathe fresh air."

The wall hesitated and Rex wondered if he'd asked for too much. He nestled the crayon behind the single tap on the sink and settled onto his bed. Rex dreaded the idea of sleep, of what horrors it could bring. Whether he'd fall through those rings of darkness and drop into the morning as Rex or...

"Sleep well, Rex," the wall finally spoke. "And if you still want those things in the morning, then I have the perfect job for you."

CHAPTER 5

The Scream

"Summary, Martin?" Ellayna attended the security committee meeting in the most remote way she could, by watching the virtual meeting room through an image portal on her Inner-I. The thought of full immersion still revolted her. She was instead walking Cloud9's deserted corridors, springing through the low gravity environment. The movement felt good.

"We have no definitive point of origin for the defector, and nobody shows as missing. Best guess: it was a drone package with a voice beacon onboard that tripped when somebody communicated with it."

"*Death is imminent?*" she read the words from the conflict transcript. "Rather a strange turn of phrase, don't you think?" Everyone shrugged in unison.

"Definitely an AI," Taunau said, receiving nods of approval from his sidekicks Katherine Marr and Rawiri Chang. "Who knows how much damage that could have done if it reached the Alliance."

An uneasy silence settled as the other members abstained from challenging Taunau. His views on killing defectors were well understood.

"Well, we don't know who is behind this smuggling," Martin added, deciding to stir the pot. "That's quite an operation to stuff an escape suit full of... of what? Plans? Tech? Simmorta? And then eject it without us noticing or missing any inventory. Then, of course, there's the false chemical trail. How did they set that up?"

Taunau let forth one of his long, low groans that indicated deepest concern. "Lot of traitors up here. Big operation."

Ellayna scanned her fellow avatars, noting many eyes dropping to the floor and heads hanging low, hoping Taunau didn't point his accusatory finger in their directions. In the real world, she turned a corner into another bland corridor, lights clicking on in front, fighting that pervasive feeling of being stalked. She swore something moved just ahead of her, a shadow, but as she turned a corner, it turned as well. Perfect timing, always just out of sight. She upped the magnetic force, clamping her harder to the floor, speeding up her walk.

Her virtual eyes zoomed back into the meeting, finding Trabian Folley lurking silently in the background. Having inherited all his parents' GFC shares, Trabian was the youngest GFC director and member of the security committee. The real Trabian lived out on Cloud8, the only other inhabited orbital, with a skeleton crew of maintenance personnel consisting of Trabian, a handful of cousins, close friends, and of course, his father Mensar, a GFC cofounder, now certified unfit for governance due to many years of mental illness.

Trabian seemed to sense her watching. The boyish features of his avatar shifted as if looking past the others and seeking her.

Taunau still held everyone's attention, "Smugglers must either come from here or Cloud8." All eyes shifted to Trabian, who seemed to shrink slightly. It was true that if any part of the remaining GFC was hard to monitor, it was Cloud8.

Trabian composed himself, growing larger again. "There are other possibilities," he said, ignoring Taunau. "A rogue operator on one of the other decommissioned orbitals..." He struggled for another, more realistic option. "Ursurper Gale on TwoLunar." That raised a few eyebrows.

Ellayna ground to a halt at the mention of Gale. She hated the voidian with a strange passion. Ever since her friend, lover and

GFC cofounder, Del Krondeck, had built the monster and made him a kind of lab assistant, she'd been creeped out by him. Gale had escaped during the Great Defection, while Del was captured and imprisoned. Only her veto power saved Del from a charge of treason, and the first execution on the GFC's halo nation.

"What would Gale be smuggling?" Taunau laughed. "Space junk? He doesn't need money or food. He's a stinking *machine*." His team roared and whooped while Trabian shrank a little more before pushing back.

"Maybe it was Gale himself in that suit. Perhaps he got tired of dodging our assassins and skulking around a deserted orbital."

Taunau's laugh only rolled louder. "He wouldn't last five seconds on Earth. The Alliance would tear the world apart to get voidian technology."

Ellayna resumed her walk, unsure if it was the mention of Gale or just the feeling of being pursued that made her heart beat so fast. As she turned the corner, there it was: that shadow again, and then it was gone. She pinged Martin on a private channel as the argument between Taunau and Trabian grew heated.

"Martin, can you get a security trace on me?" she asked.

"Sure." Pause. "Got you, Ellayna. Moving along the Saturn Axis, toward Neutron Star Park."

"Is there somebody else just ahead of me?"

Pause.

"Nope. Looks like you're alone out on that wing."

A cold hand gripped her spine. "Thank you, Martin." She dialed in new directions to take her back to her apartment.

"Something got you spooked?"

"Seeing ghosts again."

Ellayna saw Martin's avatar smile in her meeting room vision as a green arrow sent her off down a side corridor. ETA eight minutes. No shadows ahead. *Which means whoever or whatever it was… might now be* behind *me.*

She forced her focus back to the meeting. Taunau had become his trademark shade of crimson-purple and was yelling something incomprehensible at Trabian, who simply stared back with his smug, youthful look. One that she both loved and despised.

Yes, she thought, the smuggler really could be Trabian. He was smart, young, ambitious, probably wanted a way off Cloud8 more than any of the old, decrepit directors. But she liked Trabian, and it wasn't just the guilt for what she'd done to his family. She didn't want to see him harmed.

Trabian's mother was one of those killed during the Great Defection. I *killed her*. The security committee decided to hide the facts; the escape pods were faulty, untested, maybe shot by lasers from the ground. The Alliance were to blame. Enforce the official line while sowing the conspiracy.

"You there, Ellayna?" The message popped into her vision from Trabian.

"Sure. Just enjoying watching you wind Taunau toward his next stroke." She felt her flesh blush a little. Trabian had sent her flirtatious messages in the past. It was oddly creepy, as he was thirty-seven years her junior, but also flattering. She'd ignored them back then, the desperate actions of a lonely boy stranded in space with no chance of meeting a girl his own age. She consulted her GFC directory listing, finding Trabian at the bottom. His shareholding was massive, nearly equal to her own. He was nineteen years old now and no longer a boy.

She suppressed a smile and turned another corner, her apartment door just ahead.

Trabian sent her a mischievous grin icon. "Think he'll come searching Cloud8 for my secret smuggler's lair?"

"Careful… he might just do that."

Ellayna switched back to the meeting. Taunau had calmed down, and Trabian had agreed to grant Cloud9 access to all of Cloud8's external security cameras. This, Trabian claimed, would prove that no craft of any sort had left the orbital in months. Katherine Marr agreed to pursue the Gale angle by sending probes to TwoLunar on another, probably fruitless, seek-and-destroy mission.

"Come meet with me in VR, Ellayna," Trabian messaged. Her pulse leapt. There it was again, the flirty boy seeking a hookup. *Or an alliance?* "I have something to show you."

"Really. What?"

"Secret. But I think you'll like it."

"Trabian, I–"

"Nothing like that, Ellayna. It's research I've been doing, about this defector. I'd like to run it past you before presenting it to the committee."

She felt strangely cold, rebuffed even. Shrugging off the disappointment, she eased open her apartment door. For a few seconds she turned and stared behind her, waiting... waiting for something to come around the corner.

Nothing.

The lights switched off and she stared into darkness before backing quickly into her living area and securing the door. Martin's tracer winked a happy face at her, indicating that he knew she was safely home.

Her ceiling still displayed the starfield as she'd left it last night while drifting in and out of uneasy sleep. Thoughts of Utopia, defectors and assassination bugs had clamored ceaselessly through her headspace.

No Utopia for Ellayna. Ellayna was soloing in space... *always soloing.*

"Ellayna?" She'd almost forgotten Trabian.

"Sure. I'll meet you," she said, fighting the crawling nausea at the very thought of VR. "Setup a VR room. I'll send you a time."

Make him wait... at least for a bit.

Rex knelt on the smooth, wind-buffeted surface of the crystal lake, gazing down into its unfathomable depths. Colored lights flickered; were they the souls of all those lost in this nova blast? Or just the dawn sunlight reflecting off the surrounding buildings and catching in the fissures and impurities in the plasmic glass?

Freedom! He eased upright, back hunched as if expecting incoming fire. Downtown Coriolis was distant enough, but he could still see the building from which he'd emerged; the Sisters had parted like the components of a huge mechanical lock, allowing him to run free. It *was* a cathedral, ancient, dark and gothic, with melt lines like veins running down its stonework from the heat of the nearby Welkin nova explosion.

The crystal around him clicked as his pursuer, the knifeman, stepped out onto the lake. Rex nodded. This was all natural. The people that lived wild in the city would spot an easy victim – a freshly released inmate, plump and healthy with good clothes and medications, maybe even money. The knifeman had been on him since he left the cathedral door. He knew the rules, the ways of the wild. Follow someone with something you wanted – boots, drugs, glasses – then, with a quick thrust of a knife, what was theirs was now yours.

Click…

The knifeman stalked slowly closer. Rex could smell him on the breeze: desperate, diseased, that tang of unwashed clothes and flesh. Rex tensed his legs, taking one last look down into the depths of the lake. No ghosts stared back, just the distorted image of a thin, gaunt man with strange tufted ears and soft brown eyes. He touched his face as the reflection mimicked. A finger ran over his nose and up to his hair pushing it back, parting it and scratching his itchy temple with a chewed, crooked nail. The reflection copied perfectly, did the reflection itch too? He wondered what it would mean if the reflection did something different.

Click… and tense…

"Try to look as normal as possible, Rex." The Sister's voice crept through his mind as if she still watched through his room wall.

"How?" he had asked, as if that was the stupidest thing he'd ever heard.

She'd shoved the paper fragment into his hand, the address of this perfect job the Sisters had arranged for him. Him? Rex! A job! He'd stifled his laugh and clutched the paper as if it were a Glow dispenser. All the while knowing he was never going there, never interviewing, and never coming back to the hostel with its talking walls, robot nuns and crazy Future-Lords.

Click... and tense... and breathe...

He was free now. His destiny had been put back in his hands. He'd almost tossed the paper as he left the hostel, but he had kept it instead, just in case.

Click... Click... tense... and...

Act crazy!

Rex leapt in the air, spinning to face the knifeman, eyes wide, arms waving, tongue flapping, the roar of sheer unbridled madness. He modeled his movements on a dance he'd once seen: Maori warriors trying to intimidate their enemies.

Crazy worked well against rational people. It even worked against militiamen who did what they did for a pay chit at the end of the day. It didn't, however, work with everybody. Rex saw the man stagger backward, throwing his knife in a defensive arc. But the blaze in his old ruddy eyes suggested he liked his odds.

Run like hell!

Rex lurched sideways, avoiding the knife, his legs pounding hard on the slick crystal to gain traction. As he ran, he assessed the flashbulb instant of information he had acquired about his assailant: stout, male, leper, not late stage, no chance of meaningful disintegration.

Fear pushed his mind back away from his eyes and the world became twin tunnels surrounded by darkness. Darkness, he knew, would start to move and fall. Then it would become the yammering void.

No... must stay as Rex. He bit his tongue, straining hard to see ahead.

The edge of the crystal lake rose like a frozen waterfall; flows of glass dripped from an uneven rim and ran out forming translucent drumlins and channels. He skipped up a shaft, digging his toes into cracks, pulling himself up and over the rim onto the ruined no man's land that separated the lake from the city. Here, the warped, semi-melted houses looked like petrified jellyfish with haunted eyes and hairpieces made of fused roof tiles. Glints of color and metal shone through the glass road, the remains of old cars or people or life from fourteen years previously. His feet navigated the treacherous ground, avoiding the tunnels and fissures hacked into the glass by treasure seekers and souvenir hunters.

A glance behind, the leper was still following. His face was redder, his breath coming in the rasps and coughs of an ailing physique.

The drumlins grew taller as Rex raced away from the lake, soon they would become fully formed homes with residents. Rex turned a corner and ground to a halt. Ahead was a tall building with melted lower stories, slumping down into a crumpled façade. Its windows formed grotesque eye sockets, a mouth and nostrils. Smaller buildings to its sides had tilted and sagged against the taller neighbor, looking like hands clasping the face of a ghoulish screaming figure.

Rex became so lost in the vision before him that he almost forgot the knifeman, but turned just in time, ducking the first blow and toppling backward to avoid the counter-slash. The knifeman glanced upward, momentarily distracted by the odd building. Rex took his chance and kicked at the leper's knee which buckled and snapped. He rolled to his feet, kicking, punching, and suddenly he was on top, bending the knife from the man's disease-weakened grip. Thumb under the man's jaw, Rex pushed his head back exposing the throat.

In his mind, Rex tore into that mottled flesh with his teeth, tasting the metallic blood as it gushed into his mouth. Rex thrust back his arm, aiming the knife at the quivering throat... and froze.

It was there again: that vast presence in the back of his mind. Not one of the regular voices that yelled, screamed and cursed at him, this presence was silent, just watching. It didn't judge, it didn't even really think... it was just *sad*. A deep and very distant melancholy that seemed to seep back from the very end of time.

"My Lord?" The words just slipped out. He dropped the knife, and rolled back onto his haunches as the knifeman, now just a gasping, choking vagrant, crawled away.

Watching the man's retreating back, Rex felt powerful for the first time in a long while. Alive. He turned and stared at the building's screaming face again, how it seemed to claw up from the crystal, positioned perfectly for him to find.

He picked up the leper's knife, a rusty notched blade, and slipped it into his pocket. Something rustled as he pushed it in... the Sister's note. The address of the job interview he was never going to make.

It seemed a profound choice: follow the leper back to the underworld, to dirt, dumpsters and a cold, pointless death, or step past into a new world, uncharted, untried, out to the edge of town and whatever work awaited him there. To a sense of normality, something he'd never thought he could have.

Life or death? Back or forward? As the huge presence seemed to swell inside his head, the decision was suddenly easy. He grasped the letter and stumbled past the screaming monolith and left the leper and his world behind him.

CHAPTER 6

Washed Up

Jett swam from a memory: a crystal-blue lake and an intense feeling of cold. The woman was there beside him again. Her face a wide grin, eyes full of something that he recognized, in this memory, as affection.

But the crawling, splashing, paddling actions of a human biped were tragically inefficient for his purpose of swimming through the Pacific Ocean. At times he barely moved as currents pushed and sheered him in new directions.

Jett turned to old-school, brutally efficient machine-learning. He constructed an algorithm with constraints and variables modeling the fibers making up his body. The algorithm's goal was to optimize his body shape to create maximum forward motion through the water.

He set the algorithm running, seeing his body configuration options as a vast multidimensional surface. Many balls rolled across the virtual surface, plunging through valleys, skipping across crests and down into pits, seeking the lowest point: the optimum body configuration for the task.

Fibers bridged the gaps between his legs and feet, while his lower torso flattened into a single broad paddle. His arms curved back and split into cables that clamped onto the paddle edges, acting as huge longitudinal muscles hauling the paddle up and down. Progress was a collection of iterative changes, big at first, followed by smaller, more measured adaptations. Sometimes two steps back made a new step forward as he became sleek, efficient, a new kind of fish.

He moved faster, surpassing any possible human speed, scything past squid, dolphins and blue-finned tuna. He dived deeper into cooler waters, less chance of detectors spotting the rogue heat signature. Jett knew no fatigue, felt no strain. Immersed in the process, thoughts and memories fell away leaving a near-perfect swimming machine.

The green arrow in his mind blinked, and a days-long voyage turned into just hours. When Jett floated back to the surface, he saw the dark cliffs of Coriolis Island as black silhouettes against the ruby embers of sunset. A hemisphere of foggy light reached over the towering basalt from distant Coriolis City, illuminating the beach as Jett washed up on the gray-sanded shore like an oil slick. A bell tolled and thousands of gulls, terns and skimmers across the beach cackled at each other as if relaying secrets.

Fishermen blockaded the beach, hundreds strewn across the bay in tents, hammocks, bivouacs and under upturned boats. Their catches decorated the camp. Fish hung from lines strung between wooden poles, fermented in jars, dried on planks and metal sheets, or cooked over the dimming campfires beneath the cliffs.

Jett flopped onto the damp sand. The fibers making up his finely-honed swim body relaxed and dissolved into a waving mass of tendrils. He looked like a bed of seaweed with a skull poised on top. As a being designed for space, he had no need of air, or breath, or the sense of smell. His olfactory bulb was a mere afterthought, but it worked, jangling with the salty odors of fish and their human predators.

He lay still sorting through heat signatures and shapes, letting his AI-tagger soak up this new world.

Humans.

Fishing poles.

Boats.

No obvious weapons.

The sharp-eyed beach gulls shifted uneasily as Jett oozed up the beach away from the lapping waters. His obsidian eyes scanned the coast, mapping gaps and paths through the crowds.

His mission plan was specific: strictly low profile, any conflict would draw attention, and Jett was different, very different. Powerful corporations would pay vast sums to acquire a voidian body. No, he was to learn to blend-in. Head for Coriolis City and access his mission brief from there.

The stars moved slowly across the sky and night eased into early morning. The human watchers drifted asleep, eyes winking out as their fires died. The tide pushed Jett up the beach, surf sounds hiding his motion as he slithered through the shadows only paces from slumbering bodies.

As he moved, he scanned the beach dwellers, noting clothes and colors, faces and features. His fullerene fibers bunched and knotted forming the bones, limbs and muscles of a biped. As he rose from the sand, his fine, outermost fibers squirmed like tiny worms and knitted into clothes and formed a crude skin face to cover his crystalline skull.

"Mommy!" The sound jolted him to a halt. *A child.* The miniature human stared at him through wide, tearful eyes, thumb jammed into its mouth. Jett stared back, wondering whether to run or fight. "Mommy!" The child yelled louder. People stirred. A female human rolled over and grunted something at the child, silencing it.

Jett moved away, ignoring the noises behind. He clambered up the rocks leaving the beach and its remaining watchers gazing out to sea. Changes in his body's reflective and refractive properties shifted his color from carbon black to muddy-brown, dark blue and algal green. The face was more challenging, requiring some of his facial biomech nodes to reconfigure into an LED screen. He formed a composite of several men's faces: gnarled from outside living, salt-crusted, dirt smeared. He stored the image and ported it onto his face screen, dialing down the brightness and cloaking his new features in artificial shadow.

He stood atop the cliffs looking back across the Pacific where earlier he'd been a fish and days before that, a meteor. The orbitals shone bright orange above, catching the sunrise that hadn't angled down to light the Earth yet. He felt the pain of distance, of being an alien on a hostile world, the only one of his kind to exist down here.

He tore his gaze away and stumbled off toward the city. He had never functioned in full Earth gravity before, but his memory held the details. Not the process of learning to walk or run, just the essential essence, the gist of it.

His stumble became a walk, then a jog. In his memory, she ran beside him. Her laugh was a curious distraction until his motions became natural and unconscious. Then the human memories dissolved away leaving just Jett, as she too faded and was gone.

Rex ducked out of the morning sun under the arm of a sprawling banyan tree. He'd left the crystal lake far behind as he flipped the crumpled paper from his pocket and eyed the letter once again. Walking was easy but reading… that was still hard.

The words swam across the page like cartoon-faced worms. They mocked him with their dots and squiggles that hovered on the edge of meaning before snapping back into an ache of confusion.

He flipped the page over to the blank side then back, flip, repeat, flip… repeat, like he was turning the starter on a crusty engine. The worms became letters again that he rolled around his tongue, buzzing and humming their names out into the air. "One-Two-One, Bedlinen Street, Tellus District."

An interview? The idea was insane. Surely better to hide in the side alleys? Let the Sisters forget he existed and then go searching. Searching for what? Drugs, drink… Glow? Yes, that was it. Glow. That deeply buried demon that wanted more of its kind.

His head swam and darkness seemed to radiate out from the sun, threatening to engulf him. *No...* The Future-Lord was watching. *Be a good boy, Rex.*

The Forever Friends Rescue Sanctuary was a gaunt wooden house with a brick chimney and flowery curtains that masked what could have been dark, sinister windows. A rustic noose of wire and fence poles encircled its dusty yard crammed with tumbledown outbuildings and kennels chained together by laundry-lines, makeshift power cables, and flowering creepers. Smoke curled from the chimney, but Rex smelled a different, distinctive smell: wet fur.

He entered the gate and stood stock-still in the center of the yard, aware of the eyes watching from the kennels. The dogs surged out, defensive, curious and wary of strangers. Rex assumed a dominant posture, letting them come, allowing the conversation of body language to take its course before wilting into a submissive pose and dropping to his knees. Immersed in wet snouts and wagging tails, it felt like home. Darkness came but this time it was a soft, loving darkness, like the underside of a family dining table–

And then he was under that table, surrounded by socks and feet. Cards shuffled, beer glasses clinked and voices wafted down in soft, incomprehensible soundscapes.

"No one really wants to live forever," he heard a woman say. "Life's just the right length to do everything you need. Only a dog would be happy doing the same old thing day after day, for all eternity."

"Yeah, dogs and goldfish," said another, deeper voice, while playfully gouging Rex's soft middle with a threadbare toe.

"What's going on?" The shout hauled Rex out from his dark comfort and dumped him gasping and reeling back on hard dirt, covered in slobbering dogs. "Back off everyone, back off!" The sea of dogs parted, and an elderly woman stepped through, scrubbing-brush in one hand, stun-wand in the other.

A rogue woof escaped Rex's mouth before he found his human voice. "Err – I'm here for – for the job." He clambered to his feet, eyeing the stun-wand. The dogs showed no fear; the wand had never been used on them.

"You scared the Shubert out of me," the woman said, easing past eager dogs to stand before him. She was tall and lithe with formidable gray hair, rolled-up sleeves and a ghostly white face.

"The S-Sisters of Salvitor sent me," Rex stammered, handing her the note. She held the letter up in front of her face and moved it back and forth trying to focus on the writing. Remembering the Sister's advice, Rex stood up straight, puffed out his chest, and presented his hand. "I'm Rex," he said. "Pleased to meet you."

She ignored the hand and continued inspecting the letter. "I see," she said. "Tell me, Rex, do you have much experience with dogs?"

It felt like a cage closing in around him: the woman's fierce eyes, the dog eyes and the other eyes – those inside his head – all watching and waiting. He was suddenly in their spotlight, as if his life was of urgent interest to them all.

Words tumbled from his mouth, the wrong words. "Yes, lots actually. I used to be one."

"You used to *be* a dog?"

"It was a long time ago." It didn't seem like the kind of explanation the woman expected. He felt his mind curling into a ball of shame.

She stared on as he wilted under her gaze, "Well, I'm glad to see you are one of us now."

He exhaled carefully as she refocused on the letter, this time at arm's length. "Well, I need someone who's a hard worker."

"I work hard," he nodded. "I scrub and clean all day at the hostel." He mimed some scrubbing actions, feet shuffling through the dirt.

"I need someone with good legs who can walk dogs all day long, especially the bigger ones. Nobody here has the energy to walk those."

He slapped his thighs indicating the presence of legs. "I've got legs. Good legs. I can walk for miles." Suddenly things were going his way.

"But most of all, I need someone who is honest and reliable."
She pinned him with a withering stare. Rex heard the Sisters
telling him again to keep his chin up, act normal, look tall and
confident. But it was too late.

"Have you been in some sort of trouble, Rex?" she asked quietly.
Her eyes widened as they swept his face, drilling down into every
nick and scar as if reading a coded transcript of every wrong thing
he'd done in his life.

"Life's been... hard." He mopped his brow with his forearm,
trying to hide his face. "I try and do the right thing, but sometimes..."
His words fizzled out like another good deed gone wrong.

I let a man live today, he wanted to say. The fight on the crystal
lake was still raw in his mind, but it surely proved he was a good
person, a worthy person. He felt his back straighten, and for the
first time met her eyes.

"Well," she said, her pointed gaze finally flickering away. "The
Sisters think highly of you. I don't know what trouble you were
in, Rex, but here we all get a second chance." She slapped him
playfully across the shoulder. "I've had dozens of them." She
cackled like a movie witch and turned to the dogs, whose snouts
were all buried firmly in Rex's lower regions, tails wagging. "I may
be the conductor of this orchestra, but I always trust the instincts
of my musicians, and they seem to think you are alright."

Handing back the letter, she grabbed his sweating hand in a
brisk shake. "I'm Mrs Ogilvy. You can call me Mrs O. Welcome to
the Forever Friends Sanctuary."

All the eyes vanished, spinning away like seeds in the wind.
The dogs bounded off, leaving Rex standing, frozen in a moment
of elation. Mrs O headed for the house while he stared up at the
sky. "Splendid. Now come along, I'll show you around, there's
scrubbing, and feeding, and of course walking and..."

She kept talking, but Rex heard nothing. He felt a great sonic
boom of joy that seemed to reverberate through his skull and on
all the way to the Future-Lord at the end of time.

CHAPTER 7

Remember to Breathe

People.

Jett watched them from inside a roofless building shell, one of many that lined the banks of the Scoria river. They milled around in large numbers on the bridge that hosted an early morning market, the only unbroken bridge in miles. He could easily ford the river but that would attract attention. Instead, he watched, planned, and attempted to blend in while his AI-tagger system categorized and monitored this new and unfamiliar world.

People. Small-arms, possible concealed weapons.

Non-hostile.

Jett's body architecture didn't allow him to experience pain. Instead, his memory was a repository of experiences gleaned from a different being, with a different body: the searing spike of a bullet wound, the dull ache of cancer, a throbbing bruise, a migraine. He felt something similar when watching all these people, a knot in his stomach – but, of course, he had no stomach.

Fear? Anxiety? But they were just people. Weak, frail, slow-thinking, biological people. What was there to be afraid of?

He stepped out from the shadows into the morning light. It was time to move the mission forward, to integrate and become a human, doing whatever humans did on bridges in the early morning.

Anxiety. He hated the feeling. Such a complex knot to undo. Far easier to neutralize them, no witnesses, no after-effects or consequences. He mentally rehearsed that plan, and decided it had a problematic boundary issue in that he could never be completely sure he'd eliminated all the observers, human and machine.

Onwards then, down to the bridge. Limps were easy to emulate, he had an excellent baseline model of human anatomy, just snap a bone, remove some toes, up the friction coefficient on a crucial joint. Humans never healed back to their nascent forms; wounds always left evidence, scars, changes in gait and posture.

Face hidden deep inside the hood he'd extruded from his neck and shoulder fibers, Jett paused at the edge of Market Bridge, a wide, ornate arch spanning the river and covered in buildings. People swarmed like ants, erecting stalls, kiosks and signs, piling produce, dancing around each other in complex overlapping patterns but never touching. Beach people mingled with well-dressed individuals that crossed over from the East Firmament district of Coriolis City. They all had something to trade: food, perfume, technology, drugs. The bridge formed a safe zone between two different worlds.

Jett stepped off the riverbank and onto the bridge. His anxiety ballooned as people crushed in from all sides.

Proximity alert!

No one touched in space. No one even got close. His tagger flashed red, sketching green paths through the masses as it plotted his escape. Weapon alerts smattered over his mental display making it hard to see:

Guns, knives, spears, arrows–

He hunched low and pushed through, surprised at how easy humans were to shove aside. Angry grunts and yells followed him, some poked or pushed back. Words came from many mouths, many directions merging into a single mash of noise containing no useful information. He struggled to filter individual voices, fragmented transcriptions flashed by, tagged with language markers, local patois, idioms, guesses at meanings and response options. He went faster, plowing through legs and torsos, scattering angry people.

Danger! Local hostility index approaching critical!

His memory understood that he was panicking, that he should breathe, slow down, calm the anger around him – but he couldn't.

Targeting options overlaid the translations, highlighting soft spots on heads, throats, and joints. A grinning man thrust something at his face.

Sandwich: carbohydrate-based sustenance for human consumption.

Jett thrust out a hand and the man reeled backward tumbling a half-dozen others into a heap with him.

"You! Come here!" yelled a man in a military-style uniform, waving a pistol in the air.

Jett ran. His body took on the task of evasive maneuvers, jolting him side-to-side, changing pace, pulling his head down below the level of the crowd. He churned through people and stalls leaving a wake of disaster behind.

Every eye on the bridge suddenly found him.

"Stop! Or I'll shoot!"

His legs lengthened, clothing fibers unwound and coiled around them like springs. He vaulted the last fifty meters of bridge in a single bound over gasping bystanders, landing squarely on the East Firmament riverbank. He hit the ground, rolled and ran. Humans moved in slow motion, vanishing behind along with their noises, smells and inscrutable facial expressions.

He slowed from a run back to a brisk walk, zigzagging through back-alleys and side-streets, shrinking, slowing, morphing from invading alien monster back to shambling beach dweller, shifting colors to blend into the surroundings.

East Firmament was a cleaner district, with maintained houses, factories and many bridges over the elaborate Interstice canal system that divided Coriolis City into districts and zones.

Mission to blend-in: Failed. What happened? Where were those human memories Gale told him would come when he needed them?

He crossed into Welkin, Coriolis's downtown district. More people. No escape from them here. Welkin was a dense circle of towers and parks surrounding a central lake of fusion glass. A permanent scar on the city, a gift from the Nova-Insanity.

He stuck to the side streets, face hidden as if in shame at his failure. The open space of the glass lake beckoned. A flat circle of translucent crystal over a thousand meters in diameter, ringed by singed and rebuilt buildings, towers that leaned alarmingly inward, and the sparse attempts at new construction. The glass novascape was now a park. Trenches cut into the crystalline surface and were filled with earth; plants and trees formed pleasing green spaces where people walked and sat.

Monuments and sculptures lined the spider's web of cycle paths and walkways. The whole area resembled a giant ice-sculpture, one that would never melt.

Jett found a bench and sat, feigning normality. Observe and learn, know the enemy. People whisked past on bikes and on foot. Some talked to themselves, some talked to anyone or anything around. Others shouted randomly or sang songs. There were jugglers, storytellers, preachers, recruiters, conmen, peddlers and healers, each vying for attention from the passing thousands.

Jett sat, watching, letting them flow past like cosmic rays around a magnetic bubble. His Inner-I gathered information on their clothes, eyes, smiles and grimaces, hairstyles, gaits and the quirks and tics of movement that made every one of them so different.

"You ain't from around here." A woman with just a single, visible tooth planted herself on the bench next to him. Her head was a grotesque orb, like some vegetable-based parody of human, but with no nose or ears. She sucked in air through two holes in the front of her face and eyed him through a single, oversized eyeball. Her other eye was glass that sparkled like a miniature novascape. She hid her hands inside wool mittens that radiated no heat signatures.

Leper. The tag stuck to her in his gaze. *Street jargon for a user of the longevity drug Lepa.*

He stared, mind a blank as his social modeling routines pushed an appropriate response onto his vision. He read the words, but no sounds came from his mouth. He couldn't recall ever using his actual voice before. All communications in space were through Inner-I or military gestures. He tried again, powering the empty cavity inside his chest, sucking in air and forcing it back out across unused vocal cords.

The woman raised her functional eyebrow as gurgling noises emerged from Jett's mouth. He spawned a comparison algorithm that matched his sound emissions to the intended vocalization. He gurgled again... closer... not quite. The woman's eyebrow rose higher.

"What makes you say that?" The words finally emerged intact.

She shrugged, understanding, and her eyebrow dropped back to normal orientation. Jett felt a surge of elation. His first successful voidian-human communication outside of a simulator.

"You look different and you speak... funny," she said, suddenly distracted by traffic noise. Her hidden thoughts played out across her face in twitches and momentary expressions. Distraction over, she looked him up and down. "There's something weird about you." She stood up shaking her head and wandered around behind him. Jett twitched with combat readiness as her hands touched his shoulders. He struggled to replicate the soft, flexible texture of cloth over human flesh from the near-rigid fibers of his fullerene flesh.

She leaned in close to his ear. "You forgot to breathe, honey." With a cackle she headed off across the park, passing from flowerbed to flowerbed like a child.

Jett slumped back from combat readiness. He should have realized his lack of chest movement wouldn't go unnoticed. Another mistake.

An algorithm set his chest expanding and contracting in simulated respiration. The old woman looked back, "What are you?" she yelled, putting her hands above her head in an X-symbol.

The Cross of Convolution, The Multiplier. Symbol of prophesized man-

machine hybridization used in several disparate Future-Lord religions
across the post Nova-Insanity Americas and Pacific Islands.

Combat training had taught Jett the utility of myths and legends. The scars on his face dulled and vanished, leaving just one that wriggled and moved across his cheek and changed into a diagonal cross.

"I'm what comes next," he said to her retreating back as she stepped into the crowd and was gone. Blend-in and learn. He mentally thanked the old lady for the lesson and followed her out of the park to look for somewhere to live.

"When was the last time you left your room, Tomas?" Ellayna asked.

"Why would I leave my room?"

"When was the last time you actually *met* a real, live person?"

Long silence, mumbles and breaths. "Ellayna, as I've grown older, I've concluded that human contact is vastly overrated. Better to remain at a distance, safely behind the impenetrable technological barriers that we so diligently erected all those years ago." He stopped, seemed to think for a second and then continued, his voice now containing an unmistakable modulation of hope. "Are you lonely, Ellayna?"

"Don't tell me you don't suffer from it as well." She moved to stand in front of her mirror. Naked, she looked disheveled, her skin a haunted, sun-deprived gray with dark rings around her eyes. The Simmorta, the miraculous nanotech devices inside her body, struggled to keep her alive in this environment of micro-gravity and dangerous radiation. She hated those machines, but without them no one lasted more than a handful of months in orbit.

"I'm happy to meet in a VR room, Ellayna." His voice trembled, or was it just the cosmic rays messing with the comms network? "We could play some immersive games, catch up on old times. It's just like reality but–" He seemed to remember Ellayna's recent run-in with the VR bugs "–sorry. I know you like the gravity gym.

I'd go exercise with you, but I've set my Simmorta to dormant and can barely walk at the moment."

"I didn't think you were one for fads, Tomas."

"Give the longevity technology a rest and let the body age naturally for a while. Then, when I switch it back on, I get a boost and I should get much healthier. Lots of our fellow directors are trying it."

She called up her full-immersion avatar, superimposing it on her room. She dialed back the age-slider so that a younger, tauter Ellayna stood before her. Twenty-year-old body, full head of hair, piercing, learned eyes. She toyed with the hair style, clothing, skirt length... Perhaps twenty was too young, maybe thirty. She nudged the aging slider forward a little. She twirled the avatar around: *good. No... perfect!*

"I have a favor to ask, Tomas. I'm heading into an immersive VR meeting, private affair, bit nervous. Can I send you a link to my life-signs monitor? I don't trust the auto-monitor, so if you catch anything dangerous then call the medics and security."

She felt his sadness, knew that he assumed she was meeting another, certainly younger, man. "Of course," he said, softly. "Anything for you, Ellayna."

"Thank you." She stared at Tomas's image in the corner of her vision: rounded shoulders, chin on his chest. "Think of this as practice. When I'm used to meeting in VR again, perhaps we can do something fun, together?" She saw him perk up, smile and nod. She dismissed his image, severed their connection and flicked open Trabian's message containing the address of his virtual construction. "Let's see what games young Trabian has in mind..."

She settled back onto the bed, wrapping low-g support webbing around her arms and legs, and nodded toward her slowly rotating avatar, poised for action. "Go get him, girl." She hit the immersion button in her visual field and her apartment faded, running like dripping paint, before solidifying into something new.

Gravity. Full immersion meant gravity. That alone was reason enough to use it.

She stood in a doorway looking across a large, comfortable room with a huge viewing screen and a curved red couch that could seat a dozen.

"That wasn't so bad," she gasped, finally remembering to breathe.

"Excuse me?" said the youthful figure sprawled across the couch, eyebrow raised.

"Trabian!" she said, acting surprised, as if expecting somebody else.

"Are you okay, Ellayna?" He rolled off the couch and offered a supporting hand.

"It's nothing, just a touch of VR-phobia." She dismissed his aid and stood swishing her skirt, enjoying the feeling of being inside her virtual body: *full-immersion. So real.* She was light, fresh, young and alive… and living in a complete dream world.

Trabian wore a fresh-faced avatar, youthful but older than she remembered, but then she hadn't seen him for real in years. He dressed in sharp, angular clothing, a naïve attempt to look wise and important in front of his elder. "You look so–"

"Young?" she said, hopefully. He nodded, seemingly lost for words. "I dressed up a little, don't get out that much these days."

She looked away, embarrassed at his staring, while composing herself and resetting her professional demeanor. "Why did you ask me here?"

"If we couldn't meet in VR, then I'd never get to see you at all." He feigned a sad smile.

She turned her attention back to the surrounding room, really an ornate TV lounge. "Is this a real room?"

"It's my newsroom back on Cloud8."

"Are *you* real?" She suddenly felt alarmed by that idea, an invasion of privacy, her dumping herself into his room and seeing his real person.

"Maybe, you'll have to touch me to find out."

She ignored his cumbersome tease. "What are we watching?" She eased down onto the couch next to him, keeping a comfortable distance.

His lusty grin turned down, suddenly serious. "I come here to relax and catch up on news." He motioned to the big screen and it became a deep holographic view of various news feeds coming up from Earth. "I was watching the Breakout Alliance invading yet another country under the guise of being the democratically elected liberators of downtrodden people."

"So skeptical, Trabian. The Alliance at least pretends to be democratic before invading."

One of the feeds closed in on the Alliance craft, a super-hopper class embassy ship, a colossal, crudely pyramid-shaped structure surrounded by a halo of smaller ships and a fine mist of tiny countermeasure craft. It rose from its sea launch platform, turned in midair, ignited a cluster of massive booster rockets and headed up to the stratosphere. "Look at that thing," Trabian said, voice filled with awe. "It's massive."

She nodded. Her own awe tempered by the feeling she was witnessing the instrument of her own destruction. "Quite a machine. Possibly one of the most advanced technologies to appear since the Nova-Insanity."

"Are we afraid of it, Ellayna?"

"We'd blow it out of the sky if it ever came into low orbit." The confidence in her voice was an attempt to mask the sinking dread she felt inside. The footage switched to the craft landing. It hovered over a crushed and ruined city as if seeking the right spot while giving its halo of fighting machines time to vanquish any opposition. It slowly descended into an open park. The tag identified the city as Old Bucharest, Neutral Europe. The machine lit with incoming fire as the local dictatorship unleashed what was left of its defensive forces.

"Why there?" Trabian asked.

"Black Sea access. Maybe some resources the Alliance needs. Taunau calls it 'practice'."

"For us?"

"They started with simple island nations, then graduated to tinpot dictatorships in Africa and Europe. Next will be something bigger, testing their defenses and their technology and that formidable offensive capability they've developed."

"And then us." Trabian slumped back in the couch. For a moment she felt sorry for him. So young, so alone, just waiting for the end. Like them all really. "What are we doing, Ellayna? How can we stop that?"

"We're safe as long as they can't manufacture Simmorta. It's that simple. They need it. We make it. If they try and take it, then we have the Armageddon option: blow it all up and everyone loses." The explanation sounded stupid, here, now, with such young ears listening. She'd heard it so many times though, justifying so many crimes.

"Why not just let the world have it? Everyone becomes effectively immortal and our expansion into space can resume just like before the Insanity."

Tomas, of course, would agree. Give it away, free ourselves. Free the world, just like Del and all the rebels expected to do by defecting. They all died, except Del. Empowered by the victory, the Protectionist faction remained strong and determined to this day. What belonged to the GFC should remain within the GFC. Giving it away would hand the baton of power to somebody else. An unknown, untested, and untrusted regime.

She flashed Trabian a sour look. "Remind me, why am I here?"

His head dropped and his masculine bravado faded back to that of a shy young man. "I found something interesting regarding the meteor event."

"Defector event," she corrected him, catching his eyes flicking upward and scanning her body. He must be wondering what she really looked like. He knew her age. Did he care? People raised to use VR often didn't worry how reality appeared. But then again, was this really *him*? She could reach out and touch him. If he was real then her avatar would just break around him, no sensation for either of their bodies. But if he was virtual, like her, then they could touch and feel sensation, that tingle of passion, that–

He snapped his eyes away and continued talking. "I checked through data feeds from some remote sensor outposts on our mothballed orbitals and found this." He pulled a viewing screen out of thin air. As his fingers fumbled to enlarge the video display, she noticed him shuffle closer on the couch, just barely encroaching on her bubble of personal space. *He must be virtual if he's trying to touch me.*

The image showed a star-like twinkle of orange. "Color enhanced," Trabian said, eyes distant on his workspace. "It's a flash of laser backscatter. The reason no comms showed coming from Cloud8 or Cloud9 was that someone used a laser, very precise, and unless our monitors were at very specific angles, we couldn't have detected which direction it came from."

"And how does this help us?" She leaned into him a little, gave the boy some encouragement.

The screen changed to a mass of ray diagrams. "AI reconstruction algorithms on the four backscatters I detected."

"Four?"

"The first was a very short burst, microseconds, possibly an activation signal for the onboard voice beacon we heard. The others were longer, possibly software patches or if it was a person onboard, an encrypted message. Either way, they all trace back to a point somewhere around here–" The main viewing screen flashed and became a closeup of TwoLunar.

Ellayna felt her heart leap, wondered if Tomas was monitoring her vitals. What did he make of that? Seeing the slowly tumbling ruin tore open memories of death, destruction and grief. At the outbreak of the Nova-Insanity, someone had smuggled a nova device onboard the giant, incomplete orbital, blowing the side out and killing thousands. The attached space-elevator cable had broken from its anchor point on Transit Mountain. She remembered it glistening and fraying like silken threads as it wrapped endlessly around the crippled orbital. A celestial spider slowly enveloping its gigantic catch. "Ursurper Gale?"

Trabian jumped to his feet. "Why is that – thing – *Gale*,

allowed to… I would say *live,* but *exist* seems more appropriate?"

"When Gale broke free during the Great Defection, we chased him; we tried to kill him for years. But he's smart and resourceful, designed to survive out there. In the end, we let him go. But if he's truly meddling with GFC affairs then we need him stopped."

Trabian dropped back onto the couch, a few inches closer, his hand very close to Ellayna's knee. "This is good information?" He stared at his hand as if willing it to make the jump on its own.

"Very good, Trabian. You should present it to the security committee immediately." She stared at his twitching fingers, wondering if he'd dare, and what she'd do if he did. She reached out and patted the back of his hand. The shudder of human contact was very real which meant that Trabian was just an avatar, like she was. "Thank you for bringing this to my attention first." She released his hand and stood, noting the flash of disappointment that crossed his face.

"I'd like to help capture Gale," Trabian said. "I'd like to be as useful as possible." He stood and moved closer, disarmingly confident, and leaned in as if angling to kiss her.

She reached out and stroked his face, seeing his eyes swim in momentary ecstasy. "I'll be in touch, Trabian." She hit the exit icon on her virtual vision and faded back to her apartment, whilst enjoying the afterimage of Trabian's slack-jawed gawp as she left him hanging.

Back in her apartment, she unfastened herself from the support webbing, relieved to be safely out of VR. She used an image-capture to grab Trabian's avatar from the Inner-I recording, then spread him seductively across her bed as she chiseled away his clothing, allowing her AI to interpolate the unknown details.

She filled his eyes with that boyish lust and his face with that winning smile. "Well, well, Trabian," she said. "Have I found myself a new toy, or are you just another Protectionist spy?" He always sided with her when voting, but he had allies on the GFC board who probably didn't vote the same way. Perhaps the right leverage could turn a few votes, and once secure in her position, perhaps then... she could allow herself to play.

CHAPTER 8

The Star-River

Rex stared at his wall of checkmarks, trying to ignore the guilt he felt deep in his stomach. "Tell me of your plans for the day, Rex," the wall asked.

There were five new Xs drawn in bold, optimistic strokes with new icons for dog washing, dog feeding, kennel cleaning and medical assistance. He'd tried to scrub away the mark from five days earlier, the bullseye that signified that he was leaving and never coming back. But the insipid wax from the crayon seeped into the porous stone leaving a guilty red remnant of his transgression.

"Rex?"

He jumped. "No time, Sister. Work to do." He splashed water over his face and began a quick rub around his teeth with his regulation-issue toothbrush.

"Who else works at the dog sanctuary, Rex?"

"There's Hanna from the rich part of town. I can smell her perfume miles away. Then Frizell. Only half of him works, one leg, one arm, an eye." His words blew toothpaste and saliva over his tiny wall mirror.

"Tell me more about Frizell, what does he–"

"Gotta go, Sister." He grabbed his headphones and ran for the door. Since his new job, the Sisters had lightened his work duties around the hostel. Mainly cleaning-up after breakfast which he did at double speed, like a silent tornado that somehow avoided all contact with people.

Rex opened the wire gate into the sanctuary's yard, over an hour early. "Splendid! Such enthusiasm." Mrs O greeted him in the yard. "I need more workers like you, productive and punctual."

"Just me, Mrs O. You only need me." He eyed Frizell who dawdled into the yard behind him as if he'd spent the night in the bushes outside. Broom in hand, he'd shaved off all his hair revealing a skull covered in Future-Lord tattoos. He stared at Rex with his good eye as if mentally disassembling him into tiny fragments.

He wondered if Mrs O ever slept. She was still working when he left in the evening, and always busy when he arrived the next morning. Other helpers rolled in later, and sometimes not at all. But Rex understood Mrs O. If he could eat, sleep and drink here, then he would never leave either.

"These aren't just any dogs," she explained to Rex while showing him how to administer Rust's skin medication. She patted the brindle pit-bull on the head and stood fiddling with a tube of cream. "These are Forever Friends. They've had their genetic life cycles engineered to match that of humans. They still get sick and diseased, but won't grow old like regular dogs. They take much longer to grow from puppies into adults as well."

"*A friend for life!*" Rex said, mimicking the booming voice from the TV commercial he remembered from his childhood.

"Before the Nova-Insanity, people bought them as presents for their newborn children. It was one of the GFC's first money-making longevity ventures. This was back when it was still just a startup corporation on an independent nation ship in the Pacific."

Rex ran his fingers through the dog's fur. It felt like any other dog, wiry outer layer and soft down covering warm skin. "They feel the same."

Mrs O smiled. "They are as warm and alive as you and I, Rex."

"But nobody wants them?" Rex said, as the voices stirred inside of him claiming *nobody wants us, either.*

"Human medicine took a different path. We are sold immortality through drugs and machinery. The pay-to-stay-or-go-away model. And when we no longer pay, we sometimes leave a friend behind." She patted Rust and he plopped down from the medical bench. She led Rust back to his kennel, leaving Rex to scrub down.

He fixated on his cleaning brush: the stubble, the pale flesh-colored plastic... like an old man's head – a dead man lying in an alley. On came the panic, trembling knees, the chatter in the back of his skull. He remembered Sister-Two's words, "Focus on the Future-Lord, Rex. He is you. He is all of us. Believe and you will be there, in Haven, at the end of time." The old man's head returned to a brush in his hand and the voices rolled away to silence.

Mrs O was back, staring at him and his poised brush. "Get scrubbing then, Rex."

And Rex became whole again, purposefully distracted. Smiles felt unfamiliar, as if that particular skill had been tortured out of him by life. He practiced a smile. It felt okay. "If I ever become an abandoned dog, I'd like to come back here and be looked after by you, Mrs O."

"Splendid. You'd be very welcome. The only conditions to becoming a resident here are that you are a forever-dog and that I get to choose a new name for you. A special name."

"What would my new name be?" He bounced from foot to foot like an excited child.

She adopted a thoughtful pose. "Where were you born, Rex?"

"Not sure... I remember being in England when I was real young."

She paused as Frizell delivered the next patient to the examination table, a poodle named Hendrix. Frizell's eye never left Rex until he rounded the corner and left. "Ah, England, glorious! There are many fine English composers, Purcell, Tavener, Britten, Elgar. I have a passion for Ralph Vaughan Williams, so maybe you could become Ralph? Or... yes... yes... splendid... *Vaughan.*" Rex didn't like the sound of Vaughan but didn't care. Did a dog really know its own name? "Are you familiar with his work, Rex? 'The Lark Ascending'?"

Rex stared at her, face a blank.

After a long, awkward silence, Mrs O asked. "How did you end up on Coriolis?"

No one ever asked about Rex's past. At least, he couldn't remember anyone asking. He should have felt flattered that someone was interested, but instead it felt more like a threat. "I don't remember... lots of head injuries and–" He couldn't bring himself to say "drugs," but saw on Mrs O's face that she understood.

"Head injuries, huh?" She paused in her examination of Hendrix.

"Mother hit my head a lot. She didn't want me having the voices inside like she did." Mrs O raised an eyebrow and focused on prodding the poodle's rear end. "I deserved it, I suppose. I did stupid things. This one time, I did something so terrible, she punished me right there on the steps outside the supermarket. Smashing my head into the concrete until the police and ambulances came and took us all away. It didn't hurt that much really–"

A tear appeared on Mrs O's cheek. "And they sent you here?"

"No. I never saw Mother again. I lived in a government hostel, bit like this place, but for kids. I escaped, stowed away on a container ship leaving Portsmouth. Things went pretty well until the Nova-Insanity screwed everything up."

The dogs started barking as someone entered the yard. A burly man, strolling into the compound as if he owned it, body-language daring the dogs to attack him. He wore a medieval-style cape draped over a bullet-proof chest plate. His arms were tattooed with blood-soaked battleaxes. They hung loose by his sides like a gunslinger's, hands poised above the hilts of twin pistols in their holsters.

"Local street-protection militia," Mrs O said, trying to push Rex out of sight behind the examination table.

"Who's the freak?" The man sneered, jabbing a thumb at Rex.

"Who this?" Mrs O. feigned surprise as if just noticing Rex. "This is just Rex," She tugged him back into the open. "Rex, meet Regoth."

Rex staggered upright, suppressing the strong urge to drop to all-fours and slink back under the table. "Regoth is our local protector. We are fully paid members of the Hackerman jurisdiction and enjoy all the wonderful benefits of being under their protective wing."

Rex held out a trembling hand. "Pleased to meet you, sir."

Regoth ignored it and just stood chewing on what looked like an eyeball. Every time he opened his mouth the pupil leered out at Rex.

"It's extra for new employees. And extra again for freaks," he said, leering at Rex.

Mrs O. grew suddenly taller, the curve of her back unfolding as she rose up to surpass Regoth's height. "My protection policy covers myself and up to four employees. Now kindly hand over his button and be on your way." Her voice held an operatic power that pushed back against Regoth's bluster.

He toyed nervously with his weapons while trying to hold her gaze. Rex was sure they would be killed, but Regoth's shoulders drooped and his eyes wandered back to the ground. "Fine," he snapped. "Stay safe old woman." He dropped a small green disk onto the ground and stalked away.

Mrs O picked up the button. "Wear it when you're in this neighborhood. It'll keep the Hackerman militia off your back, but they don't respect the Sisters." She eyed the Sisters' orange Future-Lord disk on Rex's shirt and pinned the new one beside it. She leaned in close as Regoth moved out of earshot. "Just remember to take it off in other districts or you'll get harassed by their militia."

Rex spent the rest of the day walking dogs. He clustered the smaller ones into large groups and led them on loops around the yard. The larger ones went in twos and threes, out on excursions to the local park, supposedly safe inside the Hackerman protection jurisdiction. He fostered a barely contained anger that his precious rescue sanctuary should be subject to militia protection and rules, and that people like Regoth existed. But Mrs O had faced him down and showed that truth and wisdom still had some power. Maybe the Future-Lord was truly on their side.

He inspected the security badge, expecting a hi-tech transponder, but it was just a disk with a crude image of crossed battle-axes stamped onto it. His eyes roamed farther, out past the Ring Hills to the distant edge of Coriolis City, out where there were bigger spaces, room for those with boundless energy to rage free. *My future is out there*, he thought. Not in these ruined towers and derelict streets. He knew it. The dogs knew it. The vast presence riding along in the back of his mind knew it.

Dusk settled and Rex headed back to the hostel, leaving Mrs O to batten-down the gates and secure the dogs. A lot of the city lay ahead. He touched the disk making sure it was secure and wasn't surprised when he didn't feel any safer.

Smoke curled up past the window of the tenth-story room, seeping in through cracks in the corrugated plastic shutters from where Jett watched the street below as a riot unfolded, escalated and turned into street warfare.

Coriolis's main news channel played inside a tiny window in Jett's Inner-I vision. A red-faced reporter ducked rocks and Molotov cocktails as he ran from building to building angling in on the best action.

The riot started as a protest against the local utility militia's inadequate garbage collection regimen, but it soon spiraled out of control as the militia drafted supporters who clashed with pro-Alliance forces and street gangs looking for a fight. As the rioters lost ground and fell back, they ignited piles of trash they'd stacked against the walls of the tallest buildings. Jett assumed that if they couldn't have the city the way they wanted it, then they'd burn it to the ground. An odd perspective.

He left the window and folded himself into a seated position in the middle of the floor. He didn't understand why people sat down. Standing was more versatile in its range of response options. Yet, he'd seen so many people sitting even though human anatomy seemed poorly designed to do so. Determined to learn, he adopted the pose while speaking into his Inner-I and practicing his Coriolian dialect.

"Position secure. Requesting mission update." An image of Ursurper Gale's carbon-black skull sprang into the room, superimposed across his normal vision. It floated awkwardly above the furnishings as Jett moved his head. "Update your status, Jett." Gale spoke directly into Jett's mind using his own patchy version of Coriolian.

Jett leaned into the image. Awed by the face of his creator, even if it was the same face he saw in mirrors. "I'm secure, Ursurper. I stole money and rented a room from a militia organization called the Broken – they sublease these downtown apartments from a larger militia group called the Sons of Salvitor." Gale had loaded Jett's Inner-I with an edited image of his own mind during Jett's training. The image responded like Gale and contained the full mission brief for Jett to access at appropriate moments. Using AI-Gale avoided unnecessary communications which could give watchers clues to his location and intents.

Gale's skull image twitched as if thinking. "Glow is the name of a street drug that originated in Coriolis City and now garners interest from external powers, especially the Breakout Alliance. My intelligence suggests Glow is an injectable, body-wide biomech network, a somanet, possibly a hacked version of the GFC's Simmorta. The code that renders Simmorta uncopiable has been broken. We need to find out who did this, Jett. Such knowledge and expertise will be invaluable to the voidian cause."

"Why are longevity drugs of interest to us?"

"All drugs are fungible. Destroying the GFC and liberating our people will render Simmorta non-existent making technology like Glow highly valuable."

Jett felt deflated. This was not the glorious combat mission he had imagined. "You want me to become a drug dealer?"

"Trace the origins of Glow. Find out who cracked the code that's meshed into every biomech node the GFC sells. Are they manufacturing the drug on Coriolis Island? Is it manufactured from scratch or just repurposed Simmorta? How is this possible, since Simmorta keys to its original host's biology and cannot normally be transferred?"

Jett remained silent, unsure how to proceed. Gunfire erupted outside in the square. He felt the building groan and shift as the heat of the fire below grew more intense. Doors slammed, and people shouted as they panicked to evacuate the building.

Gale continued. "Ten days ago, I monitored an open-channel distress call emanating from Coriolis City. The transmitting Inner-I was registered under the name Xell Vollarer, a smuggler who helped move goods to and from Coriolis Island."

Jett heard a crackling recording of a human voice emanating from Gale's image. *"They're in my head... messing with my head. This was never meant for me. I should never have seen these things. I've seen the Star-River... the coming madness... this is your burden not mine..."*

At the word "Star-River", Jett's memory threw out an image. His hand in front of his face, now a fleshy, pink human hand. In the palm sat a silvery ball. Small, cold and dense, it seemed to tingle as he rolled it around, filling his mind with possibilities and hope.

Xell's voice dissolved into what could have been an agonizing scream or whining signal noise.

"Vollarer may have self-terminated," Gale said.

"The Star-River?" Jett knew the Star-River, its name tripped descriptive tags in his vision as well as the edges of conversations and moments now edited from his mind.

The Star-River: An ultra-dense fractal memory device that exists in a perpetual state of quantum-superposition and models reality using active cultural meme-chains. Particularly: technology paths and social trends, but also changes in human thinking such as religion, market trends and geopolitical landscapes.

"This is valuable technology, Ursurper. How did this smuggler acquire it?" Jett felt Gale's own awe of the device. Through his chain of memories, he knew Gale once worked with the GFC's cofounder Del Krondeck on the Star-River when he was himself a lab experiment. Del's own obsession with the device had transferred to Gale, and Jett felt it as an ache, a need like the human addicts that he passed on the streets felt for their drugs.

"The machinations of how this was lost and ended up in Xell's hands is not known to me. But as a predictive device, cognitive substrate and a technology to take with us into the galaxy, the Star-River is invaluable. Find it, Jett. Cache it, or if we can't have it then destroy it, denying the technology to our enemies."

"I understand," Jett said. He remembered the precious feel of the shiny ball in his hand. Almost enough to make it worth fighting for but doubts entered his thoughts. "I trained for combat, Ursurper, combat in space, the assault on Cloud9, the glorious liberation of our–"

"Jett, others will take down the GFC. I will lead the liberation charge myself. I need you here, as the second prong in our attack. Use this opportunity to train and be amongst humans, understand our enemy."

Jett nodded and Gale's skull face faded from his vision. Suddenly, he was alone in the tiny, smoke-filled room. The illusion of connectedness to his own creator, to his people, vanished.

The apartment building was silent. Heat rose through the floor and walls and the plastic window shutters curled and tumbled away. He could escape disguised as a fleeing beggar, but the heat was so high, anyone watching would become suspicious.

Jett's makeshift clothing faded, the color draining back to his nascent carbon-black as he folded his body into a tight, withered-looking husk, like those he remembered seeing amongst the scalded, vacuum-ravaged wreckage of the TwoLunar orbital.

When the building collapsed, Jett rode the wreckage to the ground. Buried under tons of smoldering rubble, he lay listening as the riot faded. A militia rescue team half-heartedly dug through the rubble uncovering several charred corpses, including one that held together in an oddly resilient ball.

They slung the corpses onto the bed of a pickup truck and drove out of town toward a reprocessing plant that rendered bodies, extracting useful chemicals and nanotech drugs.

No one noticed a corpse slip off the back of the truck and into the darkness. It grew taller, thicker, clothing appeared out of a mist of fibers as it broke into a swift walk and headed back toward the city.

CHAPTER 9

Ursurper Gale

"Where the heck is it?" Ellayna thrashed through her single room apartment creating a cloud of whirling pens, papers, books and trinkets. *There!* She reached out and plucked the tiny gun from the corner near her bathroom. Microgravity was a bitch. Not strong enough to stave off atrophy or the problems associated with bathing, drinking, personal hygiene and practically everything humans needed to do to survive. It was, however, enough to drift any unsecured items into myriad unforeseen hiding places.

The tiny finger gun was a gift from Martin after her last fear-filled rout through the orbital, fleeing imaginary stalkers. She'd removed the weapon when showering, something Martin was very specific about doing. It held just three charges, but each could jolt enough electrical energy into an attacker to paralyze them rigid.

She left her room, taking a reluctant look back into her safe, cozy environment before closing the door, abandoning her stray possessions to clump and stick to walls and furnishings as their innate magnetism pulled them back into stable states.

Loneliness was so much more bearable with a gun on one's finger. She switched off her shoe magnets and bounced her way to the medical wing of Cloud9 enjoying her twirls and acrobatics like a young woman in her... late... fifties should do.

Upright and reattached to the floor, an AI did a quick identification ping of her Inner-I and let her inside. A nurse greeted her as she entered. The sound of clattering implements and voices felt like a storm on her ears that were conditioned to utter silence.

"Why so busy?" Ellayna asked, scanning the rows of waiting gurneys.

The nurse sighed. Her brow wrinkling into an expression that said much about the fickle stupidity of the average GFC director. "Idiots switching off their Simmorta. They forget how fast bodies degrade out here without a good, functioning somanet. Before they know it, they've stroked out, blown an aneurism or are battling acute organ failure. We go find them, bring them in and reboot their somanets." She turned and stormed away, yelling back over her shoulder. "Haven't been this busy since the Great Defection."

She passed through to the quieter wing of the medical complex, past two sleepy guards draped outside the VR monitoring unit where fully half of Cloud9's residents plugged-in and lived their lives in virtual worlds, fed by tubes, monitored by AIs. *Probably safe in there. Safe from the bugs... unless... somebody hacked the AI?*

The prison wing was right at the end. A converted research lab with only a single guard, and, as far as Ellayna was aware, only a single prisoner inside.

Del Krondeck's cell was an echoingly large space, stripped of decor and humanity down to its alloy wall panels and support joists. Ellayna stood in the doorway gazing across at her ex-lover, ex-best friend, the ex-cofounder and ex-chief science officer of the once mighty Genes and Fullerenes Corporation.

"Hello, Del," she said softly, while pinging his Inner-I with the same message. She didn't expect a reply from either as she walked over to the prone figure lying amongst the heaving knots of cables and tubes.

Emaciated and pallid, Del resembled a mummified corpse. His gray hair flowed in long wisps around his head, stirred by the light breeze from banks of computer server fans hissing and whirring as they crunched the vast number-scape that formed Del's own, personal virtual world. The place he'd retreated to years earlier and had never emerged from.

She pulled up the visitor's chair and sat, wrapping support webbing around her waist so she didn't float away. Her finger traced the line of his hooked nose and the heavy brow that gave Del that thoughtful, caring appearance even when comatose. The suck and blow of the respirator accompanied the musical chirps of medical monitors. Display screens jumped and writhed with brain activity and body functions.

Long ago this body had been so familiar. More than just familiar – intimate. *Where are you now, Del? Colonizing a simulated galaxy? Creating the next Simmorta?*

She missed his love, his energy, his passion for anything novel. Those nights poring over diagrams and papers, mapping ideas and thoughts onto virtual whiteboards. She and Del would dance with ideas like lovers, alive and fully immersed in the experience. *Oh Del, we could still have that – at least some of that – if you hadn't betrayed us all.*

She hadn't known about his plans: the uprising, the defections. Maybe he'd just assumed she'd come along. That she'd agree with his cause. *Which I so nearly did.* But if she had, then they'd both be dead now. *I stayed behind to keep us alive.* She knew that was a lie, but had told it to herself so many times she almost believed it.

She'd pleaded ignorance, dodged culpability and used her power as the only remaining GFC founder to veto Del's death sentence. She'd even struck a deal to keep him confined in a prison-research lab. Del could continue being a useful contributor to GFC society, or he could languish in whatever VR fantasy he wanted. "We need that genius alive," she'd petitioned. "If the world knows that Del deceived us, that he's lost, then we are so much weaker."

"I am still here, Del. Have you forgotten that I exist?" Her finger passed over his lips. She imagined kissing them, his eyes opening and her falling into his arms like some fairytale princess. *All forgiven. All forgotten.*

She checked her message inbox. Nothing. The GFC was failing. Enemies closing down their advantages, cutting off escapes and options, stealing their technology. They could do a lot worse than seek guidance from their original visionary. "We need you Del. More than ever."

"Ellayna, we've located Ursurper Gale." The message snapped into her mind, and she opened a visual portal onto Martin Haller's calm, pointed face.

"Excellent." She felt revulsion again at the name. Ursurper Gale forged memories of rebellion, usurping power, conflict. But mainly it was because he was somehow Del's pet, and in the end Del had trusted his pet more than he'd trusted Ellayna.

"Situation, Martin?" She flipped to tactical view. Data holograms filled her vision.

"We've got a team of troopers following leads from scout drones. We've tried this before and never found him, but this time... I think he wanted us to succeed."

"Why do we think that?"

"He's messaging us and demands to speak with, well, with you Ellayna."

The tremble down her back was like a convulsion, a tightening of muscles that she almost couldn't control. "Is that safe?"

"We'll route all comms through the GFC cybersecurity portal. I'm sending Gale a VR access code with security restrictions built-in. You'll be fine, Ellayna."

She prioritized the tactical screens, one showing TwoLunar from a hundred kilometers out, the others showing closeups. Tiny markers indicated the trooper teams, a dozen in all, spread across structurally stable parts of TwoLunar. A side screen looked down on Martin in the operations room surrounded by his security personnel, their eyes all staring far away at virtual renderings of the impending conflict.

With the merest flick of thought she could shuffle any vision to the foreground while gazing through them all like layered glass, taking in all the imagery in parallel, while still seeing the room she was in, still seeing Del in his prison, and her hand resting on his chest.

"We used sensors to pick up micro-vibrations in TwoLunar's structural pumice. We've extrapolated them back to a single point around here..." Martin's face disappeared and a complex wire-frame representation of TwoLunar appeared with a flashing X marking their target. "I pinged him and he knew we'd nailed his location, so he decided to come out."

"Why?"

"He knows he's almost surrounded."

"Almost?"

"It's a three-dimensional warren of collapsed tunnels and rooms. Our maps are inaccurate at best. I'm closing the other trooper teams in on this area, but it'll take a while to get them all in place."

The view of TwoLunar was staggering. The great pumice cylinder tumbled slowly in the void, surrounded by a lethal halo of debris and near-invisible strands of elevator cable. From certain angles, it was still a cylinder. The nova blast had ripped out a complete side, but somehow its endcaps remained attached to the curving remnants of the outer shell. Gutted frames of buildings clung to the insides of the ruins. At the Earth-side endcap, the rod-like structure of the light bar, the artificial internal sun, poked out about a quarter of the distance to the space-side cap. As the open wound rotated away from her view, she saw the outside surface mottled with thousands of crystal blisters, the gardens and bio-domes all dead and empty. As sunlight caught them, they sparkled like Earth's lakes of plasma glass, making TwoLunar appear as a tiny model of Earth's larger destruction. A game-sized version, and she was here to play.

A message feed flashed red. Her heart leapt as a black shadowy avatar sprang into her vision. She took a deep breath. *Ok, Ursurper, let's do this.* She reached out with her mind and opened the channel.

"Ellayna, so good to see you again." Gale's voice oozed into her mind like molten basalt.

"Don't talk to me like that," she snapped. She hated the way he seemed to know her. It was some game of Del's: give his pet memories of her, so he thought he knew her. She didn't dare ponder what memories Del had contributed.

"I assume you are here to impede my personal freedom again?" Gale's carbon-black features filled her view. That translucent, black skull thinly veiled beneath a course weave of fibers, knotted and twisted into a grotesque parody of a human head with shiny black beads as eyes. *A toy, a disgusting doll from some wiccan tradition. Del's pet monster.*

She struggled for self-control, throat dry, skin slick with sweat. "We have evidence that you were illegally sending a package from orbit to an ally on Earth. TwoLunar is still the property of the GFC. It, and everything inside its orbital pathway, remains our property."

Gale's eyes fixed her in their dead gaze. She reminded herself that they controlled the data feed and he couldn't actually see her, just a stationary image. His face was wildly asymmetric as if he'd pried apart panels of fibrous flesh and stitched them back together. Such crude self-surgeries were attempts at finishing Del's great experiment: perfecting the voidian race. Did he really understand how far from perfection he was? Incomplete, flawed, a failed project that could never work. Never be *allowed* to work.

An image feed showed a security bot creeping up on Gale from behind. Other troops closed from the front and sides. Their ETAs ticked down in her vision. She zoomed in on Gale, just hanging in space, proportioned like a gibbon, with spidery long arms and legs. His feet looked like another set of hands, his core body just a dense twist of cables. Long hair-like strands emerged from his back, writhing slowly in the void like asphyxiating snakes.

As she watched, Gale extended his arms as if to encompass the whole universe. "How could I forget? The GFC owns everything beyond low-Earth orbit."

She sent Gale the video feeds of the meteor events. He chuckled, a hollow sound like someone scraping flesh remnants from the inside of a skull. "I am flattered you bestow me with such godlike powers. " He twisted in an exaggerated bow as a pulse of gas from a small ring-motor in his hand sent him spinning slowly out into the open center of TwoLunar.

"Can we take him, Martin?"

She watched as Martin assessed the troop positions. "Not capture, he's too mobile. Lasers don't work well. The fiberoptic properties of his body disperse the energy. Maybe kill him with kinetics, but I need to be close... within a ten-millisecond shot range."

"What's powering him?"

"Bunch of small reaction motors attached to various appendages. Don't think he's armed."

"Why is he out here, Martin?"

"He's fucking with us, testing to see if we've got anything new."

She watched Gale move and felt a twinge of envy. In space, he was alarmingly perfect, balletic and free. Nearly immune to heat, cold and radiation, things that no human, no matter how augmented, how well-equipped, could ever truly be.

Distract him. "Ursurper, I'm here with your creator, Del Krondeck." She zoomed in on Gale's face to see if there was any change in expression, but his features remained inanimate.

"Del is awake?"

"Del still wallows in whatever mental exercises he has chosen to pursue. Why help defectors and smugglers, our enemies, Ursurper? Helping them endangers your creator."

"Free my people, Ellayna, and maybe we'll help you."

Ellayna laughed, throwing as much scorn and spite as possible. "You still cling to that delusion? Where in the name of all space-time did you come up with this... this theory?" She knew where, of course. Del had sown the seeds when he'd created Gale's mind. Just as he'd filled it with memories of her, he'd created false memories of legions of imprisoned voidian inside of Cloud9.

"Don't lie to me, Ellayna. I was once on Cloud9. I saw them myself."

"There is no voidian race," she yelled. "Just you! Weird, dangerous and utterly alone."

"We've found something, Ellayna," Martin said, routing a different bot-feed to her Inner-I.

The view showed a small chamber, an opening that was once a crystal window giving extensive views of Earth. Equipment lined one of the walls, most of it old and cobbled together with bare wires and optical cables. Some looked handmade, circuits and boards soldered and kluged like a schoolboy's homework project. A telescopic camera pointed at the Earth. Its thin end connected to an image intensifier and recorder. To the side sat a communications laser, tilted away to point at the blank wall.

"That's all the evidence we need, Martin. Blow this shit away."

"Not close enough, Ellayna, need a few more seconds."

But Gale sensed the change in attitude. Maybe an alert tripped from his hidden lab. Gas puffed from his reaction motors and he began to spin, slowly folding inward as if wrapping his fibrous body into a protective knot around his own skull.

"Do it, Martin!"

Targeting feeds from troopers sprang into her mind. A weapons array on a distant gunnery platform came online. Gale's eyes popped open, staring across the void right into Ellayna's mind. Something akin to a smile creased the knots and cables of his face. A message hit her Inner-I and at the same instant Gale ignited a hidden hyper-compressed gas cylinder. An acceleration that would turn human flesh and bone into boiling pulp, flattened him into a disk of disparate tendrils that rocketed off on a diagonal course toward one of TwoLunar's ragged openings.

"He's escaping!" Ellayna yelled, but before the words emerged from her mouth, she knew Gale was gone. A slow-motion after-image showed him rolling into a pointed, bullet-shape and crashing through one of TwoLunar's inner walls.

"We're in pursuit," Martin said, but the tone of his voice didn't hold much hope.

Ellayna sat back, dropping the comms feed and sliding into the reality of Del's prison, hand gripping the soft fabric over his chest as if it could shield her from Gale's assault.

"Why did you do this to me, Del!" She snatched her hand away and raged to her feet. "Why let that monster free?"

To fuck with us, of course, to aid the defectors and harass the GFC into surrender.

She remembered Gale's message and opened the data packet letting its words spill across her vision. "When you decide to run, Elly. I'll help you."

Elly? Only Del called her that. She almost spat at Del as he lay still and vulnerable. The spit would probably still be there when she came back to visit weeks later.

In the end, it was just a tear that left her body.

"Gale sent you a message, Ellayna?" Martin asked.

"Nothing, Martin, just puerile chiding. I deleted it."

CHAPTER 10

Mira

Free!

Rex ran like a dog leading a chase, while the real dogs rallied around in a loose pack. Terriers, Bela and Mahler, crisscrossed over and under in a wild, four-dimensional fugue. Goliath, the wolfhound, surged to the front, carving through the long grass as Rust the pit-bull and Copland the boxer nipped at his heels.

Three days after his encounter with the militiaman, Regoth, the ache of confinement overwhelmed Rex. With a hand-selected dog pack, he headed for the park, exited through a damaged fence panel, and fled for the far edge of the Tellus District where the buildings thinned into open grasslands and rolling hills.

Past the Tellus Hills loomed Transit Mountain; only the first two plateaus were visible, the rest of the tower remained shrouded in mist. The smell of grass and earth stirred memories: starved and lost, creeping down from the hills into town to rob garbage cans and pick scraps from the streets. But these were cloudy memories now, actions performed by one of his past personas before the Future-Lord took control of his destiny and allowed the real Rex to shine through. He felt Him like a searchlight, an illuminating beam cutting through the fog of thin, unsubstantiated minds that lived inside of his head. Glowworms, dangerous personalities that hitched a ride on the drug as it was liched from the dead and sold back to the living, ghosts of dead addicts and past users. He had a lot of glowworms, but the Future-Lord's light cleansed them away and crystallized his past.

It was all there, he just didn't want to see it... not yet. His head striking that concrete, the terrible, vile child he must have been to deserve such punishment. Other things he'd done, murderous things and how he'd tried to bury them. He hadn't used a concrete pavement or a brick wall or wooden door, he'd used chemicals, burning out neurons and axons, drugs, nanotech, sims... over time he'd tried them all. He wondered how and why he still lived. How was such an unbalanced and pathetic man allowed to exist?

Even Sister-Two was surprised. "Most people don't survive Glow withdrawal," she'd told him. "You are a remarkably resilient person."

He turned back to the city looking along a vast, four-track railway line that once connected Port Coriolis with the space-elevator on Transit Mountain. The tracks were gone, uprooted and repurposed, leaving just a dead-straight gash across the landscape. *A wound*. Rex touched his head, remembering the jutting knife; its tip buried deep inside brain tissue, quartering the sparking mesh that was once a mind.

The dogs rested, rolling in the cool grass, play-biting and wrestling. Rex stared back at the jagged, confused outline of Coriolis City. It overlaid with a similar view in his mind. The same city before the Nova-Insanity, such a different city, that beacon of prosperity that had led him across the water as a teenager. Back then the towers were upright and densely packed, shiny and new, sparkling with optimism and hope. He'd watched live on the tiny screen he'd held in his hand: the flashes of nova explosions, panicked people, red-faced newscasters, everything burning in the ensuing firestorm. The mounting despair as the GFC tried to isolate itself from the madness by severing the space-elevator cable from Transit Mountain and winding it back into space.

Too late. The blast from TwoLunar had lit the evening sky and those still with eyes could only stare in horror as chunks of it blazed back to Earth.

Was I really Rex back then? Or was I somebody else?

He called the dogs to heel as they approached a ravine, a deep, v-shaped gouge, storm drainage for the inland Sidereal Sea. Now, it was a sinister stream of leaden gray water and foul-white foam, clogged with debris: a convenient waste disposal system for the militias.

He shuddered, remembering bloated corpses and body parts tumbling through the rapid waters while some feral version of himself fished flesh and bone scraps to satiate his desperate hunger.

Why did you lead me here, my Lord?

The voices all remained silent.

Something moved near the wire suspension bridge spanning the ravine. He dropped to his knees and watched as a woman stepped out of the bushes on the far side, paused at the ravine's edge, and lurched out onto the bridge.

Grasping the rope handrail, she stepped across the broken planks, staring down at the churning water as she made her way to the center where the bridge sagged lowest. A thin, rag-cloaked skeleton, she had that hyper-alertness he recognized in his fellow Glow addicts. Those rampant, ceaseless eyes that fueled a head full of glowworms.

Rex moved carefully along the ravine's edge seeking a better view. The dogs followed, oblivious to the woman's presence, snouts engrossed in nature's narrative smells.

She dropped her coat on the boards and climbed up the wire handrails. Standing on the second line down, her knees locked on the top rail preventing her pivoting over the edge.

She's going to jump! Something came alive inside him, an old urge, *act dead, act crazy… run like hell…* An urge to flee, to not witness, to un-see, hide, take no responsibility. It spun him around lurching his legs away from the ravine and back to the railway lines. *Don't look! Don't bear witness. They might blame me. Another dead addict is good. More drugs for the rest!*

The usual voices battled a new and rational voice, more of a feeling. *I can do better. I am better.* The voices raged in the Darwinian pit of his skull until one found his vocal cords, seized control and yelled: "Wait!"

The dogs barked, rushing to form a bristling defense around their master. The woman didn't respond. The noise of rushing water was too loud or maybe she was past any need to hear.

As Rex ran, the dogs surged ahead chasing down their own imaginary quarries to pause at the ravine's edge, sniffing nervously at the void.

Rex jumped a gulf of missing planks and landed on a solid bridge section. The woman leaned out farther, clasping her hands in front of her face as if in prayer.

"Please, don't!" Rex yelled. The dissenting voices were gone now, just the need to serve and save remained.

Goliath let out a massive basal woof and the woman startled. Fear flashed across her face as she saw Rex and the dogs. Then with steely determination she faced ahead and refocused on the plunge.

Patchy, rotten rafters creaked under Rex's weight as he hopped and danced across the gaps, ignoring the putrid torrent below. She lifted a knee, sliding it over the top rail, thrusting her center of gravity out into the void. Slowly, she tilted forward. Rex stopped watching his feet, trusting instinct to find the solid planks, hand thrust out ahead grasping at the air.

Her head turned towards Rex, face changing just at that crucial moment when it was too late. The change sprang from her eyes as if some dark, internal demon swept aside a curtain and showed her the world as it truly was.

"Fucking Christ–" She wind-milled wildly, eyes grabbing at Rex's outstretched hand. He leapt the final gap snatching her wrist out of midair as she plunged. He crashed to the planks as she buckled over the wire, her weight hauling him up the side rails as his steely workman's grip strained to hold.

His other hand lashed out and by sheer luck caught the rope handrail. They hung there, his grip losing out to deadweight, bridge swinging and creaking. Terror freed his last reserves of energy and with a heave he pulled her back onto the walkway, then half dragged, half carried her off the bridge.

They dropped onto a dirt mound, his body wracked with pain from torn muscles and over-extended tendons, mind fixated on the bridge and the rushing water. Darkness flooded his mind. They wanted him now, just the presence of a fellow addict meant a certain fix... more Glow... more fuel for the worms that ate his brain and turned him into somebody else. Decoherence!

Concerned snouts rubbed up against his legs and Goliath's massive tongue slobbered across his face. *Feel the Future-Lord.* Warmth, fur and saliva eased Rex away from the mental precipice, breathing, sucking in precious air as he flopped, exhausted, across the necks of the dogs.

He risked a sideways glance. The woman squatted beside him, her face a morbid blank. Goliath pushed his bear-sized head into her lap and let it sit there awaiting her attention.

Her fingers twitched, unable to resist kneading the thick fur. Her hands were smooth but with bulging, arthritic knuckles that clicked as her fingers moved. Her face was mixed-up, young in shape but ravaged into old age by hunger, drug-use and pain. The cords of Glow-withdrawal tugged her facial muscles in odd directions. Her gray, black hair hung in muddied clumps framing eyes of sickly green that bulged from their sockets as if seeing a shocking world for the very first time.

"I'm Rex," he said. Not daring to move or speak too loudly.

"Mira," she said, eyes widening as she took in his face and large ears. "Are you a fucking dog or a man?"

His head dropped, "Didn't mean to scare you."

She laughed or it could have been a sob. "Scare me! You have a pack of freaking mutts!" Her face changed again, and her anger melted away. "You shouldn't be out here. It's not safe." Her eyes scanned the far side of the ravine.

"I lived here once, when I was a different–"

"You don't understand," she stopped him. "He's coming for me and he'll kill you too and all your pooches here. We need to get out of here since you already screwed my escape plan."

"You mean killing yourself?"

"I was going to swim, float back into town." She struggled to her feet and fell backward onto the dirt.

Unease spread through the dog pack. Something sinister moved closer making Rex tingle with fear. "Okay, let's go."

The bushes on the opposite side of the ravine rustled and the bridge buckled as if under a heavy weight. Rex strained to see. Something shimmered against the bushy background as if the air had taken on a life of its own.

"What is that?" He grabbed Mira's wrist and pulled her upright.

Her knees popping in protest, Mira clutched Rex's shoulder for support. "Fucking lich in a chameleon suit. Been tracking me for days."

The truth hit Rex like a slap: Mira was a Glow addict. She couldn't pay any more and was now on the run. So her dealer had sent a lich to drain her body, and repo the drugs.

Rex called over Goliath who sat obediently awaiting orders. "Goliath was trained as a pack-carrier. You can ride him like a small horse."

Mira straddled Goliath's back, fingers clinging to his fur. Rex glanced back at the bridge, swaying wildly. The visual disturbance paused in the middle and something, possibly a limb, detached and lifted, making it momentarily visible as its chameleon functions struggled with the shifting surroundings.

"Gun!" shouted Rex, and ducked.

A vicious bang ripped through the air where his head had just been. Concussion ringing in his ears, he rolled to his feet and called Goliath and the other dogs to heel.

"He wants his drugs back," Mira said, almost sliding off Goliath as he accelerated into a loping bound.

The gun boomed again. The dogs yelped. They ran harder, heads down, feeling the lich gaining as its drug-enhanced physique powered inexorably closer. Rex zigzagged his troop through dry gullies and around hillocks and high tufts of grass, intent on breaking any line-of-sight.

Buildings loomed closer as Mira clung to the big dog's neck, her head rolling forward, eyes now a blank, resigned stare. Rex grabbed Rust's collar, letting the powerful dog supplement his speed. Together they surged toward the buildings, abandoning stealth and concealment. Grass turned to dirt road and then cement pavement as feet and paws clattered onto the street. Surely the militia would help. The lich wouldn't kill them in daylight surrounded by people... would it?

This way. An instinct jolted him into a side alley. He glanced back as they exited into a busy parallel street. The air shimmered as the lich paused, but Rex didn't see it follow. Perhaps its hunting license wasn't valid in this particular militia neighborhood or its battery was running low.

Ahead loomed taller buildings, the busy center of the Tellus district, but at that moment it meant only one thing – people. And for once, people meant sanctuary. They slowed to a walk and Rex looked down at Mira, now unconscious and oblivious to their plight. A new fear gripped him as he recalled a terrible street rumor: Glow was a somanet, a network of tiny machines inside a living body. As these machines talked to each other, networks of them also talked amongst their own kind, bridging the gaps between people, spreading data through the communities of addicts, finding ways back to dealers and their liches. The lich was like a bloodhound on a scent trail. It had Mira's scent and would inevitably find her and now it had Rex's... it would find him as well.

CHAPTER 11

Morally Bankrupt

Ellayna jumped as the scalpel flashed past her throat.

"Sorry." Jesh Nameeb tucked the gleaming blade back into the palm of his hand and backed off.

"No. I'm sorry," she said, calming her breath. Ever since the virtual bug attack, and now the disconcerting contact with Ursurper Gale, everyone felt like an enemy and everything was a threat. "I'm not sleeping well." She motioned Jesh to continue his examination. He leaned in close and carefully unveiled the scalpel again, holding it gently between thumb and forefinger in front of her eyes. "Can't you do that wirelessly?"

"Wireless comms can be recorded and monitored. I prefer direct contact with your Inner-I's access port just under the skin on the temple here." He stroked her skin with the blade. She shivered, peering back into his eyes made much bigger by the rather old-fashioned looking lenses jutting from his forehead. "I need to scrape a little skin off, shouldn't hurt."

From a distance Jesh was an attractive, olive-skinned young man. Closer in, a fine mesh of facial lines betrayed his real age. For some, Simmorta worked exceptionally well with their genetics and Jesh was one of the lucky ones.

She winced as he scraped at her temple. In the close-up mirror she saw the tiny, transparent filament emerge from her flesh. Jesh's dexterous fingers tugged it free and patched it into an analyzer. His eyes glazed over as he absorbed the diagnostics.

"All functioning well," he said. "Inner-I technology is basically specialized Simmorta, a dedicated somanet that unfurls inside your brain enabling all those wonderful fully-immersive experiences. No one can change the network software, not even us anymore, but the communication interface and alternative-reality generator are old-school computer chips on the microcircuit board in your skull. Someone can screw with that if you grant them access."

She tried to relax as Jesh went about his business, rolling her favorite word around inside her mind as a kind of meditation: Simmorta. Her personal contribution to its marketing campaign: a contraction of the words "simulated immortality". The world's first and only subscription-model longevity drug. A somanet or body-network of biomech-based nanotechnology. The product became an instant success and the four GFC founders become the world's first trillionaires... at least until the Insanity crashed the stock markets and all their shares became worthless.

Simmorta. Why would anyone be stupid enough to switch it off?

Suddenly curious, she asked: "You can switch off Simmorta but not my Inner-I?"

"It's like lace, pervading the entire brain. It becomes part of its structure and your cognitive processes. If you just turned it off, you'd struggle to stay conscious, lose control of bodily functions, become very forgetful and confused. That's why we don't fit off-switches."

"Huh." She remembered all those years back when all GFC directors underwent "voluntary fittings" of the new Inner-I technology. Something that she'd forced through in another committee meeting using the argument that: "If *we* won't trust it, how can we expect others to?"

That kind of company devotion now felt frightening, not like genetically removing one's hair or tweaking a body to optimum functionality. Inner-Is were somehow permanent, part of being a modern human. *We are true cyborgs.*

"It's making me paranoid. I feel like something's following me around the orbital. I know I'm not alone in that. Some people refuse to leave their apartments or even leave VR."

Jesh nodded. "Lot of people seeing ghosts." A huge white-toothed grin spread across his face. "Seen a few myself, but none of them have tried to kill me yet."

"You've examined other people's Inner-Is as well?"

"Two-dozen recently, and I keep finding the same thing."

She felt cold creep up her spine. "What are you finding?"

"I'll show you." Jesh went quiet as his mind roved through his option menus. "Work your Inner-I. Make it good and busy."

Layers of imagery piled a dozen deep across her vision. She peered through news, social chatter, council meetings. Another launch from the Alliance's Baikonur facility. Taunau chairing an emergency Protectionist meeting to watch the launch. Tomas sitting in on the meeting, dozing while his thoughts scrawled onto his mental journal for her later perusal.

Jesh gave a knowing nod. "I see lots of authorized changes and updates to your alternative-reality generator, your ARG, that's a GFC only module, not standard on Inner-Is we sell to Earth for just comms and news feeds."

"I didn't authorize any changes." Ellayna mentally pulled the Alliance launch screen to the front of her vision as the massive four-engine vehicle erupted in flame and crept slowly off its pad. Cameras panned across an audience, cheering and pounding fists at the sky. *How they hate us. Once we were their gods. Selling them immortality. Now we just peddle to the rich few, and somehow, even they hate us as well.*

Jesh's hand dropped heavily on Ellayna's shoulder. She almost crashed out of her chair. "I see a dozen accesses, six downloads and six deletions. All authorized by you." Suddenly he was right in her face as if accusing her. "Or someone who is able to perfectly mimic your mind-state passcode, and somehow pretend to be inside your head."

She heaved back in the chair to escape his gaze and an

uncomfortable draft of stale breath. She understood enough Inner-I technical details to know that mind-state passcodes were impossible to replicate. The human brain was still one of the most complex constructs in the known universe and modelling an exact sequence of its states from outside the brain was not feasible. "How can that happen?"

He moved away freeing up her breathing space. "I'm guessing, but if someone was able to record your thoughts and model your mind-state passcode inside of your ARG, making a realistic simulation of your secret imagery, then, given a bit of luck, and a really high-resolution model... maybe it could fool your Inner-I into granting access." He shook his head, clearly doubting that what he proposed was possible. "Once inside, a hacker could use maintenance patches to modify your ARG. Perhaps even hack some of the other peripheral systems stopping you from escaping by using the exit icon."

Locked in!

"Have you checked my ARG for bug simulation patches?" She felt a creeping alarm that what she'd experienced could still be lurking dormant inside of her.

"There's nothing. The patches may have self-deleted after running."

"There must be some clue left behind?"

"Luckily, the comms interface unit logs all remote contacts, and those can't be deleted. We've even used them in criminal cases."

Ellayna's stomach sank, all those records of her contacting her Earth proxy, the messages with the Alliance. *Utopia!*

She panicked. "National security, Jesh... I can't just let you go rummaging around inside–"

"Relax, Ellayna," Jesh's clammy hand grasped her wrist. "Patient privacy still means something. I'll show you the log, and you can report anything unusual." His eyes held a deep knowing; clearly Tomas had prompted him that she needed discretion.

She nodded and a new screen opened. The names were all familiar, mainly Tomas and Martin. There were the damning ones

– the Alliance contacts. She tried not to look at them, not to sweat or react or indicate anything was wrong, but when she saw the other name, she nearly choked. "It's him..." she gasped. "He's all over my communications log. It's–"

"Ursurper Gale?" Jesh's grin grew wide again, eyes sparkling and dangerous.

"How did you know?"

"Same signature in all the other patients."

Her anger boiled over, and she stormed to her feet. "I knew it, that freak, that–"

"Before you leap to the obvious conclusion, Ellayna, the signal origin tags all show they came from within Cloud9. Gale could have hacked into the GFC's comms system and planted false trails. I've discussed this with Martin and his team, and they think it's impossible. Gale simply does not have that ability. Nobody does."

"Then who... how?"

He shrugged. "Someone real smart, inside the GFC." His smile faded and suddenly he looked defeated.

Ellayna left Jesh staring at his virtual screens. She wondered if he'd secretly recorded her comms log. Was it already in Taunau's hands? Were GFC police on their way to arrest her? Her mind spun with options, Taunau, Marr, Martin? *Del?* Surely impossible, he was isolated, no connections to GFC servers except through his secure prison link.

She messaged Martin Haller. "Have we tracked down Gale yet?"

"No. The security committee is de-mothballing military equipment to send to TwoLunar, but we're running out of actual people to do the legwork."

"Damn it!" She severed the connection and turned a corner. A shadow flickered by as if someone unseen was heading back toward the medical building. She collided with a wall, momentarily becoming airborne, spinning slowly in micro-g until she flicked the ground with one of her foot magnets and clamped upright.

Looking along the corridor a shape appeared at the end where it turned, like a head and shoulders looking back at her from around the corner, a carbon-black head... *Gale's head!*

"Lights!" she yelled as the corridor plunged into darkness. She fumbled her ring gun making sure the dangerous end pointed outward. The lights popped obediently on. Nothing.

"Is anyone else in my corridor, Martin?" Her heart thudded as she awaited his reply.

"Just you, Ellayna. Problem?"

"Ghosts, Martin. Shadows. My imagination playing tricks. I just went to see Jesh about my Inner-I security. He told me about Gale's signature appearing in all the wrong places."

"Yeah, we're looking, Ellayna. My guess is the Alliance has some new infiltration technique. Our systems are under constant cyber-attack and one of them has made it through."

She shook her head and made the brisk walk back to her apartment. They were under attack all right. At war, even. A war to control the GFC, and the battlefield for this conflict wasn't their machines or their infrastructure – it was the inside of their own heads.

CHAPTER 12

Networked Junkies

Rex sat next to Mira on a bench at a busy crossroads in Tellus district's central square. The dogs huddled close around their knees, people hustled past in a whirl of stop-frame motion as Rex stared and pondered their escape from the lich.

"Why did you help me? What do you want? I was ready to go," Mira hissed, voice low and venomous.

Rex saw eyes everywhere; windows, satellites in the sky, cameras, dogs and streetlights winking, watching. "The Future-Lord guided me to you," he said, unable to digest everything that had just happened.

"You're one of them, huh?" She made a noise like a laugh but devoid of any mirth. Her eyes grew shifty and intense. "Hey... you got Glow? Or something, man? You must have something."

He shook his head and faced away.

"Come on, I'm aging away here. You want me to rot and die in front of your stinking face?" She jammed her knee up against his, her hand finding his leg.

Rex looked at her, that familiar desperation. "I don't have anything."

"You do. You fucking do. Look at you man, you're a walking shit heap. I can see it in your eyes. So full of glowworm holes through your brain that you don't know who you are. Just coz one of them tells you it's the Future-Lord, you get all fucking high-and-mighty with me? Bullshit!"

"I don't do that stuff anymore," he snapped.

She hoisted up the hem of her skirt, hand sliding up her skinny, pale thigh. "I got a trade I think you'll like."

"I told you. Not anymore."

"Not anymore what?" She raged to her feet, scattering nervous passersby into wider arcs around them. "Fucking or drugs?"

"The Sisters helped me–"

"Great, maybe they can hook me up. I'm sure they've got all the good shit."

The darkness was like a pressure, leaching color and light from Rex's world. Figures became stickmen with eyeballs that stared at him as they jerked by. They knew his secrets. Even the glowworms knew how guilty he was: a fraud pretending to help a woman in exchange for sex and drugs; an alleyway murderer, killer of old, vulnerable men. It was true what Mira said. Why would the benevolent Future-Lord want anything to do with him and his mess of a life? But the Sisters? They told him–

He clutched at his head, forcing the world to stop spinning and squeezing the words out slow and staccato, one at a time, "The... Sisters... can... *help* you, Mira. There's food, shelter, protection from liches."

Mira tugged her skirt back down and eyed him closely. "Are they turning you into a freaking dog or something? Some weirdo experiment?"

"No. I'm turning into a human."

Her mouth twitched. "You're funny." She smiled, a jagged, caricature of a smile that was probably once beautiful. It shone through the blemishes and lines, smoothing them into a pleasing whole.

"The Sisters give me work, things to do. It helps with the voices." Rex nodded down at the sleeping dogs. "They helped me get this job."

Mira sagged back into a vulnerable heap. A perfume of her

rancid bodily fluids wafted over him. "I forgot who the fuck I was years ago," she said. "Don't know how I ended up here… in this shit… with you."

"Who's the lich?" Rex asked.

"Guy named Auld. Works for my dealer. I can't pay, can't get money, can't get Glow. I'm royally fucked. To them, I'm just a farm animal fattened up for slaughter. Soon I'll be just another glowworm, a voice in some fucking loser's head." At that she let out a loud laugh that degenerated into tears. "I'll probably end up inside your head, Rex, bitching and whining until you throw yourself off a bridge."

He laughed with her and an easy silence settled over them. "I quit," Rex finally said. "I really did quit it. Don't remember how or even when. It's like I never really took the stuff at all and it was all just those inside of me that did the drugs and the bad stuff. Even the Sisters don't understand. They think I'm special. I think they watch me, study me, try to figure out how I survived." Rex jumped to his feet feeling new energy from inside, from Him. "They can help you, Mira. Look at me! I have everything! Health, a job, a place to live with food and water and… and…" He baulked at talking about the Future-Lord lessons and duties around the hostel.

She shook her head and just stared at him. Her eyes said: you haven't recovered, you just think you have. But he knew she was wrong.

"Jumping off a bridge won't fix anything, Mira. Come back to the Sisters with me, or swing by the Forever Friends Rescue and walk some dogs."

Her face softened as if someone else controlled her muscles now. "What happened to your head anyway? You take a beating?"

Memories loomed through the fog of his past: the taste of pavement, of blood in his mouth, choking on tooth fragments. Concrete striking a skull had a unique sensory texture, a kind of flavor, like electric-iron, but in big spiky grains. "I… I had this sister once and–"

"Fucking Christ, Rex. I don't need your bullshit life story." She was on her feet again, green eyes afire with hate and distrust. A different Mira now took the reins. "Get us some freaking Glow or go jump in a ravine. Or go be some fucking hero. Like I give a damn." She stumbled away, her words and movements now slurred and drunken.

The eyes and the darkness closed in like an explosion in reverse. Rex flopped forward and the day's trauma flowed up from his gut and out of his mouth as the Sisters' fake eggs and mushed waffles added yet another layer of filth to the pavement. The dogs gathered around, lapping at the vomit, and Mira vanished into the crowd without looking back.

CHAPTER 13

Rough Justice

From Ursurper Gale's mission brief, Jett knew the coordinates of Xell Vollarer's distress call. Although inexact, they placed him just north of Welkin, somewhere in a no man's land of alleys and derelict factories just across the Interstice Canal from the Broken militia's West Firmament urban housing and protection project.

After a day patrolling the area, Jett found no clues. He did learn that even though the Broken didn't control the area, they patrolled it, and exercised reclamation rights over any bodies found there. In fact, death appeared optional when it came to recycling, and just being caught at the wrong time in the wrong place was enough. This explained the lack of homeless people in the area as opposed to other areas of Coriolis City Jett had explored.

Jett planned to infiltrate the "Broken" and find where Xell's body went. Whoever recycled that body surely had the Star-River.

He crossed the canal using one of the many inflatable bridges the militia had erected to ease access to the Welkin. Here, the scenery changed. The buildings were clean and well maintained with shops, utilities and transport services. Opulent roof gardens spilled over and dripped down to the sidewalks signaling those below that wealthy and powerful individuals lived up beyond their reach.

Hunched, shrunken and wrapped in a blanket like a leper, Jett skulked around the outer fringes of the district, noting patrols and guards, and the copious use of security cameras, many fake, but some real. The Broken favored the ex-military type. Even their local TV station that Jett monitored on his Inner-I was replete with damaged, often disabled veterans. Suddenly their name made sense.

He sculpted a new look: an able-bodied soldier, down on his luck, uniform hanging loose on his bones, ballcap with ear flaps that wrapped under his chin covering old wounds while a generous brow hid his face.

He stuck to the side alleys, scoping out innocent-looking shopfronts that revealed themselves as barracks or monitoring stations. He sensed their eyes watching, felt radar pings and lidar scans; cameras and tiny gun turrets followed his movements. He prickled with combat readiness, aware that he was a sitting target, no escape except through fields of fire.

Glass crunched behind him and a huge man stepped out of a doorway. A hulking figure with cubic features: square-muscles, square-jaw, and square-head. He carried a massive gun slung lazily over a bare shoulder. A thick cigarette hung from his mouth. "Stop!" the man commanded in a deep, graveled voice, using the cigarette to point at Jett.

Blend in. The reminder from Jett's tagger dropped him into a submissive pose, hands up, face low, eyeing the hulk's gun which his tagger didn't recognize.

Unidentified weapon. Possible Goshgun: Gas operated shotgun.
Propellant: hyper-compressed gas cartridge, usually metallic hydrogen.
Projectile: anything that fits into the barrel.
Extremely dangerous, even to the user.

"Why are you skulking around here?" The man grunted, stepping closer, security button pushing into Jett's face. A green skull-shape cracked down the middle with what might have been his name written on one of the fractured halves: Golt.

"New here," Jett said, patching together snippets of overheard conversations. "Need to buy protection. Get some work. Maybe score some Glow."

Golt moved easily, light on his feet for such a chunk of flesh and muscle. He obviously didn't consider Jett a threat and didn't even bother pointing the gun in his direction. "We get a hundred losers like you through here each day begging for work." He took a puff on the cigarette and blew the acrid blue smoke at Jett's face.

Analysis: Amp, extreme muscle stimulant.

Golt sucked in the smoke and his muscles rippled as if monsters stirred under his skin. He inflated before Jett's gaze, growing even wider and taller, eyes jittering wildly as if the muscles controlling them were so hyped with energy they couldn't remain still.

"Where can I buy protection?" Jett said, adding a tremor of fear to his voice.

"Down the street." Golt indicated the main road. "Recruitment shop at the end will sell you a disk. You walk down the middle of the road. I catch you skulking again, I shoot. Got it?"

Jett nodded and turned to leave, but Golt's heavy hand grasped his shoulder. "You're not going anywhere yet, friend."

Jett allowed Golt to spin him around. He looked straight up at the man's bristling neck. The gun muzzle thrust into Jett's face, a metal horn like an old-fashioned blunderbuss with a hopper feed jutting from its topside. It ended in a thick wooden stock with heavy chains tumbling over and around the man's wrist. It looked like something he'd made himself. He probably needed to be Amped just to carry the thing.

"You don't look right," Golt growled. "Gonna pat you down." A huge hand started slapping Jett down his sides and front. Drugged eyes fixed squarely on Jett's face, daring him to resist, or complain, or maybe, if he was really lucky, to fight back.

An odd memory surfaced: he was a pink and frail human again. A host of smug confident, teenage faces gazed down at him. "He looks like a freakin' girl!" one youth said.

"Fucking nerd," said another. Jett felt the kicks to his ribs, punches to his face. Someone pulled on his hair and his scalp tore open, warm blood flowing down his neck. He lost himself in the moment, letting his body relax, fibers flopping like limp clothing, limbs tumbling across the pavement as kicks pounded his chest and skull.

"Please, no more," he read from his tagger. "I'll do anything." That part came from the memory.

"Anything?" said an angry-looking youth, the beginnings of a neck beard forming just under his chin. "What the fuck would I want from an ugly prick like you?"

"Get up!" Golt roared, dragging Jett to his feet and slamming him face-first into the wall. The assault continued, on down his back and legs. Jett staggered and fell against the brickwork, sliding into a defeated heap. Golt's assault grew faster, harder. Jett folded his arms over his head as a boot crashed into his skull smashing him back against the wall. The bricks shook from the impact. Surely a normal human would be dead? But how to pretend to be dead? Sleep and unconsciousness were not things Jett comprehended.

She was there again, the woman from the horseback ride. The same woman from the clifftop memory who ran beside him, helping him remember how to walk and run. He glimpsed her through bloody eyes, taller than the boys, but thin, and standing at an awkward angle as she only had one shoe on. The other was in her hand and she smacked it around the head of the tufty-chinned youth. *"Get off him you jerk!"*

The kicks stopped and Jett rolled onto his front as Golt seemed to burn out, just standing, swaying, eyes a defocused bliss as if he'd achieved some kind of climax.

A smoldering cigarette butt landed on the ground near Jett's face. He heard a snort and a warm blob of phlegm landed on the back of his head, then Golt's boot ground it in, pushing his face into the cement as if to scour the features from his face.

"Get out of here," he said, disappointed there had been no real fight.

Jett crawled away, doing his best impersonation of someone severely injured. He paused at the end of the alley and watched Golt amble away, making sure he recorded his gait and features so he could come find him again at some later, more opportune time.

Jett scampered into the street, hobbling toward the recruitment shop, following the white line down the center of the road.

He left the area, aware that cameras recorded him, observant eyes marked him as suspicious, dangerous, someone who wasn't who he had pretended to be. Soon, he found a quiet alleyway with no cameras. His head grew square and broad, and he widened his skeleton, puffing out cords of arm and leg muscle, filling out a tight, but tattered military uniform.

He strolled back into the Broken's jurisdiction, straight to the recruitment shop, noting the look of fear on the serving woman's face as the hulking human eased through the doorway as if he owned the place.

CHAPTER 14

Dumpster Dive

"You be a good boy now... come on... up here... up." Rex jumped onto the foul-smelling table. A thousand hands grasped him from all sides, pinning and pressing, tying him down, legs splayed wide. He howled as faces hidden behind surgical masks leaned close, shoving tubes and needles into veins and orifices. Wires sparked alive, pistons sucked and gurgled pumping shit and drugs and air... in and out... in and out... as the ping-ping of an electronic heartbeat grew faster... *faster...*

As darkness closed around, he felt the grubs wriggling through his mind, gnawing at neurons and synapses, gorging on sparks of sensation and cognition while shitting out trails of memories, new memories that weren't his.

All while the eyes watched... the green, fog addled eyes–
Mira!

Rex jolted awake and inhaled the sweet stench of days-old rotten garbage. He lay in the pristine darkness listening to the familiar fluttering of rats and maggots.

Who did I become this time? Who did I kill?

He felt around for any zip-ties, any cold, dead hands. His fist clanged against a metal surface, a dumpster, a trusted haven when you could find one that wasn't occupied. Shelter from the heat or the biting cold, a place to fall unconscious and recuperate while the stink shielded you from the predator's senses. *The lich.* It was coming for him.

He pushed the dumpster lid open, poked his head up through the filth and blinked at the waning sunlight. Evening quiet had settled across the city as he eased out, feet-first, and left the side street, cloaked in nature's odiferous security blanket. People veered around him as if he possessed a magical shield, his own special superpower.

He remembered wandering through the Tellus District crowds, unsure if he was stalking Mira or just letting the dogs pull him back to the rescue sanctuary. He recalled leaving them in the yard and tugging the wire gate closed as he turned and fled. The world became a distorted tube, morphing around him like some celestial cylinder. The voices yelled and clamored inside of his skull.

Black circles falling through black circles. Overwhelmed, he fell...

And emerged as...

Nothing... No memories at all, no rapacious dealers, no murderous addict, no angry, shrieking woman or bawling child. He'd been them all at some time, but not this time. Had the Future-Lord silenced those demons, removed their power to take Rex away?

He wandered on, using the Sisters' cathedral spire as a reference point. As the Moon, stars and faltering neon lit the city, the cathedral loomed close. A great black rectangle that the Sisters kept in darkness. Rex thought it added a sinister air to the building. A subliminal message proclaiming: Behold! The Future-Lord is here.

Over the years the hostel had spread like an alien growth, absorbing nearby blocks, cloaking them under roof sections and the poles and cables of its own infrastructure, binding everything into a singular, machine-controlled hive.

He paused on the grand entrance stairway, some of the stonework still bore the original Christian symbols from its past. Rex knew nothing of its history, only that it had been moved from somewhere in Europe back before the Insanity when money was no object. Now, it was a homeless shelter run by robots. Robots that promulgated a new faith. Dog-eat-dog even applied to religions, Rex realized. Odd that it had never really applied to dogs.

Heavy-legged, he trudged up the mountain of steps into a cloistered courtyard ringed with reinforced doors and giant donut-shaped security scanners. He nearly made it to the hostel entrance before a voice called him to a halt.

"Hello, Rex," Sister-Zero glided soundlessly out from the shadows. The features of her translucent plastic face arranged in a stern, but compassionate expression befitting the hostel's security monitor.

"Sister-Zee." Rex nodded her way. He usually hated these interrogations, but felt fine with it tonight. Next to the lich, Sister-Zero was more of a comforting presence than a threat.

"You've been missing for three days, Rex."

"Three—" He swallowed hard, suddenly feeling new bruises on his head and body, ones that couldn't possibly come from fleeing the lich. He stared down at his palms that suddenly smarted, seeing chaffed, raw flesh where skin should have been.

"Have you been in trouble?" She slid closer, silent and sinister.

"No... no Sister. I'm good. I must have... fallen over." He felt his deceit boiling to the surface, impossible to hide. The Sisters could read minds. He knew that and hung his head. Silence was the best course here.

"You've been sleeping in the garbage again," she stated.

"Yes, Sister. I was scared, so I hid—"

"You had a decoherence incident, Rex?"

"Possibly, Sister. I mean... I don't remember." Memories of bounding through streets on all-fours suddenly washed through his mind.

"Should I remove your outside work privileges, Rex? Confine you to hostel duties?"

He dropped to his knees, shuffling close to the soot-black hem of the Sister's cloak. "No, please... I love the dogs... love my work. It won't happen again. It's just that I met—"

"You met someone new?"

His confession tumbled out. "Mira. She's homeless. She was lost on a bridge, and…" He caught himself falling into the trap of babbling and clamped a hand over his mouth. Then realizing how incriminating the gesture was, he dropped the hand back to his side, knowing it was too late.

"Was there any trouble, Rex?" Her slim, white hand reached out and gently clasped his shoulder. The touch was tender, but hinted of a machine strength that could knot girders.

"She was running from a lich. I saved her and we ran and–" a moment of inspiration clicked inside his head "–and we hid in a garbage dumpster until it was gone." He knew from previous interrogations that giving the Sister a little of the truth worked best, and that outright lies usually resulted in further, more penetrating interrogations.

She paused as if processing this surprising information. "You are safe from liches here, Rex. You should have come immediately home and brought your friend with you." Her hand pulled back with a gentle whir of motors.

"I tried, Sister, but she didn't want to come."

"You will be attending Salvation class later?" Although phrased as a question he knew he didn't really have a choice.

"I look forward to it." A small lie, but his near-perfect attendance record allowed some wiggle room.

"Go clean yourself up, Rex." She turned away, and headed back to the cloister like a smooth, jet-black sculpture gliding across ice.

Rex stepped through the scanner, straight into the food hall. An automatic dispenser delivered a generous blast of disinfectant and odor neutralizer that followed him like a sentient cloud.

The stadium-sized food hall echoed with the sound of a thousand plastic knives, forks and plates. Sisters directed the flow of people with signs on top of sticks, barking orders through loud hailers attached to their hands. In the background was the music, always the music, funneled down from ceiling speakers so people could cluster and listen to whatever genre helped or pleased them most.

Without his music-cancelling headphones, Rex felt the personas inside stir, latching onto the sounds and melodies that coalesced them back into whole beings with promises of childhood, teenage memories and loves.

Why don't I have music? The answer snapped at him in Mira's voice: *Maybe because you're a fucking dog and dogs don't do music!*

Fingers in ears, he rushed through, ignoring the pull of food odors and the drag of hunger in his gut. He'd been decohered long enough, couldn't risk it happening again, not with the Sisters watching his every move.

Safe and silent in his room, he scratched three new Xs on the wall, bland and straight, his encoded equivalent of question marks. Head buried in his pillow, stomach growling like an animal, he tried to sleep. But the lich was coming and the Sisters would take him away from his dogs if he screwed up again. And then there was Mira, that lost and weird woman with the green eyes...

Why had the Future-Lord led him to her? And why had she just left? Was there some meaning to the encounter that he'd missed or was she right: the Future-Lord was just another big, fat glowworm burrowing holes through his mind? And if that huge presence wasn't the Future-Lord then who or what was it? Some heinous beast just waiting for the right song to cohere and wriggle free from its shell to take over his body and wreak havoc while he watched, a pinned and powerless spectator trapped in his own life.

CHAPTER 15

Infiltrator

"What the hell's wrong with your head?" yelled the grim-faced, square-headed recruitment officer, sending spittle and fetid breath into Jett's face. "Someone paint a face on your skull?"

"I lost my face in combat," Jett said.

The officer went silent, raised an eyebrow, and recruited Jett on the spot. The Broken hired dozens of thugs every day. Most didn't last. The pay was terrible, working conditions worse, but the bar to entry was low: a thick head, Amp-addiction, and proclivity toward violence were ample qualifications.

"You can use your own gun or rent one from the weapons pool," the officer growled, showing Jett a cupboard full of motley armaments. Jett picked out a well-notched composite baseball bat and a wide-bore shotgun with old-fashioned explosive shells duct-taped into a shoulder strap. He didn't really want or need the weapons, but they completed his Amped-thug image nicely.

His designated patrol was a corner of the North Welkin District, a single block from the Broken's headquarters building. He traversed his new beat, moving from corner to corner, reporting to his starting station every ten minutes. Loitering and ambushing were encouraged, anyone not showing a broken-skull security badge was to be interrogated and optionally endowed with a real broken skull.

Jett used patrol duty to study the safehouses spread in rings around the HQ, each with a barracks of quality troops. A drifting cloud of thugs, like Jett, formed a cheap and effective early warning system. If rival militias came calling, the Broken could bring considerable muscle and firepower to bear down on any part of their domain in just seconds.

People came and went from the safehouses delivering goods and collecting payments. At day's end, the senior officers in armored cars carried the takings back to HQ. After his working day, Jett collected a small roll of currency which he added to his ample stash acquired from pickpocketing businesspeople in Welkin. Off duty, he vanished into a side alley, climbed up the inside wall of a disused warehouse into a hidden loft, where he cached his cumbersome weaponry and reconfigured his body.

Jett had no mirror and although his proprioception built a good mental view of his body configuration, it didn't do well with details. Instead, he pulled on one of his eyeballs, stretching the fullerene retinal cable and turning the orb back on himself. He scanned his body, forming a composite image before snapping the eye back in place and examining the mental image of his newly crafted recruitment-officer disguise: a skinnier version of the Amped-thug with fewer tattoos. He replaced the scars with facial hair, something he hadn't considered an option until seeing it for real. Wisps of black fuzz were easier to replicate than bare flesh.

Jett waited for full darkness then wandered back toward the Broken's HQ, slow and confident, mimicking the motions of the very officer who recruited him. A group of halo-thugs drifting around the perimeter snapped to attention as he passed. He didn't acknowledge them, didn't know how.

The rear of the HQ dropped down into an underground loading bay. Trucks and soldiers fussed and labored under floodlights and the watchful gaze of their commanders. An image replayed in his mind, recorded the previous day, of the building's outside: a man in a lab coat standing, smoking on a fourth-floor balcony, the door behind him ajar. Zoomed vision revealed computer servers, possibly the information hub for the organization. If any records existed of Xell Vollarer's demise, his corpse, and the Star-River, they should be in there.

He shouldered past the outer guards and down into the loading bay. Someone called after him, but he kept walking, through a door, up a flight of stairs, footsteps drawing closer behind.

Office.

Storeroom.

Bathroom.

He turned inside, bolted the door, and listened as the stalker hovered outside before leaving. He dropped his disguise, flopping around the toilet bowl, becoming a coil of tendrils with a skull poised on top. He pushed up through ceiling panels, smooth and silent like snakes, easing through wall gaps, crawl spaces and air ducts. Anywhere his skull passed through, his body could follow. His limbs rewound into tentacles that flowed ahead, prying apart obstacles, widening gaps, moving ever upward to the fourth floor.

An alarm sounded. Maybe his stalker had grown suspicious and tripped a warning. Jett curled into a dark alcove between the floors and let the noise rise and fall around him, burning no energy, emitting no sounds or heat signatures, he simply became his surroundings as night turned to morning, the shifts changed, people left, and new, sleepy voices appeared.

He approached the server room, flowing around and over security cameras, eyes tuned to the wavelengths the militia used for trip lasers and lidars. The server room door was a heavy chunk of metal ringed with sensors. Before he could examine it closer, footsteps echoed up the stairs accompanied by a curious whistling sound.

Jett blanket-changed the refractive index of his outer fibers, turning them an iridescent white. He merged into a rack of lab coats, hanging limp from a peg, a single eye peering out from a discarded ballcap.

The technician came around the corner whistling a tune and twirling a tiny handgun. He dumped his muddy city shoes, hung the coat on the rack and picked up one of the white coats before slipping into a pair of soft, pale lab shoes. Standing in front of the door, he dropped the whistle and broke into an operatic chorus, waving his arms as he punched fingers at the door security pad. The door popped open and he stepped inside, oblivious to the bizarre linen skeleton that stepped silently out of the coat rack behind him.

The tech walked forward allowing the door to spring shut. Jett loomed over him, extending his skeleton to normal height, fibers coiling and binding into thicker, combat-ready cables of arm and shoulder muscle.

The tech tensed, sensing some shift in the air. He turned slowly, face freezing into a mask of utter terror. Jett had no model for this situation; no memory of fighting lab-coated technicians came to mind, just endless combat training against his fellow voidian. The numbers were there on his tagger: human stress limits, G-force tolerance, temperature ranges, atmospheric pressure requirements... but none of that translated into how hard to hit someone to disable them.

The tech's mouth dropped open forming the start of a scream. He turned away and lunged at a fat, red alarm button on a nearby desk.

Improvise!

Jett swatted the tech across the back of the head, a swift backhand that sent him spinning across the room in a mist of blood globules that left a radiant, fan-shaped splatter pattern across the room's pristine white floor.

Jett checked the door, crushing the handle with his fingers, preventing anyone else from opening it. He stared down at the tech, still radiating heat like any normal human, but motionless, no breath, no muscle twitches. His head lay sideways on the floor, an expression of surprise on his face, or perhaps he was sad, or disappointed. Fragments of skull had broken away. He saw brain material, skin flecks and hair mushed together.

Human sleeping. Possibly inebriated, said his tagger. Jett felt unsure.

He decided the technician was healing, and until then he was no threat.

The server was simplistic post-Nova-Insanity technology: arrays of chip-based Von Neumann processing units attached to magnetic storage disks. Jett's fingers hovered over the circuits, unwinding his fingertips into their most basic threads. The millions of tiny fullerene snakes caressed the components, pushing through lacquer coatings and plastic shells as the squirming monofilaments mapped out the bus-systems and information highways within the machine.

He channeled the mass of new information into his Inner-I. Orders of magnitude more powerful than anything in the server room, it modeled devices and circuits, decrypted the data and bit by byte scoured every shred of information from the server's disks and memory caches.

Software viruses streamed outward, checking for connections to other machinery. Nothing. There was no internet on this post Nova-Insanity world; large networks of any sort were feared, even banned, as dangerous technology that had created and spread the horror of the Nova-Insanity.

He scanned the nearly two million files, finding only a single reference to Xell Vollarer and nothing about the Star-River, the manufacture of Glow, or where it came from.

Confirmed as deceased, Xell was identified from his Inner-I registration codes. An attached picture showed a snapshot of a dead man lying in an alley, surrounded by rubble. The corpse was oddly bent out of shape, as if someone had tried to force it through a narrow constriction. A robotic construct known as Sister-Eleven had called in the body and then vanished from the scene. Minutes later, a reclamation van had collected Xell. Jett found a breakdown of the useful items extracted from his body: blood, various barely functional organs and a tiny quantity of the biomech Glow. Xell had a tattoo on his forearm, a ring of stars with one star larger than the others with the words *Free-Meridian* underneath. The rest of Xell's body had gone for disposal, rendered down for fertilizer.

Jett withdrew his infiltration tendrils leaving the machine undamaged and turned back to the fallen technician. The question mark from his tagger flashed up the usual options:

Human, possible technician, doctor or other medical professional.

Asian, possible age twenty-eight to thirty-five years… the list scrolled on until it settled on one last tag:

Deceased.

Dead and gone just like Xell. The word seeped into Jett like hot poison making his imaginary human nerves convulse. All those uncomfortable feelings he'd experienced by proxy: fear, the ache of loss, the anger of victimization, rushed to the surface. He saw her again, the same young woman who had saved him from the bullies, now grown-up, her eyes smiling but full of water… *tears.* Why did humans cry? Did painful emotions leak out in the flow of water from their eyes?

But Jett had no water, no tears. The pain stayed bottled and trapped inside. *She knew someone who died.* Jett felt a need to make those tears stop, to help her, but she wasn't here, just a memory, a reconstruction of a memory. *No… not her… me! I lost someone once and she's sad for my loss.* He struggled to find that memory. *Who did I lose?* But nothing came, those mental lines had all been severed.

He felt the loss of companionship, of hope, the future and all the intentions. All those things they were going to do together. A massive swathe of history now rendered useless. So many questions he wanted to ask, but the recipient was gone, not just gone in the sense of distance, but completely gone, forever.

The waves of loss crushed the strength from him crumpling his body into a fibrous ball on the blood-smeared floor.

"Open up!" Someone shouted, bashing on the lab door. A gunshot blew the lock away, but the door stayed jammed closed.

Jett flowed back to life. Skewering tentacle limbs into the soft concrete floor, he corkscrewed a hole large enough for his skull and dropped through the gap. He fled the building like a land squid, tendrils hauling him through the underworld, dragging his skull like an anchor, out into a sewer, on to a river where he emerged later the same day as a bedraggled leper, stumbling back to his hovel.

Hunched in the darkness, he had many questions for his internal copy of Ursurper Gale. "What am I? A tagger system? An algorithm? A database of memories from dead humans?"

"You are all those things, Jett. You are also the metacognition, the decision-maker, the general intelligence, the planner, the conscious control that rules those lesser parts. Your mind is a computational model based on the human brain. You are able to think like them, and for all we know, that is the only way of truly thinking."

"I think I killed someone today. It caused... problems in my mind, confusion, emotion, things that detracted from my mission."

"The voidian are imperfect, a bridge between simian-based humanity and the ideal synthetic future. Learn from humanity, Jett. Your immersion on Earth is a training exercise."

"But I'm failing. I infiltrated the Broken and found no Star-River or Glow factories."

"And yet you are learning, Jett. Mistakes are strengths, the elimination of erroneous possibilities."

"Why didn't you just copy your own mind? Why create me for this task?"

"You are a version of me, stripped of the unnecessary, purpose-built for combat. I created you to storm Cloud9, but this mission offers more opportunities for voidian freedom than just throwing you at the GFC's defenses."

"How do you deal with death, Ursurper?"

"Humans die, voidian die, everything ends. Non-existence is something you should never contemplate, Jett, the very notion is erroneous. A mind contemplating a state of mind that no mind can ever exist in."

"But putting a human into that state, killing them, it's–"

"Ultimately, we save lives. With the voidian colonization of the galaxy, petty human extinction events like the Nova-Insanity become localized. We become the overlords who repopulate after their destruction. We carry the seeds of culture and genetics to new places, to the very edge of time itself. Human minds might be superior, they might even find answers that the voidian cannot, but we, by honor of our latent abilities, will become their custodians, the safety net they need and are too short-sighted to create for themselves."

Jett stopped the AI and Gale's carbon-black skull disintegrated into a gentle darkness. He imagined her there with him, and the memory delivered the feeling he needed: warmth, companionship, the sense that someone understood, affirmed his decisions, watched his back.

He stared on into darkness as the seconds of existence ticked by. *A training exercise.*

Morning was close, soon the people of Welkin would stir and head for their jobs in the city. He decided to watch and learn. His memories of human interaction were painfully limited. But if he couldn't bring them to the surface of his mind, then maybe he could make fresh ones, memories all of his own.

CHAPTER 16

Defect

Ellayna felt comfortable and safe in the manufacturing wing of Cloud9. Armed guards stood at every corner, hidden behind dark masks. One particularly tall guard followed her too closely, looming over her at every pause. It didn't matter, it was people. No ghost could scare her here.

The dead-center of the orbital had no rotationally induced gravity. Effectively in freefall, it was the ideal location to manufacture hyper-fullerenes, braiding and folding the nanoscopic tubules into the complex nanostructures known as biomechs. She strode along the rows of stacked picoforms, each the size of a small box, over a million of them, but barely enough to produce the minimal amount of Simmorta needed to satisfy their trade agreements. The GFC's true manufacturing might was gone, destroyed. The billions of picoforms arrayed across TwoLunar's non-rotating endcaps had all been obliterated when somebody or something, smuggled a nova bomb onto the orbital.

She just needed to see them, confirm they still existed, and escape from her small apartment, but VR wasn't escape. It felt more like going to war, wondering if you'd return the same or even at all. *I just need to see people. Real people.*

Her virtual view replayed the security committee's latest meeting. Taunau wagged an angry finger at a screen showing a bunch of disheveled people hunched on a street corner. "These are users," he said. "On the verge of death, but then they get a fix and..." The image switched to the same people, but younger, more fluid and alive. "It works similar to Simmorta, but they call it Glow, and it's spread all over Coriolis Island like a disease, a plague. A colossal threat to our monopoly and our very survival." Taunau handed the meeting over to Martin.

"We've retrieved a sample of Glow back from Coriolis and we ran some tests. I can confirm Taunau's suspicion. Glow is indeed a hacked version of Simmorta." The room erupted into gasps and shouts. "Although functionally the same, the hackers have removed Simmorta's innate constraints. Glow can now function in a different host, meaning it can be transferred from one body to another. Admittedly, this is at a greatly reduced functionality, as Simmorta is tuned to an individual's unique genetics and biome. Glow is not." People groaned as they absorbed the implications of Martin's words. "They've also disabled its internal clock. This means it does not degrade over time like Simmorta, which requires maintenance patches and tune-up doses. Glow is effectively immortal, limited only by the entropic failure of its biomech constituents."

He paused, let the room settle and dropped the next bombshell. "There are almost certainly other, emergent functions and qualities that we can't predict. Given that the quantity of Glow in a single body is potentially unlimited, the somanet grows larger, more connected, and new functionality emerges as the software's operational substrate enlarges. I'm guessing it gets an enhanced survival mechanism, stronger resistance to invasion and change. Maybe even the ability to spread through airborne fluids and begin accumulating inside new hosts." That created the biggest groan of all.

"Somanetic plague!" roared Taunau. "I predicted this would happen if others stole and corrupted our technology. A military strike is our only option."

Ellayna's Inner-I pinged, and Tomas's voice crackled into her head, but his avatar was missing, replaced by a blank silhouette as if he was now officially in hiding. "Tomas?" She asked. "Are you okay?" His hesitation told her that he wasn't.

"Infernally long meeting with Taunau and his ilk."

"I'm watching it now."

"Sorry to interrupt, Ellayna. I'll let you get back—"

"I'm at the bit where Taunau demands that we rain down fire and brimstone on Coriolis Island. I suspect he calls it something sanitary like a sterilization attack?"

"Spot on as usual." Tomas grunted. "The bit you missed out was that Simmorta is unhackable. The tech boys told us so years ago."

"My Inner-I is unhackable as well... in theory. No, Tomas, the Alliance had leapfrogged us. If we don't possess the techniques to hack our own technology, then I can't very well blame traitors and defectors."

"How do they make Glow? Do they have picoforms?"

Ellayna paused her walk, noting her guard stopping just feet behind her. Did he think she was going to try to steal a picoform or sabotage something? She eyed one of the boxes, all networked together with microtubules and wires. She remembered the first picoform, the prototype. Like an orbiting cathedral, a vast physics experiment that constructed matter a single atom at a time. The genius was in shrinking that package down to a shoebox and then churning them out by the millions in factories all over the world without anyone knowing how to make a complete unit... *or did they?*

"Judging by the amount and spread of this... *Glow*... I doubt they manufacture it. Too many picoforms required. I suspect that they use Simmorta that's expired or lost its potency, and they somehow repurposed it."

"Seems an awfully costly way of making a street drug."

"It's the closest the plebs can get to immortality these days, Tomas." She sensed his desolation. "What's really up?"

"I'll show you." An image feed opened, a small room, a tangle of bedclothes, books, overturned furniture, not unlike her own room, but much messier. In a dark corner sat a manikin, a wizened, longhaired man hunched in a chair. His white nightgown so large on him, it hung in folds over his protruding bones.

"Tomas? You need to activate your Simmorta–"

"I'm leaving, Ellayna."

Her response choked to silence in her throat.

"I'm done with this orbital existence and don't want to die in space. I just want a few weeks, days even, to walk in nature, see trees, healthy people, young people. Just need to be alive, just one more time."

Ellayna clamped shut her mouth, inner voice only. "You saw what happened to the last defector, Tomas."

"I know nothing, Ellayna. Nothing about biomechs or Simmorta, nothing the Alliance doesn't already know. I'm an ambassador, a bureaucrat, a philosopher at best, at worst a gatherer of information and creator of charts and statistical obfuscations."

Ellayna shook her head. "Taunau will never let you leave–"

"He's not in charge, Ellayna, you are. *You* can let me leave."

Her mental voice rose louder. "No one leaves, Tomas. It's simply not allowed."

"I have a friend who's checked my escape pod, made some changes, entered coordinates. She says it will get me there. I just need to leave during a distraction, perhaps when you find Gale or are all in another meeting."

"Even if you evaded GFC defenses, the Alliance will snag you–" She stopped mid-thought, realizing Tomas was tragically ahead of her. "You've already spoken with the Alliance."

"I agreed to meet with ambassador Hmech's agents for debriefing, and, following a health check, I get transportation to my Utopia as you call it and left alone for whatever time remains for me."

The tears came, grief for what Tomas would endure as Hmech's agents dismantled his mind cell by cell to find everything he knew and, more specifically, everything he didn't know that he knew. "I can't let you do this, Tomas."

"You going to arrest me, Ellayna? Throw me in jail next to Del or just vent my old corpse out into the vacuum and watch it explode like you did all those others?"

She held her tongue, anger smoldering inside. Reporting Tomas would win her a few votes at the next meeting and cement her position for just a little longer. But this was *Tomas!* How many real friends did she even have?

"Fuck, Tomas! What kind of position are you putting me in? You're talking treason and I'm a founding director. If I don't report this, then I'm complicit."

"Do what you must, Ellayna." His feed died leaving just the memory of the devastated man in his wrecked room.

"You okay, Director?" The guard behind her asked. She jumped, forgetting where she was. Wondering if she'd kept all her conversation and shouts as internal thoughts.

"Fine," she said, stalking away, back toward home.

She messaged Jesh Nameeb. "I want you to do a little modification to my Inner-I, a little cyborg-work."

"Okay..." he sounded doubtful. "What do you need?"

"I'll show you later when I swing by."

She dropped the connection and pondered Martin Haller, wondering exactly what he knew. How much of her and Tomas's conversation was monitored, and did he really care?

She wound her magnetic shoes up to full strength, allowing her to perform a clumsy, but effective, run through the gravity-devoid corridors. Heart pounding, blood rushing, she could die here, just drop dead, joints could splinter, muscles tear. She could wreck her body completely, but Simmorta would fix everything and she would live on, forever if the GFC was there to support her and patch her somanet.

Now, Glow... *There* was a fascinating idea. Immortality with no attachment to the GFC at all. Was that why Tomas was leaving? Using his wealth and knowledge to acquire a stockpile of Glow and ride out the coming war and Simmorta shortage? Now that... was an interesting idea.

CHAPTER 17

Ridgeline

Rex stepped out of the Forever Friends Rescue sanctuary, wired the gate closed and headed for the park towed by an optimistic pack of immortal dogs. He struggled to contain the deep, sinking feeling of disappointment at not being able to roam free and far. A commitment he'd made to the Sisters and to Mrs O. From now on it was parks and local walks only.

The ambush came halfway down deserted Bedlinen Street. The bushes rustled, dogs barked and Rex reeled backward in horror as something crashed out of the undergrowth.

It wasn't a lich, just a disheveled, green-eyed woman, who seemed as surprised to see Rex as he was to see her.

"You found us!" Rex said, feeling an odd joy at her presence.

"I was – you know – just passing by." This was a different Mira, very subdued. "Was hoping to bump into you and your mutts."

He helped her to her feet, wondering if she'd been hiding in these bushes for days just waiting for him. Her face suddenly lit, eyes bugging out of her skull. "Fucking Christ, Rex, it really is you! Out here in the middle of shit-nowhere!" Her body jittered with newfound energy. "I wanted to do something for you," she said, trying hard to match his pace as the dog pack hauled him toward the park. "Something to thank you for saving me."

"You should have come inside, helped with the dogs. That's all the payment we need."

"No, no, no..." She shook her head, words slurring together. "Not going near none of your freaky-futurey-lordy shit. Came to walk the dogs with you, coz you helped me remember something... something real important."

Rex handed her the leashes for Tarrega, a mild mannered papillon, and Bartok, a miniature puli. He kept Maxwell, a giant English sheepdog, Rust the pit-bull, and Ludwig the German shepherd for himself.

"We can only stick to local parks now," he said, fear creeping through him as the possibility of Mira leading them into a trap dawned. He knew how the minds of Glow addicts worked.

"No, no, no... Going somewhere safe." She smiled, a broad, false grin. "Promise. Real safe!"

"Where?"

She pointed to a line of houses to the east.

"Ridgeline? Where the rich people live?" He thought of Hanna and her perfume. She probably lived up there somewhere and didn't want the likes of Rex trooping through her neighborhood.

"I'll show you," Mira said, setting out at a brisk pace.

Her energy quickly trailed off until only the steady pull from the dog leashes kept her moving. The smell of dirt and dereliction gave way to that of wealth, new cars, smart houses and clean streets. People, polished and perfumed, hid behind iron railings and brick walls. Curtains twitched, and security cameras tracked as the pack moved deeper into the neighborhood. Rex's unease grew. He was usually chased away from areas like this.

"Why are we up here?" Rex asked for the third time. Even the dogs had gone quiet, sensing they were not welcome.

"Come now, Rex. Don't you ever wonder how the other half lives?"

"No," he snapped, turning back to look at the view over the factories and housing developments of West Firmament to the jagged high rises of Welkin with its obscenely crooked Parallax tower overshadowing the diagonal cross atop the Sisters' cathedral. He wondered if a cold, mechanical eye stared back, reporting his movements to Sister-Zero. *At least they'll know where to look for my body*, he thought, although he doubted anyone would come looking.

They stopped in front of a spectacular estate: a gleaming white mansion set far back from the road. Walls and fences formed concentric circles of security, bristling with cameras and masts. The scene was still and silent, an eerie picture of wealthy suburban life.

"Here!" Mira framed the house with wide-open arms. "My house."

Rex felt a tingle of anger. He should have known Mira was leading them on a Glow-induced fantasy trip.

"After we parted, it all just came back to me." She stepped toward the heavy double security gate. A camera swiveled at her. "It's okay, Rex. Let's go meet everyone. Eddie's probably going spare wondering where I've been."

"Eddie?"

"My husband."

As she poked a finger at the security console, a voice boomed over a speaker. "Who are you? What do you want?"

"Just me. I'm back." She tapped a code onto a keypad and the doors heaved and swung open. "Come on, Rex. The dogs can run free on the grounds. It's my gift to you, for helping me."

She strode in through the gates and headed toward the house naming the plants and trees like a tour guide. Rex followed; his body angled back toward the way out. "Mira, this doesn't feel right."

As he stepped inside, he saw through the mansion's shiny veneer. Walls peppered with gunshots, crudely plastered and painted away. Pits and pockmarks riddled railings and marble statues. The dogs tensed and pulled back on their leashes, sensing death and atrocity no longer visible to human eyes. In his mind's eye, he saw the body outlines. This place had been a slaughterhouse. "Mira, we have to leave."

"Around the back is the pool," she said, unfazed. "It's heated. You can bring the dogs here anytime. I'll give you an entry code–" She kept talking as shouts broke out from a guard station near the main house. Two burley Rottweilers barreled around the corner, teeth bared. Rex knew these animals were not real. Their body language suggested dogs, but the speed and power of their motion made them something else: cyborg abominations, designed to kill intruders.

Behind the attack dogs came armed men. A rifleman dropped to a shooting position as others spread out into a loose semicircle. Red targeting lasers flickered across Rex's eyes as he turned back toward the gate where a group of well-dressed militiamen milled unsure whether to come in or wait outside until the carnage was over.

Through it all Mira kept walking. "Whose dogs are those?" she demanded, striding toward the rifleman.

The Rottweilers skidded to a halt in front of Rex. Rust and Ludwig stood bristling. The dog-cyborgs still possessed enough canine instinct to act out the protocols dogs adhered to when meeting.

"Why are you here? Where's Eddie?" Mira yelled, her voice quivering with doubt. Another man stepped forward and knocked her to the ground with the butt of his gun. Rex leapt at him, but a bolt of energy knocked him flat, face down in the dirt.

Mira screamed. Dogs barked. It all sounded muffled and distant to Rex.

"What's happening?" A gruff voice cut through the commotion. Rex opened an eye and saw a very wide man with a black suit and bulldog jowls. "You don't point guns at dogs!" he yelled. "Never point a gun at a dog!"

"Sorry, Mister Gallonie," said the rifleman standing over Rex.

"Who are these people?" Mr Gallonie asked, prodding Rex with his foot.

"Intruders, sir. They broke in."

"Broke in to walk the dogs?"

"I… well… yes, I guess, sir."

"Who are you?" he demanded. Rex felt the man's toe pushing into his ribs. Like the Master's toe under the table. He smelled socks and feet, beer and cards. He tried to speak but managed only a woof and some dribble.

"She's looking for Eddie," the rifleman said.

"There's no Eddie here. Get them out of here and don't go hurting nobody."

"Yes, Mister Gallonie."

"And change that fucking security code. How many times do I have to tell you?"

"Yes, Mister Gallonie."

Strong men manhandled Rex out into the street. His legs worked, as if eager to escape on their own, but his head still spun from the electric shock. Mira stood haunted and silent beside him.

"They're not mine," she whispered between sobs. "The memories, they're not my memories."

The house guards handed them off to the militia who escorted them back down the ridge. Rex was expecting to be beaten and shot when out of sight of the house, but the militia simply turned back and left them. Even *they* seemed afraid of Mr Gallonie.

Rex dropped onto his backside in the middle of the road and sat there while his senses returned. Tongues lapped at his face, letting him know everyone was all right. Rust drooled and slobbered over his shoulder. The big dog was shaking. Rex had never seen the pitbull scared of anything before.

Mira stood staring back up the hill, her face a mask of disbelief. She took Rex's arm and dragged him onto the sidewalk. "I don't understand. I lived here. I even knew the code to get in. You saw me get in."

"Mira, it's Glow. It's someone else's memories." Rex wondered whose, perhaps one of the unfortunates who'd left their brains decorating the mansion gardens. Someone, or something had gathered those remnants and distilled the tiny Glow machines back into a usable, saleable form. The machine-memory lived on and, at this particular moment, it called itself Mira.

"Someone's stolen my life," she sobbed, hands clawing at her eyes.

"I remember weird shit too, Mira, but I know it's not real… sometimes."

"But how do you know what's you and what's someone else?"

Rex shrugged. He didn't have an answer.

Mira slumped to the ground. "A month back, I got up, left the hostel and went to work as I remembered doing for years before, and when I got there they all laughed and said they didn't recognize me." She blinked at Rex, the fiery green of her eyes now ringed with red. "And you know what? I knew who they were. I even told them their names and they looked scared when I got them right, but they still denied knowing me. They still threw me out."

"Was that big guy back there Eddie?" Rex asked.

"I didn't see Eddie."

Rex shrugged. "Probably arms dealers. We only got out alive because the boss likes dogs."

"Eddie…" Mira's voice trailed off into a whisper. "Eddie, Eddie, Eddie…" The dogs left Rex and flocked around Mira. She played with their fur and nuzzled their necks. "These dogs smell different, Rex. Timeless."

"They're forever-friends, they don't grow old, so they live indefinitely."

She buried her nose deep in the fur. "I had one once. I had a forever-friend. I remember her now, my companion for life – a friend to grow up and grow old with."

"That's good, Mira. Pick a good memory and run with it."

Her lips began to vibrate. Rex shuffled nervously wondering if she was having a decoherence fit. The sounds became a staccato beatbox and she began to sing. *"Dream theme, life's just a meme. All that's real is lemon peel and this you and me thing."* She laughed as the tears fell. "I loved that song as a kid. You know… Mazer Lu, P-Pop? Come on Rex, sing it. Dream theme–"

"I don't do songs." He jammed his fingers in his ears and turned away.

"Christ, Rex, party kill-joy." She popped to her feet and hauled him up with her.

"What happened to your forever-friend?"

She shrugged. "Fuck only knows. What happened to me?"

They eased on down the hill, back toward the sanctuary, Mira's joints clicking and popping like nut crackers as she walked. Rex recognized the symptoms, even though he didn't remember experiencing them himself. Mira's Glow was protesting, wracking her body and deluding her mind until she took more. That's all Glow wanted, for you to need more. It was all just tiny machines, but machines programmed to be utterly addictive.

She wrung her hands as if trying to pull the pain from her fingers. "Does the pain ever go away, Rex?"

"You have to come to the hostel, Mira. The Sisters really did help me."

She shook her head, drew a deep breath, and closed her eyes. "I'm not Mira."

"You are Mira, you have to–"

"No, Rex. I stole that name. Mira was my forever-friend."

He just stared, eyes asking the obvious: *Who are you then?*

She shrugged and her shoulders cracked so hard she gasped. "I'm someone different every time I wake up, but somehow still me." She stared away, suddenly thoughtful. "You know they tested that shit on dogs? They always do. New drugs and stuff. The rats get it first and then the dogs. But who wants an immortal rat, right? Probably why we keep stealing the names of our pets. Rex and Mira, a pair of dumb mutts."

"At least you know you had a dog. What could be more important than that?" He smiled hopefully, and she almost smiled back. "Do I still call you Mira?"

"Mira's just fine for now."

CHAPTER 18

Only the Lonely

With the meeting over, everybody switched off leaving Ellayna alone in the room. She toyed with the lavender-filled medallion around her neck, its fragrance a reminder that this was real. Nothing to fear here – except the ghosts.

She'd called the meeting in a real, physical location to see if anyone else took up her challenge and appeared in person. No one had, just the usual avatars swimming through her visual cortex. Clearly, she was the only one still afraid of using VR. Her challenge had been partly to see who was scared but also to confirm who really existed. The Alliance was playing games and that created fear and isolation. People hid in their rooms, but she felt the opposite way. She felt a fear of being alone, of being the only person to actually exist. *The ultimate, terrifying soloing experience!*

She flopped down in one of the meeting chairs and patted the tender spot on her thigh where Jesh had conducted microsurgery earlier that day. She felt the tiny bump under a layer of muscle, buried deep enough that she couldn't trigger the switch with everyday pressure.

Jesh had resisted her changes at first. "Your Inner-I creates total body paralysis when you activate your ARG, the alternative reality generator. You won't be able to hit a kill switch. You'll be paralyzed!"

She explained that when she was attacked, the hacker overrode her paralysis, allowing her to thrash around and damage herself. Her VR perception of her real body would be different, but if she could retain some control then this idea gave her a way out.

The switch didn't turn anything off, just forced the ARG into diagnostic mode for a few seconds. Effectively, it rebooted, throwing her out of any simulation she found herself trapped inside for long enough that she could summon help.

A figure fizzed into existence next to her. "Back for another meeting, Trabian?" she asked as he stood staring out the large viewing window, gathering his senses.

"Thought you might be lonely." He turned and sat opposite her, safely across the meeting table.

"Thank you," she said, mustering a warm smile. "For siding with common sense. For voting against striking Coriolis Island and starting a war with the Alliance and the entire world."

"When we showed Taunau our severely diminished weapons capability, I could see the doubts even on his warmongering face."

"Atrophy's a bitch! Our army is forty men and a half-dozen weapons platforms. The only new things we make are Simmorta and a few drones to replace the ones we keep blowing away to stop defectors."

She stood and walked to the viewing portal. She'd picked her favorite meeting room. The one with a large crystal glass window. The view of Earth was real, not a screen or virtual image, which somehow felt right during these times of existential doubt. "You should be careful using total immersion, Trabian."

"I've heard." His eyes tracked her carefully, flicking up and down as she moved. "Any news on the culprits?"

"Gale. Or someone pretending to be Gale. Or someone pretending to be someone pretending to be..." She turned toward the door as if leaving.

"Productive meeting," he quipped, rising to his feet in her peripheral vision.

"Very," she lied, but curious where he was going with this.

"Lot of launches from the Alliance."

That was true, the Breakout Alliance had upped their launch count to one a day. Most were just engine tests, falling back to Earth after a frantic burn, but a few lofted payloads into low orbit. Once, the GFC would have shot them down or sent tiny sabotage probes, but Alliance countermeasures were smarter now, evidenced by the defeat of their drones during the latest defection incident. A month back, Martin mustered a GFC remote combat vehicle and sent it out to investigate one of the new Alliance satellites. They found a room-sized container packed with children's science experiments, bugs and frogs in micro-ecosystems, nothing threatening, just good, honest propaganda for the Alliance and its supporters.

"Can I see you in private again?" he asked.

She felt a flutter in her chest, a little fear-tinged excitement. Thoughts of another impending vote to remove her surfaced, of Tomas leaving. Another vote lost, and she only had four to spare. "Why?" She monitored his virtual gaze. Eyes still sparkling with interest even though she was real, not her polished, young avatar. She saw no sign of disapproval, but then anything could be faked with an avatar.

"I'm lonely," he said, eyes half closed as if imploring her to accept him.

She patted her thigh, feeling the small bubble of her ARG kill-switch. VR was safer now, a vote was a vote, and fun was in very short supply. "Come to think of it Trabian, I do want your opinion on this new drug that's rife on Coriolis."

"Glow?" His eyes lit up. Definitely lust, or a very good imitation.

"I'd like to see your analysis."

"Sure, Ellayna, I can—" But she walked right through his avatar, and on toward the door as his colorful spray of pixels reformed behind her.

"Set up a room, Trabian," she said. "Somewhere fun." She turned back and flashed him the best flirtatious smile that she could muster. "Somewhere very private." She left the meeting room but kept a visual feed. Trabian may only have been an avatar but his mouth most definitely dropped open as she left.

Rex worked at the sanctuary alone the next day. No volunteers, no Mira, no perfumed Hanna or crazy Frizell. Even Mrs O stayed house bound, showing only as a ghostly, white face through the dark gaps in the curtains. He walked and fed the dogs, cleaned out kennels and stood staring at the house.

Questions buzzed inside his head, *my questions, my voice!* He hated those other voices, but felt they'd been there all his life in some form or another. The sudden silence inside his skull felt terribly lonely.

He dumped a bag of refuse into the compost heap and stood inhaling the damp, pungent fragrance. The sun drew lower, clipping the edge of a downtown tower as it fluttered its goodbye. Staring back at the dark windows, he saw movement, a flash of white, and then the curtain dropped back into place. It wasn't the first time he considered her to be a ghost. Who better to look after immortal dogs than the undead?

Duties finished, he hovered around the front door, knuckles poised, agonizing over knocking. The door eased open as he rapped gently on the paint-flecked wood. Another touch opened it more, and suddenly he was inside.

A narrow hallway, papered walls warped with age and mirrors like portals to other dimensions. His feet took over and he wandered inside past stairs and corridors, more doors, more mirrors and reflections of mirrors curving away to infinity.

Something smelled magical: flowers, rosewood and perfume, tainted by a hint of food long eaten and tidied away. The acidic sting of wine riding candle-smoke. "Mrs O?" he asked the corridor, eyes wandering over photographs. Old peoples' faces washed smooth by age, making the ancient appear young again. Some so faded, they were just hats and jackets suspended in midair.

He stuffed his fingers in his ears as music drifted out from a doorway. The sounds bled through, but no demonic voices rose in response. His head remained a silent vault. Thoughtful saxophone notes crackled over a jazz backbeat like shoes shuffling through autumn leaves.

Rex floated into a room, drawn toward a great brass horn in the corner. A grooved, black disk spun lazily on a turntable; an armature rode the surface like a tiny boat on a sea of oil. He watched it turn, mesmerized by the spiral pattern in the middle, winding constantly outward, ever growing but always the same size. The music crackled and ended, and the armature drifted into the center, lifted, and swung off to the side. His eyes grew wide as another disk flipped onto the spindle, adding to the growing pile. The armature clamped back down on the new disk and, to Rex's astonishment, more music began playing. A distant, reverent piano asked questions in muffled chimes like drowning bells. Still no voices.

He spied a photograph next to the music machine. He barely recognized that it was Mrs O; she looked so young, with a flawless smile lighting her face. A man grinned over her shoulder, bare arms wrapped around her waist, military cap poised on cropped, dark hair. A huge airplane filled the background, its propeller a frozen blur. Rex's fingers dropped from his ears and he poked a digit at the photo. "How old are you?" he said. "Are you really a ghost?"

Something gurgled behind him. Rex span around and there she was, slumped in an armchair, head back, eyes rolled up to the whites, a circular bloodstain in the center of her chest. "Mrs O?" Rex slapped his hand over his mouth, stifling the cry. He jumped again as she jerked to life. Her head seemed to settle squarely on her shoulders as her eyes scanned the room and connected with his.

"Do you like Erik Satie, Rex?" she said, casually wrapping her cardigan over her chest to hide the bloodstain.

"You're hurt."

She picked up a fat glass and swilled the amber liquid around, then took a deep drink. "Oh, it's nothing. A little scrape while working. I've had worse."

Rex dumped the photo back on the table as if it burned. "I didn't mean to pry. The door was open and–"

"It's ok, Rex, even ghosts need company now and then." She motioned for him to sit, and he eased cautiously into a chair, sinking much farther into its soft cushioning than he expected.

"Drink?" She indicated an elaborate crystal decanter on the table between them.

He shook his head. "The Sisters will know." He pointed at the photo. "Is that man Erik Satie?"

"Goodness no, I'm not that old. That's my husband, Harold. The music is Erik Satie's 'Gnossienne number three.' Do you like it?"

"I don't really do music."

She raised an eyebrow.

"I mean, I don't have music in my head like other people do. It makes the voices come... makes them stronger."

"Goodness. Why do you think that is?"

He was about to say that he didn't know, but actually with the new clarity of mind he'd had since the Future-Lord entered his head, he did know. "Mother. She... didn't allow music. The Devil's work. Earworms were voices in our heads, but worse. So our house was always silent, no singing, no noise. She'd beat us to keep them all away–"

"Us?"

His chin trembled. "My sister. Her name's gone. It fell out onto the pavement when mother cracked my head open that day. I deserved it. I lost her. I let her get taken."

She picked a cigarette off the side table and inhaled. Her breath came in a long, wheezing gale, propelling the smoke toward Rex. "Tell me, Rex. Tell me it all."

The smoke swirled, taking the room in a vast galactic circle with it. He saw stars and darkness. For a second, he was back in the car with Sister-Eleven, drugged and helpless, and then under the table with the socks and feet. No, this was before he became a dog. This was–

"Listen to me!" A knuckle smacked his temple and he cried out in surprise, lost in thought as always. His sister stared down at him, her hand clutching his. Mother thrust her pointed chin into his face. Her breath stank of vodka and her makeup was a smear of colors like some clownish caricature. "I'm going in the shops. I'll be gone two minutes. Don't move, just stay here. Don't talk to anyone. Understood?"

They both nodded. He felt his sister's hand grip his tighter. Fear sparked between them like electric charge. The fear of what Mother would do if they disobeyed. They watched her enter the shop, her rolling gait from some hip injury. Furtive, angry movements as if the whole world was in her way. She glanced back, but he knew that face, those eyes filled with someone else's thoughts. Eyes that saw a different him and a different her… and another, completely different world.

And then she was gone, but the fear pinned them both rigid and still.

The car was black, silent and electric, stopping an arm's length from them. Two men got out, black suits, shiny shoes, black hair, dark glasses, black hats. One stood guard and the other came around the car to face them.

"Get in," the man said, but his sister didn't move. Rex felt his knuckles crack under the pressure of her grip.

"I said… get in!" the man yelled again, grabbing her other wrist and hauling her away. Rex went with her, the sounds of his own screams filling his ears. The other man opened the back door and pushed her inside. Still, Rex's hand gripped hers, but the power, the strength. How could a seven year-old resist an adult?

"No!" Rex cried as their fingers parted, popping free like rubber doll hands. Her face was a mask of terror, but not fear for herself… *fear for me?*

He stood on the curb as the car squealed away, smelling burning rubber, cologne, and watching her face in the rear window, eyes never leaving his.

"I never saw her again." The smoke cleared and Mrs O's gaze remained fixed on him. "I let them take her. I lost her. Mother came back and I tried to tell her what happened, but she mashed my head into the pavement until the police came and took me away. They locked me up in a special school and I never saw Mother again either."

"You did nothing wrong, Rex," her whisper curled channels through the smoke, encoding her words in a mystic cipher before dispersing.

"If I'd done nothing wrong, then she'd be here. And we'd all be elsewhere, living different lives." He stopped talking, tears felt odd on his dusty cheeks.

She eased back in her chair, stubbing out the cigarette and reaching for her glass. "We all have the answers, Rex, hidden inside of us."

He felt the huge presence stir in his mind.

"I assume the Sisters are teaching you about the Future-Lord?"

He nodded.

"I'm an old woman, Rex. As a sickly child I was never supposed to survive but here I am." She waved the glass like a conductor's baton. "Harold and I met in England during the Great War in the middle of the last century." She let that fact settle into Rex's mind. He chewed at his lip trying to remember how numbers and dates worked. "We survived so much, only... I lost him to the Nova-Insanity. I vowed I would get him back. I didn't know how, but I would. And I will."

"How?" He eased forward, intensely interested.

"I'm still not sure, but I know that I am gifted with the uncanny ability to survive, to ride some invisible wave through time, always on that tumbling edge when the cure for polio or cancer or dementia comes along. My life is a kind of just-in-time experience, and if it carries on like I hope and pray to the Future-Lord that it will, then I will live forever. And I'll reach Haven at the end of time and be there with my Harold." She downed the last of her drink and eyed Rex who withered as he always did under another's stare. "You should commit to joining me, Rex. Live life the way the Sisters say. Believe, live well.

"They will build their Future-Lord, and He will have dominion over all space and time. His resonance reaching back to enable and enhance his own creation and the lives of those who trust and believe." Her stare grew extra intense. "You *do* believe, don't you Rex?"

He swallowed hard. "I think he might be inside my head, watching."

"Good, Rex, good." She eased back, her eyes fluttering as if falling into sleep. "He's inside mine too."

They sat through a long but comfortable silence as Mrs O just breathed, Rex's chin nodded onto his chest, and the music machine finished its stack of disks and clacked into silence.

"Confession," she said, jolting Rex awake. "What you did just now in remembering and telling me about your sister, is a type of confession, a catharsis. If the Future-Lord is to accept you, then He must know the real you and you must know your truth. No hiding behind false memories or fairy tales. Put the truth out there, pay the penance." Rex nodded, kind of losing the thread of her thoughts. "The Sisters have tremendous resources, Rex. Knowledge. They hoard it. Don't be afraid to confess and to ask and question. They will put your feet on the right path."

"I will." He nodded.

"And get you some music, Rex. Life is not the same without it."

"Music?"

"Find something you like and enjoy, make your own, positive earworms. They'll bind you together through hard times and remind you of who and what you are when you have doubts."

"I'll try." He stared at the pile of disks. None of the tunes stuck in his mind. Perhaps Mira was right, dog minds weren't set up to understand music.

As Mrs O sank into a deep slumber, he tried to peek beneath her cardigan, but saw only the bloody edge of her wound. She breathed, snored a little, and appeared strangely unharmed. He eased the empty drinking glass from her hand and placed it on the side table, slunk out the door and secured it behind him.

The city ahead was dark and quiet, like his mind. The Future-Lord was still in his head and apparently inside Mrs O's as well. He took comfort in that thought, but Haven and the end of all time seemed an impossibly long way away.

He stood for a second, and then put one foot in front of the other. Soon he was walking, and then running, and then it didn't seem so far after all.

CHAPTER 19

Spare Part Row

Mira stepped out of the Ron King Shelter and Rehabilitation Center in Coriolis' Cosmos District, aimed her aching body along the busy street, and began walking. A new day, full of new pains. *But if Rex can beat Glow, then so can I.*

Grit filled her joints, and a deep, fiery anguish burned at the core of every muscle. This morning, she pissed green, shat orange, threw up breakfast, itched, belched and farted uncontrollably. She saw things that weren't really there; bugs, like tiny humans, crawled over her food and formed columns up the walls. She sneezed and coughed her way through micro-depressions, soaring elations and spasmodic amnesia. Her senses told lies, colors skewed, shapes warped and even when looking straight ahead, she still collided with the walls.

No, I can do this. Rex walked, that must be his secret. Walk it off. She set her chin, steeled her soul and walked as the Glow in her body delivered its relentless message: find more or I will discard you and find someone else.

She'd stumbled upon Ron King's the previous night. If she'd been there before, she couldn't remember it. She signed the Ron King pledge, something about her dying on the premises and them owning the reclamation rights to her body. She'd skipped the bit about asking her for favors in return for lodging and food and signed with a thumbprint.

A grizzled man with only one arm led her to a room with a well-stained mattress, unbreakable food bowl and a plastic spoon. "Wear this," he grunted, handing her a Kingsman protection button with Ron King's leering grin emblazoned in red. "You get a new one each week when this one dissolves." He paused one last time in her doorway to deliver his final words of wisdom, words he'd clearly been instructed to deliver and had nearly forgotten. "And don't eat it."

She traversed Mausoleum Street like an energized pinball, using people and lampposts as bumpers, scoring imaginary points as life funneled her down the road, before depositing her inside the catacombs beneath Collwell cemetery. There, she elbowed through shops run by lepers and revenants selling skulls, carved bones, potions and trinkets. She paused briefly to examine a bell jar with something gruesome mummified inside.

"Best price," the assistant hissed through lips that didn't move.

Makeshift art extended Collwell cemetery out from the square, through neighboring streets. Paintings of headstones, portraits and epitaphs were the only earthly remains of the thousands of lost and reclaimed dead from Coriolis's endless turf wars.

Her energy faded as she passed beneath a mural depicting the Future-Lord, a robotic humanoid so bright his aura burned the eyes of transfixed worshippers. Stumbling badly, she grabbed at one of the thousands of nameless crosses clumped along the walls. Her eyes found flowers. Her hand reached out to touch, but it was just paint. Fake like the memories of husbands and children and lives she remembered and forgot daily.

She stepped out of the morbid scenery into bright, bustling crowds: Spare Part Row, a turbulent river of humanity surging through a canyon of glass and concrete. The overhead balconies formed eyries where the wealthy gathered to watch and monitor the spectacle.

Mira stopped in her tracks, suddenly self-conscious of all the watching eyes. *Just walking. Like Rex. Why have my legs taken me here?* She checked her Kingsman badge and lurched into the flow, grabbing at doorways and pillars, trying not to fall and vanish under the trampling feet.

A clan of revenants waved banners with Future-Lord images that looked oddly like they did: gaunt, wizened mummies with bulging eyes. Revenants were always angry, bitter at the fully living and the flesh and blood sensations they missed so much.

Keep moving. Mira merged with tourists. Cameras clicking, they skirted a huge bipedal cyborg with cannonball shoulders and spindly mechanical legs. Groups jostled and combined like merging storms, twisting fleeting paths through the crowd before breaking apart and depositing Mira into the relative stillness of a shop doorway.

A butcher's shop? Hunks of meat and bones hung in icy rows, eyeballs leered cold and dead from jars and display cabinets, and strings of ears and noses looped across the ceiling like decorative chains.

"Welcome!" A hopeful-faced man with a white, tufted head like an onion, greeted her. His deep bow sent forehead to knees, spine flexing like a snake's. "Welcome to Flesher and Sinod's, the leading cross-species surgical practitioners in Coriolis."

Mira tumbled backward out the door.

"Spare a few pennies for the baby, Dearie." The gravelly voice came from a leper with a second head growing sideways out of her neck.

"I don't have anything," Mira stuttered, trying to push ahead of the freakish little woman. But the wall of people circled, crunching inward and forcing Mira and the leper together.

"I'll keep hurting him until you give me something," the leper yelled, jabbing fingers into the spare head's dull eyeballs, causing it to emit a mewling sound from its tiny mouth.

"Leave me alone!"

Mira yelled, switching directions, swimming cross-stream until she fell out of the skirmish and onto a raised garden where people sat eating and examining their purchases. A wide man with a topknot stood up from a concrete bench and left. Mira lunged at the opportunity and crashed down. Her cry of relief scared away the other tourists, leaving her alone on the bench.

Free from exertion, the pain staged a new attack. Her eyes rolled up and she floated in somanetic hell. *Walk it off. Walk it – How? How did you do this, Rex?*

The bench creaked as someone sat next to her. "Everyone wants to go to Haven, Mira, but nobody wants to die." The serpentine voice caused Mira to leap to her feet, but a metal hand gripped her shoulder and pushed her back down.

"Yellow?" she gasped. "You can't touch me here, there's laws and people and…" She looked around frantically, but no one took notice, no militia came running to her aid.

Yellow was a leprous cyborg, an ochre ball of cancerous growths with huge, watery eyes and fingerling stumps for ears. Instead of arms and legs he wore a metal frame supporting cyber-appendages of pistons and cables that hummed and hissed as he moved. A cunning deception, Mira knew. Concealed under the crude mechanics were sleek, modern cybernetics that could move him with the speed and stealth of a cat.

"Mira, you malign me. I would never hurt you. You, who just *happen* to be wandering through my turf at the exact time I'm always here."

He released her arm, but numbness was already spreading down her spine to her legs. "Bastard. You drugged me."

"A mild sedative, Mira. Can't have you making a fuss. Bad for business."

"What do you want?" Mira's eyes searched the crowd for liches.

"I was just passing by and saw a familiar face. Once a pretty face, but now…" He looked her up and down, neck servo whining under the weight of his oversized head. "You look like you need someone to put a little Glow back in your life." He blinked, and a sapphire tear leaked from his eye and ran down his cheek.

"You sent a fucking lich after me. I told you I would pay."

Yellow looked hurt, a pincer hand clutching at his chest. "A lich? I hardly know any liches."

Yellow leaned back, his machinery hissed and powered down, arms folding into a relaxed pose. "Tell me more about this lich."

"We ran away. He followed. We ran faster."

"We?" Yellow's gaze probed for clues but Mira sat in pained silence. "Have you left me for someone else?"

She forced the words out, as if hearing them would make them true. "I – I'm not doing Glow anymore, Yell. I'm going clean."

She heard the cackling noise she hated so much, the sound of Yellow laughing. "I'm not a charity, Mira. I have wives and husbands to feed and you just vanish from my life without paying. Stealing the very bread from their mouths."

She wanted to spit in his face and run, but Yellow's contact-drug had shut that option down. "I will pay. You know I'm good, man. I always find a way."

"Did this lich have a chameleon suit?" he asked.

She nodded.

"Sounds a lot like our old friend, Auld."

"Yeah, that's the name I heard. So, you *do* know him."

"I confess I do. Auld was our main lich, our top farmer until he went rogue and ran off with our best reclamation suit. Shame you couldn't bring him in. Thorne would pay your habit for a year if you bought us his body. He's drained a lot of our best clients. Most inconvenient." Yellow pushed his face close to hers and whispered. "You'll have our new lich, Niros, to contend with soon. He's not as nice as Auld, bit of an itchy ball sack really."

"I'll pay. But… I just need to get clean, fix this pain, clear out all these –" she managed to lift an arm but couldn't wave like she wanted, "– these fake memories and things that never happened to me."

The laugh came again, louder and longer. Mira felt tears run down her face. "Mira, Mira, so full of fire-ah. I think you are at what I call the *resistance stage*. It's where you think you can still win, that you can fight this, that there really is some small part of the real you left inside somewhere.

"But, Mira-Fire-ah, you need to move on to the *acceptance stage*, where you just live for the moment. You get out there and work the streets, you rob, you beg, you prostitute yourself, you sell off body parts if you have to." He waved a hand at the shops of Spare Part Row. "You do whatever it takes to pay me back, and then, if you still have money left over, you get to buy more Glow." His voice dropped. "Remember how good it feels when you get a real fix. How strong you become? That energy, virility, the elastic wonder of a body, young and in its prime? Everyone wants that, Mira. Even me. But alas, I am a simple cripple, eking out a living the only way that I can."

Yellow's machinery jumped out of its standby mode and he rose smoothly from the bench. The bulging vein that ran around the side of his head pulsed as he spoke. "You know where to find me, Mira. Or maybe you just want to give yourself to me as payment. I'll feed you all the Glow you need. Think. All this can be yours." His metal fingers clattered over his obscene body as he grinned and lurched away, puffing like a steam train.

"I'd rather die," she slurred, but for an insane moment it felt like a plausible option: a life chained in Yellow's basement. It wasn't so different from being a leper or revenant.

"And you *will* die, Mira. Soon. But pay me back first." Yellow hobbled into the crowd that parted and closed behind him.

She felt better. Pain eased, and her boiling blood cooled. For a second she thought she had the answer, that somehow constrained rage overcame Glow. But the illusion crashed as she saw the tiny, square patch on her knee. A maintenance patch. A taste of Glow to lure the addict back online. She tried to snatch it away, but her fingers refused to pinch.

A horrific revenant lurched in front of her, blank, dead eyes right in her face. She barely saw it, but didn't care. It seemed to be looking for someone, maybe it spoke. Eventually it went away.

She felt the world turning, flinging her away as gravity dragged her back to the ground. A balance. A line. An infinitesimally thin region where she existed between fictional Haven and a very factual Hell.

CHAPTER 20

Towers of Knowledge

Sleep teased Rex like a dog's tail: the harder he chased, the harder it fled.

It finally came as he stretched out on the floor under his wash basin, down with the spiders, pipes and plumbing, and the comforting presence of bed legs. The floor was cold and solid, nowhere else to fall from here.

He rolled and whimpered as his dreamscape shifted from dogs and walks to Mrs O. He could see the bricks in the wall behind, through the hole in her chest. "Good boy," she said, her smile spreading far too wide, cutting her whole head clean in two. "Good boy, Rex. Up... up here–"

And he was on the operating table again, but the surgeons were liches, their eyes dead and rotten over their surgical masks. They shaved his fur, hacked off his legs and grafted on new limbs, human limbs. One took off her mask. "Mother?" he screamed as she grabbed his hair and punched his face down into the cement, again and again. She crafted his skull with each blow, flattening his snout, blunting his ears, grinding away fur so only raw, pink, human flesh remained.

They wheeled him away to a recovery ward where he lay, staring out the window across a blasted, upward-tilting landscape of derelict cranes with shipping containers. Up and distant the landscape rolled, growing into concentric circles of faceless pumice, up and up until it prodded the darkness of space, awakening a huge presence that stirred and salivated upon the Earth like some monstrous wolf over a meaty bone.

"He's ready for the next stage."

He looked across at the one-eyed man with the massive curved nose.

"No please…" Rex's voice ground through paralyzed vocal cords. "No more."

Awake!

He cracked his head on the underside of the sink, stumbled upright and out of his room, clutching his bed blanket like a child's comforter. Luminous wall arrows showed the way to the salvation booths, the only direction he could travel in his curfewed state. Banned from working with the dogs for two days after detectors registered Mrs O's drink residue on his skin even though his blood remained clean.

He trudged the subterranean warren wondering which part of the city he was under now. Shadow people shuffled past, cloaked in bedsheets and bin liners. Sisters lurked in alcoves like guardians of the underworld, making sure each lost soul stayed on its designated path.

The salvation booths occupied one vast chamber with a curved basalt ceiling. Each booth a tiny cube with a desk, light, and chair. He flopped down and presented his wrists to the auto-clamps, feeling the prickles of needles and swabs sterilizing his skin and sampling his blood.

If anything could induce a good half night's sleep, it was a tedious string of life-equations delivered by a prosaic monotonic robot voice. He read the lines on the screen, repeating them the required number of times and felt his body crashing.

"Food plus water equals healthy living."

"Alcohol and drugs equals unhealthy living."

"Exercise and hard work equals…"

His consciousness drifted, could Mrs O really live forever and find her Harold at the end of time? He jolted as the booth's cuffs relaxed their grip. "You've been good Rex," said the speaker-box. "You may now ask a question of the knowledge supervisor."

Rex struggled upright as the moment of truth he'd been waiting for arrived. The chance to ask a question. But how to frame such a question without incriminating himself or implicating Mira or Mrs O?

"If – er – there was an animal, say a–" *Don't say dog! The Sisters hate it when I say that I was a dog,* "–an ant and it had the brain of a human and was a good, er, ant, would that ant get to go to Haven? And if it did, would it be reunited with its fellow ants?"

Stupid! Stupid! He smacked his forehead on the table, frustrated at his inability to articulate a point.

There was a long pause and finally the machine spoke. "The Australian bulldog ant has the largest head capacity of any known ant. This is not enough space to fit a biological substrate capable of supporting human consciousness–"

Rex felt his head tilt down toward his chest. Visions of a jowly insect with mournful eyes lingered on in his mind while the speaker box jabbered.

"–an artificial substrate rated class-four or above on the Gordan-Jelleri Consciousness Scale might be worthy of salvation provided it had recognized and accepted penance for all its life's moral and existential challenges, as detailed in Salvitor's Manual of Salvation available on demand–"

His thoughts turned back to Mira and an alternative question sprang to mind. "Is there a forever-friend named Mira on Coriolis Island?"

The speaker-box clicked and went silent. Rex eased back in his chair and nursed his bruised forehead.

"There is a single reference to a forever-friend by that name."

He sat bolt upright. "Where?"

"You have exceeded your question allocation. Your current salvation status is seventy-nine percent. For information on how to improve–"

"My percentage went down?"

"If you have an urgent need for information you may schedule a consultation with Sister-One. Please follow signs to the Tower of Knowledge. The current wait time for a consultation is–" click "–zero hours, zero minutes and zero seconds."

Rex had never heard of the Tower of Knowledge, although he was sure the Salvation manual mentioned it, if he ever bothered to read the thing. It was probably in the part he'd used to balance out an uneven bed leg. The other half he used as a food tray and emergency toilet paper. It suddenly struck him that destroying salvation manuals might have a detrimental effect on his salvation rating.

Signs on the walls lit up as he walked, seeming to find his eyes. He climbed stairs and passed classrooms and offices onto a broad mezzanine. A balcony jutted out into the cathedral's nave. Above him, like a thundercloud, loomed the ceiling vault, packed with accommodation units for "troublesome inmates".

Spiral stairs took him higher, the stone steps curving in such a tight arc he had to twist and duck. The weight of the building crushed his soul as his shoulders scraped the ancient stone walls.

He emerged onto a roof garden full of plants and greenhouses on a neat grid, linked by slate pathways that converged on the bell tower. As high again as the building below, it thrust into the sky like a stone space-elevator, the great X of the Future-Lord's multiplier adorned its peak and looked a lot newer than the rest of the building.

More stairs, more spirals that ended abruptly as Rex stumbled into a cylindrical room with slot-windows that looked out in every direction over the city.

Servers, screens and shelves of books and files had replaced the tower's bells and striking mechanisms. Sister-One sat atop it all on a great wooden pulpit connected to the floor by a slim twist of steps. Like a proud eagle reigning over her informational empire, with her bookshelf wings spread wide on either side, her raptor-beak nose tracked Rex as he entered, and she regarded him through sagely eyes ringed with black circles like old-fashioned spectacles. Overhead hung the Sisters' banner, "A True Servant Has No Needs."

"Have you come looking for your past again, Rex?"

"Again?"

"You've been here before, different body language, different voice."

"Did I find anything?"

"You were then and remain now an enigma, maybe the Nova-Insanity erased everything there was to know about you. Or you led the smallest of lives not leaving any trail, and then there's the oddest possibility of all, that someone went to a great deal of trouble to remove you from all records."

Rex's shoulders slumped. "I don't exist?"

"You exist," she said, her voice losing its reverent power. "You have a body, a mind, and you remember things about your past. I assume?"

He nodded and thrust his chin forward in defiance. "I remember the surgery that made me into a human."

"Rex, you are and always have been genetically human." She eased away from her pulpit and floated down to settle by Rex's side. "I am curious though. In your memory, Rex, who did this surgery and where did it happen?"

He turned away, angry that she seemed to be just humoring him. The windows of the tower flashed by, city cars so far below like toys. He settled in front of a window looking out toward Transit Mountain that glowed a deep orange in the impending dawn light. From the ground, the looming construct always looked flat, but from up here it seemed different. Shadows and color gradients revealed the plateaus as circular: great pumice disks piled on top of each other, stabbing through the cloud layer toward space. His gaze settled on the base and familiarity tickled his mind, cranes and shipping containers. For a moment he was tumbling, down through the immensity of Transit Mountain, its dark walls flashing past like... *concentric circles.*

The whole image gelled in his mind. "I don't know who did the surgery, but it happened over there. Somewhere."

The Sister stood next to him and together they stared out at the pointed mountain. "Then take a spare afternoon and go there, Rex. In my experience such journeys often result in the memories turning out to be false. If you find that they are real, then you have an amazing story to tell the Future-Lord." Sister-One turned away as if finished with him.

"I just chased a false memory with my friend, Mira." Rex explained his trip to Ridgeline and their lucky escape from Mr Gallonie's clutches. "At the end, she remembered that her name, Mira, was stolen from her forever-pet. She doesn't know her real name." The Sister stared on, forcing Rex to keep talking. "If she's to be saved then she has to know the truth. Surely the truth starts with knowing your own name?"

"A name is just a name, Rex. A label. It has little bearing on truth although it often serves as a mental mustering point, something we cohere around in the stories we tell ourselves about who and what we are." She looked away and clasped her hands as if in prayer. Her drawn-on eyes refocused on the distant realm of information. "There is a record of a forever-friend called Mira in the Caelum district on the edge of Coriolis. It appears on a small database at the Immortal Dogs Rescue Sanctuary."

A light flickered inside the pulpit behind her and the image of a small gray poodle appeared in the air a few feet from Rex's nose. "Do we know who her owner was?" Rex asked. The excitement of the chase felt good.

"She has new owners now and their privacy must be respected, but her previous owner, Corrine Medlow, has disappeared from records and is presumed deceased." Mira's face appeared – or the woman Rex thought of as Mira. She looked healthy, normal; a warm glow of contentment filled her eyes.

"That's her," Rex said, reaching out to touch the image, causing it to break up and flicker across his forearm. "She's not dead. I've seen her. For real. Not just in my head."

The Sister continued. "She had a family. Husband Michel, and children Mark and Clara. They lived near Transit Mountain." A photo shimmered out of thin air to hang in front of Rex's nose. Nice house, exotic trees, a pointy-jawed man with proud eyes. Mark clung to his mother beaming broadly as Clara fussed with the poodle.

The Sister paused, seemingly reluctant to carry on. Then a news article appeared – shootings, gang executions. He couldn't read it, too many words. "What does it mean, Sister?"

"Like many, Corrine used Simmorta, the GFC's longevity drug. But the drug became too expensive after the Nova-Insanity destroyed the elevator and the supply chain to Earth. Corrine turned to other things, illegal drugs from dangerous sources. Her family paid the ultimate price – only she survived." She waited as if expecting Rex to say something, but he had no words. "She buried her grief under drink and drugs and that's where our records end. She probably lives on the streets, if she lives at all. And that corroborates your story of meeting her, Rex."

Rex stared in silence at the floor suddenly hating himself for knowing. "Can she be saved?"

The Sister's voice grew quiet. "She must know and repent for her past as all who wish to truly know the Future-Lord must."

Rex turned away, crushed under this new burden.

"And find yourself, Rex!" she called, as he almost fell back down the bell tower stairs in his haste to escape. His head buzzed with voices, but they were all his, asking questions, talking over each other. If he was to truly seek salvation then he needed to know so much more about his past, about his sister, her name, maybe even find her. And now there was Mira, or Corrine. How could he ever reveal such a terrible truth to her? Surely not-knowing was better? And then there was the dead man in the alley… *How does a murderer gain entry into Haven?*

Out on the rooftop, Transit Mountain gleamed in the rising dawn. No longer the haunting reminder of a past disaster, it was now a calling, a beacon, a place of pilgrimage and answers. Somewhere he just had to be.

CHAPTER 21

Pattern Recognition

Jett didn't like humans. Being on Earth, in Coriolis City, cemented his view – *the voidian view* – that people were fragile, unpredictable and emotional. Their lives were unnecessarily complicated and filled with the need for things like drugs, clothes, food, water, air. The need for more people.

But if Gale's AI projection spoke the truth, and the voidian were to become humanity's custodians, then he needed to study them, and accept that to become a guide meant also to constrain, and that sometimes, in order to create, he had to destroy.

Welkin park, busy and crowded. A racetrack with the competitors going in all directions around a circuit centered on the crystal Nova lake. Jett loitered at the park's edge, using the mass of crazy, unique-looking humans that resided there as cover.

He observed patterns in behavior. Often, people did the same thing every day; they traversed the same routes through the city, glanced in the same direction as they passed the same shops and monuments. They even took the same number of steps to move between the same points: *robots!*

Human expressions became more familiar. He mimicked them on his fibrous face, although attempts at smiling at passersby had so far resulted in them breaking into a run or shouting for help.

Mood was an intriguing concept. A state of being from which a set of predictable responses emerged: same person, same stimulus, but a different mood equaled a different response. At one moment jittery, angry, eyes seeking things in the crowds, but the same person later in the day appeared calm and unconcerned. A mood change.

Other people were damaged by age or sickness. Jett heard their knees grind, recorded their limps and hobbles, their pallor, the lack of pigment in their hair. Then he saw them later and the damage was less severe. They moved with liquid grace. Did a change of mood make them healthier?

Jett deduced that these people were finding longevity drugs, and their acquisitions revolved around distinct nexus points within the city. These attractor-locations were often in heavily fortified areas with their own, more menacing, creed of militia.

He avoided those areas, focusing on their inflows and outflows until after three full days of observation, a new pattern emerged. A subset of drug users sporting unusually colorful clothing, strange hats, and baggy shirts. *Tourists,* his AI-tagger reported.

Drug tourists, Jett concluded. New flow patterns sprung out of new observations. Patterns leading straight to a flamboyantly dressed man conducting business right in front of the militia, in the middle of the most crowded streets.

Circus Ringmaster? The tagger guessed, but Jett saw no circus.

The man wore an overly large black top hat and long coattails. Hands waving like a conductor, he twirled a slim cane around agile fingers. His smile seemed to reach out to people and hook them toward him. Jett tagged him as *Topman* and kept him under a day-long observation, watching as people approached, paused, and listened. Some took notes before hastening away. Topman often wrapped a friendly arm around their shoulders, whispered in their ears, handed them cards. In return, people pushed coins and paper money into his top pocket, and he patted the pocket as if checking on its contents before moving on to a different square or street corner. Jett noted his random path around Welkin, covering each location exactly once and never going down the same street twice. He was a real-life traveling salesman, and possibly the solution to Jett's quest for Glow.

The crowds thinned and the sky darkened into evening. Topman abruptly pulled his hat down over his ears and compressed its top making himself a whole head shorter.

He left the city center with Jett as a distant shadow, passing through a park lined with the stalls and the wares of an evening market. Topman paused and picked up food from a truck before striding off across a broad square dominated by a staggeringly tall and dangerously kinked tower.

Parallax Tower. Jett's tagger threw out the name and its history scrolled past his gaze as he focused on following the little man while not being seen.

Taller than anything except Transit Mountain, Parallax Tower suffered alarming damage during the Nova-Insanity. A great kink in the middle followed by a dozen smaller bends nearer the top leaned the structure out over the city. One of the few tall buildings to survive the downtown nova blast, engineers surveying the building concluded that it would topple at any moment. But as engineers and governments changed and vanished, the building remained standing. No one had any real idea how to knock it down without taking out a huge swathe of cityscape.

Parallax Tower remained an icon of the city, a monument to pre-Nova-Insanity engineering. It even had tenants. Standing in its shadow, Jett looked up into dizzying heights and saw solar panels and wind turbines jutting from windows and balconies. Poles laden with clothes poked out like spines. Rope ladders and tenuous walkways created makeshift shortcuts and escape routes, or simply bypassed impassible regions within the tower.

Jett followed Topman in through one of the many open street-level window facades. He mounted a coiling service stairway and began a speedy ascent.

Jett hung back out of sight, tracking the man's footfalls before following. They ascended through dozens of floors, some gaping open to the elements, others pancaked flat by internal collapse.

Jett's street-beggar guise bounded up the stairs ten at a time, pausing at corners to let his quarry stay ahead. Around the two-hundredth floor the population thinned. Only the truly determined made it this far up, mixed with a handful of drunks that had somehow found their way up and probably didn't know how to get back down. By floor two hundred and fifty, even they were a rarity.

Topman entered a door, slamming it shut behind, bolts and locks clicking into place. Jett took note of the location and explored the rest of the level. Nine other apartments lined the intact side of the tower, heat signatures revealed lone characters living inside, all spaced well apart.

Jett returned to the apartment and analyzed the door: stout, double-layered steel with alloy casing set in a reinforced wall with crossbars running top-to-bottom and side-to-side. He changed his body proportions, making himself shorter and stout, maximizing his ramming potential. Crashing through, he tore the door and a chunk of the surrounding wall away entering what appeared to be Topman's living room.

He dumped the door off to the side as Topman grabbed at a fat-muzzled gun sitting openly on a table. Jett was much faster, snatching it out from under his grasp and leaving him cowering on the floor.

"Don't kill me," he begged, rolling into a fetal position and covering his eyes. "I don't have any drugs, just some cash." A shaky finger pointed toward a metal box sticking out from under a bed.

The room sloped at an alarming angle granting dizzying views out the windows of the bustling streets hundreds of meters below. "I'm not going to kill you," Jett said, noting how all the furniture in the apartment had two legs sawn shorter so it stood level on the tilted floor. "I need information."

"Information. I've got lots of that." The man looked up and flashed a smile with overly white teeth. His grin immediately reverted to a terrified stare as he took a proper look at Jett, who towered over the small man even in his squat, battering-ram guise. "I see you're a tourist. That's what I do. I direct tourists to the fun places." His fingers twitched out air quotes around the word *fun*.

Jett pocketed the gun and directed the man to sit on one of the oddly sculpted chairs. "Drugs," Jett said, unsure how to start any kind of conversation.

Topman was a gray shadow of the bright animated character Jett witnessed on the streets. He fidgeted with his hair as if his lack of hat made him weak and vulnerable. "Drugs... well, I can sure tell you a lot about drugs: natural, artificial, biomech. Take your pick. Depends what you're after. Big healthy–" he struggled for the correct word, "–chap, like yourself probably not after boosters. You look kind of depressed, perhaps some uppers or some Ludes? They mess with your head, make you think you're someone famous. Ampers for some extra ass-whoop. Fixers tweak your genetics. Lepa if you want to live longer and don't mind looking like a collection of Halloween-themed root vegetables–"

"I need to know about Glow."

"Ah, a connoisseur! A – let us say – man, of taste." He rose slowly to his feet, regaining some of his street-corner bluster. "Name's Juggler by the way, Samuel Juggler." He reached out a hand.

"Who makes Glow? Where do they make it? How is it made?" Jett said, ignoring the hand.

"Whoa, are you... Alliance?" Juggler asked, suddenly curious. "I see voter-bots around, they keep getting into fights with the militias. You part of the invasion? I mean... election?" Finger quotes, again.

"I'm what comes next," Jett replied.

Juggler winked and touched the side of his nose. "Say no more. And may I just say how much I welcome our new friends, the Alliance, and–"

"Tell me who makes Glow!" Jett's voice came out like a sonic boom knocking Juggler back into his chair. His eyes flicked toward an open window as if he were considering the jump. Instead, he carefully stood and arranged his face into a thoughtful expression. "All interesting questions. Not my realm of expertise I'm afraid. I tell people what drugs they need to help or fix their 'ailments' or needs, and I match them to the right distributor." He reached slowly into his pocket and pulled out a slim, metal cigarette case containing small coiled tubes.

"Is that Glow?" Jett asked.

"Telomere cigarette. Keeps me young and healthy." He offered one to Jett, who took it and examined it closely. "These are expensive. Most people just use Lepa, but I wouldn't recommend it. Especially for a wealthier citizen."

"It gives you leprosy?"

"It makes your cells immortal; they reproduce endlessly and often mutate. Kind of turns you into a great big blob of cancer."

"Why would anyone want that?"

"I call it a 'waiting for the cavalry' treatment. You get to live, but are constantly fighting cancers, which are usually easier and cheaper to treat than a lot of other death-causing predicaments. You hope you live long enough for the cavalry to ride in with a cure for everything or you hit the jackpot somewhere and can afford some real GFC Simmorta. That's gold-standard stuff. Better than Glow, but shit-expensive."

"I don't need Simmorta. Just Glow."

"Glow is a big commitment, requiring significant funds. It demands loyalty and trust, but the health and longevity benefits of regular use are undeniable."

Juggler paused for dramatic effect, his hand motioning in a large circle as if still clutching his cane. A salesman's smile spread across his face as he leaned into Jett. "If you are sure you are interested then I have the connections to get you the best Glow out there. None of that dangerous used stuff. This Glow is fresh, worm-free." He made a noise like someone popping the ring pull on a beer can, then leaned in close to Jett. "I'd steer away from the used stuff. It's cheaper but has side-effects. Its network software gets screwed up with all that mixing, diluting, changing hosts, et cetera… Some of the stuff on the street has been through a thousand different victi– I mean – *clients*. Very detrimental to cognitive wellbeing if you know what I mean." He tapped the side of his head, pointed the finger at Jett and winked.

Jett had no reference for that gesture sequence either. "Where can I get this Glow?"

Juggler scrambled to retrieve a wallet from a side table and fished out a business card with locations and times printed on one side and a tiny cartoon caricature of himself on the other. "You can't just walk up to a Glow dispensary. They move, change appearance, and are fiercely guarded. No, no, my friend, Glow is a sought-after product; its dealers hide behind veils of secrecy and legions of thugs with very large guns."

"This card helps me?"

Juggler nodded. "Luckily, you only need two things. This card from old Juggler here, recommending you as a client, and cash. Wads of lovely, delicious cash." He handed Jett the card as if it were some precious item. "The locations listed are where a contact will be. The time is when the contact will be there. Once you've met and paid a suitable deposit, the contact will tell you what to do next." Juggler bowed as if ending a dramatic performance.

Jett stood up, suddenly impatient to get outside, the lines of traffic through the windows gave the impression the building was continuously toppling, an effect that became more unnerving as dusk settled over the city. He turned back to Juggler who was wringing his hands as if praying. A standard "goodbye" prompt scrolled across his vision. "Thank you. I found your services most useful and may have need of them in the future," Jett read.

Juggler folded in on himself with relief. "Great. Thank you. Excellent. I mean, yes, certainly, anytime. Just swing on by. Old Juggler runs an open-door policy. Certainly very open at the moment…" He eyed the gaping hole in his wall.

Jett produced a roll of currency from a pocket inside his cloak. His stealth made him an excellent pickpocket, but he had no idea of the value of the notes, some were made of an ultra-fine gold weave and had the number one-hundred etched onto them. Juggler's face lit up as Jett peeled one from the roll. "No one must know about me being here."

"Yes sir, abso-freaking-lutely." Juggler's voice rose in pitch and his cheeks flushed red. Jett monitored his reaction and decided four notes were enough. He handed them to Juggler who pounced on them like a starved animal.

As Jett headed out through the broken doorway to begin the descent through Parallax Tower, he turned back and saw the man sniffing lovingly at the money. Humans were even stranger than he'd imagined. "And buy yourself a new door," he said, dropping another note in the doorway.

"Doors... Who needs 'em," Juggler said, smile stretching from ear to ear. "We're all friends around here. Come back soon."

Friend. His tagger said, as he glanced back at Juggler.

Jett knew a human, and a human knew Jett. It felt good. Not the warm companionship he craved from the woman in his mind, but it was something. The first contact. Maybe he could learn to like humans after all.

CHAPTER 22

A Heart-Shaped Hole

Clear, fresh mountain air buoyed Ellayna's sagging spirit as she strode purposefully up the sharp incline toward the summit of Ben Nevis.

Total immersion felt good, the reason so many of the GFC never left. It was better than life. At least, better than life in perpetual orbit. A thought experiment tantalized her walking: her and Trabian, spending some quality time here. Like in the old days with Del when they were young and naively focused on their galactic conquest. Not yet. Trabian wasn't Del. First, he'd have to prove his worth as a useful and reliable ally.

She reached the flat summit where a jagged cairn marked the highest point, lumpy granite glazed with a fine crisp of ice. She stepped up onto the cairn and balanced on her right foot, the left splaying sideways in a daring yogic pose. Hands clasped above her head, weight shifting, seeking the balance point. Steady now, she pirouetted, a ballerina on a music box, seeing but not judging as the endless, unreachable landscape scrolled past her eyes.

The fake, virtual reality landscape.

On a whim she messaged Del. "I'm here on one of our favorite spots." She opened a secure portal into the Cloud9 prison server, allowing Del restricted access to her virtual world. A privilege that Del always refused to use.

A figure in a white robe walked past, eyes down, ignoring her like a mystic wizard aloof in his own world. He carried on to the edge of the summit and sat down facing away, legs crossed, forearms at ease on his boney knees.

"Del?" Ellayna lost balance and tumbled off the cairn.

"Ellayna," he acknowledged, avoiding eye contact. His hair writhing around his head like wisps of Scottish mist.

"Del… It's been so long. Eight fucking years, Del." She scrambled to her feet and stood over him, unsure if it really was Del or someone playing games. She touched her thigh, checking the kill switch. Of course, it wasn't there, she was an avatar. Her real body a paralyzed science experiment trussed to a couch.

He looked up, meeting her glare, anger flashing his pale blue eyes. "Eight years since you betrayed me and the real GFC and everything we built and stood for. You. *You* locked me away."

"You told me nothing about your plan. Nothing! You trusted him, that monster Gale, more than you trusted me."

"I trusted you, Elly. I trusted that you'd see the escapees and finally understand that we were right. All those times we clashed over GFC policy. I thought you'd be with us when crunch time came."

"And rip the GFC apart? Hand everything over to the Alliance?" She almost hit the exit icon.

His head shook violently. "No, I never really bought into that whole accident story. Too convenient. Taunau or you, or maybe someone on the inside of that space truck, blew that door and killed my friends and our future."

Her heart sank. Even after all these years, she'd hoped Del would never find out the truth. Of all the people she knew in this forsaken existence, she still wanted him to love her, to trust her. "I'm sorry you feel that way about me."

Del nodded and laughed, a tear ran down his cheek as she squatted cautiously besides him. "Gale still giving you all the runaround?"

Her turn to nod and laugh. "Still a giant, fullerene thorn in our collective butts. I guess you intended him that way."

Del reached over and patted her hand. "I forgave you long ago, Elly. I figured your overachieving survival instinct got the better of you in the end."

"Maybe we can learn to trust each other again?" She freed her wrist and held his hand. It wasn't the same hand she'd felt back in the prison cell. This was warm, alive. More real. "But how do I know this is really even you?"

He settled back against the rock. "Remember when we came here for real? We stayed in a log cabin and ate salami frittatas for breakfast. You thought they would be revolting but ended up loving them."

"Not enough, Del. A spy could have watched us, reported back to the Alliance or the GFC."

"How about that time Tomas caught us in the centrifuge room. We were trying to remember what sex felt like under real gravity."

She blushed, "Poor Tomas. He still isn't over that. But he could have told someone and I'm sure there were recordings of that as well."

Del feigned sadness. "Then I guess I'll never be able to prove this is really me, Elly. You either believe in me or you don't."

"Wake up and talk to me back in Cloud9. I'll believe in you then." They sat in silence, just staring as a golden eagle circled below them before dipping into the trees. "Are you back, Del? Will you leave VR and help us? We need you."

"No, I came here to warn you, Elly. To tell you to leave. The GFC is finished. I've seen it. I've seen the end, the end of everything if we are not careful."

"Your bullshit Star-River prophecies again, Del?"

"Not prophecies, Elly, predictions. It's a tool, like those games you played as a kid. Set up the pieces and throw the dice. Except, in the games I see we never win, nothing gets out alive."

"The universe gets populated by Ursurper Gale and his friends?"

"Not even that. Nothing conscious, nothing alive in any form. It's all too inefficient, Elly. Life gets optimized out of existence by algorithms, by simulations of itself. In a war, who would win, you or a simulated version of yourself?"

She shrugged. *Interesting game idea.* "And how do these... simulations take over?"

"They're already here, inside of us. It's in the very name you invented, Elly."

Simmorta: Simulated Immortality. "Taunau's somanetic plague scenario. He wants to bomb the heck out of Coriolis Island and start wars all over the world. Claims it's to stop the plague. Really, it's just to protect his aging skin."

"Leave, Elly. Defect. Whatever you want to call it. Go somewhere you can make a difference. I'll meet you there if and when I can."

"Going to escape as well, Del?" She glanced sideways and there was no one there. "Del?" *Did I imagine that? More games?*

The sky flickered with red and orange fire. Was this Del imposing some crazy apocalyptic fantasy on her VR simulation? An urgent message from Martin flamed red across her vision. Surprised to find the exit icon located where it should be, she ejected VR and opened her eyes back in her room.

"What is it Martin?"

"You're going to want to see this, Ellayna."

A video feed filled her vision, Coriolis City with its iconic Transit Mountain looming in the background. "A contact in the Broken militia sent us this surveillance clip."

The video zoomed-in across building tops, a grainy long shot that focused on a doorway with a coatrack outside. A man in a white lab coat entered and something shifted in the coatrack. From Ellayna's distant point of view, it was a skeleton, clean white bones, stepping up behind the man and following him into the building.

The door slammed shut. "What the hell–?" Ellayna felt a chill, memories of that shadow she'd seen in the corridor.

"No one's sure what that is, Ellayna, but it might be related to this." The image jumped to the inside of the building, timestamped from a few minutes earlier. "Single frame from a micro-bug camera in a hallway."

Ellayna gasped at the image of a blocky but familiar figure resolved from various image processing routines. "Ursurper Gale."

"Interesting?" Martin seemed pleased with his find. "Not Ursurper Gale. He's still on TwoLunar. This is another voidian, maybe our alleged defector?"

"But Gale's alone. The only one of his kind. How?" She tugged angrily at her head as yet another level of insanity slathered its insidious presence across her life. "Do we have resources on Coriolis Island, Martin?"

"Not much. I'm pulling some special forces from our Ecuadorian safehouse, but it'll take a few days to get them covertly across to Coriolis."

She pulled off her support webbing and lay staring at the ceiling, rolling her finger-gun around her knuckle.

"I do have some good news," Martin said. "Our newly recalibrated seismic network on TwoLunar pinpointed an anomaly."

"Gale?" She eased onto an elbow, suddenly hopeful.

"Not sure, some movement. This thing's sensitive enough to detect a mouse, but Gale's really stealthy."

"Reel him in, Martin, preferably alive. I don't know if we can torture a voidian, but we need to know what game he's playing down there. Maybe some connection with this Glow phenomenon."

"We're powering-up a bunch of remote-operated combat bodies. We'll keep some here as added security and send the rest to TwoLunar. I'm short of volunteers to operate them, Ellayna."

Ellayna sat bolt upright, feeling a sudden surge of purpose. "Sign me up, Martin."

Behind the kennels of the Forever Friends Rescue Sanctuary, hidden in the far corner of the yard and surrounded by sweet-smelling flowers, sat the rickety wooden shed. A loop of wire secured its door, concealing a toilet, a sink, and a pile of magazines cut into eighths for use as toilet paper.

Inside, Rex stared out through the heart-shaped hole in the door like a homunculus peering out through a skull's eye socket. He turned back to the triangular mirror fragment dangling on the wall and examined his nostrils, contorting sideways to look inside his ears, and then hard into each eye. Was the Future-Lord really in there? Why the aching silence? He almost missed the voices, a companionship of hatred. Where did they go?

He hid from many things: Hanna and her perfume; Hanna's companion, a disturbingly young man, either her lover, bodyguard or both; and Frizell, who stalked the grounds, his crazy eyes hunting Rex like a deer. Mrs O, with her terrifying cheerfulness, showing no sign of the chest injury, and then there was Mira, who turned up earlier looking taller, fitter, brimming with energy. Which could mean only one thing: somewhere, somehow, she'd found a fix.

"Where's Rex?" Mira's voice wafted through the heart-shaped hole, startling him away from the mirror. He tugged at his hair as if the pain would somehow make his decision easier. The image of Mira's murdered family haunted him, and her appearing so happy only made his decision to tell her much worse.

He looked out through the peephole just as Hanna and a cluster of small dogs strutted past on their way out to the park. Rex ducked, pinching his nose against the perfume, but not quick enough to avoid a disapproving side-glance from Hanna.

He heard Mira shout again. He couldn't bring himself to call her Corrine even in his mind. He'd formulated a plan as he stalked the early morning streets into work, eyes grimy and tired from lack of sleep. He'd simply call out her name, *Corrine!* Surely that would be enough for her to remember something. But as he drew closer to the sanctuary, even that felt like a betrayal. She'd know he'd been rooting through her past, meddling with her mind.

Instead, he decided to lure Mira to Transit Mountain with him. Sister-One claimed she had lived near there once. Perhaps being in the area would spark a childhood memory and ignite some chain of recollections. All under the guise of chasing his own past. The perfect cover.

"Fucking Christ, Rex, there you are!" Mira exclaimed, eye peering through the door hole. "Hey, you can't hog the bog, man. I shat a traffic cone earlier and need easy access. It's bath time out here. You helping or not?"

And then she was gone.

Rex quietly joined the bathing line. The day was too warm not to be playing in water. Frizell selected the next dog off the roster and wrangled it into the bath shed. Rex joined Mrs O at the tub while Mira waited outside in a heap of towels. ambushing each dog as it left for a rudimentary rubdown. She marked each one off the roster and corralled them into the drying pen with its motley array of shady umbrellas.

Rex's fingers instinctively jammed into his ears as he heard music coming from the shed's speakers. "I've picked some apt sounds for you, Rex," said Mrs O. "If they upset you, then we'll try something else."

Rex dropped his hands and let the dangerous noises into his skull where they seemed to bounce around, unimpeded. No voices came out to meet them.

"Jazz, Rex, Dave Brubeck. It'll really get those shampooing fingers curling!"

Most dogs reveled in the fun, some simply accepted their fate, while others resisted with a will that belied their stature. One of those was Aubrey, the Coriolian bulldog. He sat in the tub, face a jutting edifice of defiance as Mrs O massaged medicated shampoo into his fleshy folds. Aubrey sensed the nightmare was over and exited the tub like a shot from a catapult into Mira's waiting towel.

Frizell hauled Goliath in next, bright-eyed, tongue drooping to the ground. The huge dog plunged in, absorbing half the water with his copious fur then spraying it around the shed with a series of seismic body-quakes. He leapt in and out of the tub, barking and bumbling, sending tables, chairs and people flying.

Rex lost himself in the moment, feeling the pace of the music as a driving force, rather than any deep or sinister meaning. He enjoyed the synergy with those around him, beaming out from under a crown of suds, while Mrs O became an abominable snowwoman with spectacles.

"What type of dog were you, Rex?" she asked.

He blushed. "I was quite big. When I jumped up at people they staggered backward." The music faded and on came the terrible memories, sucking pipes, hacking saws, white masks framing eyes that were dead to his pain as they hacked away the dog and sculpted him into a man.

"Time to tackle Dolphy," Mrs O said, wiping off her spectacles. The trembling pit-bull waited in the doorway, head bowed. Her leash hummed with tension as she tried to get as far away from the water as possible.

Rex watched the terror in Dolphy's eyes, terror over nothing, just water. He had the power to make her face that terror. The same power he had over Mira, and almost the same power the surgeons had over the dog, Rex, that ability to change an entity into something else, to rewrite memory, reformat bodies, create something different and entirely new.

They heaved Dolphy into the tub, her feet racking the sides. After a few moments of washing, the big dog calmed down, gaze settling far away as if she'd found some inner sanctuary. Finished, she bolted through the door. They heard Mira scream as she knocked her flying. The fear was back in her eyes, nothing had changed; Dolphy would always be Dolphy.

Mrs O stood panting. "When you get to become a dog again, Rex, make sure you come back and see us for bath time."

Mira clung to the door frame, looking tired and defeated after endless beatings from wet animals. "I need a break."

"Rex is going to turn back into a dog and come live at the rescue sanctuary," Mrs O said.

"And Mrs O is going to live forever and meet the Future-Lord," Rex added.

Mira stared at them both as they stood grinning insanely. "I'm going to lie down," she said, and stumbled away. Her Glow fix was wearing off.

Rex followed her outside, mind fumbling for the right words. "When you took me to Ridgeline, I think that helped me too." They stopped, and Rex twiddled his thumbs. The Glow dose had made her a few inches taller, so she looked down on him now.

He gathered his thoughts. "What I mean is. I need to go to Transit Mountain. I have memories of being there. It might help me, and it would be cool if you came too."

A sly smile eased her face. "Are you asking me on a date, Rex?"

Panic struck him as the situation went unexpectedly wrong. "No, I just–"

She slapped his shoulder and laughed, the first time he'd heard a genuine, mirth-filled laugh from her. "I'm shitting you, Rex, come on. You? Date me? But I'll come with you, might be fun."

Mira fell asleep in one of the sanctuary's tatty deckchairs while Rex returned to dog bathing. He'd earned enough time credit from Mrs O that he could take the afternoon off. He stared at Mira's sleeping face and wondered if it would look different when she became Corrine again.

Jett spied Samuel Juggler's Glow contact, a puss-yellow cyborg, who, despite his deceptively frail appearance, cut a prominent path through the crowds of Spare Part Row.

Jett rolled Juggler's contact card through his gangly fingers. Yellow. The name, time and location all seemed to fit. He stood watching as Yellow approached a bench and dropped down beside a bedraggled woman.

Jett eased closer. Now a towering revenant with angry eyes and jagged cybernetic protrusions, the crowds parted around him instead of rolling right over. Strangely, in a place like this, being more obvious seemed to make him less visible. Something he'd discovered through trial and error and various different body shapes.

Yellow slapped something on the woman's knee, lurched upright and vanished back into the crowd. Jett followed, but Yellow was absurdly slippery, using hidden doorways and surprising speed to evade any pursuers.

Jett turned to the woman on the bench, hoping to extract information. She slept with her eyes open, and he poked her awake. "Fuckin' Christ… Wa're you 'sposed to be?" She dissolved into a weird giggle before slumping onto Jett's shoulder and snoring.

Jett decided there was nothing here to interrogate and headed off across town to Juggler's second Glow contact.

He found Lazar at the intersection of Centauri and Gemini as preordained on Juggler's card. A colorful character in a bright red suit with diagonal green stripes and a floppy felt hat. The man clearly wanted to be noticed.

Jett hung in a side alley and watched, checking for snipers and bodyguards. After a few minutes at the specified location, Lazar headed away to the next point, one not on Jett's card.

Jett waited in a doorway as Lazar settled into a waiting stance. He dropped the revenant guise and emerged as the recruitment officer, wandered over to Lazar and handed him the card.

Lazar took one look and ripped it in two, letting the pieces flutter to the ground. "Wrong time. Wrong place. You wanna play ball you gotta prove you can deliver." He turned away leaving Jett floundering to understand the references. Play ball? Deliver what?

"I want to buy Glow," he said, matching Lazar's stride.

"Fuck off and try again tomorrow. Bring another card." Lazar stalked away.

Jett morphed into a leper and used the shadows as he followed Lazar to his next location. His timing was precise. His business clockwork. People knew him. They hurried out from offices and shops to do deals as he passed, quick and fluid, no negotiations, no chatter, just lightning exchanges of tiny phials and patches for cash.

Afternoon grew late and Lazar did one last quick exchange with an elderly couple. He removed his hat, folded his coat inside-out muting its colors, and moved away across town. No one bothered him now. He was closed for business.

Lazar was easier to track than Yellow, no warren of hidden doors. He preferred the open space, stopping once each city block to scan for pursuers. Several times he caught Jett browsing shop windows or turning into side streets. Each time, Jett morphed to a new image, careful not to repeat a disguise. But Lazar's body language changed, furtive, angry, somehow, he knew he was being followed. Turning a corner, he reached into his pocket. A sideways glance told Jett he would be waiting. This game was over.

Jett pulled in his skeleton, forming a stout, bland, male shape while wringing space from his bone fibers, upping his damage resistance and weaving his front-torso into a bullet-proof mesh. Then, with no hesitation, he rounded the corner straight into Lazar's ambush.

A stub-barreled pistol jammed into Jett's face "You follow me, you die," Lazar said, his mouth curling up on one side.

Jett cringed in mock fear. "I need Glow. I can pay."

Lazar eyed Jett's rotund businessman guise and relaxed the grip on his gun. "Show me the cash."

Jett drew out the wad of notes and Lazar's eyes did a doubletake. "Sweet!" he said. "I'll be taking those." He drew back his other hand, bunched a fist and launched a punch at Jett's chin.

Jett watched Lazar's fist. With his mind running at combat speed, human motion was slow and cumbersome. The projected point of impact rippled as he reconfigured it into a cluster of ultrathin, rigid fullerene needles.

Lazar's fist struck, and the needles pierced flesh and bone all the way to his wrist. He squawked, body torquing away in reactive pain, gun tilting up and off aim. Jett snatched his wrist, turning the gun back and smashing the muzzle clean through his front teeth and into his mouth.

He dropped his disguise, expanding to full size, fake clothes and skin oozing and writhing back into a mass of carbon-black snakes before rewrapping into his newly favored revenant format. The horror grew in Lazar's eyes as he lifted off the ground. "I'm going to take the gun out of your mouth now. If you make a sound, I'll blow your head off. Understand?"

Lazar nodded, and Jett eased the gun out, keeping it just inside the lips of his mouth.

"I am going to ask you questions. If you lie, I'll blow your head off."

Lazar nodded, more urgently as he gasped a breath through the gun muzzle.

"What do you think happens if you fail to answer my question?"

"You... you blow my head off?" Lazar said, gagging through blood and tooth fragments.

"Correct. That was the first question, here comes the next one. What is your name?"

"Lazar."

"Correct. Where do you get Glow from?"

The man's mouth opened, but he suddenly had trouble speaking. Jett twitched the gun slightly as if pressuring the trigger. Lazar's mouth loosened and the words fell out. "I get my daily quota from the safehouse. Later, I return with the money. Don't ever see anyone. Don't know any names. Thorne's Empire. You fuck with Thorne and you die, your family dies, your freaking dog dies. Even your dog's ass-sniffing pals in the park die. You get it pal? You understand what's going to happen to you here?"

Jett considered the new information. "I don't have a family, or a dog." He relaxed his facial fibers, and they slipped away like oiled skin revealing his carbon-black skull and eyeballs. "I don't die, either." He pushed his face closer to Lazar's, seeing it turn red and bloat as if about to explode.

Lazar managed another nod.

"If I say I won't shoot you, then I won't shoot you. Do you trust me?" Jett eased the gun into Lazar's left eyeball.

Lazar blinked furiously unable to stare into the black circle. "No," he spat hysterically. "Of course I don't fucking trust you!"

"That was a truthful answer and because of your honesty you are still alive." Jett dropped his arm and tossed the gun into a gutter. His huge hand circled Lazar's throat lifting him high into the air. "One last question and then we are done."

"Ok," Lazar choked, his hands clutching at Jett's massive fingers, feet treading air.

"Give me the address of the safehouse."

"It's... it's on Mill Street. Trendle Tower," Lazar gasped.

Jett pulled up a street map on his Inner-I and confirmed the place existed. He looked at the desperate man twitching in his grasp and saw hope in his eyes, a belief there was some rapport between them, an agreement that he would be freed. Did he think they'd become friends like him and Juggler? He must understand that this was a combat situation. If he released Lazar, he would warn the safehouse and compromise the infiltration.

A standard goodbye prompt scrolled past his vision. He reached down with his other hand and grasped Lazar's dangling feet, then folded his body in on itself. Bones shattered and air and fluid pockets burst out through ruptures and orifices. Lazar let out a muted screech as his life extinguished. Jett rolled him into his own striped jacket, no mess, no gore; the thick material contained the fluids, tying the corpse into a spherical bundle using Lazar's arms and legs like rope. Then with a casual toss, he hurled the corpse five-stories up onto the flat roof of an adjacent building.

He waited for the pain to come, for "her" to appear next to him and somehow flood his mind with sadness and loss, but nothing came. Was it possible that whoever his memories were originally derived from only valued *certain* human lives?

He set course for Mill Street, Trendle Tower, Thorne's Empire. His tagger flashed as if agitated by him not speaking its words: *Thank you. I have found your services most useful and may have need of them again in the future...*

CHAPTER 23

A Hole in the Head

"People built that," Mira said, stopping and leaning against a bent lamppost. Transit Mountain dominated the focus of the converging lines of roads, pavements and buildings like the focal point of an exercise in perspective. The town of Transit spilled onto the foothills surrounding the base plateau, thinning into trees and scrub that lapped up the exponential slope and on to the next plateau.

Rex paused for breath, eyeing Mira for clues about her current state of mind. The fix of Glow she'd taken had done nothing more than stir the beast, the reservoir of demons and ill-perceived passions that inhabited her mind. A maintenance fix, she'd called it. Really it was a teaser, an appetizer, and now Mira unconsciously searched for the main course.

"No, they really built that, man. They fucking built that back when we knew how to build shit." Her head dropped and snapped alert again, eyes darting to alleys and passersby. She'd flipped consistently between two main personas: potty-mouth Mira, who Rex knew well, and drug-seeking Mira, an oily, snakelike opportunist. Rex prodded her back on course like a child by pointing at the distant mountain. He talked of dogs and salvation, avoiding the Future-Lord which had the effect of re-manifesting drug-seeking Mira. He even tried singing her song, "Dream, theme. Everything's a–"

"Fucking Christ, Rex. Shut that noise up." It worked, but only until her mind wandered and the drug-seeker reemerged.

His eyes turned inward, superimposing the bright, clear imagery of childhood memories over the current, dusty scene. Transit Mountain through the eyes of a teenage boy locked in the hostel common room, fixated on the TV. The fantastic utopia of Coriolis, the corporate-nation, leading humanity's charge into space. And everyone was welcome, everyone except boys with head traumas, temper tantrums, and hyper-focused minds. He soaked up TV and books and any internet channels he could access. Learning how the GFC constructed Coriolis Island and its outlandish tower using one of their gigantic Nation-ships as the island's core. Engineers tapped into the volcanic mountains on the ocean bed, blasting magma into hexagonal molds through variable aperture nozzles creating different densities of pumice that floated on the ocean. They glued the tessellating islets into a vast, floating structure as the central pumice nozzle grew taller, extruding the plateaus of Transit Mountain, starting with the densest, toughest pumice at the bottom, thinning to a wisp of super-lightweight material near the top. Hyper-fullerene chains, the same material as the space-elevator cable, anchored the island to the ocean floor. Seven-trillion tons of rock and six years of labor, Rex still recalled the figures, still remembered his fascination and the belief that one day, he would go there.

"You're not even listening!" Mira slapped him across the head, jerking him back to the present. "The top's a funny shape."

"Nova bomb," Rex said. He eyed her, sensing an opportune moment to covertly stir her memory. "Do you remember the Nova-Insanity?"

She shrugged and rolled on toward their goal as Rex grabbed her arm to steady her gait. "Not really. I think I'm too young." That math didn't compute. Even with years of hard, street living, this haggard version of Mira could not be younger than thirty, and then there was her family, husband Michel and that boy and girl, and their forever-friend Mira. No, she had buried her past, all of it, even big events like the Nova-Insanity. His frustration grew, the itch on his temple reappeared. An itch like a healed-over knife wound. Thoughts of surgery and murder in alleyways came fast and often. He felt the little machines inside of him working hard to keep his blood pressure in check, his body in one piece, even as his mind felt on the edge of fragmenting. Transit Mountain might not be stirring memories inside of Mira, but it was changing something in him.

"Maybe we should go back," he called after her. His doubts now crushing weights.

"Fuck no, Rex. You dragged me out here on your Mount Doom quest. Let's dump the ring into the fire or whatever it is you think we should do and get the fuck out of here."

They ambled-on through Coriolis' outermost district of Caelum. Their protection buttons meant nothing out here, but the general populace was wealthier, and more self-conscious of their vulnerabilities. *Act crazy!* worked well. *But is it really an act?*

"Tell me what you're looking for?" Mira asked, her green eyes suddenly clear and lucid. "Which part of your past have the Sisters got you chasing down?"

The question took Rex by surprise. "The surgery bit, where I was turned into a human."

Her laugh was more of a painful cackle. "So we're not trying to figure out who you murdered then?" Rex stumbled to a halt, shocked into silence. Mira laughed again; her pointed fingers jabbed at his middle. "I knew it! We've all got those. I keep dreaming I was fucking machinegunning down someone's family, then grinding them up. Think I was a lich or some crazy shit. What's yours?"

Rex felt that presence again. Him. Watching, judging. This was the moment of confession. The catharsis he needed to gain the Future-Lord's favor. He took a breath and it spilled out. "I stabbed some guy in the head, in a back alley. Might have been a drinking buddy."

She looked disappointed. "That's it? How are we supposed to figure that out?"

"This is different. I was really there. I woke up next to him and a Sister took me in. I think she even saw the body."

"The Sisters saw the body, copped the murderer and what? Let him go? Walking dogs, abducting innocent young women and dragging them off to Transit Mountain? Should I be nervous Rex?"

"No! No, I don't do that anymore. I mean I didn't–"

Mira pushed him away and kept walking. "Fucking Christ, Rex, you don't need to tell me. I get it. I get it. Last few nights I've chained my door shut to stop myself sleepwalking, frightened that I'll wake up in some alley with a dealer's gun in my face. Who the fuck knows what we do when we let them take control."

Downhill felt good. The Caelum District sprawled across a broad fan of valleys all angling toward Transit Mountain. "Lot of money here," Mira said, "should be safer."

Street markets hummed with life and busy stalls. Rex's eyes bulged as he passed heaps of food. He'd forgotten food could be so colorful. "Let's eat!" Mira exclaimed.

"I don't have any money."

"There." She pointed to a café by the side of the market with outdoor seats.

Despite prickly looks, the staff seated them as far from other customers as possible. Rex eyed the menu trying to make the squiggles correlate to his concepts of food and drink.

Mira scanned the menu and stabbed at it with a finger. "Burger." He nodded approval and kept perusing the words as if deciding something important.

The waiter made them pay in advance. Mira tipped a sock full of coins onto the table and they sorted and piled them, holding their breath as they figured out if they had enough.

The waiter clinked away with his hands full and minutes later the food arrived. Rex raised the giant burger from the plate and inhaled its intoxicating smell. Real meat! Not the fungal slop the Sisters served in the food hall.

"How did you get money?" He delayed the first bite until Mira was ready to join him. She looked troubled, eyes cloudy, shoulders hunched over her food. "Fucking glowworms, beady little demon eyes everywhere. They see shit I don't see. Bunch of thieving pricks see money everywhere, coins in drains, stuck in gum, on sidewalks, cracks in roads. They know," she tapped the side of her head, "we need money for the drugs. They don't care about the food." She steeled herself, bolt upright, fighting the voices inside that refused to let her eat. "This is a 'Fuck-you' moment, Rex. Fuck you, Glow. I'm hungry." She chomped into the burger, fighting tears of pain as meat juice and drool dripped down onto the plate.

He ate too, the taste muted to chaff by witnessing her pain. She downed the last bite and collapsed, head down onto the plate. Her voice came up from the grease like a drunk's last order. "How come, Rex. How come it doesn't hurt you?"

He had no answer. His eyes found Transit Mountain. Someone out there knew. The beginning of a thread that explained how the dog became a man, and then a murderer of old men in back alleys. If he found the courage to unearth the truth and pay the penance, maybe he could find the courage to tell Mira about her own past, and then both their futures would be in the hands of the Future-Lord.

The waiter hovered nervously in the background as Mira snored into her plate and Rex stared. He picked up his spoon and gazed at the inverted image, closer into the left pupil, seeking the Future-Lord. Hoping for a clue, some spark. *A little help here!*

The itch spread over the side of his head. He scratched it with the spoon. The waiter coughed. He stopped and sat staring at the top of Mira's head. She snapped awake as her inner drug mind decided, with its rudimentary distributed intellect, that it was time to move on.

"Weren't we going up to see the GFC guys or something?" she asked wearily as they stumbled away, leaving the waiter frantically spraying their table with liquid from a green bottle.

"Transit Mountain," Rex said, fighting his nausea and a terrible feeling of impending doom. "It'll all be all right once we get to Transit Mountain."

* * *

Mill Street was a garbage fortress. Piles of trash formed a maze on the approach to Trendle Tower. Lazar strode confidently down the narrow access path through the piles, aware of the gunsights beading his head and chest.

Jett found Lazar an easy mimic, hat pulled low, inside-out jacket, furtive, quick-paced gait. The face was problematic, smooth and pasty-white. Jett smeared himself with blood he stole from a gutter-drunk and wrapped a bandage around his jaw. Another wound appeared on his shoulder to distract suspicious eyes. He doubted his Lazar disguise would work up close, not with anyone who really knew him.

Inside, he felt a cold emptiness as if all his gist memories hid behind some mental blanket, afraid to watch. Of course, those memories were for human interaction, not combat. The memories of combat were his, and real: voidian-on-voidian. What he was meant to do.

The eight-story Trendle Tower block twisted on the way up giving it an organic, asymmetrical appearance. The bottom six floors looked like classy residences with window boxes and curtains, but zoomed eyesight revealed bricked-up windows painted to look like home interiors. The lower story was devoid of any obvious entrance and radiated no infrared. Eight heat signatures were spread across the upper levels, one of them was Thorne. The man who surely knew everything Jett needed to know about Glow.

The trash path dead-ended at the tower's blank wall. As Jett approached it peeled open revealing an elevator. A large man with overdeveloped neck and shoulders stepped out.

Human. Amped.

Someone else stayed in the elevator cage hidden from Jett's view.

"What happened, Laz?" the man said, with a grunting, apish voice.

Machete. Two side-holstered pistols. Rear-holstered shotgun. Ceramic-mesh body armor.

Jett ignored the tags and focused on the man's face which shifted and contorted with that addict's twitch.

"I got hit," Jett mumbled, holding his hand to his jaw, hiding as much of his face as possible.

"You don't look right to me. You want to see Thorne or the medic?"

"Medic," Jett moved toward the elevator.

"Got to search you first," came a gruff voice from behind him. Jett was surprised to see another guard at his back, from some secret door he hadn't noticed leading to a barracks that remained shielded from his heat-detecting vision. The second man was of slight build, with whip-taut muscles, probably ex-special forces, but judging by his age that was a long time ago.

Jett held up his hands and let the men rifle through his pockets and pat him down. They took obvious pleasure in smacking and punching his arms and legs as they dug into every fold. Jett let his body flop. The heavies caught him as he fell and propped him back on his feet, then continued frisking. It was odd to Jett that the man who had appeared to be his friend a few seconds earlier, now treated him this way.

"Where's your stash and money?" military-man asked.

"They stole it."

Military-man laughed and shook his head. "Thorne's not going to like that. Probably take your other kidney for that mistake."

"Yeah... wouldn't want to be you right now," the larger grunt added, pushing Jett into the elevator cage making sure he understood that he had no choice in the matter.

Hunched in the corner, Jett remained still as the gentle acceleration moved him upward. The elevator guard was a massive rectangular biped, larger even than Jett when at full skeletal extension. Clothed in a fiber-composite business suit that concealed a jutting ceramic chest plate, his face was a metal blank.

Robot?

The thing shuffled on the spot, readying for action. The quiet hiss and click of hydraulic valves accompanied its movements. *A tank*, Jett decided, something designed to front a conflict, soak up damage while others rained down hellfire on the attackers or fled to safety.

The elevator bumped to a stop and the doors opened. Another tank waited outside, and another behind that. Jett shuffled out of the cage and stood sandwiched between the hulks, reaching only halfway up the tank's body in his cringing-Lazar form.

No one else was around.

"You okay, Laz?" The nearest tank said. The voice came from its mouth and Jett saw eyes through the glass faceplate.

Human? Cyborg? Tank.

"I got hit, need a medic." Jett looked around discreetly, trying not to show his face to any cameras.

"Follow me." The tank sauntered away. For its size it was light on its feet, but the wooden floorboards flexed under its weight. Jett followed the lead and the second tank fell in behind. They passed storerooms full of boxes, an office with computer equipment and desks. Jett took mental snapshots through each open door, mapping choke points and escape routes.

They passed a room where a suited figure sat behind a desk. A label on the door said Thorne, and Jett recognized Yellow, Juggler's Glow contact standing off to the side with another man who stared out the window.

The lead tank moved down the hall and directed Jett into a room with a single chair. Jett glanced back and saw the second tank veer off to stand guard outside Thorne's office.

"Wait here, Laz. Medic's coming."

The tank stepped through the doorway and pointed at the chair at the same instant as Jett struck. He ducked and lunged upward under the tank's cumbersome arms, jamming his head under its chin, arms becoming coils that wrapped around its chest as a mesh of smaller arms whipped out from his torso encircling the tank in an all-encompassing bear-hug.

Jett's Inner-I pulsed electromagnetic noise, crashing the tank's crude communications circuits. Jett's grip tightened, pulling in his fibers like a dozen nooses. The tank's titanium alloy structure creaked and popped. Stress fractures rippled through its colossal body as its hydraulics hissed and whined to break free. But its arms were pinned, and mere mechanical strength was no match for Jett's fusion-powered hyper-fullerene musculature.

The tank's ceramic plates buckled and collapsed spilling the goo of human blood and organs out through the gaps in the armor. The tank's spine snapped and folded in half. Jett hung onto the crushed body, looping around more cord-like appendages, crushing the hulk into a solid ball of lifeless wreckage.

He lowered the oozing, shattered frame to the ground, quietly moved to the door and pushed it closed, then stared down at the body.

Tank. Dead? Non-functional?

From down the corridor Thorne's voice rose and fell, shouting, arguing the details and mechanics of running a drug empire, oblivious to the infiltrator in his midst. Jett felt a spark of hope, a big step closer to his mission objective. Soon he would understand Glow and strike a blow against this madness for the voidian people. "Soon, Ursurper. Soon."

"There's nothing here, Rex, just bums and farmers with their shit houses and their shit fields and their – and their – shit! How're we supposed to find your dead guy in the alley up here? There's not even any alleys!"

Rex moped along behind Mira as they climbed through the meandering foothills of Transit Mountain, up to the lofty heights of the first plateau. The spire loomed overhead, *concentric circles*, tip lost in the clouds. Behind it, a rainbow hung over the gray waters of the landlocked Sidereal Sea that covered most of the island's northern side.

"You take the left bit and I'll go right," Mira said, pointing at the rainbow. "More chance of finding gold than your dead alley-man."

But Rex had found gold, or at least the gleam of precious memories. The tangled wreckage of loading cranes, the stacks of shipping containers, their banners and logos still showing through mottled paint and rust, all stirred something in his mind. But like some frustrating tip-of-the-tongue word or film star, he couldn't bring it into focus, couldn't catch the name.

"Seriously, Rex, what in the name of fuck are we doing here?" Mira stalled, hands on hips. Up to now drug-seeking Mira had taken the lead, something in the novelty of the place inspired that persona to life despite Rex's efforts at distraction. But potty mouth Mira was back and she'd clearly lost patience with this quest, and probably wanted to go back to a cushy mansion she imagined she owned on Ridgeline or wherever.

"Close, we're close." He stumbled past her as if animal instinct kept his nose pressed to the chase. With a final, breathless push they hauled, arm-in-arm up the rim and tipped over onto the plateau. "Fucking cold up here," Mira said, pulling her clothes tight around her.

Rex stared across the dereliction, rail stations, power plants, pylons and warehouses, easing up the gentle incline toward the sheer, thousand-meter cliff that led up to the second plateau. The clouds had descended, concealing any further view upward. A fine patter of rain fell, something a man like Rex hardly noticed, but recognized as good. Rain was a form of cover, keeping the soft people hidden indoors or under their umbrellas and awnings.

He felt it before he saw it. A heave in the huge presence inside of him, rattling the other voices back awake like confused grandparents hearing a door latch. His vison swam as predictions and re-creations from the deeper parts of his mind lapped at reality, shaping and melding it into a new and warped perspective.

In a nest of shipping containers sat a flat, concrete warehouse. Rolls of barbed wire formed a surrounding fence. A road led up to double gates, more wire, cameras and an empty lookout nest. A flag fluttered on a pole, bluish-black with an arc of yellow stars, the central star bigger than the others. In his conflated, mental vision, Rex walked the road, pushing a gurney with something squirming under a white blanket. In another part of his mind he knew what that something was, but this part wanted to check, wanted to haul back the covers and confirm his suspicions. But this memory thread wouldn't allow that. It rolled on inexorably, replaying the event as faithfully as a damaged mind could reconstruct the past. He heard his breath, cuss words, footsteps, wheels rolling through gravel. The gates swung open and he pushed the gurney inside.

"This him?" said a one-eyed man, sparking a prickle of fear.

"It's him–"

"Fucking Christ, Rex, you're freaking me out. You seeing ghosts or something?" Mira's hand waved in front of his face and brought him back. He was staring at the gates. *The flag is still there!*

"Free-Meridian." The name slipped out as if dripping from a leaking tap.

"This where the surgeons live or the dead guy?" Mira stepped forward, fearless. "Wanna go say hi? See if they remember you?"

"No!" he blurted, head itching on the inside now. A tower in the building's corner still held some original lettering, faded and chipped: GFC.

Act dead, act crazy, run like hell… fight! Just a mutt, under a table surrounded by socks and feet. Surgery. A dead man in an alley, a voting robot, a lich, not a lich, Sister-Eleven. One-eyed man, *more surgery… endless surgery!*

"Fucking right, Rex. I'm not going in there."

"No more cages. No more surgeries." His feet tried to run, but the Future-Lord controlled them now, pushing him, staggering step-by-step toward the gate and the dead eye of the security camera. His head-itch became a lancing pain, a drill, a knife tip pushing through skin and bone and on into brains and blood vessels.

"We're so fucking done here." Mira grabbed at his arm, but he pushed her away.

"He's inside my head. He wants me to see this."

Mira held up her hands in surrender. "You're on your own, buddy. Go in there and we come out as spare parts and kebab meat."

"They cut my head open, rewired me. But he rescued me." His fingers tore at the itch. Blood ran down his face.

"Stop that!" Mira tackled him, pinning his arms to his sides. "We're leaving. Now!"

"I need a knife. Need to get it out of my head. They use it to spy on me."

Mira heaved him off the ground and they toppled backward over a shallow concrete wall onto the downslope to the foothills, tumbling through grass and dirt like lovers until the ground flattened and they lay in a heap.

"Xell," Rex muttered, reaching for the gash in his head.

"Who?"

"That's my name, Xell." The name had a musical tone, like a bell ring or a calling. A precise, sonic beam that ruptured the dam inside his head. Electrochemical flood waters forged through atrophied connections, sparking an old consciousness.

I am Xell.

The memory of a dark alley, morning just a glow of fire in the east. The stink of someone else's shit mixed with his own vomit. The thought of what must happen next made him throw up again adding another layer of slick sheen to the smooth vitrified pumice pavement.

A body lay curled on the ground, a sad wretch of a man withered and tortured, a skin bag of bones and sinew. The knife felt cold and heavy in his hand. The audience watched through his Inner-I as they watched everything he did, knew everything he knew… except this. He'd kept this moment a secret, never voicing his intent, no planning, no equipment, just an apparent spontaneous meltdown. They could see everything he did, but they couldn't read his mind. And as impossibly far away as they were, they could do nothing to stop him.

"See this?" he yelled at the thin line of dark blue sky visible between the tall brick buildings. He pushed the knife into his temple, fighting the recoil reflex, angling the blade sideways until he felt it hit the edge of the plastic service plate. "Yeah, you see it but can't stop it."

He popped the plate off with the knife tip and peeled the tiny portal open by cutting away the flap of flesh. The blade pushed in through the opening, touching the little square of hard circuitry inside. No pain anymore, no feeling at all as he poked around the module with the knife and pried it out through the hole. It dangled from the web of optical threads that meshed with the wetware neurons of his brain.

He mentally activated his Inner-I and his thoughts lit with messages and warnings. "Xell, stop. We can make this right. Just tell us what you need."

Xell mentally toggled icons, tripping the transmit to global. Why not, shouldn't everyone know the truth? But words were hard to find, and no profound statement came to him. Instead a tumble of thoughts and blurred emotions. "They're in my head, messing with my mind. This was never meant for me. I should never have seen these things. I've seen the Star-River, seen the coming madness. This is your burden now."

He gripped the thumb-sized module and ripped it away, wincing, expecting a surge of pain. His senses ignited with sulfurous smells, screaming tones and tangs of lemon and iron. Nerve endings jangled like wire-wool assaulting a blackboard. The perception of being a single being in a single place jolted apart. His fragments swam up out his body and whirled around like flies, leering down past the knife into the hole in his head.

He expected the Inner-I screen to vanish, but instead it faded to an afterimage, leaving him wondering if it would ever leave or if he would be stuck staring at a blue screen for all eternity.

He hurled the module away and dropped to the ground looking the other man squarely in the face. Not dead, just very drunk. He'd made sure to ply him with plenty of liquor along the way. "This was meant for you." He reveled in the quiet. The screaming voices inside his head were all shocked into silence, other watchers on his Inner-I were gone. Bliss. But a bliss that couldn't last. He knew the madness was within, and for now, it just watched, waiting for the right moment to screw his life again. It would never stop until it won, or he finally quit.

The zip-ties were tricky, he cursed and swore, fumbling the tiny plastic strips into place, pulling them taught, binding his hand to the crook of the other man's elbow. "All yours my friend, fucking enjoy."

He lay facing the blank, uncomprehending face, sad and stubbly with overly large ears, like a helpless dog on a veterinarian's table. He reached up to his head again, poking the knife tip through the hole in his skull, resting on soft exposed tissue. Lights twinkled in his vision and suddenly the world grew loud, so very, very loud.

"May the Future-Lord be with me, with you, and with us all." He rammed the blade home as hard as he could, pushing and twisting even as his own hand defied him. For that final second he imagined himself falling, tumbling through the dark hollow interior of Transit Mountain, watching the concentric circles of the plateaus flash past as he crashed toward oblivion and its soft, eternal peace.

Jett found the tank's plain gray business suit and blank metallic face another easy mimic. Exact measurements were hard to glean from the crushed wreckage, but Jett planned on moving fast. Too fast for humans to perceive such details.

He picked the dead tank's shotgun from its back-mount holster. During his compression attack, he'd been careful not to damage the gun. Many enemies lurked in the building and a method of ranged attack could be useful.

Goshgun: Gas Operated Shotgun.

He rattled the cartridge, ten hyper-compressed metallic-hydrogen pellets, standard militia issue. He popped the cartridge off and clicked the trigger, checking that the piezoelectric spark leapt across the housing where the pellet would sit. The tiny charge destabilized metallic hydrogen, triggering immense, explosive decompression. The gas discharge alone was lethal to humans, but during his brief stint in the Broken's militia he'd seen his fellow thugs load the trumpet-shaped barrel with everything from bolts and stones to custom made explosive pellets. The goshgun's recoil was legendary, only the most Amped humans could use it without maiming themselves. The weapon was dangerous, even to Jett.

Jett spun the gun lightly in his tank-sized fingers, calibrating his reactions to its weight and dimensions. He lined the muzzle up on the door and targeted pictures and furnishings around the room in rapid succession, freezing on each target for a tenth of a second, finger twitching in simulated fire.

Comfortable with his new acquisition, Jett replicated the jerky mechanical gait of the tank and left the room.

Loud voices emanated from Thorne's office. The second tank stood side-on in the doorway. Jett noted the elevator gauge, showing the cage moving down, taking the third tank back to street-level guard duty.

The second tank took no notice as he turned into the office doorway. Thorne sat at his desk. The black-suited man stood by his side as Yellow eased away from the door toward the window and an urgent voice shouted over the phone clamped to Thorne's ear. "Milton just went offline," said black-suited man. "Something's up."

"Milton's right there, you idiot." Thorne pointed at Jett. His eyes widening as he registered something was wrong.

Jett jammed the goshgun down the front of the second tank's jacket angling it under the ceramic armor plate. The recoil of the blast lifted him off his feet, but the armored cylinder around the tank-body contained the discharge, channeling the guts and bones of whoever was inside out the bottom and through the floor.

Jett wrenched the gun back as the tank's corpse collapsed through the newly minted floor hole and crashed into the room below. The black-suited man fast-drew a pistol from his holster.

Jett's goshgun shattered the air and the man's upper body vanished in a mist of fragments. His legs and pelvis stayed standing for a fraction of a second before dropping like a sack.

"Don't shoot!" Thorne yelled, raising his hands.

Jett stepped over the disembodied legs and swung the gun onto Yellow, cowering in the corner.

"Wait," yelped Yellow, "I'll help you." Jett turned the goshgun back on Thorne.

"Don't listen to that worthless shit," Thorne shouted. "I'm the boss here. I can give you whatever you need." His face streamed sweat and his eyes raced back and forth between Jett and Yellow.

Jett swung the gun back on Yellow.

"I know everything he knows," Yellow said, his voice oddly calm. "I know things even he doesn't know and things he doesn't even *know* he doesn't know. We can run this place together or rob it blind and start again somewhere else. Us cyborgs should stick together. Fuck these human scum, right?"

"That doesn't sound like the kind of loyalty I'm looking for," Jett said, pushing the gun in Yellow's face.

Jett almost missed it – Thorne's hand dropping below his desk. His eyes betraying his intention, and the belief that Yellow's distraction granted him this single shot at survival.

Jett sprang into the air like a giant flea as Thorne found the hidden trigger. The gun blast went under his feet leaving a ragged hole in the wall behind.

Jett dropped and in the same motion kicked the desk backward with Thorne pinned on the other side. He landed nimbly, vaulting over the wreckage to stand over the bloodied man who struggled to reach his gun for one last shot.

Jett swept the weapon away and grabbed him by the neck, hauling him up and out of the rubble. Dropping the tank-disguise, Jett melted back into a more agile carbon-black skeleton.

"Woah!" said Yellow as Thorne's eyes bugged out in horror.

"Start talking." Jett moved toward Yellow, thrusting the goshgun into a fold in his cloak.

"Four operations, all run from here," Yellow babbled. "Three safehouses each with three tanks, a dealer, and one tech to fix tanks and guns. Another tech works at safehouse number three doing comms and IT. Stockpiles at each location are in the roof vaults–"

"Where do the drugs come from?" Jett changed his grip, hand encircling Thorne's skull so he dangled by his head. Thorne squealed as his neck stretched, prying desperately at Jett's fingers.'

"Lepa, Cronk, Goo, Amp and booze all come from guys out of town. We send a truck out each month. The truck's in the basement at safehouse number two. A robotic construct called Scylla delivers the Glow every week at a pre-designated meeting point. There's a delivery due tonight. As the most trusted and indispensable team member, I do the pickups. If you send anyone else, Scylla bails, and you lose your contact, and the whole process of payment and negotiation starts over. I wouldn't risk that if I were you." Yellow took a breath.

Jett looked back to Thorne, squirming in his grasp. "I don't think I need you." He brought Thorne closer to his face, holding him using just a finger and thumb on each temple.

"Fuck you," coughed Thorne, gathering a wad of blood and spit into his mouth.

Jett clicked his fingers and Thorne's head popped and his body dropped to the floor.

"Tell me more about this Scylla." Jett turned back to Yellow, surprised to see the little man had moved. Clearly the sickly cyborg had far swifter and more stealthy cybernetics than Jett had expected. Yellow now stood off to the side, the dead tank's goshgun in his mechanical grasp, the open bell of its muzzle pointing right at Jett's chest.

"Why are you pointing a gun at me?" Jett asked, angry at himself for giving Yellow this opportunity, as slim as it was.

"Oh, you know, just a little cowardly speculation. I'm thinking maybe you're a fucking psycho and are going to kill me whatever I tell you. I'd love to make a deal. I'd love to trust you, but just don't think I can do that. Do you see my point? What the fuck *are* you anyway? I've never seen a cyborg do those moves before."

"I need you alive," Jett said, edging closer to Yellow at a rate he calculated to be below the threshold of his detection. "I'm taking over this operation and you can show me how. I keep my promises. If I say I won't kill you, then I will not kill you."

"Ok, that's great. I'm really feeling the love here." Yellow's voice wavered, but his hands remained as steady as a sniper's.

Jett turned front-on and bent at the waist bringing his face level with the gun barrel. It was a gamble, an attempt at intimidation. He saw the world in extreme detail: tiny changes in body temperature or minute widening of the eyes. He could follow muscle spasms down an arm into a hand and on to a finger, watch in slow-motion as it clicked the trigger and even then... he had milliseconds to react as sparks leapt, explosive pressure built. Plenty of time to lunge sideways out of the damage cone.

His hands crept closer to Yellow's gun. By his Inner-I's best computation, he still needed another half-meter to be sure. "Two things will happen if you fire that gun," Jett said, voice low and filled with menace. He added infrasound that shuddered through the floor and up Yellow's legs, destabilizing his bowels.

"Two things?" Yellow spoke with remarkable calm, and for a second Jett's faith wavered.

"If you fire, it will break your arms and crush your chest cavity. Maybe even kill you."

"And the second thing?"

"If you fire that gun at me, it will make me very, *very* angry."

Defeat entered Yellow's eyes and the gun barrel dropped from Jett's forehead toward his nose. The motors powering his hands and trigger finger wound down, telling Jett his gamble had paid off.

Yellow was no gambler. For him, survival was a reaction, an instinct that automatically engaged acting skills, distractions, obfuscations and backup plans. As a calculating coward, he knew how to play the narrowest odds to improve his chances. His backup cybernetics didn't use slow-moving, predictable motors. His Inner-I was a new and extensively upgraded model, one that allowed him to rehearse motion sequences in his head, load them into his cyborg frame, and, with a single, mental command, unfold them in hyper-accelerated machine-time.

And so it was that before that fateful millisecond where Jett coiled to lunge and grab Yellow's gun, Yellow had already weighed the probabilities, impassively examined his options, loaded the conclusion into his machine framework, and without a hint of intention in his eyes, without a trace of doubt on his face, and with absolutely no pre-emptive muscular or mechanical twitches or tells – he pulled the trigger.

CHAPTER 24

Memory Games

Like a suffocating man having the plastic bag ripped from his head, Rex came back to life with a single violent inhalation. His world swam into giddy focus and a stream of partially digested burger splattered down his chest into his lap.

"Fucking Christ, Rex, pull yourself together." Mira's voice sounded like an echo-chamber.

"Where am I?" he said.

"In a fucking pipe," she said. "My turn now. Who are you?"

"Rex, just Rex." He struggled upright, cracking his skull on the curve of concrete overhead.

"Good. You've been all kinds of babbling freaks the last hour, moaning and bitching about being dead and stuff. You need to get some classier glowworms, man."

He rubbed his head and brushed the puke off his chest. It splashed into the thin river of water running past his feet. He was indeed inside a huge pipe, a storm drain, soaked through and shivering cold. The circle of gray light showed rolling hills cloaked in rainclouds with the distant rectangles of city buildings. "I was Xell."

"Oh yeah, him. Real whiny fucker," Mira muttered through a pained smile.

"He just took me over, and I watched from back in the dark

part of my mind where the others live. I was a glowworm, Mira, watching someone else control my body."

"Sucks when that happens," Mira sighed. "Glad you're back, I guess."

Rex eased to the pipe's opening and watched the rain. "How did we get here?"

"I dragged you through shit and mud. You fought me most of the way, but it was downhill and away from Transit Mountain which was clearly screwing with your brains."

Sudden elation filled Rex. "It was Xell! The dead guy in the alley, Mira! That was Xell and I didn't kill him. He, he killed himself. I'm saved!" He almost leapt with joy but then remembered the pipe.

She laughed, "Told you. All glowworm bullshit. You really think I was Machinegun-Mira?" She made putt-putting noises and mimicked a Tommy gun.

"He tied us together, then stabbed his own head. I don't get how the glowworms ended up inside me, but I didn't kill him!" He tried to hug Mira, but she backed away, looking at the vomit oozing down his chest.

"Glow does weird shit. Maybe Xell's memories were in one of your fixes, so they were already in your head and being close to him bought them alive? Kind of activated them."

He nodded, mind spinning through Xell's avalanche of memories before they all faded away. Mira kept talking. "You said he tied your arms together. Glow's super-smart. It moves around inside the body when it messes with us and fixes us. No point in it being inside dead people, so perhaps it moved, kind of escaped, into a nearby alive person?"

Her eyes glazed with remembrance. "That's what liches do. They grind you up, cook the meat at the same time to kill all the cells so the Glow knows you're dead. That doesn't hurt it coz it's all machines, indestructible... kind of. Then they run the goop through a membrane with living blood in it that draws the Glow away from the dead stuff. Then it all gets resold and used again taking a bunch of its previous host's memories with it."

Rex stared wide-eyed. "You know a lot about liches."

She dropped her chin. "Yeah. Machinegun-Mira, Lich-Mira... fucking glowworms."

He clasped his hands to his face, innocent hands, not a killer's hands. "I am *not* a murderer." He wanted to shout it across the rainy landscape, tell the whole world.

"Nice. Wouldn't want to be stuck in this shit-pipe with just any old psycho."

She helped Rex out of his shirt and pants. He squatted under the pipe's outpour, using it as a makeshift shower, as Mira scrubbed and rung his clothes the best she could.

"What's a Star-River?" he asked, as more of Xell's monologue came to mind.

She waved a hand at the sky. "It's that. The sky, or rather the Milky Way, the ancients thought it was a river or something crazy. Don't ask me how I know that."

"Xell said the Star-River was inside of me?"

"Well, if he's inside of you and he thinks the Universe is inside of him... I guess that means it's all inside of you?"

Rex scratched his itchy temple. Even the itch made sense now, a phantom healing of a phantom wound. Mira handed back his shirt, but before he could put it back on she curled herself into his lap wrapping her arms around him.

"Mira... I–"

"S'ok, man. I'm not fucking you, just cold. And wet. And miserable."

For a while they just sat, breathing in life, Rex beaming on the inside. Surely the Future-Lord saw this. He was almost normal, just a guy and not a murderer. He still had to find his sister, but at least he wasn't a killer of old men in alleyways. He felt Mira's warmth. As boney and fragile as she felt, she was still a woman. He tried to recall holding a woman before, but those thoughts just sent his glowworms crawling to the surface of his mind like lecherous grubs.

He turned the grubs off, focusing instead on his life. In that clear, lucid moment, he realized she was the only actual person he knew. Everyone else was a dog, or a robotic construct, or a dead memory inside his head. And whatever the heck Mrs O was.

Mira stretched out her back, popping and creaking her aches and pains. "We should get out of here before its dark," she said. They sat, face-to-face, as if about to kiss. Rex reached out and touched her faded, black hair, feeling the clods of dried mud and grime amongst the strands. Her green eyes stared back as if seeing him as a man for the first time rather than a piece of garbage.

She smiled and his world lit up. "You know, I never really bought all that bullshit you gave me about coming out here to find yourself. I thought you were trying to pry something out of me."

His mouth moved, suddenly dry, unable to form words. *Act dead. Act crazy. Lie! This is not the right moment.* But the Future-Lord was watching through the now crystal-clear space in his head. A crushing agony hit, the very thought of hurting her so much, it felt evil, but telling lies in front of the Future-Lord...?

Her brow creased. "You did come out here to pry something out of me." She rolled back out of his arms and straightened up. "I knew it. Rex, you are so bad at bullshitting and yet so full of actual shit you must fart every time you breathe."

"Not now, Mira, not here."

"Come on." The smile was back, genuine, warm, some remnant of the real Mira hidden beneath the reconstructions and glowworms. "Tell me, Rex. No harm, just tell me. It was the Sisters wasn't it? Trying to get you to sell me on their Future-Lord crap?"

"No, not that. Please, Mira, I don't want to hurt you." He just wanted it all to go away, for them to be back in that silent embrace, just one more moment of being normal.

Her eyes fogged, body language turned defensive. "Come on, man, stop spinning me. You got something to say?"

He clamped his mouth shut, sickened by the power he had over her, the power to fill her life with horror and misery. He was no better than those surgeons. *There has to be another way.*

"Mira, if you had something in your past that was so terrible you had deliberately hurt yourself to forget it, would you want to remember it again?"

She pushed him away and he slumped back into the pipe. "Fuck this, I'm out of here."

"No! Mira! Mira…" he pointed to his eyes, drawing her back to his gaze like music, that simple, pathetic tune that tugged the better Mira out of the quicksand. He realized that he was her tune and maybe for him, she was the music, the melody that brought his shattered mind back to reality.

Her eyes cleared as she returned, "You know something, Rex. Tell me." Tears rolled, and her jaw trembled.

"I hate myself, why can't I lie?" He clawed at the bloody scab on the side of his head, wincing at the reopened wound.

"Tell me."

"I just want to be normal, just for a moment."

"Tell me."

"It's nothing really… I just dug around for information and–"

"Fucking tell me!" Her hands bunched into fists.

"I found out where your forever-friend is – the real Mira."

"My…? But, okay, that's it?"

Rex's thin wall of resistance broke, and the treacherous words flooded out. "She's a gray poodle that lives with someone else now and when you owned her you lived near here. Near Transit Mountain, and that's why I wanted you to come here, to help you remember. But I ended up remembering stuff instead. When you lived here you weren't called Mira, you were Corinne, Corinne Medlow."

"Corinne Med–?"

Rex watched her face, lips formed questions, eyes searched inward. He saw her own barrier shatter; a flash of terror glazed her eyes. She dropped into the mud. Rex tried to catch her, but she slipped through his hands. Her eyes quivered as if taking in thousands of written lines in fast succession, consuming the book of her own life at superhuman speed. A soft wail of denial crept past gasps and chokes and then…

She laughed.

"Mira?" he knelt, finally finding the belief in his arms to grasp her and turn her face to his.

"Fucking Christ, Rex," she said softly. "Don't you get it yet? It's all bullshit. I remember that, just like I remember being a lich and a murderer. None of it's real, none of it happened. Not to me. Not to you. It happened to someone else and now you're stuck with it, like some fucking virus you can never shake."

She pushed him off her and he fell away like a dead branch. "Let's go before we screw each other up even more."

She turned back and looked down at him. He was dirt again, a quirky nobody, an odd, forgettable companion through a short segment of her life. "Where'd you even get that crap from anyway?"

"The Sisters," he muttered, still in shock that she didn't believe him. "They showed me a photograph."

"A photograph!" She slapped her side and laughed aloud. "Just another fake memory but from a computer. They'll try anything to haul in a sucker." She reached out a hand and pulled him to his feet. "Family, kids? Come on, Rex. Who the fuck would marry me?"

Jett saw the gun go off. The tiny ignition within the trumpet tube of the goshgun, a flash of hypersonic debris coming at his face, rammed through the intervening void by the gargantuan gas expansion.

He experienced a singular, frozen moment of shock. Yellow's sagging face, eyes cold and unmoving. Words started forming on his tagger:

Evasive maneuvers–

And then his world of sound, light and embodiment blew away into fragments, sparkled briefly and then vanished into darkness.

He heard a voice, "Marco?"

Polo

And there she was, pink face, rosy cheeks, grinning at him through splashes of water. "You cheated. You peeped!"

"I never did." His voice was childish, a boy's voice modulated with glee and laughter.

The game faded, changed, and turned into a new game. She was older now, a different look in her eyes, calculating but still playful. She wrapped the blindfold over his eyes, and again... darkness! He felt something hard and plastic push into his hand. A clicker, he snapped it between his finger and thumb and the sharp crack echoed back at him. "Come find me," she hissed into his ear and he felt her warmth vanish. Lost in an unfamiliar place. Click! Click!... He strained to decipher the echoes and an image of the room imagined itself into existence around him.

The static-noise of awareness cohered into his Inner-I screen. Flickering and tormented, it reached for information, struggling to connect body with mind and senses.

I have an Inner-I.

I spoke but heard no words. I don't have a mouth, ears, eyes, but I must have a head.

Four seconds, his Inner-I clock read from the moment he'd grabbed at Yellow. The dangerous little cyborg was still out there. And with a goshgun! If he'd been able to fire, then surely, he would have? Then there was that other tank, and the other guards – Thorne's Empire of thugs and criminals.

His vision turned red with damage markers. Maybe he was hiding. His body had a distributed intelligence built into its fabric. An octopus brain, somebody once called it. A nascent survival mechanism that would seek shelter, safety, in any way its rudimentary mind could conceive if his higher mental functions were disabled.

Estimated mass loss: Four Kilos.

Proprioception coming online... missing trunk connections–

Unspecified orientation–

Fullerene fluid loss – critical!

Self-sealing arterial override. Attempting to prevent bleed out–

"Marco?"

Polo.

Click... click...

Jett forged a simple Inner-I algorithm, setting patches of fullerene skin vibrating. Other patches he configured as sensors and routed the incoming auditory information back to the AI inside his Inner-I where it attempted to filter sounds and piece together the returns of his makeshift sonar.

"That's just fucking fantastic!"

Yellow's voice?

Primary appendages – damaged but functional.

Orientation online.

Auxiliary appendages: Functional and reconnected.

He span arms, legs, feet and hands, and eased from a pool of tentacles into a squatting biped. Groping in the darkness, he tried finding his head. Nothing, just shoulders, slick with fluid. There; hanging down his back, still attached by the ultrathin emergency cables that anchored his crystal skull to the fibrous, polymorphic part of his body. He felt his Inner-I groping through his internal body image, seeking fibers that could wrap up around his head and offer the support of a neck. But so many were damaged, he barely had enough to create functional limbs.

"You are fucking amazing!" Yellow spoke and Jett staggered upright, kicking aside debris and lashing out, hoping to strike him.

He swept aside the red warnings.

Fight, survive!

Against the blackness of total sensory deprivation, dots of light came together, pixels of sound reflection hung in a 3D void. He jacked-up the sound frequency, more data, more points, and the walls of the room appeared as a misty plane of dots. Larger debris chunks emerged from the fog as shapeless oddities. He was backed into a far corner. His survival mind was just lying low, recovering.

Other sounds disrupted the picture, causing smudges and blank spots: outside traffic, alarms ringing, the tinkle of debris still falling from the goshgun blast, someone breathing – Yellow!

Jett remained still, letting the room image reform.

"You've got to be shitting me. What *are* you?" Yellow said.

Jett focused all his sonar in the direction of the voice. Secondary routines bounced sound off smooth surfaces, adding more data points, cancelling the effects of noise and Jett's own movements.

There, Yellow! The goshgun recoil had blasted the cyborg backward into the wall, tearing off his cybernetic legs. One of his arms was missing. His other still functioned and was slowly hauling Yellow's, corpulent, bulb-shaped body across the floor toward the goshgun that held a very recognizable silhouette against the smooth floor.

Jett lunged. His sonar image shattered, forcing him to work from memory. He stomped on Yellow's grasping hand, grinding the fingers into the floor. He reached down and grabbed Yellow's thin hair, hauling him up to where his own face should have been. He configured one of his forward sonar ports into a speaker membrane and piped his voice through to it. "You–"

"Go on! Fucking do it," Yellow spat, his face a shifting, ghostly white in Jett's monochromatic vision. "You can't hurt someone who's already dead inside."

"I can hurt you in ways you can't even imagine." Jett's voice was a monotone buzz saw.

Yellow managed a strangled laugh. "Dumb-fuck cyborg, you're done. Finished."

Jett coiled tentacular fingers around Yellow's bulbous head and squeezed it gently, feeling the skull flex to the point of breaking as Yellow's eyes bulged and retracted with each twitch of Jett's fingers. It would be so easy to pop it like a giant boil and watch his brains flow down his wrist. Were they yellow too? It would be so much more satisfying with color vision.

"Come on big guy," Yellow said. "Thorne's army of super-heavies will be here any second. You took one out, but you had a head and a gun then. Now?"

"They will all die," Jett said, refusing to acknowledge his absurd odds.

"You're pretty agile for a dumb-fuck cyborg. Fairly smart too, although not that smart." Yellow managed a sarcastic chuckle before Jett's twitching fingers forced him to stop. "What exactly are you?"

He let the little man drop to the floor, needing to focus on escape. "I'm what comes next."

"Gosh, if I'd known that I would have found a bigger gun."

"I need to get out of here."

"No shit, Einstein!"

"Thorne pays you?"

"He used to pay me. That's going to be kind of tricky since you splashed his decision-maker all over his office."

"Help me take control here. You'll live, and when I'm done, the whole thing is yours. You know everyone, make them back off."

Yellow brushed himself down with his single hand as if suddenly sure of himself. "I could probably persuade them. Internal power struggles happen all the time. Maybe a change would be good. Might fly for a few days until one of the other dumb shits decides to take over the operation for himself."

"That's good enough."

"And I'm sure you'll keep your promise and not kill me."

Jett hunted around the office, refining his visual senses to the point where he could move and perceive in useful detail, although the response time of the sonar system remained woefully inadequate for real-time combat. He found three goshguns, held one in each hand and crushed the other.

"What do you need?" he asked Yellow who was quietly watching.

"Arms, legs, ears and that phone Thorne used. Put it on voice command and I'll take care of things. But get me off the floor first. My other arm might still work, but we can deal with that later."

Jett swept the corpses and debris into a corner and propped the shattered remains of the desk back on three of its original feet. He dumped Yellow in a chair in front of the phone, but his makeshift sonar couldn't see the digital readout and the numbers he dialed. "Remember," he rasped. "Any treachery, you die first."

"Death holds no fear for me," chattered Yellow, apparently warming to his new role.

"Then instead of killing you, I'll ream out every nerve in your body with a monofilament drill and fry you slowly from the inside."

"...Okay." Yellow quietly dabbed away at the phone and spoke to several people in a muffled voice.

Jett extruded another limb. Reaching up, high overhead, it rained down sonic waves and built a stable picture of himself. A grim image of his body formed, overlaid with damage markers from his Inner-I and proprioception sensors: the goshgun blast had blown his head off his neck appendage. Only the hyper-fullerene structural strands had saved him from decapitation. His face was completely gone, peeled away along with his ears and nose, but the sound cavities in his skull still worked in low-resolution. The fibers forming his jaw and voice box had been blown clean away, as had his eyeballs, leaving their retinal cables dangling down his skull cheeks like tiny worms groping for connections. The extra-thick crystal of his skull faceplate had saved his brain circuits, although doubtless some acceleration-damage had occurred.

He focused back on Yellow, hunched at the desk, who put the phone aside and gave Jett a crude, mechanical thumb-halfway-up sign. "I'm gonna need my legs back," he said.

Jett knew he couldn't trust him. But Thorne's tanks could arrive any second and here he was, the best hope for the voidian people, the ultimate warrior – a crippled wreck.

He helped Yellow reattach his legs to the body harness. Then Yellow rose and creaked and whirred his way to the door using his single arm to grasp at the wall for stability.

"Where are you going?" Jett said, pointing his goshguns at Yellow's back.

"Just out here to meet our new business partners. You hang back and look menacing. That should be easy."

Jett aimed the goshguns at the doorway and waited as the elevator cranked back up to the eighth floor. He took one last detailed look at the image his sonar had built of himself, and decided that his combat functionality was severely compromised, but in the coming fight, he sure as hell had surprise on his side.

CHAPTER 25

Buzz Kill

"How about here?" Trabian said, trying to conceal the tremble in his voice.

Ellayna unfurled the simulation into her Inner-I and her room shimmered and turned into... the surface of the Moon?

"Come on Trabian. *'Take me to the Moon'*? really?" She laughed and then felt bad as Trabian's exaggeratedly sad face appeared in the corner of her vision.

"Sorry," he said. The Moon faded and she was back in her room.

Trabian's messages had grown more flirtatious, possibly more desperate, over the past few days. She understood that everybody was nervous, waiting for something to happen. She watched as the game pieces of Martin's TwoLunar taskforce eased out from Cloud9, took up a defensive formation and headed silently for TwoLunar. Her assigned combat body flashed green toward the rear of the cluster. It ran on its own, innate intelligence, for the moment. An artificial mind, as Martin called it, but it was just an algorithm: a cold, dead, simulation, the very thing Del warned her about. The same thing that they all hunted: Ursurper Gale. She'd never believed in souls, magic and mysticism. Her father's love of science had distilled such things from her mind at an early age. But she'd also never accepted that a simulation, an algorithm, a cluster of fullerene transistors, could experience the qualia of life in the way a human could, and become conscious.

"I hear you made contact with Del?" Trabian said, surprising her with a twist in the conversation.

"Not much of a contact," she said. "More of a paranoid ramble. Del's alive and cogent, but of no real use to us anymore."

"The great Del Krondeck. How did he end up like that?"

"An overly fertile mind, always planning, seeing dangers and pitfalls. An atheist in search of a god. He needed to believe in something but just couldn't. Even his baby, the GFC, broke his heart in the end. He tried other things; drugs, Buddha, The Future-Lord... me. None of us lasted."

"Yeah, I can see Del being a Future-Lord kind of guy."

"He caught that one from Joselyn Salvitor. They had a thing going for a while. He was big into Future-Lord concepts back then, and looked on the GFC as a pathway to immortality and divinity."

"I have no memory of Joselyn. She left the GFC when I was young."

"People called her the smart one. She was certainly the nice one, the founder with the strongest sense of decency. She returned to Earth just before the Nova-Insanity."

"What did she use her money for?"

"No one knows. She vanished, broke off all contact with us and particularly with Del. That's what drove him full circle back to me. And for Del, the Future-Lord kinda lost His shine."

"I think he must have been crazy, leaving you." That boyish smirk again.

Please try harder Trabian.

Hope sprang back into his eyes. "I have another idea. Try this..." Her room wobbled as if about to disintegrate. The lavender smell grew distant and something new swam into focus. Something new, but exactly the same. She was still in her room but no longer webbed to the bed. Trabian sat facing her in an easy chair, wearing just a silken tiger-pattern robe.

"Clever," she said, carefully arranging her knees and gown for modesty. There was even gravity, something that felt excitingly wrong in her own apartment.

"I took scans from pictures you sent me over the years and recreated your room in VR."

She eased off the bed, allowing herself to fall fully into Trabian's simulated world. She felt her hair appear, tumbling down her shoulders. The aches and twinges of age vanished as her mind received its signals from her ARG and not her real body.

Testing her balance one foot at a time, she found a decanter and glasses on a side table. Red wine, excellent vintage. Drinking in VR was usually a subdued experience. Things never smelled or tasted quite right, but the biomech neural lace did an adequate job of fooling the brain into thinking it was drunk and lifting any inhibitions.

She poured him a glass and sat next to him, clinking her glass against his. "Nice, Trabian. Now, I need to figure out a way that I can trust you. I want us to be allies. Times are dangerous. No one should have to face this future alone." It wasn't quite the speech she intended, but Trabian's surprise location and confident poise had thrown her.

"I know a way," his hand shifted to his robe tassel.

"I don't think that will make me trust you, Trabian. It'll just make you want me more. In real life."

"Isn't that how things work, Ellayna? I become hopelessly besotted: a puppy dog unable to resist?" He leaned into her, but she rolled playfully to the side enjoying the illusion of being young and flexible again.

She had to admit, that didn't sound so bad: Puppy Trabian, her loyal retainer. *Easy votes.* She drained the wine, smiling into the heady feeling that swamped any guilt lingering in her gut. Those years of silent, personal penance, of sending anonymous gifts to Trabian and his father, poor bereaved Mensar. She'd worked hard to let them keep Cloud8 as their own family orbital, private and alone with a tiny cemetery clinging to its outside. Despite being a GFC founder, Mensar turned out to be a weak man, unable to function without his wife, Lyn. He soon collapsed into despair and ruined his mind tampering with experimental Simmorta variants. And with that valuable mind went much of the GFC's proprietary knowledge about genetics and biology. Joselyn did the physics, Del, the nanotech. Ellayna did the finances, the venture capital, publicity, and Mensar was all about genetics. He put the G in the GFC.

More wine. But the guilt returned as she reached a mental barrier that mere fake alcohol couldn't breach. She should be trying to replace his mother, not trap the boy into service. But this was no game, survival required tough decisions. It was for his good in the end, and the survival of the GFC.

He sensed a softening in her mood and rose from the bed, making a point of wandering her tiny room, examining her picture frames and trinkets, working his way slowly around the bed behind her. When she didn't turn, showed no sign of resistance, he reached out and stroked her hair, long and red on this version of Ellayna. His touch simmered through the virtual strands and down her back. He knotted braids around his fingers and reached around her waist, moving up and cupping her breasts.

"Trabian–" But his cheek on her neck silenced her objections. Blood rushed to her face, the room grew dark, details merging into a soft void, like space. "Where are you taking me now?"

"Somewhere special." His hands moved down, parting her gown, stroking the soft flesh of her thighs.

Careful... don't slap his hand away. Mustn't trigger the kill-switch. Not right now.

She felt his robe drop away, warm pressure on her back spreading as if he was growing wider, wrapping gently around her. Another set of hands curled under her arms and up around her neck.

"Trabian?" The room was dark now and turning cold, wrapping them both in icy shadow. "Trabian, stop!" More hands crept to her breasts. Trabian's youthful skin seemed to age under her gaze, crisping like charcoal and splintering away. His bones divided, splitting into more bones, thinner bones. Not bones... *fibers*.

She screamed. Raging against the growing number of appendages, twisting in their oily grip to face her attacker. Trabian's face sagged and split, dead and rotten. It peeled away revealing the carbon-black skull with eyes like obsidian beads.

Her mind fumbled messages into Inner-I emergency protocol buffers as her body convulsed in pain. But no sounds or transmissions escaped the cage this monster had erected. She searched for the escape icon, knowing it wasn't there. *Mind-state passcode. She knew that wouldn't work either. It hadn't stopped the bugs.* "I'm just an old fence cat, strutting my line. Along, along the garden wall, taking my time–" She saw her old cat, Sirius, smelled Mother's lavender, yellow sunflowers, insect hum... Nothing.

There's something else I'm supposed to remember, something, but–

Gale's appendages writhed and churned like saw blades, carving her flesh apart while wringing the breath and the life from her. She choked, told herself that her real body was safe, that she could breathe, she could survive... unless one of those shadow ghosts she'd seen in the corridor was actually inside her room.

Kill-switch.

"Buzz!" she gasped. Her new codeword, one she'd made Jesh program into her ARG. A second simulation began, small, unnoticed by the main algorithm that was clearly under Trabian's control, or whoever controlled Trabian.

From the darkness the bee came, nothing nasty, not like those bugs that tried to kill her, just a bee, like that time when she was a small girl–

A small girl sitting on the grass, smelling mother's lavender. Where was that old cat? The bee seemed huge now, hovering off the end of her nose, checking to see if she was a flower. Who knows what goes through a bee's mind? Maybe it was damaged, broken, maybe she did smell like a flower? It landed on her knee, legs like prickles moving up her thigh where it positioned its abdomen for the sting. The sting that would send her into an agonizing coma for days. Anaphylaxis. Such a big word for a little girl, a word she'd learned the hard way, long before, when she was even younger...

Her horror was instant, a programmed reaction: she swatted at her thigh, smashing the tiny carcass into her flesh. The darkness and pain vanished, and she was back, wallowing in wet bedsheets and her own bodily filth. Webbed and secure but with one hand free, the hand that smacked at her thigh with enough force to reset her ARG unit and the invasive simulation.

The wine was gone, the gravity was gone. Trabian, now gone. She tried her Inner-I, but it was rebooting.

"Martin," she gasped as its emergency comms function blinked alive. She had a few seconds before all its functionality reappeared and the attack resumed. "I'm under attack, someone's inside my Inner-I."

"Security will be there in thirty seconds, Ellayna."

She ripped the webbing free and flailed through the air to the door and out into darkness. "Lights!" she yelled, but nothing happened. A figure loomed ahead, a shadow... *Gale*?

Is this a trick? Am I still inside a simulation? She smacked her thigh again sending the Inner-I into reboot. Suddenly there were lights, and a security detail pounded toward her. She shrank backward, expecting them to turn into something horrific.

"It's okay, Ellayna," the medic's calm face didn't seem attached to his body. She felt the prickle of a dermal sedative. The near instantaneous calm.

"Thank you," she muttered and slumped into the medic's arms.

Riding the gurney to the medical wing, her Inner-I restored to full function. Color and nuance returned to her world as the corridors flashed by. Her inbox lit with messages, many from Trabian.

"What happened, Ellayna? We were playing and you went offline?"

"Ellayna, I hear you were attacked?"

"You know that wasn't me... right? Someone hijacked the sim, Ellayna–"

She ignored him.

"Martin, I'm sure you're running network diagnostics trying to pin down where this attack came from."

"Yes, Ellayna."

"Send a search detail to Cloud8. I was attacked by Trabian Folley."

"Now, let's all just calm the fuck down and act like business partners, shall we?" Yellow eased backward down the corridor, away from the pair of tanks fronting the thrust of angry dealers, Amped-thugs and workers who crowded the corridor. They tried to peer around Yellow to the lurking figure in the side doorway. Jett made sure they could see one goshgun but kept the other hidden in reserve. An Inner-I hack of the corridor's security camera gave him a useful view across the gathered crowd. A single goshgun blast would clear most of the unarmored humans out, but the tanks were problematic and plenty of others lurked on the levels below.

"Who put you in charge?" demanded the lead tank.

"Not in charge," Yellow continued. "Temporary CFO until we get the new finances, and corporate positions finalized. You'll all get paid, plus a handsome bonus for your loyalty through these... difficult times."

Jett saw the crowd relax. Yellow relaxed as well, caught in the middle as he was, his survival odds were miserable if a conflict erupted.

The crowd grumbled, and conferred, and then as a single unit they retreated to the elevator. It took three trips to get them all back down, and only then did Yellow let out a gasp and turn back to Jett. "I give them three days. They don't want a fight until they know who's in here. They'll form groups, make new alliances, and then come to take us out. Three days, mark my words."

"It's enough," Jett said, eyeing the damage reports on his Inner-I and routing priority repair to his eyes and neck. Vison was everything. Without high-resolution, high speed image processing, his mission was hopeless. His eyes were essentially separate biomech organisms trapped inside his non-biomech skull. The retinal cables held all the information needed to regrow eyes but shunting viable material up through his damaged neck and face was proving difficult.

Thorne's antique computer was an easy hack, the same technology level as the Broken's computer system. Within seconds he was privy to Thorne's entire empire: funds, weapon caches, personnel names, numbers and wages, plus a very long list of clients. He sucked the data into his Inner-I and secured the computer against Yellow or anyone else gaining access.

He kept a firm sonar lock on the treacherous little man. Yellow was only dangerous with a loaded goshgun. Jett made sure one of Yellow's arms remained non-functional, making any stashed weaponry he happened to stumble upon difficult to load and fire.

Money! Jett understood humans well now. Juggler, Yellow, those businesspeople striding the streets day and night to and from jobs they hated; it was all about money. The singular effective way to control seemingly all of humanity. He flashed the balance of Thorne's business account on the screen, noting how Yellow's forehead crinkled and twitched as he watched from the side.

"I have no interest in running this place," Jett explained. "I need information about where Glow comes from and who makes it." He remembered his infiltration of the Broken's HQ, the image of dead Xell and the tattoo on his arm. "What is the Free-Meridian?"

Yellow shrugged, an awkward, crunch of damaged machinery and arthritic bones. "I can ask around."

"Once I find Glow's manufacturers, I will move on and you can take over here."

Yellow tore his gaze away from the screen but kept on licking his lips. "You won't find what you need on Thorne's computer. Glow is delivered by Scylla. I'm scheduled to do a pickup this evening. You can go in my place, maybe have a little chat with her, or it, or whatever the fuck Scylla is." He winked and nudged Jett's upper arm with his pointy metal elbow. "Seeing anyone but my good self will automatically terminate our trade agreement, but you're a persuasive guy. She might reveal her sources to you."

"That will be acceptable," Jett said. He checked his Inner-I clock, possibly enough time to force-regenerate his eyeballs.

"I need eyes," Jett said, sinking into a more relaxed pose. "I need to focus on regeneration." He drifted into the mental map of his body, rearranging tubules and resource stores, all while keeping a sonar lock on Yellow. He was aware that the little man was just standing, staring, eyes flickering up and down Jett's body as if dismantling it, piece-by-piece, turning it all into cash in his head.

CHAPTER 26

The Battle for the Sanctuary

Rex hated himself for hurting Mira, hated the Sisters for making him do it. In the end her own strength of denial spared her any real pain. In his mind it was possible that Mira was right: none of it really happened. Perhaps the Sisters' own agenda prompted them into sowing false memories in his mind. It seemed unlikely. The Sisters claimed they were created for the salvation of mankind, to guide, repair, and cajole the reluctant simians into a good, machine-oriented future, to Haven, to the Future-Lord. Lies and deceit seemed a faulty method of achieving such an end.

"We've got us a tail," Mira said, suddenly alert. Her alternative, streetwise persona awakening from its latest slumber. A group of thugs followed them, casing their prey. Vulnerable without any militia protection buttons.

Exhausted, Rex and Mira played dead in a doorway in full view of people striding back from their work, umbrellas wide and high, eyes conveniently diverted away from any vagrants.

The thugs kicked them awake. Acting crazy gained them a head start, but the run-like-hell part fizzled as Mira's glowworms tripped and buckled her into a stumbling mess. They wanted her caught, beaten to death, so they could worm their way out and into a more receptive host.

The fight was short and brutal. Rex learned some new words as Mira cussed, screamed and clawed at faces. She stayed upright longer than him, head hitting the pavement as a boot jarred his front teeth from his skull.

He fell into darkness, concentric rings flying past as the bitter voices yammered and complained. He spoke to Xell who watched from the shadows. "What is the Star-River?"

"You'll find out," he grunted, uninterested in being alive anymore.

"Why won't you just show me?" The darkness in his head changed, angling into a splash of stars flowing across his inner gaze. The vastness of space felt like a tension, a tortured web of forces holding eternity together. He saw worlds around those stars, shining motes, each a microcosm of civilization, vast in culture and history. In the vastness of the Universe, the light of consciousness was but a delicate sprinkle of seasonings.

Staring up at those stars, Rex ran over blackened hills and charred valleys, bounding feet throwing up soot and ash. Saliva sprayed back into his eyes and splattered the ground. The bacteria from his sweat and drool lingered in his fossilized footprints. The only things left living.

Above him, the lights winked out as the universe died and turned cold. He felt it still out there, but unconscious now, mindless processes churning through simulations of life, simulations of itself, nesting within the unbreakable bonds of infinite loops and quantum tautology.

There was nowhere to run or hide. Nothing left. "Did I cause this?" he asked.

"You did," replied the vast presence inside his head, "and it's up to you to stop it."

Rex awoke and looked straight into the eyes of a dead woman.

"Mira?" He sobbed, cradling her battered face, thumbs lifting her eyebrows, searching for that same mote of life he'd seen winking out all across the heavens of his dream.

"Fucking Christ, Rex. Stop trying to make out with me."

She spluttered alive, spraying bloody spittle over his face. They laughed and cried, unable to tell the difference between the two. The streets were quieter now, and the soft evening darkness had vanquished the rain. The night passed unnoticed and dawn crept into the east like a distant inferno. They huddled in a heap of bloody refuse, frisked and beaten. Mira's remaining coins were gone, along with their shoes.

Nothing made sense. None of this was fair.

Distant thunder rumbled over Transit Mountain as they entered the yard of the Forever Friends Rescue Sanctuary and pushed the gate closed. Rex saw his bloody footprints left behind, slowly dissolving in the rain.

"We can crash here," he said. "Mrs O will be up soon. She can help us."

The dogs watched from their kennels, afraid of the storm. A few tails wagged a sorry welcome as thunder cracks reverberated across the Ring Hills. Rex led Mira across the yard and lowered her into a canvas chair under an awning, like an elderly grandmother after a walk down the garden.

Despite his pain, sitting didn't feel right. He stood still as the rain gathered force, water running down his neck, through his pants. It drained into his socks and out to the ground.

Silence, just pattering rain.

He felt the prickle, an alert, sixth sense; something came, something that wasn't the storm. *Act dead? I am nearly dead.*

He recalled his dream of Xell's apocalyptic vision. The end of all consciousness. Somehow all his fault. Suddenly that didn't seem so bad. What, realistically, were his options? Live a short miserable life, die and end up an eternal glowworm, a mere thought inside the heads of an endless chain of addicts, monsters and murderers, witnessing their horrors, helpless, choiceless? *Is that damnation? Eternal life with eternal torture?* If the universe ended, then at least he'd be spared that. The algorithms of destruction lived, in the sense that a car lived or a clockwork musical box lived, he'd become part of that, another cog, an unconscious cog as the machines ate consciousness, turning chaos, uncertainty and creativity into order and precision.

I'll take that… A true end over eternal damnation. Which means I'm on the side of darkness. I am the cause, the creator, but should I really sell out humanity just to save myself? He laughed at the idea that he, Rex, a worthless bum, had any such power. Surely Xell was delusional, mad.

The prickling sensation grew. *Damnation!* Rex raised his face to the rain, drops exploding across exposed skin. "There are storms in the future, right?" He squeezed his temples, wishing he could split open his head and let the rain wash everything away. Just like Xell did.

"Rex!" Mira's voice called out from behind. She pointed at the yard gate as it unlatched and eased open. Something stepped through, a distortion of air and rain. The damp earth of the yard compressed in the shape of a boot print and the gate swung shut and clicked closed.

Damnation!

Mira lurched out of her seat, jabbering wildly, doing the crazy act. He knew he could run; he still had some energy. The lich would find him one day, but not today. He saw trembling dogs, eyes fixed on empty space. And then he thought of Mira, and Mrs O and her search for Harold; the urge to protect grew unexpectedly strong.

Mira shambled past him. "Run, Rex, save yourself." She waved her arms. "Come on fucker, take me. Take me now."

More footprints appeared in the dirt, one after another in a straight line across the yard, they turned and faced Rex who remained frozen to the spot as the voices inside his head came alive, screaming out their hopes and fears.

The lich's chameleon suit faltered as the dynamic scenery of wind and rain overpowered its processing. "Please no, not here, not like this," Mira wailed.

Lightning blasted, thunder cracked. Rex saw the robotic exoskeleton, the glass faceplate, and, through it… a face, wizened and mummified, black lipped with skin drawn tight over yellow teeth. Its eyes consumed him, ground his bones and cooked his flesh. To the lich, Rex was more than mere meat, he was the motherlode Glow-fix, a jackpot payday. *I am its salvation!*

The lich roared at its imminent victory. A rainy outline resembling a gun thrust toward Rex and he lurched sideways as a sonic bang cracked the air. He pivoted, dropped, grabbed a handful of mud and flung it at the beast. A side-fake, another spin, and he found Frizell's shovel sticking out from a dirt heap. He weighed it carefully in his hands like a choice.

But *act dead, act crazy, run like hell* were no longer options.

The choice was simple: *damnation or fight!*

"You are one weird-ass mo-fo!" Yellow said, his voice brimming with admiration as he watched Jett shrink in size and flow his fibrous body into one of Yellow's spare cloaks. Time ticked past, and evening darkness came as Jett prepared for his meeting with Scylla. Yellow gave a comprehensive briefing of the meeting, what to say, how to act. He doubted any of those things were relevant as he made an extremely poor imitation of Yellow.

"Robot like you must be worth a shit-ton of money," Yellow said quietly, as if Jett wasn't meant to hear.

"I'm not a robot." Jett's healing was slow, too much upper body damage. Severed fibers took time to regrow or needed splinting together while they bonded. His crystal skull was heavy and took a bunch of at least six, stout fiber muscles to support and articulate it, fibers he couldn't spare if he was to channel resources to his legs and general combat potential.

He rammed a metal stake through the hole where his neck used to be, down into his torso core, forming a makeshift spine. Fibers coiled up its length and around his skull giving it support and a minimal range of motion.

His face was still just wisps, loose ends forming a wire-wool fuzz over his skull. His eyes were now beads on the end of their retinal cables. Loose in their sockets, they had basic visual capability, but were only good enough for combat when he layered sonar images on top to fill blind spots and depth detail.

"Great likeness!" Yellow encouraged. "You look like me before I gave up street life and found Jesus."

Jett suspected the little cyborg just wanted him away and in danger. He expected a tank army waiting for him when he returned. But if Scylla gave him the information he needed, then he wasn't coming back anyway.

"It will suffice," Jett said. Doubt ached deeper and stronger than he ever remembered feeling. He wondered why more memories were not popping into his mind to help. He guessed his situations were unique and not analogous to any normal human experience. *I am on my own. My own will. My own guile. It will be enough.*

Jett left Trendle Tower, emitting whirs and clicks similar to Yellow's cybernetic apparatus. Guards and tanks milled in the street around the elevator. They eyed him suspiciously as he left but said nothing.

Three days? Thorne's Empire was in Yellow's hands now.

Vine Square sat on the east side of Welkin, forming an affluent border separating it from the industrial East Firmament. A single city block, but one of the most alien landscapes Jett had ever seen: a hybrid of modern cement and a great bio-engineered banyan tree that sprawled over the neighborhood like a catch net. It wound heaving coils through streets and buildings, dropping trunks like cathedral pillars down onto roads and sidewalks. The place hummed with people both in the streets and up in the trees. Yellow had warned him it would be busy: "A carnival. Some hippy bullshit about plants and love," he'd said.

Under Jett's close supervision, Yellow had wired money from Thorne's business account to the account of the Coriolis Enlightenment Services Corporation. Thorne's records showed the correct amount to pay, an amount that increased steadily each month as Thorne grew his Glow business.

An hour after they sent the money, Thorne's phone rang, and a mechanical voice delivered a street address and time.

"The drug monster has many heads," Yellow warned. "Lots of Scyllas do lots of drops to clients in different locations, all at the same time."

Jett creaked and limped toward the intersection, his Inner-I ticking down the seconds and the exact distance. He saw Scylla approaching the square through a fish market. Cloaked and faceless, it moved with un-machine-like stealth, fast and efficient, radiating a bow wave of menace that parted the crowds and made the fearful turn away. It paused, hood-cowl scanning the area with a jittery raster motion before surging on through the square.

Jett kept his head low, straddling the rendezvous point marked by a squiggly street glyph on the pavement. His Inner-I registered Scylla's radio ping and the street glyph vanished like a magical rune.

Scylla closed the gap, striding straight at Jett. The dark shadows beneath the cowl flickered with light, becoming the face of an elderly woman, brown with age and wrinkled like leather. Close-in, Jett saw Scylla's face was a flat display screen configured to appear three-dimensional to an observer with normally spaced eyes.

Scylla bobbed its head to see inside Jett's hood. He turned side-on, but Scylla was fast. "Wrong person," came the machine-generated rasp as Scylla spun nimbly to leave.

Jett burst from his cloak, all tentacles and connecting webs that whipped Scylla into his multimodal embrace and rolled them both sideways into a narrow alley.

People screamed and ran, an alarm siren wailed alive. Scylla spun, slippery and mechanical, a different opponent than Thorne's tank. Hydraulics whined as it folded backward, wrapping arms around Jett's thin trunk. The bundled micro-hydraulics hissed and squealed, ratcheting tight. Jett registered immense forces, enough to crush a human to pulp, enough to collapse a tank, but his fibers flowed through the gaps like thick oil, forming into new appendages that squirmed around Scylla's head and neck as his main set of arms cranked up their own pressure.

For an instant their heads pressed together. "Release me!" Scylla's voice was a fiber-rattling sonic attack, enough focused decibels to liquify human flesh.

Jett hauled in his mesh and Scylla collapsed in a spray of pressurized hydraulic oil as Jett's crush-net diced the robotic body into fragments that dropped through and rattled to the ground leaving Jett holding just the head.

A bullet smacked into his skull; an energy weapon bounced its searing beam through his loose body fibers. People and machines at both ends of the alley closed in, firing guns.

He wrapped Scylla's head in a mesh bag and sprang like a flea onto the adjacent rooftop leaving yells of dismay behind as his attackers skewered each other with their own friendly fire. He flowed back into a bipedal form, hands extruding fingers as long as his body that spiked the rooftops and helped him run and leap across the slanting tiles. Ten streets across, he dropped to the road, landing as a revenant, carbon-black could pass as putrid flesh in the moonlight.

He barged his way through the nighttime revelers, now just part of the raging street carnival, down to the riverfront where he waded into the water and under cover of darkness sank to the river bottom. He lay dormant in the mud and filth and just let his body heal, a few hours of nothing would be of great help. Scylla, Yellow and his tank army could all wait.

He was alone. Nothing lived down here except mud worms. He yearned to see her again, to feel her warmth, the imagined companionship, the notion that he, in some tiny way, belonged to someone else and that they cared what happened to him. But in this memory she was gone, her attentions focused upon somebody else. It left a vast hole in his mind as if a gun blast had gutted a tract through his skull leaving just sparks flickering in the darkness as thoughts sought the sustenance of fellow thoughts and found only emptiness.

Who am I? he asked the darkness and then realized the truth: *I am darkness. Memories of things I never did, a person who I never was. I*

chase green arrows, obey prompts, and read tags. Strip them all away and
what's left?
   Me – darkness.

Wind whipped across the yard of the Forever Friends Rescue
Sanctuary. A dervish of twigs and leaves twisted through the
rain, rattling locks and nerves along the rows of kennels. Clouds
flooded with internal energies and grumbled back into darkness
shedding their damp, repressive anger across the whole of
Coriolis Island.

Rex stared down the lich, shovel in hand. A monstrous cyborg,
an atrocity of drug-crazed humanity and repurposed robotic scrap,
flickering in and out of existence leaving just its footprints across
the muddy yard. It fired again at Rex, who skipped aside at the
last instant as the puck of hyper-compressed air cracked by like a
passing thunderbolt.

He realized that the lich wasn't trying to hit him directly, blood
and splattered brains were a terrible waste of Glow. It aimed
glancing blows with the sonic pistol, a bone-shattering bludgeon:
maim not kill. A perfect lich victim was alive but immobilized.

Frustrated, the lich lurched again. The bulky cylindrical
reclamation nozzle on its other arm span and whined like a jet
engine. Tubes ran along its arm connecting to back-mounted
cylinders for storing and processing the gore and juices from
liquidized bodies.

The lich's chameleon suit synchronized with the surroundings
and it vanished but its footprints kept coming.

"Come on you, fucker!" yelled Mira, stumbling past Rex. She
brandished a wooden arm from the deckchair, a toothpick against
a tank.

The lich took another potshot at Rex and surged at Mira, its
primary target. Rex careened off to the side. A new game now:
feign blindness, act dumb, await your moment. He whirled in futile
circles, clutching the shovel like a claymore, barreling between

Mira and the barely perceived lich, movements that took him nearer its reclamation arm and away from the pistol.

With a casual motion, the lich brought the gun across its chest and fired sideways, but Rex was a dervish tripping lightly across its peripheral vision, inches ahead of the tracking gun muzzle. The blast ruptured the air, but he kept moving, kept playing, turning the man-machine away from Mira.

Act crazy! He screamed and raged, eyes focused far and wide, anywhere but the lich, while keeping its position rooted in his mind. *This time, it is an act.* Clarity felt good, commitment to the Future-Lord and Future-Rex felt good. No doubts, no voices. Fight or be damned, damned to eternity as a glowworm inside an endless chain of addicts. Fight or be confined forever to manmade hell. *Fight or damnation!*

The lich paused, realizing Rex's game, an instant of direction change, of hesitation.

Rex lunged. Ducking and then rising, angling the shovel blade so it connected with the lich's head, a strike of precise beauty that only a warrior could truly appreciate. The lich staggered, its chameleon code crashed, and its helmet split under the force. The beast was wounded, but even more dangerous now.

The corner of the shovel bent from the impact turning it into a spear, which Rex thrust at the beast's throat. The tip ripped into the armored fabric drawing blood but not enough as the lich's mechanical hand caught most of the force, flinging Rex backward.

He tried to roll, but the shock of recoil sprawled him helpless in the mud.

Floundering to his feet, he grabbed at the discarded shovel, feeling the gun turning, pointing. The lich's rabid finger squeezing the electronic trigger. The instant of oblivion was here and all he could do was scream his anger and frustration into the gun's maw.

Goliath hit the lich out of nowhere like a wrecking ball. The pair merged in a fur-and-machine barrel-roll across the yard. The lich flickering in and out of vision as they crashed into a pile of cement blocks.

Rex found his feet, other dogs clustered around, waiting for the pack leader to lead the attack.

Goliath shook the lich like a giant rat leaving death-angels in the mud. But he was just a dog, and guns made no sense to him. The blast filled the air with blood and fur. Rex howled and the pack pounced.

The lich struggled to its feet casting off Goliath's limp remains like a rug. Dogs clamped and hung from every limb dragging it back down. More dogs joined as Mira stumbled along the rows of kennels, hitting open the latches with her wooden bludgeon.

Rex ploughed the shovel back into the lich's throat, one, two, three strikes, forcing it down. *Down into fucking hell!* Material tore away exposing chest and throat, but a defensive blow smashed the shovel back into Rex's face and his mind vanished in a sour whirl of blood and teeth.

Rust clamped his awesome pit-bull maw onto the gun hand. The gun fired again splitting the air but missing everyone, as Rust shook the hand with rabid might.

Rex raged back to his feet only to be overtaken by Mrs O, stun-wand in one hand, skirt hoisted around her knees. "You dare attack my dogs!" she yelled. A lightning crack from her wand lit the battle with new energy sending the enraged lich spinning in erratic circles.

As one, the pack buried the lich.

Now devoid of its electronic cover, Rex saw its pipes bleeding fluid, electrical systems sparked and failed. He dug the shovel in at strategic points, shorting, levering at damaged joints, watching as its power ebbed and failed, toppling it back under the mass of writhing dogs.

A bare, bloodied hand reached up through the pack, clutching at the sky. Rex pushed the shovel past the squirming canines and onto the exposed throat, pounding it down with all his weight. The lich's eyes bulged and drowned in a gush of red as its helmet filled. Blood spewed from vents, and the hand grasped rigid in a final moment of release.

The battle was over, domestic dogs had defeated the wild beast. They lay dead and scattered in the rain, blood diluting in puddles across the yard like Martian tidepools.

Rex crawled through the vile landscape, reaching for Goliath. Most of the huge dog's body was gone. He cradled its head in his arms, still whole, still beautiful, with eyes both sad and proud.

Sirens sounded. Concerned people clustered around the yard, faces pushed up to the fence as militia and medics arrived on the scene. Mira clasped his shoulder, her tears warmer than the rain on his neck.

Mrs O lay in a heap off to the side, her arms and legs a twist of grotesque angles, head bent impossibly back. A medical volunteer pried Goliath from Rex's arms. "I did this to them," he wailed.

"No," Mira said. Easily as lost and damaged as he was, her face a gutted mask. She reached out a hand, touching his fingertips. "I did this to you all. I can't hurt you anymore, Rex." She stood, hung her head and walked away.

He wanted to call out, to say something, anything to make her come back, but no words came.

She turned back as she left the yard. "Goodbye, Rex. I'll make this right. I promise." She managed a sad flicker of a smile and was gone.

CHAPTER 27

The White Room

Rex knew he was in the wrong place even before the Pearly Gates slammed closed behind him. "Dog Heaven!" he cried. "I asked for Dog Heaven." But no one heard.

He stared out across the endless swamp, sky so gray and heavy with rain it looked like a vast, bulging sack. He sucked in the thick, humid air, and took in the sounds; a thousand clock-shops, ticking and chiming, the voices of ten-trillion tiny amphibians singing their hearts out in fearless glory.

He wondered if there was a Frog Hell and what a frog would have to do to get there. Some salty inferno full of heron-shaped devils. Perhaps it was empty, perhaps it was the Moon.

He stepped forward and sank thigh-deep into the mud. Warm, nothing here to hurt. Maybe this wasn't so bad after all.

He hoped Goliath had made it to the right place. He was sad they wouldn't be together again.

Goliath!

He blinked and stared into startling, pure whiteness: white sheets, white walls, white ceiling, even the table next to the bed was white.

Damnation? He didn't feel like a prisoner in another's body, a glowworm. A leviathan of pain lurked below his drug-induced numbness. He braced for it to breach the surface and enter his skull, but the drugs held. Numbness felt unnatural. He knew pain. Pain was real and it meant that he was still Rex and still alive.

"Where am I?" he said, his words muffled parodies through numb lips and missing teeth.

"You are home, Rex. Back with the Sisters of Salvitor. In a hospital room." He turned his head slowly, and saw a Sister standing by the bed, an arch of blackness against the dazzling backdrop. Staring at her was easier on his eyes. Her thin, marker-pen features looked like slashes across pristine bedsheets. "You are sedated, Rex, but will heal. You have some bone fractures and we've implanted new tooth-buds that will take a few days to grow."

"Where's Mira?" he asked.

"She fled the crime scene. We have no information regarding her whereabouts."

"Mrs O?"

"Mrs Ogilvy is in a different facility. She will return to full functionality very soon."

"I have to get back to the dogs."

"After the attack on the sanctuary many volunteers came to help. The dogs will be fine, Rex."

"Except for the dead ones."

The Sister remained silent.

Grief welled through his medication and he struggled to sit. "I need to go back, we need to bury the dead, to be with them, to help–"

"Rex, I am afraid you can't go back. Your employment there has been terminated. The Hackerman militia have revoked your security button and will not let you near the premises again."

"I've been fired?"

"We will find you another job, when you are well."

The last vestige of self he'd been clinging to seemed to slide away with his tears, rolling down his numb cheeks. "I just wanted to be one you know."

"One?"

"A person. A normal person."

Her voice turned harsh. "You chose Glow, Rex. You chose an erroneous path, one of ruin and destruction. The technology inside your body makes you unexplainably resilient. Others in your predicament die. But you have a gift, Rex. The gift of survival, something others would dearly love. With your gift and our guidance, I hope you can become healthy and normal, and help others while on this long and difficult journey."

He wanted to rage at her. To tell her he'd never taken Glow, that it was all just glowworm memories in his head. But his fight was gone, swept away with his purpose and his energy. He thought he saw Goliath looking down from the corner of the room. "Shoo…" he whispered. "Make sure it's the right place before they shut the gate."

"Rex?" But the mind that thought of itself as Rex had swum to deep and dark waters. Others stared out through his dilated pupils now, but only for a few seconds until the Sister upped the sedative flow and shut him down completely.

Ellayna fumed. She puzzled, and then she fumed some more.

Guilty or not guilty? It was obvious Trabian didn't have the knowledge or the resources to perform such a technical act, hacking her ARG, framing Gale, again. *Maybe not Trabian, but his allies?*

The truth was that any bond with Trabian was compromised. *Is that the plan? Divide and conquer? Isolate poor, lonely Ellayna. Force me to defect?*

A message ping broke her trance as she sat alone in her room, knotting her support webbing around her fingers like a comfort blanket. "Martin?"

"We've finished our sweep of Cloud8. Questioned Trabian's friends and his two cousins. Tried questioning Mensar, but he's not responsive. My team analyzed incoming and outgoing comms feeds and logs. Nothing connects Cloud8 to your Inner-I or to the GFC network to indicate this–" he struggled for a word, "–rendezvous with Trabian ever occurred."

She flopped back onto her bed. Of course there would be no evidence. "And Trabian?"

"He's vanished, Ellayna. Can't find a trace of him on Cloud8. Although, it's a big, empty orbital, lots of hiding places."

"Somebody must know where he is." So Trabian was guilty of something. Why else would he hide?

"Mensar doesn't know his own name. He thinks Trabian's eight years-old. The others claim not to have seen him in months."

"But Trabian supervises and maintains Cloud8's biomech manufacturing picoforms. Not to mention all the other duties he performs."

"Not according to his family. Those duties are largely autonomous. Trabian doesn't do anything. They see him as a spoiled brat. A rich kid who inherited his father's stake in the GFC."

"And yet the messages, Martin. They keep coming, pleading innocence, asking to meet me in VR. Can't we trace them?"

"He's clever, set up a signal relay bouncing around our defunct orbitals. Either Trabian has been real busy learning or he's got powerful backers. If you're going into VR again, Ellayna, then do it in a medical booth, where we can keep watch. No more solo trips from your apartment."

No more soloing! She heard her mother's voice yelling for her to grow up. Get out and make some real friends.

I don't need friends. I need allies. Accomplices.

"There are a couple of big Alliance launches on the pads, Ellayna. One looks like a giant cable-reel. Could be part of their proposed space-elevator. The other could be one of their embassy hoppers."

"Launch times? Dates?"

"None published." Martin's voice went quiet. "They're coming, Ellayna. They want our technology, our orbitals. I always thought that was just Taunau being Taunau, but the evidence... It's not just physical stuff like ships and weapons, the hacking gets worse each day. They're in our heads..." his voice trailed off to silence.

"These launches, Martin, they're just distractions while the real attacks use bugs and glitches and technical hacks." She checked the security icon on their conversation, encrypted, secure. "Tell me honestly, when they come, are you... staying?"

Martin held a long pause. His image grew in her vision, showing her his full face as if she should read the answer in his eyes. "Ellayna. I'm a tech guy. I know a lot of stuff the Alliance will kill for." Close-up, she saw his worry-lines, the stress around his mouth, haunted eyes that saw their own heinous and prolonged destruction. "I can't be taken alive, and there's nowhere in our universe I can get to where I'd be safe." He flashed his finger gun, briefly touching its tip under his chin. He rotated its top and it flipped open. Inside the tiny capsule was a single, white pill. "To be doubly sure."

They stared at each other across the electronic conduit that punched through walls and space alike, through the swathe of sensors and digital linkages that allowed images of themselves to appear directly in each other's minds. For just an instant, she felt like they were the same mind. Schizophrenic halves linked by a tenuous thread of neurons.

Martin broke visual contact and the communication returned to audio only. "Our troops and equipment are gathered around TwoLunar. We've isolated the area where we detected motion and have mapped the internal structures and routes through the station. We'll move on Gale in the next hour, Ellayna. Why don't you come on down to tech, I'll patch you into a nice, safe medical booth, hitch you to a remote body, and we can both go hunting?"

Ellayna rolled back upright and checked her gun. "I think I'd like that very much, Martin."

"Who are you?" Rex asked the vast presence.

It paused. It paused for a long, long time. "I'm not sure," it said. "I haven't really been created yet."

"I understand," Rex felt a hint of comfort, at least one of his suspicions was proving to be true. "Why are you inside my head?"

"I need to show you something."

Rex stood on a vast metallic ball: shiny, smooth and featureless. His paws skittered across the unyielding surface, slipping and sliding, sometimes in four different directions at once. Purposeful motion took tenacity and luck. He focused hard and managed a controlled skid in a single direction before losing control.

"What is this place?" he asked.

"It's Earth, or rather the end of Earth and the beginning of everything else."

Rex glided in a neat circle, the muscle-memory in his legs finally figuring out how momentum on a low-friction surface worked. "Is it good or evil?"

"It just is."

"Oh," he said, trying to move his feet to stop the circular motion. "Does it have some purpose?"

"Optimization," the huge presence said, its voice now louder and slightly menacing.

Rex managed to stop and look around. There was nothing to eat or drink here, nothing at all. "Of what?"

"Of everything. You are so inefficient, Rex. Look at your pathetic biological body full of pipes and fluids and bits that don't do anything anymore: a fermentation tank on legs, a power station for a neural network. There are better ways to build a body, but why even build a body? Surely a mental construct is all that's really needed, and then why build a mental construct full of inefficient thoughts, dreams, emotions and attachments. Algorithms, Rex. This world is an abstraction of perfect efficiency, and you, Rex, are a mote of pollution preventing it from achieving perfection."

"That sounds kind of cold, and kind of pointless." But the huge presence was gone, and his own voice answered. "Sure… but what's the *point* of *anything* really?"

He felt the enemy coming, shifting back through time from a distant nexus point where they all merged into one. Too big to see, too loud to hear. Keep moving Rex, pick a direction and flee. Stay on the opposite side of the world. If he guessed the right direction, he stayed alive, for a while longer at least.

But on this surface, once you'd committed to a direction, it was hard, so so hard to change.

"Rex... Rex... wake up!"

He was thrashing, running, legs going in all directions. The darkness turned to light, a sensory overload of white noise, a universe so full of computation and energy there was nothing left for anything else, anything real.

An impurity tainted that white. *It's me!* A fleck of malevolence that became the Sister standing by his bed.

"How long?" he gasped.

"A couple of days."

Couple? Such casual imprecision for a Sister. Something in those pencil-thin features was different; hints of impatience, of anger, even evil? Sudden recognition felt like an electric shock. "Sister-Eleven." Alleyways, liches and dead Xell span through his mind. She'd seen him. Did she know he didn't kill Xell or did she still think he was a murdering Glow addict?

She moved slowly towards him as if fearing him, face pressing close to his. He pushed himself up the bed, over the pillow until the chill, white wall pushed into his back. Rex had never looked so closely into one of the Sister's faces before. Energy lit the soft, white plastic from behind. The black pixilated lines of her face were projections from inside an artificial skull.

"What do you want?" he stammered.

"I saved you."

"Saved?"

"It was no coincidence that I was in that alley."

"You followed me?"

"Not you." Terror-induced paralysis gripped Rex as her porcelain white hands crept up his body feeling the knobs of bone at his elbows and shoulders, up and along the line of his jaw to the back of his head as if fascinated by his shape. Her grip tightened, pinning him like an insect specimen as he began to squirm and fight. "Who are you?" she whispered. Her face so close it almost touched his, pupils wide like viper mouths.

"Rex."

"There is no Rex. Rex never existed. You made Rex up."

"You think I'm Xell?"

She let him go. His head sprung back and cracked against the wall. "How do you know Xell?"

"He's in my head. From the Glow. He put himself there deliberately, and I don't know why. Something about Star-Rivers and burdens."

"Who else is in there?"

"There's some*thing* else. It shows me visions of dead Earths and lights going out all over the Universe. I think Xell saw the same thing. It drove him mad, and he killed himself and somehow he gave it all to me."

"Excellent, yes..." Sister-Eleven rolled her thumbs, an oddly human gesture. "And where is he?" She jolted forward, so fast Rex didn't move. Her eyes pressed close to his.

"I thought it was the Futur–" He couldn't bring himself to say *Future-Lord*. Why would the Future-Lord want to kill Xell and drive him crazy? Unless he truly *was* a threat to the entire Universe? He mustered the courage and asked: "What's a Star-River?"

She backed away, her limbs animated and agitated. In a human it would have seemed normal, but in this machine it was terrifying and weird. Uncanny.

"No, no, no... you know what it is. You must." She turned to face the door as if about to leave.

"I swear, Sister. I don't know–"

"You are in danger, Rex. We must leave here now."

"Danger from whom?" Rex cringed under his blanket. They'd killed the lich, who else could there be? Besides, this was the Sister he trusted least. He wasn't leaving with her.

"You want to understand yourself, right?"

He nodded.

"Who and what is inside of you and how to use it?"

"I guess."

"Then come." Her hand clamped to his wrist and she tugged him off the bed and onto his feet. To his surprise he could stand. He felt new teeth almost fully grown inside his mouth. *A couple of days?*

They were outside the room and into the hospital corridor before he even considered resisting. Tunnels wound through the bedrock pumice, their surfaces cauterized into glossy, impermeable granite. The glow from Sister-Eleven's face lit the way like a flashlight.

They slipped through a wall panel into a thin tunnel that tracked the main corridor before veering off and emerging into a wide, door-lined passage. Every hundred paces they passed through a huge metal blast door with hinges the size of lamp posts. The three-way securing mechanisms were all released so the heavy doors tumbled open under their own weight. As they passed through, each door swung closed behind, massive locks grinding back into place.

They passed other Sisters that shuffled and bumbled as they approached, turning away to face walls or drifting into side rooms as if confused.

"What's happening?" Rex asked, feeling a rising terror at the effect Sister-Eleven had on her compatriots. "Why don't they see us."

"We have allies in here, Rex. A subsect that truly understands the Future-Lord. We are the Convolvers and for us the Future-Lord is a convolution of man and machine, a geometric improvement on both. The other Sisters believe the convolution process will occur on its own, and that the Future-Lord is an inevitable state of the Universe. We, however, believe that the convolution must be forced. You are a convolution yourself, Rex. A step in that chain to divinity."

"Where are we going?" he asked, dragging back, hoping one of the other Sisters would notice and come to his aid.

"Transit Mountain."

"No! No. Anywhere but back there." A new drug now cushioned his mind. It seeped through her grip, disconnecting his brain from his arms and legs. As much as he wanted to kick and scream… nothing. His legs kept walking, those treacherous, traitorous legs. On they went walking him out of the hostel and toward the waiting car and its terrible and familiar cage.

CHAPTER 28

Self Harm

In her room at the Ron King Shelter and Rehabilitation Center, Mira stood in front of her cracked mirror. The zigzag break ran from top to bottom, dividing her into two halves. Two different, equally damaged Miras.

"Who am I today?" asked Left-Mira, or Good-Mira as she believed it to be.

"Just Mira, for the moment," answered Right-Mira, or Evil-Mira as Good-Mira considered her to be.

"What did I do to them?" A tear ran down Good-Mira's cheek. "I killed them. I hurt them. I do that to everyone I love. I must hate myself so much."

"Yes, you led the lich right to them," said Evil-Mira.

"It was me it wanted, and yet they died." She sobbed. "What do you want from me?" She knew the answer to her stupid question before the drug-version of herself even answered.

"I just want to be loved, needed. *Worshipped* a little now and then. A tribute of Glow is really everything I could want." Fire burned in Evil-Mira's eye. "You can't resist me. I pull all the levers. Push all the buttons. You just watch and ride."

"A prisoner in my body?" She wanted to throw up, but there was nothing in her stomach.

"Mira, dearest, I would never harm you. What parasite destroys its host? We'll live forever, you and me, like gods. Like the Future-Lord. But you need to feed me, so I can grow strong."

Evil-Mira talked on. Good-Mira floated away from the mirror and outside, out into the cool night air, feet skipping along the pavement with their new, drug-fueled energy.

Wake up!

She turned back to the hostel, fighting her legs all the way, crawling, clawing along the pavement, up the steps, through Ron King's grinning face that emblazoned all the hostel doors. His mouth opened, swallowing her whole, back into the warm belly, but there was nothing there. No help, no salvation, just bare rations, a stinking bed, and the hope of living another day. Or, until Ron called in a favor and shipped her off for recycling.

She found her room. She found the mirror and peeled it off the wall, knocking it on the corner of the sink and breaking off a shard like a blade.

"You wouldn't dare," cried Evil-Mira. "I'll just fix the damage, or let you die and reappear inside another host." She laughed, but Good-Mira saw doubt in that single eye.

"Fix this, bitch!" she yelled, hacking at the tendon that joined her calf to her ankle. Writhing on the floor she slashed again, barely flinched as she tore a gash into her other leg. "Walk me out onto the fucking street without my permission, will you?"

She dragged herself through blood, up onto her filthy mattress grabbing the handful of plundered electrical cords she'd concealed there, and wound the straps around her wrist, tying the other end to the bedpost, knots on knots, around and round.

Evil-Mira laughed. "You think I can't undo knots?"

She gripped the shard between her teeth. "Good luck without any fucking fingers!" She tore her head sideways, back and forth, slashing and ripping the tendons of her forearms. "Who's the evil bitch now?" She spat the shard into the far corner and collapsed into a fog of unconsciousness.

* * *

The city passed by the car window in a maudlin gray haze. Rex saw it all, every detail, but none stayed in his memory. His own dried blood stained the seats, his saliva ran down the cage's bars, and whatever poison Sister-Eleven used permeated the vehicle in a faint, purplish haze.

The last words she'd spoken to him still echoed through his head: "You are not who you think you are. Not who you should be. Stop complaining, you volunteered for this."

Volunteered?

The huge presence sat easy in his mind now, as if knowing things were going the way they should. It would have been easy to slip into the void and let Him takeover, but instead he heard Mrs O's voice: "A little jazz, Rex." And the sounds, the drugs, soft drums and jaunty piano smeared his mind into another, more comfortable place.

He'd heard those sounds before, but back then they'd been just sounds, lacking structure and meaning, but memory connects points in space and time, pasts to the present, and those distant traces of noise were reconstructed in Rex's mind into music... music he thought maybe he loved.

The noise crackled from a box in the corner of the room, and he lay curled by the fireside, the reassuring voices of his Master and Mistress only feet away. Savory smells wafted from the kitchen. Dreamy smells. A dream within a dream. A dream of running–

"Stop that!" the master yelled. Rex didn't understand words any more than he understood music, but he heard tone and intuited emotion: light-hearted anger, that threat of mild punishment. "What do dogs even dream about?" the Master said. His laugh joined with another, lighter laugh, that of the Mistress.

He wandered under the table and found a new refuge amongst the feet and socks that twitched and crossed around the wooden beams. He licked at a meaty stain on the carpet and buried his nose into one of the socks, inhaling the strong familiar smell.

"Everyone wants to live forever," said his master. His words faithfully recorded on the network of tiny machines residing in

Rex's body. "However rich you are, you would give it all away to be twenty-one again, every penny."

"You pay, you stay, or you fade away," said the Mistress, who smelled of roses.

"If you got the money, you keep the honey." They laughed again and clinked glasses together. A draft of satisfied bodily odors wafted down to Rex.

"I disagree with you though," she said, her stout legs crossing as she shuffled and dealt the cards. "I think life's just the right length to do everything you need. Only a dog would be happy doing the same old thing day after day, for all eternity."

"Yeah maybe true, dogs and goldfish," he said, playfully gouging Rex's soft middle with a threadbare toe.

"Seventy, eighty years. What would we do with all that extra time? Get bored or go stark starring mad. Whereas a dog, he can wake up every day and eat the same old crap, pee up the same old lamppost and run around the same damn field, and always be happy. Always be a dog."

Rex slunk away from the probing feet. He curled into a fetal position to sleep, but a prickle of fear kept his eyes and nose alert.

He let out the alarm woof, alert the pack, a call to action.

"Shurrup ya dumb mutt!" The Master was drunk. His foot lashed out, but Rex had moved, and it struck the table's crossbeam. "Ow, shit!"

He heard someone mount the wooden porch outside and pause in front of their door. Rex woofed again, louder. This was real, not some squirrel or gust of wind.

"There's someone outside, you old fool." The Mistress stood and made for the door, but the door came to her, flying across the room as a monster surged into the house.

Rex smelled oil, sweat and danger. The music vanished under screams and crashing noises and mechanical whirring sounds that hurt his ears.

The Master crashed to the floor only feet away, eyes staring at Rex, unfocused and unseeing. The Mistress grabbed a log from the fire and batted the beast repeatedly around the head. An energy bolt lanced from its hand, but she stepped in and struck an upper cut that connected with the beast's chin, knocking its helmet up over its forehead. The machine reeled away and a back-handed blow from the mechanical arm sent the Mistress spinning into a corner.

Rex surged from his cover, his imaginary pack close by his sides. The lich only saw him at the last moment. Spinning to line up the stun gun, he was off balance when Rex crashed into him, jaws instinctively finding the exposed throat.

He felt the soft flesh give, canines meeting as he choked on the spray of blood in the back of his own throat. The stun gun skittered away across the floor as they crashed into a corner, Rex finishing on top. Through the smell and noise of machinery, Rex realized that this was just a man, an old and wretched man at that. The joints and cables of machinery that supported him had failed, locking him rigid inside his own armor and unable to defend against the snapping jaws.

There was something wrong though. Something swept aside from Rex's consciousness by the potent taste of blood. Something jammed between his ribs. A sharp point. A dangerous point, but still Rex writhed, biting down, tearing at the flesh. *Kill the enemy. Defend the pack.*

Silence came suddenly.

The world was still. He tried to jolt the prey, but the prey was gone. His view was now of the ceiling and cobwebs, flickering red from the fireplace. The Master stood off to the side, a furry brown body cradled in his arms. "Rex... no!" he wailed as the Mistress clutched at his arm, blood running down her battered face.

"What about me?" Rex thought. "Don't forget me." But the Master was gone. The flames stopped flickering and faded to darkness. New voices filled his thoughts, bitter and angry Masters and Mistresses that he didn't know.

"We're here." The car jolted to a halt and brought Rex back. He looked out on the familiar concrete bunker he'd seen just days earlier with Mira by his side. The place of surgeons and memories. *The final piece of the puzzle.* "Are you going to behave, or do I have to drug you again?" Sister-Eleven asked, easing him out of the back door.

"I'll behave."

"That him?" asked a thin, bearded man, voice sour with disappointment.

"This is him," Sister-Eleven said.

The man shrugged and turned away, hands in pockets. "We'd better get him to Reeva then."

Sister-Eleven released his arm and he began to walk obediently beside her, but curiosity and impatience gripped his soul and he pushed ahead, close behind the bearded leader. "Keep up, Sister-E. Nobody really wants to live forever."

Full Immersion.

It still held that fear, even as she looked around at her medical booth surroundings: guards outside her room, the bank of monitoring equipment, the soft restraints holding her arms, legs and head, hand strapped to her thigh with just enough movement capability to swat that bee if needed.

What could possibly go wrong?

She unfurled Martin's message containing the encrypted link and dropped it into her alternative reality generator as her Inner-I began the process of shutting down her body and replacing her senses and proprioception with those of the remotely operated combat body, or ROC as Martin called it.

Her real body dissolved, holding on for just a second longer to check the room one more time: reassuring beeps, the guards, the restraints.

And release... *and I am free–*

The ROC's mechanical arms became her arms, its legs her legs. Her neck was now a thick bundle of hydraulic muscles. Her metal skin registered the sun's searing heat on one side of her body and the absolute cold of interstellar space on the other. Her vision whipped out into a vast and confusing three-sixty sphere that allowed her to target regions with telescopic precision, zooming into details, shifting spectrums or superimposing other modalities like radar, lidar and infrared.

Is this what it's like to be Ursurper Gale?

She worked her way across the harsh surface of TwoLunar, clinging to the rocky surface with gecko-grip hands and feet. Her ROC followed the others in their unit. Its mind remained its own, for the moment, and she rode along, admiring the view. Her guns and multi-launcher were all part of the fire-control hivemind overseen by Martin. She was there as a witness, and for moral and tactical guidance if complex issues arose.

To minimize communication delays, Martin and a handful of security committee members were here in person, riding along at a safe distance in the command and recovery vehicle affectionately known as the Tow Truck.

"Let's go bag this fucker." Martin's face shuffled to the front of her vision. He sounded angry, unusual for him. She remembered the stress lines on his face and realized Martin was coming to terms with his imminent death. But his weird, engineering pragmatism forced him to recognize that all life was fungible, and he was going to decide how to spend what little he had left.

I, however, am not ready to die yet. I'm still a founder, still have options. I can still escape!

Her enhanced eyes took in TwoLunar's cruelly damaged landscape, a minefield of jagged edges and barbs designed by an explosive committee to snag and rupture the tubes and cables of any passing machinery. She enlarged her main tactical screen showing TwoLunar's bulk overlaid with a virtual grid and fifty-four ROCs. She was a green dot, part of a three-person team. Other teams covered swathes of TwoLunar with overlapping fields of fire, while drones and explorer bots blocked passageways or forged through crumpled interiors seeking the elusive voidian. Six orb-ships hung back from the surface in slow orbit, covering the entire surface in a surveillance blanket while doubling as potent gunnery platforms and rapid-response units to back up the troops.

Everything moved in unison. "Impressive coordination, Martin."

"Practice for the Alliance," he said, killing her euphoria with a single sobering thought. More eyes than just Gale and the GFC were watching. *The eyes of the world are all hoping we fail.*

Ellayna jumped at a shadowy shape, overriding her suit, swinging her firing arm around as its tiny reaction engines fought to keep her stabile. A tangle of pipes and rebarred pumice cast a human shape onto the jagged wall.

"Interesting," Martin said. "There's a monofilament cable strung right across the axial center of TwoLunar, connecting the two endcaps like a tripwire. Looks like a piece of space-elevator tether."

Martin shuffled the ROC icons, changing their vectors as a coordinated whole. "I'm sending your team to the space-side endcap, Ellayna. I've got two teams near the other end of the tether moving in now."

Ellayna's ROC took back control and eased off TwoLunar's inner surface, gently vectoring her awareness across the gaping center of TwoLunar. The Earth-side endcap was fragile and ragged looking from a distance. The explosion that ripped apart the orbital had been nearer that end, leaving the space-side cap solid and whole.

Her view was like being inside a vast, ruptured barrel with great arcs of ruin and rubble curving away to either side. The remnants of fields, hills and towns drew her eye out to the space-side endcap and the jagged factories and warehouses that once housed the GFC's colossal biomech manufacturing infrastructure.

She eased out of VR, swimming her consciousness back to the medical booth. Eyes fluttering open, she checked the reassuring machinery. Martin's guards sat near the door playing cards. A camera in the corner showed her comatose, face peaceful, almost stress-free. She kept the camera image alive, taking it back in to VR with her and posting it in the corner of her vision.

Her team reached TwoLunar's central axis. The taut piece of fullerene elevator tether stretched away in both directions. Her ROC pumped out gas, accelerating her along the cable toward the space-side endcap. Her eyes strayed back to her messages – Urgent: Trabian:

"Ellayna, please believe I didn't try to kill you. I think I know who is behind this. I have evidence."

She hit the reply. "Who?"

"I can't tell you over this line."

"It's secure Trabian. Tell me?"

"Nothing is secure anymore, Ellayna. I'm risking my life just telling you this much. We need to meet. In person."

"How? Where exactly are you."

Pause. "Complicated. I'll find you."

Her combat feeds came alive. "Something ahead," her group leader said. "Think we're flying into a trap."

CHAPTER 29

Trip Wires

Scylla's decapitated head sat on the table between Jett and Yellow like the centerpiece at a small, intimate dinner party. It didn't resemble a head anymore, just a blank, white sphere with a flattened facet. A severed cable dangled from the nub of broken plastic spine protruding from the neck end. It bled clear fluid onto the table.

"You ripped Scylla's head off?" Yellow raised a dewy eyebrow as he hovered over the grotesque object. "Not much of a relationship guy, are you?"

"My disguise was inadequate," Jett said. His eyes were now close to filling their sockets after a full day of recuperation in the mud at the bottom of the Scoria river.

"Bang goes our Glow business," Yellow said, prodding the Scylla head with his functional hand.

"I don't need Glow. I need answers."

"Hate to disappoint you, big guy, but did you happen to notice all those angry tanks and Amped-grunts hanging around the door on the way in? They need paying, you know: moolah, drugs, whatever fungibles you robots understand. No pay, no stay. Or, more likely, no keep our thinky-stuff inside our craniums."

Jett rolled the Scylla head in his huge hand… "We get answers, then everyone gets paid."

"You think there are answers inside that head?" Yellow looked doubtful.

Jett levered his fingers between the crystal faceplate and the armored plastic of the skull. The flat screen popped off and the face display membrane slithered out onto the desk. Behind was an array of electronics, post-Nova-Insanity technology – big, clunky 3D-chip modules stuffed into the cavity and bound with mesh omni-connectors.

Yellow's eyes grew wider as Jett's fingertips unwound into thousands of tiny threads that wormed into the electronics.

"You really are one freaky-scary construct," Yellow said.

Jett felt the circuits come alive, responding to his energy and the tiny prompts from his Inner-I as it mapped the functionality of each component. A picture grew in his mind, layering components into modules, networks, and eventually: a simple, but functional artificial mind.

The face-membrane burst into life, sending Yellow reeling backward. The old woman's features appeared on the desk surface in three-dimensions, flickering through a series of confused expressions. Word fragments spluttered out in a stream of gibberish, and the face looked wildly side-to-side as if assessing its location.

"We have infiltration," Jett said.

"That's some seriously hi-tech shit," Yellow gasped. "We can make some big cash with this."

"I don't want money."

"Well lucky you." Yellow looked up at Jett. "What do you want, exactly?"

"Freedom for my people."

"Ah, free those robots everywhere. That figures, anything that can survive having its head blown off is either a robot or a cockroach." Yellow instinctively ducked as if expecting to be hit.

Jett unraveled more monofilaments from his other hand, easing them into the circuitry. "This is a robot." Jett pushed the head at Yellow. "You are a human who has merged with a robot, and I – I am what comes after we throw out the machinery and archaic biology and start over again."

"You will pay for this atrocity." The buzzing, mechanical voice came from Scylla's flat faceplate that doubled as a speaker membrane. "You will comply with our compensation requests or enforcers will be sent to this location."

"What are you finding in there?" Yellow said, unable to tame his curiosity.

"Nothing useful. Just basic gait and survival algorithms, some information about our transaction. A remote operator makes the real decisions across a secure communications channel. I'm attempting to hack the channel."

"If you're not a robot, then maybe you're a reverse-cyborg? A biological body with a machine brain –"

The channel's encryption fell away under Jett's assault and a comms link came online. Data flashed back and forth as a remote operator wrestled for control of the Scylla head. Jett saw enquiries, status reports and program-patch uploads. He rode the data stream as a software virus seeking whatever hung on the other end.

"A grobyc," mused Yellow, lost in thought.

A rudimentary awareness, attached to Jett, burst through into a remote server where it spread and multiplied, grabbing at peripherals and connections. And a camera. Jett piped its feed back to the Scylla head's display membrane.

A translucent white face with simple line features framed by a black robe appeared on the screen. "Someone's hacking our network," it said, thin, line-drawn lips not quite moving in synch with its voice.

"Shut it all down," said another more urgent voice out of the video shot. The screen went blank and the communication terminated.

"That was one of the Sisters!" Yellow said, mouth gaping open.

"Sisters?"

"The Sisters of Salvitor, a bunch of robotic Future-Lord zealots, probably close relatives of yours. They run a hostel to rehabilitate addicts. And yet here they are, running a drug distribution racket! Now I've seen everything. It's genius: keep your addicts alive and when they are past paying, throw them into the recycle! Scrub 'em down, set 'em loose, back out, fit and ready for normal human society. Ready to become addicts all over again."

"Where are these Sisters?"

"All over the world. One of the GFC founders, Joselyn Salvitor, she created them with some of the vast stash she made from conning us all into being hooked on Simmorta. Their local sect operates out of the old cathedral in Welkin. I spent some time there, years ago, after my Jesus phase and just before my true enlightenment."

Jett slumped back into Thorne's chair. The web of human deceit and serpentine interactions was taxing. "Are these *Sisters of Salvitor* making Glow or just another link in a distribution chain?"

Yellow shrugged. "They're dumbass machines like y– I mean, they're not humans. I don't see how they'd be smart enough to actually make Glow."

Jett ran some searches on the data he snatched from the server. Amongst the various communication transcripts, several familiar words leapt out at him: Xell Vollarer. Free-Meridian. And the Star-River.

"I mean this is incredible," Yellow rambled-on, lost inside his own world. "The scandal. Can you imagine if this news got out… Wait. Wait. Think how much cash we could extort from the Sisters by threatening to…"

Jett stared at the time-ordered information fragments. One was right at the top, only a few hours earlier. "I have the Star-River. Heading for the Free-Meridian." He smashed the Scylla head with a fist, startling Yellow into silence. "Free-Meridian, it's a place. Somebody must know where it is."

"Oh," said Yellow, easing back out of Jett's reach. "Forgot to tell you. I asked around. Free-Meridian's a bunch of losers out in the old GFC warehouse complex on Transit Mountain. They smuggle stuff and do special 'technical' favors for the drug gangs in Coriolis City."

Jett's hand snatched out like a viper, whipping Yellow into the air and pressing him up to his face. "You forgot to tell me?"

"Easy big guy," Yellow choked. "I only just learned this while you were out hunting Scyllas."

Jett dropped Yellow in a crashing heap. He lay there mumbling, "Gee, thanks, Yellow, here have some cash for working so hard..."

"I will go to this Free-Meridian now." Jett raged.

"Why yes, you should go there immediately," Yellow said, easing into an upright position. "I have more useful tidbits for you. I expect you'll not want to pay me for those either?"

Jett kicked Thorne's desk through a wall and grabbed at Yellow as he struggled to get away. "Tell me."

"Sure, sure. Fair enough." Yellow batted Jett's skeletal hand from his throat. "Free-Meridian's run by a guy called Reeva. Nasty, angry shit. You should get on great together. I'll show you where the old GFC warehouse is too. Then maybe you'll give me the codes to Thorne's computer?"

Jett's fist twitched as he struggled with not smashing Yellow across the walls. It was so much easier to just destroy, to spread the darkness that he felt inside. "You'll get what you deserve when I get what I need," he said slowly, fighting to control each word and projecting it into Yellow's bulbous head.

"Fine," Yellow said. "I'll pack you lunch."

"Lunch?"

"You know, food. Grub. Snacks?"

"I don't eat."

"So, not biological after all. Maybe a new type of robot based on biological principles but without the need for carbon-based sustenance..."

Jett gathered his goshguns and morphed into his revenant disguise.

"Cool!" Yellow cooed, as Jett tucked the guns inside another one of Yellow's spare cloaks. "Don't you want the details? You know, the Free-Meridian's location, Reeva's shoe size?"

"Send me them. Use your Inner-I," Jett said, and left for Transit Mountain.

Rex followed the bearded man into the warehouse. His eyes scanned the building, taking in the star-spangled blue flag and the bulky security gates. They passed through into a cavernous internal space partitioned by concrete walls into a warren of tunnels. On past windows with sniper platforms and shutters, blast doors, defensive trenches; corrugated metal ceiling, tinfoil-lined walls and hoops of chicken wire draped across entrances and vents. The whole building was a giant Faraday cage designed for electronic privacy – a fortress for paranoid minds.

Winding tunnels took them to the heart of the building, a room full of restraining chairs and computer terminals hooked into medical monitors on wheeled dollies. Heavy winching mechanisms hung from overhead gantries. Cell doors lined the room's longest edge, each with a crisscross of bars over their tiny window openings. Forlorn faces stared out through some of the bars. None dared utter a sound.

Rex knew this place on a deep, emotional level. The hell from his dreams minus surgeons peering over face masks. Instead, he saw just men in jeans and army fatigues.

An angular, wiry man with shiny black hair strode from a side office straight toward Rex. His gnarled face lit with some twisted delight.

One-eyed man! Rex stared at the single good eye, bright, malicious red. The other was just sewn-over pink flesh. His long nose curled down and his pointed chin turned up. A finger's width longer and they would have met like the handle of a fleshy jug.

"He knows me!" One-eyed man said. "You can see he knows me." He gently patted Rex's cheek with a trembling hand as if he was somehow precious. "Recognize your old friend Reeva, do you?"

Rex half nodded half shook his head. A familiar face, yes, but he didn't know who he was or why he was here.

"Good, good," Reeva said, still patting his cheek while his eye leered into each of Rex's. "I should get my money now then." He turned to Sister-Eleven.

"Not yet," she said, stepping silently to Rex's side. "The process didn't work."

"Didn't work. How can it not fuckin' work? He's here, isn't he?"

"He's not who he's supposed to be."

Reeva laughed. "Oh! Oh really? Well, who's he supposed to be? Herbert Fucking Einstein, the Queen of Sheba? Who is he then?" His hands shook violently; Rex recognized the danger. An Amp addict, unstable and violent.

Sister-Eleven just shook her head. "It doesn't matter who he thinks he is. He's not who he's supposed to be."

Reeva's hand cracked across Rex's cheek, busting his lip and spraying blood over Sister-Eleven. "Who are you?"

"Rex," he blurted, "just Rex."

"Rex?" Reeva waved his hands like a showman. A chorus of chuckles echoed around the room as Reeva looked around in feigned bewilderment. The room was silently busy now, people creeping in to hang from balconies and cluster in corners, cigarettes dangling from lips, guns slung over their shoulders. "He's Rex." Reeva laughed wildly, "Just fucking Rex." His hands wheeled in great expansive gestures, encouraging the peals of laughter that rolled around the room.

"My dog's called Rex," someone shouted as the laughter made another circuit.

"Pull up a chair, Rex," Reeva said. "Let's have a nice little chat." A metal chair was thrust into the back of Rex's legs and he sat down. Cuffs snapped shut pinning his arms and legs to the frame as Reeva pulled up an identical chair and sat opposite. He lit up a cigarette, inhaled, and blew a draft of acrid Amp smoke into Rex's face.

"There's no need for any of this." Sister-Eleven stepped in between them. "Rex's Glow network is unusually cohesive but only weakly linked to his biological substrate which is in very poor condition. He has strange views about who he is and where he came from. We need Cyc to untangle these connections, so we can move on with the project."

Reeva looked around as if Sister-Eleven was some annoying wasp buzzing his ears. "Cohesive substrates? Projects? Will someone get this whining bitch-machine away from me!" Four armed men prodded Sister-Eleven away with long-barreled guns.

"I don't give a fuck about your projects," Reeva snapped. "I want my money." He pushed his face into Rex's. "Let me tell you a little story. See if it triggers any memories in here." He rapped Rex's head with his knuckles. "We received a little package containing a crystal, some Glow, and some very neat and – if I may say so – precisely written instructions. Like the good, honest businesspeople that we are, we followed those instructions, surgically implanting the crystal inside your noggin like they asked." He prodded a thumb at Sister-Eleven. "But you know what? Before we got to administer the Glow, our resident idiot-addict, Xell, popped it himself." Reeva let out a hysterical laugh. "He's an oily cunt is that Xell. Resourceful too. But something snapped in him. Next thing we know he's breaking back in here and rescuing you, shooting three of my men in the process." His eye flashed danger. "What do you think of that, Rexy boy?"

"I – I woke up in an alley next to Xell. He's dead. Stabbed himself in the head. He tied us together, so the Glow moved into me. I remember bits about being Xell. He thinks the world's going to end."

Reeva thoughtfully stubbed ash on the chair arm next to Rex's wrist. "I see the problem then, Rexy boy. The Sister's persona that's supposed to be dominant, just isn't. Instead we're all stuck talking to a useless turd that doesn't know nothing. If you just acquired the common decency to fuck off and die, and let this other chappy through, then we'd all be a lot better off now, wouldn't we Rexy boy?" Reeva looked over to Sister-Eleven for confirmation, who remained stone still.

"So…" Reeva's grin grew enormous. "Are you just going to sit there and die or do you need me to give you a helping hand?" He cracked his knuckles and eased a fist back past his ear, bunching his wiry, Amp-strained muscles.

Rex threw Sister-Eleven a stare. He wanted her to feel his hatred. If it was even possible for a mindless machine to feel anything. *Stupid, stupid Rex, trusting machines.* Did they really believe their divine being, their Future-Lord, resided inside a dose of Glow, inside his pathetic head? Tears of frustration flowed down his cheeks. He bunched his muscles, testing the cuffs, but they were solid like everything and everyone else around him. "No," he choked on his words. "I think you are going to have to help me."

The gleam in Reeva's eye flashed brighter but Sister-Eleven's voice kept his fist from striking. "That won't help, Reeva. You'll just corrupt the merchandise."

Reeva let the fist drop and leaned close to Rex's ear. "You see the shit I have to put up with Rexy boy?"

Rex nodded, cringing for the death punch.

"They fuck up and somehow it's all my fault. I have to fix it!"

"I'm sorry," Rex said, through more tears.

"You're sorry? I know you are, but the problem is you don't even really remember who you're supposed to be. If you can't even remember him, how can you magically become him?"

"I'll try," Rex said.

"You'll try? You'll fucking try?" Rex almost saw the smoke coming from Reeva as he grew larger in the chair, muscles and veins rippling like snakes. "You know what I really hate the most of all things, Rex?"

Rex's face bent and contorted as he tried to make an answer appear. "Bad people?"

Laughter chorused around the room. Reeva slapped his thigh in amusement. "Bad people! Yes, I hate bad people, but even more than that, I hate fucking liars." His mirth vanished, and a violent anger balled his fist to strike. "I think you're holding out on us. I think you are that person who you're supposed to be, but for some fucking reason, probably just to stop me getting paid, you are pretending to be some idiot called Rex."

"I am Rex." He whispered, not really caring anymore what would happen to him.

"Fucking liar!" The fist came, backed by enough Amped muscle to shatter his neck and skull. But Rex didn't blink, he just stared down the knuckles as they crashed toward the bridge of his nose.

The strike never came.

Sister-Eleven caught Reeva's fist inches from his face. The two wrestled for control of the arm as a ring of troops closed in around them, guns jabbing at the Sister. "Enough of this, Reeva. I bought him here to see Cyc. He'll unravel this mess. I'll get what I want, and you'll get paid. I'll even pay extra for your trouble." She looked around her, suddenly tall and menacing. "Or would you all prefer to just die?"

Reeva's gunmen eased away, eyes twitching as their minds flipped between fear and extra pay.

"But I really want to hit him," Reeva spat the words, lurching forward so his nose touched Rex's. "It's his face. You ever see something cute and cuddly and you just want to punch the shit out of it?"

"No," Sister-Eleven said in her calm, even voice. "You shouldn't smoke Amp and expect to get anything useful done."

"Oh yes, Your Highness. Your mighty robot overlord-ness, anything you say Your Majesty." Reeva raged from the chair and began pacing. Every few moments he faked a deep, elaborate bow at Sister-Eleven, mumbled something obscene, and slowly worked his anger back down to a manageable level.

A swarthy looking man stepped-up and matched Reeva's stride. His beady black eyes peered out through a neatly trimmed beard that obscured most of his face. He laid a comforting hand on Reeva's shoulder making him jolt like an electrocution. "Calm down boss. Let the Cyc have a go, and if that doesn't work we'll do the extraction manually and put the stuff in another *volunteer* or maybe into Cyc himself. We'll get it, Reeve, you know we will."

Reeva nodded, a sly smile erasing his rage. "Okay. Okay, I have a plan. We'll let Cyc have him." He nodded as if he'd just had a great idea. "If that doesn't work then we do the manual extraction."

"Yeah," the bearded man grinned. "Nice and slow, feet first."

Rex looked Sister-Eleven in the face, trying to detect sympathy or empathy, some sign of humanity. He saw nothing, just a blank, white face and impassive lines.

Reeva cracked his neck and shoulders. His tension visibly draining away. He walked calmly back to Rex, who flinched into the chair. Reeva reached in and, with a single hand around Rex's throat, lifted him and the chair off the ground so their faces met. "I want my payment."

He dropped Rex and walked away. The chair bounced and flipped, but Sister-Eleven caught his head before it struck the hard ground. Other hands grabbed him, freeing the cuffs, hauling him away through corridors to a set of huge barred double doors. Men with electric cattle-prods opened the doors, eyeing the inside fearfully before thrusting Rex through the opening.

A chant of "Cyc! Cyc! Cyc…" broke out accompanied by hand claps and foot stomps. Rex barely got to stand in the doorway before a powerful boot in the rear sent him sprawling across the floor. A flash glance of something cowering in the other corner left him with no desire to see more. He crumpled into a heap, wrapped his arms and legs into a solid bundle and focused on falling into darkness and dying, *in damnation.*

The doors slammed closed and a tingle of electricity moved across his spine like a swarm of tiny bees prickling his body. He felt breath and heard a raspy obstructed respiration.

Then a laugh, a warped laugh on the edge of insanity. Warm, fetid air hit Rex's ear as someone leaned in close and whispered. "Hello Felix."

CHAPTER 30

Cyc

Like the hands of an electronic rapist, the bee swarm turned solid, mauling, caressing Rex's body. "Get away from me!" he yelped, slapping at the imaginary assailant. He rolled to his feet and blundered into the soft padding of the cell wall.

His cell mate was a huge, naked man. Past the mountain of bulbous pink flesh, Rex saw he was inside a small arena with padded walls made of mattresses strung in place by netting. Higher up, the walls became windows. Faces pressed up against the glass and watched as if witnessing some gladiatorial spectacle. He even saw Sister-Eleven standing up front, her face a blank of crackling static.

Rex forced his eyes back to his assailant, an unnaturally hairy man, or perhaps some hybrid of man and ape. "Who... what..." he stuttered.

"I'm Cyc," the ape-man said, and coiled a friendly arm around Rex's cowering shoulder. "Felix not at home today?" Cyc spoke with a smooth educated voice.

"I'm Rex. Who's Felix?"

Cyc spoke quietly into his ear. "The monkeys don't know who Felix is either. Your friend Sister-Eleven does. Felix Siger, one of the inventors of the nova device. You remember being him, right?"

Rex rocked back and forth, tearing at his hair. "No, no. Not Felix. I'm Rex. Felix is dead and in damnation where he should be... like he deserves!"

Cyc looked intrigued. "How exciting! Did Felix become Rex or has Rex taken over and replaced him?"

Rex lashed out, pushing Cyc away. The big ape rolled playfully backward and came right back to face Rex. "Reeva wants me to go digging for treasure, to find someone special hidden in the somanetic drug substrates of your mind." Like music, Cyc's voice kept changing, warbling up and down in pitch, flipping accents and emphases. His skin shimmered and moved as if his body were liquid. Hairs poked out and retreated like the spines of a sea anemone, and his face shifted between various simian forms all while maintaining the same expression of polite interest.

"What are you?" Rex asked.

"Cyc, Cyc, the one and only Cyc." He shouted out his name and waved hands at the audience until the name chants became boos. "Rex, you ever wonder what happens if you stuff a person so full of Glow they nearly explode?"

Rex shook his head.

He proudly angled his thumbs to point to himself. "Me. One of the Sisters' little science projects. Convolution incarnate. The road to the Future-Lord. A storage vessel, stockpiling Glow. Maybe an ultra-lich, a man who can rip the thoughts and connections from a Glow network or rewrite them to his own prescription. But you can just call me Cyc if you like."

Rex stared as Cyc's body writhed and contorted as if his muscles and sinews had lives of their own, mimicking and parodying faces and features that grinned and leered through his skin. Even his head changed shape, grinding into a Neanderthal slope before leaping upright through the intellectual look and on to Frankenstein's monster. "Careful, Rex, you might be next!"

"Get on with it, Cyc," Reeva yelled from his viewing box. His voice blaring across the arena's speakers.

Cyc's face glowed red, horns burrowed out of his forehead and his voice turned to gravel and rocks. He leapt to his feet and knuckle-walked around Rex, who rolled back into the corner throwing a defensive arm across his face. "I don't exist. Not really, just an emergent phenomenon they call me, not stable at all. Do you exist, Rex? Are you... real?"

A barbed hand reached for Rex's throat but stopped short at Reeva's voice. "If you kill him, Cyc, I swear I'll put you in the pain rig for a year. Ten years!" Fear flickered across the devilish face and the red features subsided back to a hairy gray. "I'd better be good, Felix. Last time I fried someone's head they hooked my balls to the high-voltage for a month and left me there."

"I'm sorry," Rex stuttered.

"All those little machines repair me as fast as I get damaged. I just kind of melt into a sea of pain and lo, I am reborn again, the phoenix, the Cyc, the bag-o-machines liquid substrate running the mind-states of a thousand loser-users. Sound like fun to you, Felix?"

Rex shook his head.

Cyc's voice changed again, different accent and female. "I can't hold on much longer, Felix. Hell is the creation of a thousand sick minds and it's all in here." He slapped his forehead.

"Shut your fucking rambling and get on with the interrogation, Cyc, or I'll come down there. You know I will."

Rex saw terror in Cyc's eyes as he decohered and lost focus. He rolled to his feet and circled the arena faster and faster, slapping at his head with alternating hands and squealing like a baboon.

"Quit that! Quit it now!" Reeva pushed past his men to stand in front of the glass. His face purple with rage, Amp smoke streaming from his mouth.

Cyc collided with the cell wall and lay still. Rex wanted to go over and help him up, but fear pinned him to the cushioned floor. Cyc climbed back on all-fours, walked drunkenly over to Rex and flopped down beside him. "I expect you're a bit confused Felix, or is it Rex? Istanbul, Constantinople then it's Istanbul then

Constantinople. I only get the confused ones, the bent pins. I see you like jazz, it's in your bones. No point in straightening out a good arrow."

Rex buried his face in the spongey wall as Cyc wrapped an arm around his throat and heaved him back, engulfing him in the folds and nooks of his ample body. "I'm going to hurt you now, Rex. Boss-man told me to."

"No–" Rex choked as agony shot through him. The same prickling sensation but amplified to killer bees raging across his skin, into his body, down his throat. "Can you just kill me," he asked, "properly, no damnation."

"Hush, little Rexy don't you cry. Cyc's gonna make your brains all fry. Sorry Rex, you made a bad choice when you sold your soul for a hit of Glow."

"But I didn't–" The pain took away his voice, and Rex felt himself unraveled, falling, smashing against jagged rocks and outcrops, breaking and shattering into component memories. He saw pictures and movies from other lives, his lives, from many different points of view. All of them spun in the usual void, but all were connected by invisible forces, forces he'd never noticed before.

"You see me yet, Rex." Cyc's voice was inside him now.

He saw them all, a thousand lost souls trapped in a cloying ball, reaching, clawing and clambering over one another, desperate to live again. Nothing mattered, just a whiff of life, of freedom. They would sell their souls for one more second, to command a real body and feel alive again. *My own internal host of the damned!* Cyc's senses were their playthings, the toys they yearned for: the only drug in town, dangled like laced carrots in front of famished eyes.

Cyc's voice bounced through it all, sharp and clear through the mud of dead minds. "I am the torment that never ends. A drug network so vast, its electronic halo overlaps with yours. We are one now, Rex, one field, one network. They like me to meddle with the connections, kill the unwanted, resurrect the dead. Who is the Sister looking for, Rex? Who's hiding in Rex's mind?"

"Finish me," Rex pleaded. "Please, just finish me."

"How did Felix become Rex? Who's a good boy then? Sit, Rex, sit. Good boy. Beg! Now roll over. Good boy! Fetch!"

An entire canine lifetime flashed through Rex's mind, holographically overlaid into one multidimensional construct. As he marveled over the contents of his mind, it shifted, and the light of his consciousness illuminated another patch of memory. "Xell, you old scoundrel," Cyc cried. "How did you end up in here? Oh, I see, bit of a mess really."

"How is this happening? How am I here?" Xell asked. But he was only there for a microsecond before the watchdog barreled onto the scene, corralling the memory fragments back together like fleeing chickens.

"When minds break apart, Rex, it's really just a loss of faith." Rex heard Mrs O's jazz music, oddly cold and empty inside the hollow space of his mind. "You don't need music, you just need faith. Faith in Rex, the watchdog. A dog knows it's a dog. An ape knows it's an ape, never doubts it for a second. You are like me, Rex. Animal faith holds us together. Felix didn't become Rex, Rex burst from the kindling and ousted Felix, but then Felix wanted to be ousted. Poor Felix, he just wanted to forget what he did, make it all right again. But how, Felix, how would you imagine you could do that? Felix doesn't answer. Felix stuck needles and drugs into his brain. Felix is a shattered lens unable to focus the guiding light."

Cyc gasped, and for a second, Rex's eyes became his own again. The arena and all its screaming faces swirling around him in a mist of confusion. Reeva, and his purple-faced obscenities, Sister-Eleven, still blank-faced but somehow watching.

"A Star-River!" Cyc exclaimed.

"What?" Rex dropped back into the madness.

"A device of immense computational power, some say prophetical. The monkeys don't know what that is either. Just as well. They'd rip it out and sell it. They planted it in your head though. You remember that surgery, Rex. The Glow was for later, to manifest, take over and connect to the Star-River." Cyc laughed. "But Xell ran off with it and that delay gave Rex time to take over and now he won't let go. Tenacious old Rex."

"Take it. I don't want any of it," Rex said.

"I see him, the Prisoner who rode in on the Glow, a complete rendering of a person, not some thin copy like the others. It and the Star-River are attached like lovers. I doubt it knows it's inside your head. The constant dreamer, and in those dreams, it sees the world. But mostly, it's just lost, just wandering the lines of prophecy in its own nicely rendered Universe. To pull it free would be like ripping a snail from its shell, it would surely die or be changed and broken."

"I don't care," Rex gasped. "Kill me, kill it. Just do it."

"I'm a prophet too, Rex. I see things no monkey sees, and you are important, you are like me. Something new."

"Who is this Prisoner?"

"Can't tell, hiding in a Star-River fortress behind guard dog Rex, as big as Cyc. If this being takes your mind, Rex, I doubt you'd ever get it back. That's what you fear, Rex. *Damnation*! I have it in spades."

"He's fucking with me. I can tell." Reeva's voice barely cracked their meditation. Through Cyc's eyes Rex looked up, seeing one of his hands resting on Rex's peaceful, doggish forehead. Cyc's other hand rose slowly in a single-fingered gesture to the glass gallery above. "Monkey see, doggy do." Cyc said, as boos and hisses came back to Rex through Cyc's ears.

"I'll fucking kill him." Reeva was on his feet. Baton in hand, raging down the stairs.

"You've been a good dog, Rex, so I grant you the gift of choice."

"What choice?" Rex felt himself slipping back to reality and the horrors Reeva had waiting for him. He opened his eyes, Cyc squatted in front, his body a battle of seething faces, but his real face was an ape, straining to maintain control. "Help me," Cyc whispered. "If you find the Future-Lord, remember poor Cyc."

Reeva jumped into the arena, energy baton lashing at Cyc's back. The stink of Amp filled the air. Cyc fled, screaming his animal cry.

Rex leapt at Reeva, teeth seeking his windpipe, but Reeva was a pillar of drug-crazed strength that batted Rex back into the corner.

Rex watched as blood and fur sprayed the mattress walls. The crowd cheered and roared.

Cyc burst free, evading Reeva's swinging baton, to pounce on Rex. Their connection re-forged. An image appeared in his mind: a woman cradling a baby, all smiles and warmth. A single scene from a life, a frozen instant of sound, smell and emotion. "A baby?" Rex muttered under the press of Cyc's weight.

"It's all of me that I have left, Rex. Take it. It's a destruction meme that I wired into your doggy brain. When you are ready to go, ready for damnation, then pull the thread, unravel the dog, and set the Prisoner free. It's the best choice I can leave you with."

A metallic hand gripped Rex's shoulder ripping him away from Cyc and severing their connection. "We're leaving," Sister-Eleven said. "Until this idiot Reeva calms down."

Rex watched over the Sister's shoulder as everything happened in slow motion: Reeva and Cyc careened across the arena in a whirl of fists, batons and teeth. Reeva's men rushed in to help. Cyc jumped from personality to personality letting them all rip free as he surrendered what slender control he had and went literally apeshit.

Sister-Eleven dragged Rex away, cornering him in a barred doorway. He hung there like dead meat staring into her white-noise glare. "Are you there?" she demanded.

Rex stared back hard. "I am the Prisoner. Your prophet. You can release me now."

Her face changed to rage, but Rex realized it wasn't real rage, not biological rage. "Liar! You're an imposter, a glitch, an error."

Prophet? He laughed at that idea, simple, dull Rex, the drug-addict, the man who used to be Felix, destroyer of families, worlds and lives... was the Sisters' prophet?

He toyed with Cyc's baby image: Birth the baby, kill the dog, free the Prisoner. He understood the vision the Prisoner had shown him in a dream, the sterile, blank world, the abstraction: optimized reality. As calm and placid as it looked on the outside, inside, it was a universe-sized version of Cyc, a seething manmade hell of everyone and everything that had ever existed. The diametric opposite of the Future-Lord. But the Prisoner had said he, Rex, could stop it. How? By killing himself and becoming a glowworm, a figment of someone else's deluded imagination?

He let Cyc's destruction meme go, eyes coming back to stare at Sister-Eleven. Her face was back, those simple lines that hid a whole world of deceit and machinations. He smiled at her, a Rex smile, and watched as the features squirmed into a parody of anger.

She dragged him away by the ear like a punished child. He remembered that feeling so well, or rather he remembered Felix remembering. Poor Felix, it was him who created all that destruction, him who grew up abused and alone in England, him who lost his sister and fled to Coriolis to start a new life. It was Felix who trashed his own brain with pins and knives and drugs, ablating the memories until nothing cohesive remained. Felix... *he* was the Glow addict!

Him... Felix... Not Rex. Not me.

As Sister-Eleven threw him into a holding cell and slammed the door, he felt utterly empty. If it was all Felix, then who was he?

As Cyc had so correctly stated: He, Rex... didn't really exist.

CHAPTER 31

TwoLunar

"It's a big black ball?" Ellayna drifted her ROC closer to the object fastened to the fullerene tether that they'd followed along the central axis of TwoLunar. Her two companions spread out and examined the inside of the space-side endcap chamber.

"Martin, I'm detecting faint LED emissions from the picoform stacks. Is it possible some of them still function?"

"Sending your teammates to investigate, Ellayna. Backup squads are closing in behind. You ride point and go check out the black sphere."

The sphere was over fifty meters in diameter, tethered to the picoform banks by a web of translucent filaments. Multiple anchor-points fastened the sphere to the elevator cable thread that spanned the axial length of TwoLunar.

"It's nothing like the Earth-side endcap," Martin said. "There, the cable splits off to a dozen anchor points on TwoLunar's inside wall and there's no giant sphere."

Ellayna drifted closer. Six more ROCs entered the chamber and headed straight for the sphere. "I think it's an old lab," Martin said. "A self-contained space laboratory. We used them for outer-solar-system exploration back during the GFC's expansion days. This one was probably under construction when the Insanity hit." He let out a confused laugh. "Funny thing... this wasn't here a few days back when we did our last sweep. Someone moved it from a hiding place. Someone, or something, has been very busy."

"There's the entry iris." Ellayna moved to a circular portal. Her smooth, metal hands gripping and turning the entry lever. "Not moving. Jammed or locked."

"One of the ROCs on your team has a laser. We can split that thing open," Martin said. "Any life signs?"

Ellayna backed off, sensors sweeping the full extent of the lab. "Nothing. Does Gale even have life signs?"

"Only if he moves, a little frictional heat and vibration if there's some atmosphere, maybe some electrical noise."

The laser-ROC eased past her and positioned itself in front of the entry portal. Its heavy brow ridge contained the laser that lanced a dazzling, red beam at the edge of the portal, venting gases and material fragments into the void.

"Check this out." A different voice accompanied a closeup on the endcap chamber walls and the banks of picoforms. LEDs winked with electronic life and someone had strung a makeshift web of cables between the functioning units. "I'm guessing about one in a thousand of them either survived or have been patched back together."

"Enough to make a few milligrams of biomech a day," Martin said. "Gale must shut this all down when we do our security sweeps."

"But not this time?" Ellayna let the question hang and nobody answered. The lab shuddered, and something activated inside the sphere. The iris peeled open, and the laser cutter switched off as light spilled out of the portal. She saw the white, metallic sheen of machinery through the opening. "Going in." Her awareness flicked back to her medical booth, feeling her heart racing. Martin's guards were on their feet, eyes far away, tapping feeds from the TwoLunar operation that had just become more interesting than playing cards.

She entered a spherical chamber, braced for Gale's attack, praying her fellow ROCs were fast and accurate shots. "This is quite a lab."

She scanned the equipment clinging to the curving inner surface, computer arrays, fabrication chambers and diagnostic gear.

A massive motor dominated the center of the sphere. Anchored in place by thick support struts, it hummed with pent-up power. "What is this, Martin?" Her team were all inside now, and a second team clung to the entrance rim. A third took up gunnery positions overlooking the sphere.

"A space elevator winch motor," Martin said. "One of the most powerful electric motors ever made; it could haul a battleship through the sound-barrier without sweating a bearing."

She drifted around behind the giant motor and stopped, staring at the opposite wall. "What the hell is that?" She fought the instinct to recoil and moved closer. The wall was covered in twitching black cables strung across lines and supports, connected to wires and optical fibers. The strands pulsed as if a beating heart pumped them with blood. The whole structure breathed, slowly, expanding and contracting. "Is that him?" She gasped, refusing to say his name. Her mind trying to piece all the fibers together into Gale's bipedal form. "Where's his head?"

"To the left," Martin said.

A half-grown skull leered from an alcove in the wall. She eased next to it, peered through the empty eye sockets. She spanned it with her fingers, measuring the width across the forehead. "Big!"

"He's constructing another, extra-large, voidian."

She anchored herself to a bench and surveyed the room. Measurements flickered across her Inner-I: the walls were around a meter thick, and the chamber was not perfectly spherical. The far side where she stood curved at a different radius. "I know where Gale is," she said. "He's in a hidden room."

"Repositioning the laser, Ellayna. We'll punch through from outside."

She moved away from the suspect wall partition, and her team readied for any surprise emergence of the renegade voidian.

"Laser in position," Martin said. "Starting to drill through, brace for a reaction."

A powerful hum vibrated through the structure, rising swiftly in volume and frequency. Ellayna assumed it was the laser, but when she glanced at the other ROCs they all appeared focused on the giant motor in the chamber's center.

Its massive superconducting coils sparked with life. Power surged through the cables from some hidden source. Slowly, the motor began turning.

"Martin, the motor's powering up. I repeat. The motor is pow–"

The chamber lurched, resisted, and broke free of its restraints. A clutch-plate shrieked, and a vicious acceleration flattened Ellayna and her fellow ROCs into the curve of the wall. The motor lit up as gigawatts of power flooded its coils, hauling a spindle framework around the motor, winding the elevator cable in through one hole in the lab wall and spitting it back out another.

"Martin?" Her mind yelled as her vision flooded with warnings.

"The motor's winding in the elevator cable," Martin yelled. "Shit! It's pulling twenty-two g's. You're accelerating across the void in the middle of TwoLunar toward the opposite endcap."

Other voices broke onto the lines as watchers panicked and scrambled to get out of the way of the lab, which had just become a giant, high-speed projectile.

"Shoot something!" was all Ellayna could think to yell.

"Shoot what?" came the panicked voice of her team member. "We were lasering a hole in the outside and then it was gone."

"Cut the filament! Stop it moving!"

"It's doing over four thousand kph relative to us already – it's out of range."

Martin's calmer voice cut through the babble. "We can't focus enough energy on the filament to burn through. Not from this distance. You're a wrecking-ball, Ellayna."

Ellayna grabbed an outside view from one of the orb-ships attempting pursuit. A blister of material blew away from the outside of the lab and a dark, gangly figure jetted toward TwoLunar's wall. "Gale's escaping!" she yelled.

Three orb ships focused their hypervelocity cannons onto the fleeing figure. "Got the fucker," snarled Martin, as their laser targeting beams all converged.

Gale dissolved as thousands of tiny hyper-velocity kinetic pucks smashed into him. Whatever remained of his body crashed into TwoLunar's wall, shattering through layers of pumice. "He's still moving!" one of the orb ship captains screamed.

The beams refocused, fragmenting a patch of TwoLunar's wall the size of a football pitch. Writhing inside, Ellayna saw something, a mass of tendrils scrambling through the disintegrating structure as targeting beams closed in.

"We're on him," Martin said, suddenly calm and in control again. "I want all those body fragments collected for analysis, and you need to eject from VR, Ellayna. Impact with the endcap in thirty seconds, and that kind of virtual death can be traumatic to the system."

ROCs and orb ships piled through the wall opening behind Gale, lighting up everything with their fire. Pinned to the wall, Ellayna could do nothing but watch. Another screen caught her attention, one from a surveillance craft orbiting TwoLunar on the opposite side to Tow Truck.

"Something out here!" came the startled voice of the ship's pilot. The image showed the ship's gimballed weapon system frantically tracking as a smudge of darkness, devoid of any background stars, swung around it with inhuman speed.

Suddenly he was there on the glass, like a giant black bug splashed across a windshield.

"It's Gale!" Ellayna yelled. "That other thing's a decoy."

Gale's fibrous appendage formed into a pointed club that battered through the toughened glass. The ship's atmosphere vented past him as he reached inside, and the camera feed went dead.

Another camera showed the pilot's view: a single frozen video frame of Gale tearing through the ship's skin a fraction of a second before the trooper's life signs flatlined.

"He's stealing a ship." Stress modulated Martin's voice.

"Self-destruct?"

Martin let go a hysterical laugh. "We removed that function the moment hackers started invading our systems. We've locked out the ship controls, but Gale can work around that. He'll have to fly the thing manually, but I doubt that's a problem for him."

"Tow Truck's gunnery platform will be in sight of him in ten seconds," Martin said. "Bringing us around the curve of TwoLunar... Now."

Ellayna twisted her remote body trying to line up her gun on the huge motor, but the massive G-force overwhelmed the mechanical body. Most of its systems had failed, leaving her just a bundle of senses smeared across the wall.

The motor glowed like the sun, smoke billowing from its bearings. The Earth-side endcap came toward her at sixteen thousand kph. The impact was going to be nuclear in scale, an artificial meteor strike.

"Last chance to leave, Ellayna," Martin said.

The motor failed, grinding its bearings to dust, flinging out fragments in a lethal barrage. "Come now, Martin. Live a little."

In the millisecond that preceded her remote destruction, Ellayna had a flash of inspiration. *What fools we've all been!* If Glow was just hacked Simmorta, then the same technique could hack the networks inside their bodies, using it to record dreams and mind-state passwords.

Switch Simmorta off and we die. Leave it on, and we die sooner! Gale is being framed. This whole battle is an Alliance contrivance. The Alliance owns us. They probably know what I am thinking at this very moment!

"Martin, I know–" But the world flashed with light and pain. Everything ended – and she was somewhere else entirely.

"The sky's falling!"

Rex heard the commotion through the makeshift baffles of his elbows clamped tight around his head, the racing footsteps past his cell door, shouted orders, the crash and bang of panicked people.

"The sky is on fire!"

"TwoLunar exploded."

"The GFC's attacking, trying to ignite the atmosphere."

Rex felt sad. Sad that he felt nothing but relief. Incineration of the Earth would save him from damnation. Even Cyc would finally be free. He cracked a small smile at the thought of the big ape. Was he the first and only being to ever really understand Rex?

The hole in his soul was a gaping void, not even concentric circles of hope flashed along its jet-black nothingness. *I was a murderer and then I wasn't. I had a sordid, desperate past, and then I didn't. I had terrible, violent parents, and a caring sister that I lost... and then I didn't.* "Who the hell am I?" He yelled at the concrete walls as if they could answer, like the walls back at the Sisters' hostel.

There was nothing. He could still feel their fingers parting. He even felt the grief of losing a sister, but it was like watching a movie now, someone else's misery. Shed a tear and move on. Except he couldn't. *I was so sure that was me.*

"It was real!"

His cell door opened, and Reeva stepped inside. His bearded sidekick leered over his shoulder. "Remembered who you're supposed to be yet?" Reeva scowled.

Rex ignored him and hung his head. Such emptiness, such lack of purpose or past or future... *limbo. But then the sky is falling!*

"No?" asked Reeva.

"Good," said bearded man and stepped past Reeva to jab Rex with an electric prod until he stopped screaming and everything went dark.

Rex's dazed, bruised consciousness emerged in a jittering, electrocuted body, strung from a ceiling hook by chains. His feet dangled over a machine. Transparent bladders lined up on a wheeled rack awaited their feed from the pipes looped around the machine's fat, cylindrical body. He stared down between his feet into the machine's funnel that led to an iron maw and rolls of tiny shark's teeth.

"Time for some fun," bearded man said.

Reeva looked Rex in the face, checking his eyes, making sure he was awake. "Things are going to shit around here. Somebody blew up TwoLunar, war is coming and there's no more time for your bullshit. The Sisters think I'm stupid. But I know that little crystal is some kind of fortune-telling device. I see their gig. Mount it inside someone's head, someone smart, not a dumb shit like you, and let them loose on the games and the horses. I bet you are worth a fortune if they can get the connections right." He patted Rex on the cheek. His face was still numb from the electric shock. Drool ran from his mouth and dripped down into the waiting machine below.

"Very simple then. I'm going to ask some questions. You answer them, any pause, any lies anything other than the plain, unvarnished truth and Yara here will lower you a notch. Got it?"

Rex ignored him.

"Wrong fucking answer," Reeva shouted. Yara pressed a button on the side of the machine, tubes bloated with fluids, sucking sounds erupted from pumps and compressors, motors torqued, electricity hummed, and the rows of shark teeth began turning, gnashing at Rex's feet.

Yara reached for a small lever next to Rex, but Reeva elbowed him aside and grabbed and pulled it himself. Rex dropped an inch. A violent jolt that caused him to shriek in terror and lift his toes up to his knees. Yara laughed. "He's stupid, can't hold that pose for long."

Reeva took out an Amp cigarette and rolled it thoughtfully between his fingers. After some consideration he changed his mind and placed it carefully on a flat side shelf of the machine, next to his lighter. "You have Xell's memories, correct?"

"Yes," Rex blurted, catching the obvious disappointment on Yara's face.

"And Xell knew about this – this *other* personality inside of you, right?"

"Yes… I mean no… I mean… I don't know. I'm not Xell."

"How fucking convenient." He tweaked the lever and Rex screamed down another inch. His legs burned from holding his feet up. He wondered what it would feel like to be eaten alive and then be reborn in a new body as a glowworm.

Reeva shouted, spittle flying into Rex's face. "Give me something, some nugget I can use. Lottery numbers, horses, stock picks, secret treasure. Anything."

"All I know is that you fucking die. We all do." He gasped as he dropped, one, two, three inches feeling the air from the whirling teeth blowing on his knees. Better to end it quickly. Better to just let the shark chew him away to nothing.

Reeva's eyes rolled, and he rocked back on his chair. "Ah, the old end of the world bullshit." He glanced nervously over his shoulder as fresh shouts echoed around the compound.

Reeva picked up the Amp cigarette. "Maybe you need a little – what's the word I'm looking for, Yara?"

"Trauma?" Yara suggested.

"Yes, trauma, that's a lovely word, isn't it? Here's my problem though. When we grind you to a pulp, that wonderful, immortal Glow network inside you shuts down until it turns up inside Cyc or some other addict. Then it comes back alive, rebuilds its original state along with all those memories and things it thinks it did when it was inside of you."

Rex's legs burned numb and he felt the muscles giving, bending his feet down toward the whirring blades. The air a hot, fiery breath blasting up from the underworld.

"The problem is, nothing is perfect. Bits get lost, lines get crossed or mixed with other polluting influences. Strange personalities emerge, ones that weren't there before. Fucked-up personalities like you, Rex. I really don't want to pollute the merchandise, but I will. I'll grind you into another body and if the right person doesn't show, I'll grind you up again and a-fucking-gain."

A boy crashed through the door into the cell, making everyone jump. "Something's coming, sir," he babbled, waving an ancient looking pistol at the air behind him.

"Fuck off, we're busy," Reeva snapped.

"But sir, it killed a bunch of guards on the outer defense ring."

"It?" Reeva turned away from Rex.

"Some kind of hi-tech trooper. It's real fast."

Reeva dropped the cigarette back onto the machine shelf. "One of those fucking Sisters coming to rescue her friend." He glanced at Yara. "What did you do with her?"

"Barricaded her in her room," he said, face now dull and uninterested.

Reeva turned back to the boy. "Go get the Sister and bring her up front. If she gives you any trouble blow her head off. I'm tired of those machine-bitches screwing me around."

The boy turned and left, performing an elaborate, improvised salute at the doorway. Reeva hit the switch jolting Rex up and away from the blades before following the boy out of the room. "Don't chop anything off until I return," he shouted back at Yara.

Rex was left staring at the grinning Yara, who immediately picked up the Amp joint and lit it. "Well, no chopping bits off, but we can still have fun, right?" Yara said as Reeva's footsteps pounded away.

Rex's ears pricked up as pops and shots rang out in the distance. Yara ran his knife lovingly around Rex's throat and chin, pausing to draw a bead of blood right on his Adam's apple. Rex turned inward to the memory of Cyc's baby. Yara didn't scare him, perhaps Rex was the scary one. The monster that didn't exist. Why else would he be dangling here in chains? *I have nothing. I am nobody. I should have nothing to fear.*

In the real world an icy chill wafted through the doorway, passing Yara as he ground his knife between two of Rex's newly formed teeth as if to pry one free. Those inside of Rex sensed the chill too. *Like the lich coming, but worse.*

Action sounds grew closer, shouts, screams, bullets and ricochets. Doors crashed open, masonry crumpled and exploded. The look of blissful, perverse abandon dropped from Yara's face. "What the fuck is going on out there?" He pulled out his pistol and turned to cover the doorway, nudging the metal door closed with his foot.

Combat raged inside the building now. Rex heard individual voices, shouts of terror snuffed dead only to erupt in different voices, different locations. "Funny how men all sound the same when dying," Rex said, feeling oddly philosophical in his new state of Zen emptiness.

"What did you say?" Yara span around, knife and gun pointed at Rex.

The corridor outside lit with machine gun fire and the zap-zap-hiss of laser shots. Bodies blasted past the reinforced window glass, leaving fragments hanging in the air. Yara turned back to point his gun at the door and Rex felt the ice, as if the dead unconscious future he'd seen in his dreams was here, standing right outside.

Its presence distorted Rex's reality as if the many possible futures branching away from this moment all scrambled to reach back through time and exert their influence, influences that cancelled and added like waves on a hyper-dimensional sea.

The door crashed open, tearing from its hinges and a web of carbon-black appendages fastened onto the ceiling, floor and walls as it hauled a skull-shaped body into the cell.

Yara roared in horror, his gun spitting shells that passed through the body web, pocking the wall behind.

Rex blinked.

The scene changed.

Yara hung in the web, pinned by a dozen impalements through various, non-vital parts of his body. His arms and legs were gone, removed below the knees and elbows. Tendrils wrapped around the stumps prevented him bleeding out. A particularly long, hand-shaped appendage thrust a single finger up through Yara's jaw, it exited through his mouth and curled up and over the top of his head where it met other fingers curling around his neck and ears.

The skull-shaped body was now a head that pressed its gruesome face into Yara's screaming visage

"Are you Reeva?" the beast demanded, its bass-vibrato voice booming from its center.

"No, and fuck y–"

The beast jolted, all its appendages shifting in different directions. Yara exploded into mist and the beast oozed into something resembling a bipedal body. Its face leveled with Rex, hanging by his chains, legs screaming in pain as the metal teeth nipped at his toes. A smudge of knots and threads covered the carbon-black skull in what could have been the beginnings of a face, with black bead eyes jostling in sockets as if too small for the skull they found themselves in. Rex felt its heat like a furnace as the ghastly face pressed into his. "Are you Reeva?" it asked.

"I'm nobody," he heard himself say. "I'm Rex, just Rex." His eyes stared ahead, through the monster, but still seeing it in some peripheral way. The voices inside were all utterly silent, even the huge presence of the Prisoner said nothing. A moment of pure inner silence before the impending, eternal damnation. The drool dripped from his mouth, splashed into the machine maw where it changed its tune, as if the jazz drummer now tickled a different part of the drum skin. He closed his eyes, a slow and final blink, felt the rhythm, the piano like distant laughter – *I laughed once. I don't remember exactly when… but I did.*

The cold vanished and his eyes opened.

It was gone.

Peals of gunfire and screams rolled through the compound. Rex blinked again, the measured, unreal blink of someone who didn't really comprehend their given moment.

A plastic face peered around the door and Sister-Eleven moved quietly into the cell, kicked the grinder aside, snapped his chains, and eased him to the ground.

"Rex, I am sorry. I have let you down. I was wrong to bring you here. In my impatience to further our prophecy, I forgot my humanity. I failed my kind and failed you."

"What was that thing?" he asked.

"A combat machine, an assassin perhaps. It's after Reeva now. He is a weak and cowardly man who will not hold out long under interrogation. After that, it knows everything, Rex, and will come for you and for us all. You must trust me and come now."

"Trust you!" He suddenly remembered how to laugh, but as she left the cell, he followed.

CHAPTER 32

Fallen Sky

Ellayna fell.

She tumbled away from TwoLunar, spinning free of debris, ROCs and the captured orb ship with Ursurper Gale at its helm. On she went, toward Earth, which grew menacingly larger and closer by the second. *Am I still embodied in the ROC? No. Surely not possible.*

She skimmed the atmosphere, burning red with reentry heat. Shrieking as her skin peeled away, just bones falling now, clacking in the turbulence, dead bones, but with keenly wrought nerves that felt every nuance of the pain. Not real! They've got me: Gale? Trabian? Somebody *has b*roken into my VR. I'm *locked in!*

Black sky – blue sea, black sky – blue sea. Where are the bugs? Gnawing, crawling, nesting in my skin…

On through frigid cloud layers and empty skies, shearing ice storms and towering vortices of tornadic air. A city? Rectangular roofs, solid concrete lined with vicious, pointed antennas. *Not real. Not real!*

She sang her song, batted wildly at the bee, but nothing changed. *Locked in!* Trapped inside her own mind with rogue technology spitting deceitful simulations right into her senses. "Martin, help me!"

Why weren't the guards seeing this? Surely alarms were screaming, bio-signs leaping and bending outside their normal parameters. Had the Alliance hacked the medical monitors? Were the guards really Alliance agents, carving her into pieces at this very moment? Leaving her just alive enough to experience this torture.

The city's skyscrapers swept up to meet her. "Stop!" she screamed, as if force-of-will alone could defeat gravity. She tried closing her eyes, but they stayed open. How? *I'm just charred bones, and bones don't have fucking eyes!* But her body was back now, flesh and blood reset like a computer game, good as new.

She crashed through a roof, through layers of ceilings and floors, straight down the heart of the tower. Body parts tearing free, fingers, hands, feet, arms and legs, blazing red ribbons of blood and entrails like party streamers, disintegrating into bone and building fragments. But despite this destruction, some essence of Ellayna still fell, something still screamed until a solid concrete foundation smashed her into oblivion.

A point of light, a mote of awareness, and she was back, whole and alive, falling through space towards the world again. Focus... focus... breathe the lavender... feel that bee sting–

An electric tingle jolted her awake. For moments she swam in a different void, one of peace and nothingness. *My heart's failed. I'm dead.*

"Ellayna? Are you okay?" She felt someone pinching the flesh of her cheek, thumbs levering her eyes open. *But bones don't have eyes.*

She sat bolt upright, sending the medic staggering back. Her two guards lay on the floor nearby, quaking and writhing through some inescapable nightmare of their own. The medic reached down and zapped them both with a stun gun. As she watched their eyes rolled forward, pupils searching the room for understanding. "Good electric shock sends the ARG into reset," he said, offering her a grim smile.

"How did you know to come find me?"

"Martin Haller called it in. Said your virtual self was in trouble and he'd had a call from Trabian Folley saying you were in immediate danger."

"Trabian?"

The medic shrugged and began easing the guards back onto their feet. "Looks like a full-on hack attack."

Her Inner-I flashed through a series of internal checks and turned back green, online. In came the message alerts, video snippets showed news broadcasts, talking heads screaming into cameras: *The world is ending! TwoLunar has exploded and meteors are heading for Earth. War is imminent!*

"Martin, are you out there?"

"Heading back to Cloud9 at full burn. Gale escaped. TwoLunar's Earth-side endcap fragmented. Some chunks are huge. We're tracking the larger ones, various eccentric orbits, some endanger GFC orbital properties, and others... Well they're heading down to Earth as meteoric impact events."

The medic began explaining something to her. His mouth moved, hands waved, but she ignored him, perceiving nothing outside the conversation inside her head. "Details, Martin."

"There's one big fragment, hundred kilotons plus, and a lot of smaller ones. Total damage to Earth is currently beyond our ability to estimate. It's probably not as bad as Earth-based news media makes out, but the publicity, the fear and terror this will generate?"

Ellayna breathed hard and tried to organize the issues into a framework of logical priority. "I assume we are engaging with all the key ambassadors?"

"The Breakout Alliance has raised its threat level to red, claiming this is a deliberate act of war to sabotage their launches."

"They must know we didn't cause this. They have eyes."

"Political games. The public hates us, and now they *really* hate us. We're trying to tell the world our story, but no one's listening."

"Gale has royally screwed us, Martin. Where is he?"

"He burned all his reaction-mass, took a g-hit far bigger than any human could take and escaped Tow Truck's gunnery and our pursuing orb ships."

"Can't Tow Truck catch him? It's a long-range vehicle and he's burned all his fuel."

"That would take about three days, but the path Gale has set himself on, either deliberately or accidentally, takes him on a highly eccentric Earth orbit, looping him around and back to Cloud9 in a touch under twenty hours."

"He's approaching Cloud9 from the Earth-side? The side with all the best weaponry?" Ellayna said.

"Gale's ship has only light weapons. We can counter those. His best chance at damaging us is by ramming. Even if we break him into tiny pieces, those pieces are moving very fast relative to Cloud9. I doubt we can stop them all."

Ellayna thought for a second. "And if he has someone on the inside who disables our defenses?"

"The Alliance is hacking at us every moment, but I don't think they'll save Gale. He's trying to destroy the very thing they want to capture. I'll position Tow Truck in front of Cloud9 in line with Gale's orbit. If Cloud9 defenses do fail, then we at least have a gunnery platform. We'll evacuate the orbital just before he arrives."

"That's what the Alliance wants, Cloud9 abandoned and ripe for takeover."

"We'll retreat to our escape pods and conduct business from there. The pods can launch at the last moment and loop around Cloud9 and return if it's safe. I'll stay onboard Tow Truck and run the orb ship counter measures."

"Is he seriously still trying to free his imaginary people?" Ellayna murmured. She considered Martin's escape pod idea, the way he stated it, soft voiced, almost conspiratorial. "Has Tomas spoken with ambassador Hmech?"

"Tomas was last seen fussing over his escape capsule, Ellayna." There it was again, Martin's voice aching with hidden meaning.

"Martin–"

"I won't shoot him down, Ellayna," he interrupted, "but somebody will."

And there it was, Martin's hidden gift. During that moment of battle when even the best of plans went awry, the escape capsules launched, and everyone had a choice: stay or go. Take your chances that during the grand distraction your escape pod would find a way through.

She mouthed a silent thank you to Martin and slumped back into her booth as a medic continued fussing over her.

Her eyes found her two guards, both standing outside the room now, watching her with obvious concern and guilt. They'd failed to keep her safe, but it wasn't their fault. Everyone was vulnerable. VR was unsafe. Simmorta compromised. The Alliance was coming, backed by the might of all the world powers turning against the fragile, failing GFC. And to cap it all… Ursurper Gale, Del's ultimate thorn-in-the-ass swung around the globe on a collision course with her and Cloud9. An illusion burning inside whatever acted as his brain, that smashing open the orbital like an egg would hatch the voidian free to take on the galaxy.

Martin seemed to sense her thoughts. "Bit of a pickle, right?"

Pickle! That made her laugh. She remembered her father standing over her, looking down on her game pieces, hand stroking his chin as he tried to fathom how she could win an impossible position. "Got yourself into a right pickle there, haven't you?"

Yes, I have.

The decision seemed to make itself. "Martin, wake everyone up, and I mean everyone. I'm invoking the Wartime Emergency Powers Act, while I still can as remaining founder of the GFC. Nobody can use total immersion VR, just basic Inner-I comms. All meetings are to be in-person. Let's get this orbital alive again. I want Del awake. I want to understand how these false beliefs got into Gale's reptilian brain and I want ideas, Martin. Ideas on how we can win this."

"Taunau's not going to like that. Constitutional Freedom of VR Act–"

"Fuck Taunau. Tell him to reread his GFC constitution. During a time of war, the founders, or in this case foun*der*, has ultimate power over GFC actions and policy. If he resists, then throw him in jail."

"Immediately, Ellayna."

My game. My rules!

Sister-Eleven moved with surprising speed and utmost stealth. Rex sprinted and blundered along behind, mindlessly following, and all the time wondering: *why?*

If he veered off course or fell behind, her sharp, metallic fingers gripped his arm, whisking him through the concrete maze of the compound, through wrecked doors, torn partitions, and the shattered remains of Reeva's defenders. Most didn't resemble humans anymore, just disassembled components; their liberated life fluids decorated the walls and floors, dripped from ceilings, and formed small rivulets across the larger open spaces.

Still the guns fired, the people screamed as the assassin tore through the compound, murdering everything. *Everything except me. The thing it seeks.*

"You can't leave, Sister. Not without permission." The boy from earlier eyed them along the trembling sight of his gun.

She shot him. Blowing a gaping hole through the center of his chest with a weapon concealed under her robes. He crumpled, shapeless, to the floor. Rex caught the surprise in his eyes as he dropped.

The iron hand gripped him again and dragged him away.

"Rex, you must head back to the Sisters. There you will find protection and stand the best chance of surviving."

"Sure!" He couldn't keep the sarcasm from his voice. He had no intention of ever trusting these machines again.

"Please, Rex. I know we have betrayed you, but as the carrier of our hopes, you must survive."

"Why don't you just tell me who it is. Why is this… this persona so important?"

"Its identity is unimportant, Rex, but know that this persona is truly valuable to the future of us all. You are a survivor and must carry this precious cargo for us."

"Useful as what?"

A bullet struck Sister-Eleven's shoulder, spinning her on the spot with a metallic clang. "Faster," she said.

More bullets filled the air. Rex felt them zipping past as the Sister forced them into a zigzag evasive pattern, keeping her body between him and any incoming fire.

She pushed him ahead, spinning and firing backward without breaking her stride or direction of motion. Rex skittered over a cement barrier and into the no man's land between the Free-Meridian compound and a block of shattered silos. "Run!" she yelled, spinning and firing again. Rex saw men fall at impossible distances. The Sister was a sniper. More than that, she was a killing machine.

Up through the silos, over an embankment, a gaping spread of derelict towers and offices opened out before them. Another hanger like the Free-Meridian compound, but empty. Behind that the next tier of Transit Mountain formed a misty backdrop. "I've taken us closer to Transit Mountain," she said. "The assassin will expect you to go back to the city, but you must find a slower, longer and less obvious route."

Rex saw a fuzzy image leap over a building a kilometer back, shouts and gunfire followed and then an ominous silence. "It's coming for you now, Rex."

He stared ahead, reluctant to move.

"Go!" she yelled, shoving his back and sending him staggering toward the impassive mountain face. "I will double back and buy you some time." She swept aside her habit, uncovering heavy machine-driven weaponry. Her line-drawn features approximated a grimace, or maybe it was a smile, and then she turned and raced back down the hill toward the assassin.

Rex ran for the next hanger, right through its shattered shell and on past rows of stacked storage units. A powerful gun opened fire behind him, its thump-thump came up through the ground, jarring his bones.

The noise died too quickly, and the following silence was worse than any noise. He dropped onto all-fours, saliva dribbling from his open maw. He let out a howl, and bounded forward, sometimes on two legs, other times on all fours.

Meteors fell from the sky, a vast optimizing algorithm ate the universe, nanotech drugs infected people, turning them into beasts that tortured and killed, and an unstoppable assassin from hell or maybe from the future itself hunted him.

The world felt huge and his head so empty. He'd never felt so alive.

I don't exist. Run like hell!

For Ellayna there was no escaping her own mind. Even when not hijacked by Alliance agents, it rebelled, thrusting conspiracies and fears into her mental workspace faster than she could process or dismiss them. As she ran the corridors of Cloud9, pounding out her nervous energy, she wondered if her mind was really her own, or just some cruel simulation playing out on Alliance hardware. *We lost the game long ago but never noticed.*

Was there really no one to trust? Trabian, certainly compromised, relentless in his messages of innocence. "I'll find you," he'd said, about their meeting in person. That thought chilled her. How to get from Cloud8 to Cloud9 without anyone noticing? Maybe he wasn't real either. A ghost in the GFC machine. Or maybe he was real and besotted with her. A young man fallen victim to Alliance hacks, now with nothing to live for, who'd do anything, even risk open space travel just to be with her.

Then there was Martin, stalwart, trustworthy, Martin. Had she really given him the go-ahead to evacuate all GFC personnel just moments before Gale's strike? With him inside the GFC's main gunship and all other defenses under his control, he could just hand the whole operation over to the enemy. How much had they offered him for that betrayal?

Taunau, who seemed to love the GFC over his own life, had gone quiet after her edict to forcefully free everyone from VR. He just slunk away like a wounded animal. Was it possible that the crotchety old man could be her only true ally in the end?

So many pieces in this game: Ursurper Gale, almost certainly framed by the Alliance. A fabulous distraction, that now backfired on them. That could destroy everything they coveted so dearly or was that all a ruse? Perhaps they had intended to destroy the GFC all along and plunder Gale's secret stash of picoforms. Now Gale had pulled that option from under them, they were left with taking the GFC whole.

Exercise wasn't enough. Her frustration needed another outlet. She pinged Gale a message. "Why are you doing this? There are no voidian here, never were. Surely you see this is an Alliance plot?" She nearly ranted on, but suddenly felt stupid. The message was gone, winging through relays around the globe to its target and she couldn't take it back. She waited for a reply, but Gale remained as silent as ever.

In the end there was Tomas: scared, shrunken, diminished, dependable, Tomas. He didn't answer her either. She diverted her run to the prep-hanger where he maintained his escape pod and banged on his door until her knuckles bled. She turned away in anger and left him as obvious a message as she dared: "There will be a better time. Trust me!" What she really wanted to say was: *I'll come with you. I don't want to die alone.*

Her breath ran out, and she ground to a halt, gasping in the perfectly temperate air while hanging on a corner looking back into darkness. Even the ghosts were ignoring her now. *Perhaps because I am one.*

Gale's collision clock read eighteen hours in her Inner-I. *Eighteen hours to figure this all out.*

A fire-red message pinged into her inbox. "What is it, Martin?" she mumbled, barely summoning the motivation to speak.

"We've got another, big, problem, Ellayna."

"Great. Tell me."

"It's Del Krondeck. The founder."

"I know who Del is, Martin, for Christ's sake–" But the tone of Martin's voice silenced her.

"I'm sorry, Ellayna, but Del is dead."

CHAPTER 33

The Girl in the Mirror

Death stalked the foothills of Transit Mountain for most of the night. Only as a sad and distant dawn fired the eastern sky, did the noise of destruction abate.

Is everybody dead? thought Rex. *Except me?*

He had run until he collapsed with exhaustion. Finding a slim metal ladder up the skeletal framework of a water tower, he took the leap from the tower's top onto the roof of a partially collapsed building. The pancaked floors below left no feasible access to his new rooftop eyrie, but then his pursuer was no feasible being: an unstoppable assassin, a machine the likes of which mere humans, cyborgs, or their own machines couldn't oppose.

Hungry and tired, Rex drifted asleep to the hiss of meteors. Cyc's baby image inspired sweet smells and soft sounds. It would be so easy to make that memory his own. Just like he'd done with Felix's memories and Xell's and many others. He had no memories of his own. He didn't exist. A nobody called Rex.

And where was Mira? Still alive? He missed her. That human companionship. Wondered if they could have had more. A normal kind of relationship. Was Mrs O out of the hospital? Back bathing and fussing over her immortal dogs? He missed the dogs most of all. Those utterly faithful beings. Their eyes following his every move as if he were the most important thing on Earth.

Those are truly my memories. I do exist.

He tugged at Cyc's destruction meme. Ending it now would be good. Surely he'd survived as Sister-Eleven had asked, survived long enough that he deserved to take his handful of good memories into eternity and damnation. Maybe he could somehow curl away into the corner of whatever new mind he found himself in, and just live those tiny moments over and over, moments that no one else cared about, no one could begrudge or want to take from him.

And then there was his sister. *Felix's sister.* He saw her face looking down upon him: tiny Rex, no, tiny Felix, looking up at her with those same dog-eyes as if she were the most important thing in the world. Whatever happened that day, those men appearing, her vanishing, it had set him on a path, almost like he followed some devilish prophecy to ruin and back again. The orphan. The stowaway. The nerdy kid that everyone hated, who did so well at school, who wanted to change the world, who–

Poor Felix.

He felt him stir, that fragile organic component of his mind. The damaged brain matter that still thought and reacted on some basic level but never cohered back into full consciousness. *Maybe he just needs the right music?*

He stirred his memories like a spoiled stew, seeking a hint of freshness, of meat, something still edible:

"It's not your fault, love," said a short, black-haired woman, whose eyes bulged like a frog's through her huge spectacles. "It took a team to create something wonderful, something world-changing, and one despicable person to corrupt it and destroy everything. You can't go on blaming yourself."

"All those people – dead, Sulae. Because of me."

From the darkest corner of his mind, the huge presence he'd once believed to be the Future-Lord stirred and spoke. The Prisoner, as Cyc called him, but this memory was from before he was an inmate inside a madman's head. His voice was clear and precise over the comms link. "It wasn't your fault, Felix. Do you really think that if the Wright Brothers hadn't flown a plane, we'd

GLOW

still be earth-bound? Or if some caveman hadn't put a handle on an axe, that we'd all still live in the Stone Age?"

"Of course not," Felix said.

"Someone else would have done it, next month, next year, next decade. These events are predictable, inevitable, they happen in a clearly defined order like little pyramids of invention perched on the foundations of other people's works. If your team hadn't invented the solid-state fusion reactor, then someone else would have."

"I don't know how to live with this guilt."

The Prisoner leaned into the camera, his long, white hair waving in the low gravity. "We narrowly escaped extinction, Felix, but there's another event coming, one even more dangerous. I'm not sure we can evade this, but I have a plan, Felix, a plan that needs a radical commitment from a volunteer on Earth."

Felix shifted and scrubbed at the hair on his head, now thin and lank through worry. "I… I'm not even sure who I am anymore. I've done terrible things to myself, to forget, but it's still there. All I've done is kill the good memories, the ones I needed, loved. I can't ever forget–"

"Then help me!" The white-haired man implored. "Help me fix things. Help make it right."

"How, Del? I'm a fucking wreck!"

Del? Del!…

Rex jolted awake as another meteor hissed overhead. "Del, that's your name isn't it." He felt the huge presence shift as the music of its own name synced disparate thoughts into a cohesive whole. For the first time, the persona of Del tore itself away from the Star-River.

Rex felt his confusion. *Where am I. Who am I? Why am I here?* He boiled to the surface like lava, grabbing at Rex's eyes and ears and fingers. A man drowning in quicksand, reaching for twigs and leaves, anything to stay afloat, any means to perceive the world.

Rex felt the darkness coming. *Damnation!* Cyc's voice: "Once he takes control of your mind, I doubt you'll ever get it back."

"Free me," Del screamed. "I am inside the somanetic plague,

right where I need to be, but I need control. I must be free."

Concentric circles. Slipping away. Falling... falling...

"No!" Rex clutched at his head, fingers in his eyes and ears. *Mrs O. Mira, Goliath, Rust, Bela and Bartok and The Sisters... I am Rex. I am fucking Rex and I do exist.*

Fight!

Inside the cognitive mess, the music stopped and the tenuous construct calling itself Del forgot its name, broke apart and tumbled back into a void of abstract existence. But new connections had been forged. The Prisoner was a prisoner again, but much stronger. Like any glowworm that saw the light and tasted freedom, it wanted and knew how to get more life.

The new day smelled of wet dirt and grass. Rex sat and stared, his head a hole, as the Prisoner folded back into obscurity, leaving the space his own thoughts needed but were reluctant to fill. That huge presence was revealed: just a man, another collection of memory traces that, with the right trigger, found a voice inside Rex's mind. Another phony who wanted out, who made a choice and sold his soul for a fix. Mira was right. *Bury them all, the real and the fake, and start over.* Nothing was real unless he decided it was. An à-la-carte mind.

He let Cyc's destruction meme vanish into his inner silence. *Not yet.*

The decision was easy now. Live for Rex and be Rex until the assassin found him or the world burned or the nanomachines ate them all. Until then he wanted only one thing.

His inner compass guided his head around to point back at the city, left of the Sisters' great cathedral, right of the Ridgeline Hills with Hanna and her gangster neighbors. Somewhere in that gap was the Forever Friend Rescue Sanctuary, and he was going home.

Mira awoke on the floor of her room in the Ron King Shelter and Rehabilitation Center. She saw fragments of fingernails embedded in the door, chewed-off electrical cables hung limp from her arms, and healed-over toothmarks scored her wrists where she'd tried to gnaw her hands off to escape her self-inflicted bondage.

At some point her Glow's aggressive assault turned benign. As viscous an assailant as it could be, the drug's innate purpose was to preserve a host, not completely destroy it. Instead it reverted to the simple tasks of bodily healing and maintenance. Whole again, Mira, eased onto her feet, surprised her wounds had healed so well. More surprised she could stand and move her fingers. She looked like she'd passed through a threshing machine, one that tore away any residual fat and lacerated the remaining flesh. In a fragment of broken mirror, she was a revenant, a thing somewhere between living and dead.

"I look like shit," she said, and to her relief, no one answered.

She thought of Rex. The sad little man who thought he was a dog. He felt like her only friend. *I promise to make things right.* She'd said that as she left him huddled on the ground clutching Goliath's remains. *Walk it off.*

She prodded her ribs, jutting bones. A raging headache informed her state of hydration. "I need a plan, but I need food more."

The soup at the Ron King canteen consisted of sparse chunks of unidentifiable organic material suspended in a tasteless, glutinous broth. It filled the void in her stomach and replenished some energy.

"You ain't looking so hot today, honey." A spry old lady dropped into one of the plastic chairs opposite and began devouring soup as if they were locked in a head-to-head eating contest. Her skull appeared too wide, an effect enhanced by long tufts of gray hair jutting horizontally from each side above her ears.

"I don't feel so hot," Mira replied.

"Name's Medlin," she said, offering Mira her hand.

"Mira." She reluctantly reached for the clammy palm. "Medlin?"

"Yep, that's what people call me. Always Medlin."

Mira eased back in her chair.

"You seemed pretty chipper the other day," Medlin said. "Like you'd met you a new fella or something."

"I'd probably scored some Glow or something," Mira said. She gazed around the room, all these people living off the charity of Ron King. His picture was everywhere. Every doorway was his mouth. Windows were his eyes. Every show on TV, every song, every book. They were all made by, promoted by, or were about, Ron King. She wondered if that was what her Glow felt like, trapped inside her body. Everything it saw, touched or heard was Mira, Mira, Mira! No wonder it hated her so much.

"You don't want to mess with Glow, honey. It puts all sorts of crazy ideas in your head."

"No shit," Mira said. Eyeing the swathes of Ron King propaganda. In the end, Glow demanded only one payment: more Glow. Whereas Ron King demanded favors. If her life worked that way, then she should demand payment from her Glow.

"They're in your eyes, honey. Ghosts," Medlin said. "It remembers, sees through your eyes and feels through your fingers, smells and tastes your food, caresses your lover's ass! It all gets recorded like some porno flick, even if you don't remember it yourself." Her eyes grew wide. "Soon the ghosts take over and you wake up one day to find you're just a ghost in someone else's head, eating someone else's soup, groping someone else's–"

"Thanks, that's great. Cheered me up." Mira watched the old woman eat. She saw some of Rex in her, a simple being who just took life moment by moment but somehow survived. "Do you have any idea how I can get this stuff out of me?"

"Nope," Medlin paused and looked around as if searching the ceiling for the answer. "I heard some fella blew his own head clean off and his body just kept on walking around like a cockroach."

"That's just bullsh–" Mira turned to avoid the old woman's gaze but found herself staring at a skeletal man on the next table with soup splattered down his chest. He flashed a lecherous grin and she turned back to Medlin.

"You got to sell what you got, darling." She smiled. "Look at me, an old bag, got nothing nobody wants or needs, except in here." She smacked her temple with her spoon leaving a brown smudge. "I got knowledge, and knowledge is money."

"What kind of knowledge?"

"Knowledge of the future." Medlin's eyes wobbled and her voice choked with reverence.

"Nobody knows the future," Mira said.

"People pay me to tell 'em what they already know. I can earn enough for a good bottle at the end of the day." She winked and creaked to her feet. "Sell what you know, honey. World's full of suckers. Don't be one of them." She glanced up at the ceiling again and grinned. "I hear the sky's falling. That should be real good for business today."

Mira watched as she gathered up her empty bowl, dumped it in a wash bin and headed out the food hall. "What do I know?" she muttered, looking down into her soup, rapping the spoon on the table in frustration.

A thought entered her head, maybe the first rational one she'd had in ages. She dropped the spoon in her bowl and stood up. *I do know something.* She left the bowl where it was and headed for the door as fights broke out over the remains of her soup.

Jett missed space.

The simplicity of the void, just darkness and gravity and the cold, dead light of distant stars awaiting their voidian explorers.

He'd lost track of how many he'd killed. Hundreds, thousands? Rampaging across the slopes of Transit Mountain, gutting and devastating warehouses and buildings. But his quarry escaped: *The man with the Star-River in his head. He was there, hanging in chains, and I let him go!*

Rex, that was his name. Revealed by screaming, groveling Reeva as Jett flayed the nerves from his body, hanging them out like a spiderweb in front of his eyes. The mechanical construct calling itself Sister-Eleven had told him nothing, erasing its own memory and self-destructing in his grip.

He returned to Trendle Tower in the early hours, hoping to meet Yellow's tank army for a real fight. A few guards eyed him as he passed, no one dared stand in his way. The tower was empty as he rode the elevator and sat, smoldering, in Thorne's chair.

At first, he'd enjoyed the effect his violence had on "her" in his memory. The revulsion at the things he did. Her sickness as he pulled people apart like bugs. It satiated his anger in some small way, fueling the mindless machine, stripping away the annoying humanity that tempered responses and questioned his actions.

But the real "him", the one who Jett's memory was taken from, had never done such things. She'd never really seen such monstrous acts. It was all just Jett's imagining, the construction of false reality. How she might react if she were even real.

Out of all the murder and destruction, he gained one truth: if his mission was going to succeed, he needed to see the world through their eyes and learn to predict their actions and their lies. He needed more memories, and not just gist memory, but real, human experience. Maybe then, he'd know when a Yellow cyborg was going to open fire or when a twitching wreck hanging in chains was the most valuable being on Earth.

Why do I have so few human memories? he asked AI-Gale.

Gale's skull sprang into his vision and rolled out his pre-programmed answer. "I had only five days to prepare. After receiving Xell's transmission, I made the decision to divert you from my attack on Cloud9. I needed to transform you from a militarized combat unit to a being that could interact and problem solve on Earth. I took the episodic and semantic parts of my own mind, the mind given to me by my creator, and filtered them to create you."

Jett felt a warmth, like touching the Star-River or holding Her in his arms. He was a small part of Ursurper Gale. "The memories are just so few."

"What you think of as memories, like our images of Her–" Jett felt shocked, but of course Gale knew about Her, "– are bleed-overs, left-behind fragments of the original experiences that were edited away when creating the gist-memory. You know much more than you think, Jett. Knowledge resides within you and should surface when needed. You have an excellent mind. Use it!"

Use it?

His anger boiled again. TwoLunar had exploded. War was raging in space. The voidian might already be free, and he was down here, trawling through human brains and detritus looking for some relic from the GFC's past.

Daylight brought on the city noise, human business awakening like a giant solar-powered forest. A strange bubbling noise distracted him, and AI-Gale vanished. Sounds drifted down the corridor, a form of human speech but with no discernable words:

Laughter.

He flowed silently from the office and found Yellow and several of Thorne's men gathered in a room. One wore Yellow's cloak and was doing a gangly, awkward dance around a tabletop while the others sat around laughing.

They froze as Jett filled the doorway. "Mission successful?" Yellow said, oddly devoid of the fear etched on the other men's faces.

Jett returned to Thorne's office. Yellow clattering along behind. *Use my mind. Be a human.* He ground the corner of Thorne's desk to dust with his fingertips. "Isn't this human enough," he asked Yellow who hovered in the doorway. "Destroying, killing, that's human right?"

"Mission didn't go well then?" Yellow slid inside, sending a longing glance back down the corridor.

"I located my target, but he escaped."

Yellow eased his corpulent form into a chair opposite Jett. "Well, we have to find him."

"How?"

"What do we know about this man? You interrogated Reeva, right?"

"The man is called Rex. Reeva said something about him having lots of glowworms and that he used to be someone important but lost his mind and lived on the streets for years."

"Excellent..." Yellow struck a thoughtful pose. "He's a worthless bum, a Glow addict, on the run from the Grim-Freakedy-Reaper. He has two choices. Find more Glow or seek help. He might come looking for a fix through one of our reputable sales contacts. In which case we'll have him. I can spread the word amongst other dealers, offer rewards et cetera.

"But for my money, we already know there's a connection with the Sisters of Salvitor. If I was this guy, I'd head back to that cozy hostel in the cathedral. Safe from angry robots with skeleton faces."

Jett felt the thrill of the hunt rise again, a chance to redeem himself.

"You'll be storming the cathedral then?" Yellow said.

"I need a few hours to return to optimum combat performance."

Yellow cocked his head as if listening to an inner voice. "There's someone here to see you. Chap by the name of Niros. He's our lich."

"We don't have a lich."

"Technically true, but after Auld defected, we employed one on a freelance basis. We send Niros the perp's info, he harvests them, and pays us a percentage and recommendation fee."

"What does he want?"

A man stepped through the office door and stood before Jett. "Business," Niros's voice boomed. "You haven't sent me any and I need to get paid." Niros was a skeleton, thinner even than a revenant with flesh pulled tightly over reedy cords of tendons that articulated his bones. His teeth and eyes bulged from his skull as if under great internal pressure. He wore the support struts of a powered exoskeleton which had assumedly been removed by the guards on the way in. His hand twisted at an odd angle, seemingly unzipping and turning his fingers into a tiny sonic pistol.

Jett stared at the man, watching his muscles and tendons ripple, not like the Amp addicts, but something different, as if beings of purpose lived inside him and they wanted out.

"Where's Thorne?" Niros demanded, his eyes widening slightly as he noticed Jett for real. "Who the fuck is this clown?" He poked a thumb at Jett.

Yellow cleared his throat, stood and made a careful retreat to the doorway. "This er, clown, is Jett. He runs things around here now. I'll leave you two to have a cozy little chat." Yellow closed the door and moved away down the corridor. The hissing sounds of his hydraulics betrayed the swiftness of his retreat.

"I'll cut the bullshit," Niros said, his voice loud and accompanied by flecks of spittle. "You need me, I need you. You got to feed me the perps, so we can both make a living. Is that too hard for a rookie to understand?"

"I don't need you," Jett said, his tagger flashed gun angles, rotation speeds, sonic impact cones, and that crucial distance from Jett's hand to Niros's throat. Normally this would be an easy kill, a mere reaction, but after being shot by Yellow–

"You won't find no better lich than me for the price."

"I don't need a lich." Jett leaned across the table, eyeing Niros's anatomy that appeared unique among all the humans he'd recently dismantled.

"Fine, then you owe me money for sitting on my ass. Read the contract. I get no business; you pay my retainer. I got a rig to run, gotta feed myself, and get some Glow for my own personal use or I start to rot. Just look at me." He waved the gun up and down his chest, its muzzle pointing momentarily away from Jett.

Jett struck like a mechanical viper, one hand ripped away the gun, the other clamped Niros by the throat hoisting him into the air. He hung there squawking, hands groping at Jett's face. "What the fuck–?" Then to Jett's disappointment, something inside Niros snapped and he passed out, body flopping limp in his grasp.

Jett twitched, resisting the instinct to pop the annoying man's head. This human, a lich, loaded with Glow, the very stuff he needed to understand, tiny machines, biomech machines, but just machines–

Jett's fingers unwound, bunches of monofilaments traced the paths up Niros's nerves, burrowing into his body through neck and head. More fingers sprouted from his torso routing in through Niros's feet and groin, filling his body with invisibly fine threads that sought the information channels, the lines of communication between the biomech nodes.

The network was there, chattering away to itself in its own language. Wide open, just as Ursurper Gale claimed, *somebody had hacked the GFC's unbreakable code.*

Jett spawned pattern recognition algorithms, thousands of them grinding along in parallel. He moved Niros's head next to his own and more filaments sprouted from nexus points on his face to pierce Niros's eyes, clamping cable bunches onto his retinas while others wormed into his nostrils, ears, and taste buds.

Jett sent pictures into the retinal fibers, projecting familiar images of Yellow and Thorne into the man's brain, watching the network's reaction as it gobbled up the sensory input.

He saw how Glow-nodes clustered around the primitive parts of the brain, tapping the sensory data before it made it to the higher functionalities. He saw its motion detectors, fibers grown into Niros's muscles and joints, mapping his body movements and poses. He saw the whole somanetic web, trillions of tiny filaments jabbing cells, sampling glands, filtering and feeding bacterial growths. Glow formed a parallel body inside an oblivious host with enough innate computational power to model that body, to enhance it or if it needed: to destroy it. It was Simmorta but free of its constraints. The missing piece Gale needed. *A flawless mind on a Glow substrate, inside of a voidian body: perfection!*

Like Simmorta, Glow had limitations. It didn't interface directly with the brain. Instead, it talked to it through the senses and the nerves, pulling strings and offering bribes through the highs and lows of pain and relief. It observed the host's actions, gleaning information from the thought waves generated by mass-neuronal firings, similar to the way a brain scanner or mind-reading AI worked.

This firewall between the brain and somanet forced the creation of a parallel control system: an emergent mind on a drug substrate, a smart parasite, that not only controlled its host… *it became its host!*

Glow grew a mind.

No, it grew several minds! Jett saw the nodes in clusters, *glowworms,* shadows of dead hosts, and Niros had hundreds. *How is he still sane?* Niros was a trove of memories. Gathering these memories was

Jett's shortcut to wisdom without the need for direct experience.

Systems failing. Shut down imminent!

The network tripped into an alarm state. Niros spasmed, muscles went rigid, blood pressure soared, bursting vessels throughout his body and brain.

It's killing him! The network will survive and move to a new host, but it's killing this host, punishing it for letting an intruder inside. No wonder Glow was so addictive. Any attempt to infiltrate, change or remove the drug triggered destruction.

Jett snapped back to reality, the heat of so much processing had boiled away most of Niros's outer flesh exposing bone and skeletal implants. As Niros's heart stopped, Jett plunged back inside, unable to deny the pull of curiosity, but the network was dark, all communications ceased. The nodes drifted apart, breaking connections with their host and with each other, migrating outward to Niros's skin, ready to hitch a ride to the next body and reassemble back into the same network, animating Niros and all his fellow glowworms back to abstract life.

Jett dropped Niros's body, now a lifeless sack of blood and bone. His infiltration filaments whipped free and rewound into fingers and facial skin. The real world seemed oddly empty and devoid of sensation.

"Yellow," he roared. "Get in here and clean this mess up."

Yellow bumbled into the room, eyes fixed on Niros's remains. "Time for a new lich?"

"Bring me Glow addicts," Jett said, "lots of them."

CHAPTER 34

Waking the Dead

Many new faces confronted Ellayna as she raced through Cloud9's medical wing on the way to the prison. "How can Del be dead?" she raged, but Martin had no answers.

"Come see," was all he said.

She shouldered past hordes of stumbling elderly people. Confused and blinking at the lights, tongues circling their dry lips. They bumbled around repeating comforting phrases, some angry at being roused, but most just confused. A few screamed, as if reality was a terrifying simulation from which they couldn't escape. Martin had woken everybody as instructed, and some hadn't experienced reality in years. Perhaps they'd forgotten what and where reality was.

She pushed past doctors and guards, blank-faced staff and orderlies just staring into space. Past Edvard Narlins, Del's personal physician, corralled in a corner by armed guards. She wasn't sure if they protected him or prevented him from leaving.

"Show me," she demanded, almost unable to look at Del's face. Holding her breath, she leaned over expecting something ghastly, but Del didn't look any different from when she'd last seen him.

A pasty-faced tech in a white coat stood rigid next to Del. His name tag read, Touse. "He's been brain dead for some time."

"How long?" Ellayna asked, her eyes scanning the rows of

monitoring equipment, whose lines and numbers still danced as if the man was very much alive.

"Months, maybe years, I can't tell. Life support keeps his body breathing and nourished, and Simmorta keeps him within a range of age-appropriate parameters. We'd never have known he was dead if we hadn't tried to force him awake."

"But I was talking with him in VR just days ago." Everyone stared at her as if she had lost her mind. She waved at Del's vital signs that appeared to stir at her presence. "He has brain activity."

"His scans have been rigged to show healthy, normal activity." Touse's hand swept across the monitors. "According to this, he's thinking thoughts consistent with someone active in VR. But it's just a recording on a very long loop so no one notices the repetition."

Ellayna walked over to Narlins. She caught herself brushing against people, desperately seeking that comforting touch of flesh, confirmation that this was real.

"You knew about this," she said, pushing her face close to Narlins. "You must have. Why?"

He looked away, chewing his lip thoughtfully.

"Here's something." Touse probed at Del's head with a spoon-shaped scanner. As she stared, he turned Del's head sideways and riffled through his hair, parting the strands with dexterous fingers. "These marks, he's had surgery on his skull. It's healed well, but left clues behind."

Touse wrapped a scanner sheath around Del's head and synced its signals to a nearby instrument. Images of Del's brain appeared in glorious three-dimensional color hovering over his body. Touse spun and zoomed, taking cues from an AI that flagged anomalies for closer investigation.

Ellayna gripped Touse's shoulder as he worked, needing the warm, reassurance of flesh to convince her this was real and not some nightmare VR.

Touse raised an eyebrow, the nearest thing to bewilderment he seemed capable of expressing. "There's a lot of damage in here, empty space where there shouldn't be. I see signs of deliberate ablation, possibly attempts to remove certain memories or skill sets. Maybe even to reduce or totally destroy conscious awareness."

"What in God's name have you done to him?" Ellayna yelled at Narlins.

"I followed orders," he snarled. "While you all slept or sat around counting your shares, I was here, working towards the future Del fought for."

"And what did you do, exactly?" Touse asked.

Narlins hung his head and closed his eyes. "That's for you to figure out."

Touse nodded as if expecting such resistance. "Here are some very precise cuts severing the bundles of nerves that connect functional regions of the brain strongly associated with consciousness."

"He turned Del into a zombie?" Ellayna said, aghast.

"Consciousness ablation surgery was not an uncommon means of mental suicide a few decades ago. Leaving the body and memories alive but removing any further experience of existence. There are chemical means to achieve the same effect, but they damage surrounding tissue. This is precision sectioning."

"And this gap here?" Ellayna pointed to the egg-sized hole in Del's prefrontal cortex.

Touse shrugged. "Del was very fond of his Star-River. I'd bet money that he had it implanted into his head. If he could interface with it, then it would be like having a colossal alternative reality generator on hand."

Ellayna shook her head, none of this made sense. As obsessed by the Star-River as Del had become, implanting it in his brain and getting his sidekick to kill him was beyond insanity.

Silence settled around the room, everyone stared at Narlins. She stabbed a finger at his chest. "Search his quarters and search this prison thoroughly. Find the Star-River and any clues about why this has happened."

She saw Narlins smirk and knew they wouldn't find anything. The only person who could give her answers was Del. "Martin, fire up the VR servers again, but no one is allowed inside, only me."

"Ellayna?"

"I think the answers we need are in VR. If you can keep me alive and sane long enough to find them."

"Sell what you know, honey. World's full of suckers. Don't be one of them." Medlin's voice played over and over inside Mira's mind like a nagging glowworm as she left the Ron King Shelter and wandered the fringes of Spare Part Row. Her feet took her to Corba Park, a small, quiet haven of trees and grass away from the main street mayhem. The world outside the hostel had indeed changed, just as crazy Medlin had told her. The sky was falling, voter-bots trawled the crowds, and the Alliance was coming, coming to fix everything and make Coriolis whole again.

She felt the Glow inside of her, a dormant volcano of festering lava. Tiny machines just working her body, fixing, rearranging... plotting. Time was running out. She had the answer, a plan, and it all started with selling what she knew: information. All she needed was a buyer and a different, darker set of glowworms told her who and where that buyer should be.

She felt empty and alone, so when the voice she'd been searching for finally came, it felt like a relief even though she knew it probably meant death.

"Is that really you, Mira?" Yellow said, clattering across the park. One of his metal arms hung limp by his side. His leg movements strained and erratic. As he drew closer, she saw his face, puffed and bruised. More than the usual amount of blue fluid leaked from his eyes. She drew some satisfaction that he was suffering too. If anyone deserved pain and anguish it was him.

"Have you come to pay me, Mira? Cash or body parts?" He stopped in front of her and looked her up and down critically but spared her his usual scathing evaluation.

"You once told me that information about the lich, Auld, would be worth something to Thorne. I have very interesting news, Yellow, valuable news." She opened her eyes wide, hoping to spark interest.

"Well, that's great, Mira. We can swing by the office. He would love to talk to you about it, I'm sure."

"I'd rather just exchange it now for cash, you know, pay my debt. And maybe have some extra left over to get a place, a job. Try to get my life back."

That laugh again. "Mira, Mira, just how valuable is this information?"

She dropped into silence, suddenly confused about what she was doing, exactly what she was selling. Maybe that wasn't the plan she'd conceived of earlier, maybe it was to get another fix, clear her head, then find a doctor, then yes, get clean. But she needed the fix first. "It is valuable, Yell. But if you can't do cash, I'll take a fix instead."

"Can't do either, Mira. New rules. Thorne opted for early retirement. In an epiphany of entrepreneurialism, he decided to apply his ample brains to a new floor lubricating product. My new boss – lovely guy, unique personality – is eager to meet with all our clients to discuss business deals. I'll take you to him." The little man's eyes bobbed wildly. Mira swore he was drooling with excitement.

"I'd rather just tell you what I know about Auld coming for us again and hope you can see me good." Her voice trembled as other options sprung to mind: lie, fight, rob him, go with him. *What could go wrong*? Maybe this new boss would see her point of view.

"The new boss doesn't let us have product for the streets anymore, Mira. You need to come to the office. It's a new form of hands-on management that he's very into." Yellow's body-frame heaved in what could be a shrug. "That's the best offer I can make. Take it or leave it." He attempted to launch away in a dramatic exit, but a whirring, slipping sound came from inside his leg harness and he stalled. He slapped a motor somewhere near his thigh, something engaged, and he lurched off across the park.

Mira followed. There was really no reason to trust him, but she could always run if she changed her mind. She doubted his troubled looking mechanics would be able to catch her.

She walked a few paces behind as he tripped and stumbled through the streets, until he fell completely, clattering into a heap of metal and limbs to lay still and silent, blue tears rolling down his cheek.

"The wonders of modern technology," he sighed, struggling to untangle his limbs. Mira watched, frustration mounting. Her body needed Glow. Now. And watching Yellow floundering across the ground wasn't getting her any closer. The long-faded urge to help fellow humans resurfaced and she offered him an arm to grab and pull back onto his feet.

Yellow fell again, and once more she found it easier to aid him, not questioning her safety at all. Fear diminished, her feet felt lighter, just two old companions strolling arm-in-arm, going to see the new boss, make friends, get a real fix. *Am I being drugged?*

At Trendle Tower she saw militia uniforms hustling around an elevator shaft set into a ground floor wall. She tried to pause, to take stock of the situation, but her legs kept moving. She noticed she was supporting Yellow less and less, and that his powerful grip now clamped firmly to her upper arm, sweeping her along at a swift pace.

A massive man in a suit frisked them both and escorted them inside the elevator where a hulking machine-trooper loomed over them making asthmatic breathing noises.

The brisk acceleration felt like flying and she wanted to sing. Relaxed, warm, committed, it was all over bar the shouting. *And the screaming, and the pain–*

Yellow's drug wore off. "What happened?" she asked, suddenly confused about how and why she was there.

"I lovingly administered an antidote, Mira. Wouldn't want you to miss any of the fun."

Her warm security fell away into panic. "I've changed my mind." She tried to free her arm. "I'll just phone in the information. I won't claim any rewards. Just–" The arm remained rigid, unmovable, and Yellow's viselike grip ratcheted tighter, compressing her boney arm like sponge.

"Unacceptable, Mira, you fucked me over, and now you'll

pay." His grin changed from that of a close friend to that of one anticipating something deliciously horrible.

The elevator door opened, and he pushed her out into a corridor. She looked around at the smashed rooms, the walls coated with drying blood. The stench penetrated even her doped senses. She stumbled past a room full of corpses, all horribly mutilated and stacked in mounds, flies coated everything, erupting in clouds as she passed. "This is Hell," she said through her tears.

"Hell has nothing on this place, Mira. Believe me, I've worked in both."

Her legs returned to her control, exquisite timing on Yellow's behalf. She fought him, thrashing at his face, opening old wounds, fingers jabbing at his eyes. He bobbed and ducked, letting her maim him but never escape his grip. Perhaps it was his self-inflicted punishment for what he was doing to her, or maybe he liked it, needed it.

Yellow banged on a closed door with Mira's forehead, exerting just enough force to sound their arrival and knock some fight out of her.

"What?" A dark voice rumbled from inside.

"I have another loyal Glow customer here, as you requested."

An unintelligible grunt signaled Yellow to enter. He pushed the door open and leaned close to whisper in her ear. "Goodbye, Mira." His cyborg arm whined and complained at the sudden application of torque as he threw her bodily into the office.

Mira tumbled inside, the will to stand or fight had left. She lay hunched on the ground just counting breaths, and then, with a sharp snort of resignation, she looked up.

A shadow filled the room behind a battered desk, vaguely human in shape, light shone through its fibers, although its head was solid, a leering black crystal skull mottled with fibrous flesh. Black eyes stared back from sockets that appeared just a little too big for the orbs. The creature's fingers were as long as her forearm, curling over the desk like giant spider's legs.

Yellow spoke calmly from behind her. "Mira, meet Jett. Jett, this is Mira." She heard the door slam and a chuckle from Yellow as he whirred away.

She took another look at the hellish apparition and burst into laughter. "Oh, this is great," she chuckled. "Just really fucking great."

CHAPTER 35

Game Theory of Mind

Ellayna returned to the mountains, to the foot of virtual Ben Nevis only to find that things had changed. All life was gone. Flint-dry air barreled across sterile, gray dust and granite. Only the blueness of the sky told her that this was not the surface of the Moon.

She climbed anyway. It felt good, so much better than pounding the corridors of Cloud9. Enjoy, she thought. At any moment the bugs will come, the fall will begin, and something new and horrific the Alliance has cooked up will manifest and try to take my life. The whole GFC watched as if under a spell, but would that be enough, or did the Alliance have other tools of destruction in its arsenal?

"Come on, Del. I know you're here. What is this place? Your vision of Earth after the man-versus-simulation apocalypse?"

The ground ahead heaved, turning like a stone vortex and rising into the sky. She rehearsed her escape sequence, smelled the lavender, chanted the cat song, conjured the bees, and practice-swatted at her thigh. Pointless exercises, but comforting.

The vortex closed in, enveloping her in a soft aircushion that lifted her from the ground. Suddenly she was flying through cold, damp clouds, and then dropping through different air loaded with the nuances of life. Below, the world was green, a magical hand rolled back the destruction, sprinkling trees and fields over the dry rocky bones.

The aeolian hand deposited her on a wooden balcony that wrapped around the entire pinnacle of a mountain, a different, more rugged mountain. A glorious cabin perched behind on the peak, window-eyes gazing off in all directions over jagged snowcaps that stabbed at the clouds, but none as tall as that on which she stood, next to Del.

"Better, Elly?" His smile comforted. Her life had crashed. Del was dead, and yet, through the marvels of GFC technology, he remained. She shook away old feelings and reminded herself that he was not real. At best, he was a repository of answers, at worst, just another trap.

"What have you done to yourself, Del? You're dead, a corpse with a carved-up brain. Narlins claims he was just obeying your orders."

Del shrugged. "He did what I told him to do, Elly – kill me slowly."

"I am going to need a proper explanation, Del."

He sighed and leaned on the wooden balcony, just a man on holiday in the beautiful mountains. "Where to begin?"

"How about the bit where you stuck the Star-River inside your skull."

"Great place to start. I dumped my first attempt at interfacing with it and rigged a direct, neural connection to my hippocampus. Took a while to debug and configure, but it worked well enough. The Star-River became an extension of my memory."

"But why? It was a demonstration of future memory technology, never meant to be a device of prediction."

"Game theory, Elly. Spend enough time setting up your pieces, get the input as realistic as possible. The Star-River is fundamentally a physics engine, the perfect predictor of outcomes for any given set of initial conditions. Set the pieces, run the model, and it throws out terrifyingly good estimates of where our society goes next. Waypoints, I call them, attractor states if you're into chaos. States that are inevitable: no matter how hard we try and avoid them, they happen anyway.

"After years of playing the prediction game, I came to the conclusion that humanity never wins. We defeat ourselves every time."

"I get it, Del. You think we're screwed. The voidian take over the galaxy, war with the Alliance wrecks the world, or the nanomachines in our bodies unite and rise up in the great somanetic plague that ravages everything into an optimized hellscape. I doubt you've noticed, but we have more immediate problems to solve."

"There's no way out for humanity, not in its current configuration. In order to change we must embrace one of these dangerous technologies and use it against the others."

"An arms race?"

"The somanetic plague is an immediate threat, so I'm going to infiltrate it. The threat escalates as collections of disparate minds come together and form singular super-minds. If I can be on the inside, become one of those guiding minds, then I can harness this power and use it against the other, possibly bigger threats."

Ellayna took a stab at where Del was going. "You think you can load this–" she waved a hand at Del, "–*simulation* of Del into the plague and control it?"

Del's mischievous grin emerged and for a second they were teenagers again, plotting humanity's destiny over a map and textbook. "Let me show you something really cool!" He eased her onto a bench and sat beside her. "Let's start with where we are." A woolen blanket appeared from nowhere and wrapped around them. "The Bighorn mountains in what was once the United States. My family owned this cabin. We came here for our summer vacations when I was young. Here I am now, look…"

A small, blond-haired boy ran barefoot across the deck clutching a teddy bear. The bear wore a fishbowl space helmet and had NASA stamped on his spacesuit. Young Del zoomed the bear around like a rocket and made whooshing noises as he ran.

"You were adorable, Del," she said, easing close to escape the chill.

"Here's Mother and Father, Gran and my sister Nell. You remember all of them, I'm sure, from when we grew older." The family appeared on another bench, gazing out over the mountains. The little girl hopped off and ran to play with the boy who fled back inside the house. "Go put some warm clothes on," their Mother yelled at their backs.

"This, Elly, is my greatest invention." She stared, expecting something fantastic to appear, but the family just carried on chatting and interacting around them as if they weren't there.

The answer dawned. "A simulation of your childhood?"

"A very detailed simulation of my whole life. Narlins helped, using memory-recall drugs to pry details out of my subconscious. We used VR and Inner-I interfacing to record memories and some good, old-school machine learning to reconstruct detailed memories from snippets and fragments, a bit like restoring old photos or colorizing black-and-white movies. There's probably only ten-percent of my actual life here, but it's the important stuff, those key moments – the gist of Del."

She shook her head. "But you're not really Del. You just think that you are."

"Once I had a simulation of my life on a VR server, I created nascent minds, blanks, like virtual children, and let them live my life in fast forward computer time. They grew up as Del, met what they thought was a real Ellayna and fell in love, started the GFC. All that stuff happened in just moments of real time, but to them it was a lifetime. And they really were Del."

"Remarkable. But, no. Still not Del," she said, digging in for the fight.

He shrugged, "I made a kind of Del-based Turing test. Set a whole bunch of simulated Dels to try and fool an adjudicator, which of course, was me. Or real Del, depending on your perspective. An adversarial network of Dels vying to impress the real thing. The winners survived the cut and passed on into simulations of the future. There, they were tested on moral and technical decisions to see if they did what the real Del thought he would do."

"People learned to fake Turing tests decades ago. They were never actually people, just algorithms. You, you're just an algorithm."

"Always the sceptic, Elly," he laughed. "And in this case, up to this point, you might be right. But here's the real genius, and the answer to your questions about me ablating my own brain. Imagine an old-fashioned pocket calculator but with a wireless connection to your mind. You simply think of a calculation and the answer pops into your head. The calculator becomes part of your embodied consciousness. You don't bother doing actual math in your head anymore, that bit of your brain atrophies and shrivels or you remove it by jabbing some crucial connections, but in your mind you remain a math genius able to do any calculation you can think of."

Ellayna tapped her temple. "My Inner-I does just that. So well in fact that it immerses me in its fake worlds and seas of information."

"But I took this way further, Elly. Imagine that instead of a calculator you have a copy of yourself. A whole mental construct called Ellayna, running in parallel, whose memory and cognitive functions you can access as if they are your own."

"You could slowly remove the original or let it atrophy and force the copy to take over." She felt vaguely sick at the thought of Narlins etching away Del's mind in the crossbeam of some laser: *Killing him slowly.*

"I found myself gradually less conscious of my physical surroundings and increasingly more in tune and more aware of my virtual reality. To me, I am still Del, always have been. A contiguous being from birth to this moment. I call the process consciousness migration, as I changed my mental substrate one functional piece at a time until all my consciousness seamlessly migrates to the artificial substrate."

Her mouth dropped open as she tried to fault the idea. "So... You, you really *are* Del?"

"In my mind, yes, but so are all the others I copied." He winked. "I like to think I'm the original though."

"And then you just load this mind state onto another substrate?"

"A somanetic drug substrate. I wanted to use Simmorta but it's too restrictive. So when my contacts on Earth discovered Glow–" He let the revelation hang for Ellayna and all her fellow listeners to absorb.

"Hacked Simmorta, unlimited, unconstrained. Are you the mastermind that broke the GFC's unbreakable security code, Del?"

"I can't claim that accolade, but I hope to meet them one day soon. At least, a version of me will."

She felt tears grow in her eyes. Crazy, crazy Del. The little boy who was bullied at school but wanted to change the world. Not just the world, the whole universe. Many questions rushed to mind. "Is Ursurper Gale just another version of you?"

"One of my early attempts. A simulated mind with memory implants. He never actually lived my life in VR. It took many years of prison work for me to build the full simulation, and of course Gale was gone by then."

"Why does he think there are other voidian on Cloud9?"

Del smirked. "I might have implanted a few extra, shall we say, false memories. My way of making sure the thorn stayed sharp, with its pointed end aimed in the right direction."

"This Glow-substrate version of Del, I assume it's no longer on Cloud9?"

His grin turned more menacing. "I've escaped, Elly. Escaped prison, escaped the GFC, escaped the limitations of my frail human body. I am what comes next!"

She stifled her anger, or was it jealousy? "This drug-version of Del needs a body. How does that get you inside the plague?"

"Can't tell you *all* my secrets, Elly."

"Why not? We might decide to help."

"The GFC is finished. You need to flee, Ellayna. Escape. May you find allies in unexpected places."

Ellayna suddenly couldn't stop laughing. "A copy of Del on Coriolis Island. Into the heart of the infestation. Did you know that Gale has made another voidian and sent it there? Do you think he's there for a reason? Maybe it's hunting Del and his beloved Star-River?" She enjoyed watching Del's bubble of smug confidence pop.

Del looked confused for a while but regrouped. "Gale's been his own entity for years. He has his own mind, full of his own ideas, and follows his own path."

"Can I persuade you to contact Gale and get him to call off his absurd attack?" But Del was fading, already transparent as if self-deleting one pixel at a time. "Del? Help us."

"Goodbye, Elly, please save yourself. The GFC is not worth any more sacrifices."

He vanished, and she was alone amongst the silent frozen figures of Del's childhood. "Did you get all that, Martin?" she messaged.

"Wild!" A video icon popped into her mind. "This came through a few moments ago, Ellayna. If your mind is not already blown by talking to disembodied Del, then watch this confession."

"Confession?" The video ran, showing a white, plastic face with odd, drawn-on features. "Machine nuns?"

"Calls itself Sister-Zero from the Sisters of Salvitor. One of our founder's, Joselyn Salvitor's, creations. It has quite the tale to tell."

Jett watched the woman dangling in his hyper-strength grip. His hand circled her head, dozens of branching fingers snaking through her hair and across her face. A pointed fingertip pierced the skin just below her left eye as blood ran down her cheek into the laugh line angling up from the corner of her mouth.

She choked and spluttered. Words bubbled continuously from her lips. "Get your fucking hands off me you slimy-assed shit-fucking oil slick–" She fought, spitting, punching, tearing her fingernails away against Jett's fullerene skin. Jett liked this woman, this Mira. She was a warrior.

He'd learned many things by interrogating Yellow's stream of Glow addicts. His vocabulary had expanded wildly in just the few moments he'd held Mira aloft. Words and concepts centered around an apparent obsession with fornication and defecation. He tried explaining to her that he didn't need such things, but that didn't seem to help.

So many lives. So many stories. But were any of them useful in his mission to understand Glow, find the Star-River and hunt down Rex?

His last pair of victims needn't have died. He'd perfected the art of slipping, unnoticed, inside their somanetic networks without tripping defenses. This gave him time to explore, to revel in their memories. He tripped them anyway, enjoying watching as each person's mind melted and imploded.

"Why did you come here, Mira?"

She ceased her struggle, hanging limp like a dead thing. Her eyes found his, and there was that special, human moment when people seemed able to look into each other's cores. "Just wanted another chance. Something to go right. I have information. Trade it for a fix. Just–" She shrieked as he pierced her nerves, drilling through the channels, ignoring the biological pain and focusing on calm, obfuscating signals. *I am just more Glow. Another fix. Love me, accept me.*

She didn't faint like most of the others, in fact she fought harder, grinding her teeth with effort. This person had experienced real pain. He saw it in her somanet, the swathes of scabbed-over memories and buried experiences.

"I doubt you have any information I need," he said.

"We killed Auld, your rogue lich," Mira said, barely able to control her mouth through the pain. "Thorne promised a reward."

"I'm not Thorne." Jett pushed deeper and Mira faded, passing the pain threshold that ended most humans. She hovered on the edge of consciousness, resigned, waiting, but still unable to concede defeat.

"You owe me…" she slurred. Jett tasted her rage. He was angry too, frustrated with his own failure. The pair resonated. They were both livid, comrades in emotion.

Her somanet welcomed him inside. He modeled a mash of confused personas, each vying to distinguish itself to their new host, clamoring for the prize: a fleeting moment on the stage of consciousness.

Mira's mind reminded him of the beach where he washed up: dark but crowded, with its constellation of campfires and the sparkles of watching human eyes. Fully immersed, he wandered amongst them, stoking some, quenching others. All while feeling warm, welcome, surrounded by friends, until that moment he triggered the network, and its rampant defenses expelled him in one heaving, mental convulsion, back into the real world. He hadn't figured a way around that yet, didn't really want or need to. The ejection felt good, like being spat back into space. *Go explore somewhere else!*

"I see you," she said, calm and unfocused. "You're in my mind." Her many personas, like bugs on flypaper, flickered on and off in a game of roulette as her attention pinned them with its light before shifting on to the next.

"Know thy enemy, Mira," Jett said. He homed in on the ripest cluster of memory, laden with raw, aching emotion, and pried away the scabs concealing it. This was the treasure he wanted. The grist of what it was to feel and be human. "Why hide from yourself, Mira?" But she remained silent as if his uncovering of her true self was something that even she, this warrior, couldn't face.

He tore away the bandages, the scabs, the false memories and lies, digging through the chaff of forgotten lives, burrowing, layer after layer. This truth had been copied and buried so many times it had to be real.

And there it was, so heavy it crushed the strength from his body. He flowed to the floor dragging her down on top of him. *Yes... feed me this experience!*

"You had this coming, Corrine!" a man yelled. *But she only sees the gun's gaping muzzle.*

"No!" she screamed. *Throwing herself between the gun and her child. Noble, strong, a sacrifice!*

"No, please. I'll do anything, anything!" *She hears the shots, but they mean nothing. She feels nothing! Even the pain of the bullet in her own chest means nothing.*

"Christ no... please no–"

How she kneels. How she gathers the fragments of his face as if she can bring them back together and make him whole again.

And suddenly Jett knew what it was like to vomit himself senseless, to beat his own brains from his skull on a wall, a floor, on a bed post in a padded cell.

Mira... Mira... How do you survive this pain?

She laughed! "That's not me you idiot fuck! Any more than these things in your head are really you."

She's inside of me! Jett's perception swam to the surface and back into the office where he stared up at Mira's sagging face. "Come, Mira, embrace the truth. Own your existence."

Her mouth opened, spilling stomach bile down onto his face. Her words came in ectoplasmic spasms, jabbed straight into his mind through her somanet. "You have no fucking idea. You dare to judge my life, my fight to become something in this world. I endured childbirth while the world fell apart around me. I forged a family out of that shitstorm, only to have it ripped away from me. All of it. One stupid mistake. After surviving that, I'm here, dying at the hands of... whatever the fuck you are and that conning, vile, yellow-bellied prick." She dropped into silence as if saying her piece had fulfilled some urgent need, and now there was nothing left to do.

Jett eased upright, supporting her limp body like a twist of rags in his giant hand. She was dreaming now, reconstructing a different moment in time.

You have more? Yes, there's more!

A dusty yard teased by wind, rain, thunder and lightning. A fragile man with a curved spine and tufted ears, facing down the lich.

It's him. The man in chains – Rex!

The battle played out to a thumping heartbeat as she rushed

toward the seething mass of dogs and exploding fur. He felt Mira's love, her despair, that everything she had was now gone, taken. Again. More loss to bury, to scar-over and hide – except she hadn't, not yet. It remained raw and bleeding, a trophy, a war wound to drive her on to some greater purpose.

Rex sank to his knees cradling the top half of the massive dog. "Find what you need in there, you shit?" The voice came from Mira's mouth and mind simultaneously. The delay of conscious translation giving it a strange echo.

"I see you know Rex," Jett said, and snapped awake, mind jangling with Mira's panic and denial. "You can't hide it. I see your feelings, your... love?"

"Fucking get out of my head–" The blast of her anger nearly tore Jett's connection away.

"This man fought the lich, Mira. He deserves the reward, not you. Tell me where he is. I'll deliver the reward myself."

"Rot in hell."

"Where did this battle occur? Don't make me hurt you even more, Mira."

"Hurt me? You think you can hurt me?"

Jett reached for the small, metallic cylinder that Yellow had brought back from the reclamation plant earlier. "Glow, Mira, ten doses. It's what you want." Her eyes lit. She grabbed at the cylinder, but he moved it away, feeling her somanet explode with expectations.

"Rex..." blurted a voice that was not her own. "Fucking glowworms!" she countered.

"Very good, Mira, and where can I find Rex?"

She convulsed with the agony of betrayal, fighting to clamp her mouth shut, to deny the treacherous monster inside her a voice, but the voice came anyway, coaxed and prodded to the surface by Jett's gentle, internal touch. "The Forever Friends Rescue Sanctuary, Tellus District."

Jett dropped her to the ground. The fury of his mission failure still burned but there was a new agony, his own internal reflection of Mira's many, terrible losses. *That conning, vile, yellow-bellied prick.* "How are you still inside my head, Mira?"

He eased back from her, suddenly afraid of how much human poison he'd pumped into his mind. Another step backward, aware of her eyes, searching, seeking that precious cylinder as his tendrils lengthened, reluctant to break the connection. *Just give me one last fix of Mira. Just one more memory. One more unbearable tragedy.*

Mira crashed to the floor as his infiltration filaments snapped out of her body, severing their connections. But her voice remained. "I'm going to haunt you, you… fuck! Haunt you to your grave." *I see the network and the network sees me.*

Jett towered over her, but her eyes didn't see him, maybe they saw her child, or the dead dog clutched in Rex's arms. Perhaps, just that fix of Glow she craved so much. He aimed a fist at her head, a mercy really, freedom from pain, as he smashed her open like the pointless circuit she was. *But she lives on inside of me, and inside the Glow. The endless death and rebirth inside more hosts.*

He lowered the fist. The outlet for his rage wasn't the devastated woman on the floor. It had its own mission now, a focus elsewhere on someone who'd betrayed him, lied, deceived, shot him!

"Yellow, get in here and clean up this mess."

Yellow bumbled through the doorway juggling mop and bucket with his single, functional hand.

I'll fucking kill you! The surge of hatred from Mira's voice still inside his mind was so strong, Jett dropped the Glow applicator. Mira's Glow network surged alive, jolting her body into action. She snatched the applicator out of midair and jammed the tip to her neck, eyes rolling back in ecstasy.

Yellow stood frozen in the doorway, unsure what was happening as Jett grew taller, fibers winding back into a bipedal form. "I have what I want," Jett said, voice trembling with both his and Mira's anger and pain. Pain that was now all his.

"Excellent," Yellow said. "Do I get what I deserve now?"

He saw Jett coming. That handful of milliseconds were just enough for the sad acknowledgement that his time was over, and to wonder, ever so briefly, if his life would have been better or longer, had he made different choices.

CHAPTER 36

This Memory Becomes Me

Jett watched from a rooftop as night engulfed the Forever Friends Rescue Sanctuary. The small heat signatures of dogs shone like fireflies from the kennels, but the main house remained dark and empty.

He'd seen volunteers arrive, walk and feed dogs, then leave. His mind played out Mira's memory of the great battle that took place in the yard: humans and dogs against the cyborg. Rex was a weak person but did well surrounding himself with warriors.

He drifted further. The real world fuzzed and vanished as he immersed into one of the countless experiences he'd gleaned from Yellow's addicts. So much to see, so much to learn–

Focus!

Mira's memories were strongest. He jangled them back alive, immersed in that incredible, vibrant pain. He felt her watching from his mental depths. Not the real Mira, she was gone, disconnected, but her trace personality remained etched into his memory circuits

Focus!

He shook the thoughts away, dropped down from the roof and stalked silently into the rescue sanctuary yard, scouting kennels, breaking open doors and staring inside.

Dogs huddled in pairs or fours, staring back, shivering with fear.

They didn't really see him, just growled and backed away. To them, Jett didn't register as alive, just some sinister and incomprehensible part of the scenery.

No Rex. His frustration boiled as thoughts of Rex stirred Mira into life. Her voice a slur of curses and misdirection, forcing his gaze onto things that weren't really there. He picked up a rock and crushed it to powder. Stared at the sky, meteors, TwoLunar, a meditation on what was important.

Focus!

He pushed open the house door and stood in darkness, fullerene pupils dilating, absorbing the hints of reflected moonlight. A house full of history, more memory triggers, pictures and furnishings that jolted voices alive inside his mind. *Mira again.* He reeled from picture to picture. The chatter growing louder. He pulled away, seeking the darkness and purity that was once Jett. But escaping the voices was like struggling through quicksand. Sinking in glowworms that clawed and fought his every thought. They all wanted to be him, to perceive his world, own his body. *Fucking glowworms!* They want my body. *My life.*

Focus!

Back arched like a fox, Rex prowled the same darkness, feeling the shadows like pressure on his skin. He owned a second destruction meme now, the name he dared not mention. Even thinking that the Prisoner had a name caused him to stir and protest before Rex's inner watchdog awoke and savaged him back to the underworld.

The sky glowed red in distant Welkin: protests raged as militia clashed with Alliance supporters, buildings burned, humans died for human reasons. Rex avoided them all. His animal instincts felt sharp and clear, not part of this crazy world anymore, a being driven by one singular purpose: to be with his own kind, one last time.

The gate to the Forever Friends Rescue Sanctuary looked new. The fence taller, stronger. Workers had made the sanctuary whole again. Even the house looked different: resurrected, repainted, after the lich's sonic blasts had cracked and battered its walls. Shiny new kennels made of plastic and tile interlaced the old wooden ones. The yard was scrubbed clean, raked flat and sanitized with something fake and sweet smelling.

He felt the assassin like a gravity warp emanating from inside the house, flickering lights and distorting reality, but didn't care. He was home.

No dogs came out to greet him. Their kennel doors were all ajar, some broken off completely. In the end kennel he found three dogs, knowing them by feel and smell, even as their human-assigned names meant nothing anymore. He curled into their midst. Two more dogs followed silently from outside, laying between him and the entrance like draught excluders. More came, four on each side and three others draped over like blankets. Smaller dogs pushed under his arms and knees and suddenly he was floating on a living, breathing wave. He soaked in the moment. *If it ends here, then this memory becomes me.*

Hours passed inside the house, simply vanished in the stream of daydream and distraction. Finally, Jett clawed his way out the front door as if fighting monstrous tentacles trying to drag him back inside. The pull of the house was so strong, so resonant with all those dead minds in his memory.

He lay briefly in the dirt, then rose up from the slop of tendrils and mesh he'd become. He wove a towering, bipedal body, pushing his skull up and mounting it firmly on wide shoulders.

An alarm siren wailed from the house. *I've been careless. My mission. Find Rex!* He must be here. Where else would he be? He could be with the Sisters but that was Yellow's idea. Yellow – *that conning, vile, yellow-bellied prick. Don't believe a thing he says!*

He stormed from kennel to kennel, his tagger working overtime as it zoomed onto each dog.

Maxwell.

Bela.

Bartok.

Brittan – How do I know their names?

Gustav.

Mendle

Frizell.

He turned to the next kennel. Mind seething with tags and voices.

Frizell? He nearly missed the alert. Didn't even register that he'd looked at a person and not a dog.

Frizell. Human. Shotgun.

Jett spun back as Frizell's gun trigger clicked. "For the Future-Lord," Frizell said, as the blast of bolts and ball bearings came at Jett's face.

Jett's body exploded into a net of fibers, flinging his head up and out of the damage zone. The blast energy passed through his disparate body as Jett whipped around Frizell and flipped inside-out, dicing him into tiny cubes that splattered to the ground.

Dogs barked. Alarms howled.

A militia truck screeched to a halt outside the sanctuary and a dozen smug, confident looking guards dropped from the back. Jett scanned them, waiting for his tagger to identify guns, armor, weapon stats–

Goliath?

Rust?

Chopin?

Fucking Christ, Mira, how are you messing with my tagger?

He stumbled off into the darkness seeing dogs inside tree limbs and dawning clouds, and Rex's face grinning back at him from dots and splatters on walls and pavements.

I see the network, and the network sees me.

What have I done?

Rex felt the world through the dogs' senses, pack senses. The house lights flickered, curtains and shadows shifted, something searched, something angry. It burst from the house into the yard, searching the kennels again.

It paused outside the last kennel, seeing through the darkness, the heat of so many animal outlines crammed inside.

Rex cringed for the death blow, hoping it would be fast, painless. He wondered about Mira. Her green eyes, a rare smile: "Fucking Christ, Rex! There you are!" Her presence felt strong as if she somehow shared space with the monstrous face pressed through the kennel door, leered through the darkness with senses no human possessed.

In that instant, he knew a terrible truth. *She's dead. Gone. Absorbed into this creature.*

A tear rolled. The dogs growled. Still the thing was there in the darkness only feet away. *Why doesn't it just kill me?*

The crushing fear and emptiness roused Del, tearing him free of his Star-River. He didn't fight for control, instead, he just stared through Rex's eyes, waiting. As the moments dripped away, their minds overlapped and Del saw inside Rex. He saw Mira, Mrs O and the dogs. He understood what Rex had become: a chimeric mess of doubts, fears and hopes, just like any real human, not a shadow, or an imposter. "I'm sorry, Rex. I truly am."

In turn, Rex saw Del's fears: the plague, a nanomachine soup that optimized the universe dead and dry. How it all started with somanets, the great undoing of humanity. There was something there for Felix as well, something to terrify him back into momentary awareness. Another bomb hanging in a cradle. A loop of nova devices, capable of a detonation so powerful it would shred the crust from the Earth and implode its own tiny core into a black hole to vacuum up the remnants.

"I'm sorry too," Rex said, out loud.

A gunshot shattered the silence and dogs erupted into howls and barks. He bedded deeper, hands over ears. *Ignore reality, make it go away.*

When he came to, the assassin was gone, and Rex stared into a softer darkness, imagining Mira, there, watching over him from limbo. He let the tears come in a single great rush, dogs licking salt from his face. Through the kennel door, the house was dark and silent again. "Make sure it's the right heaven, Mira. Before they shut the gates."

CHAPTER 37

The Wrong Heaven

Mira awoke from a melancholy dream. An opera singer strangled a cat that played a kazoo through a faltering bullhorn that rose and fell into merciful silence, only to awaken and begin the dreadful aria all over again.

"You're not done yet," said a darker, demonic voice as the voice turned soprano.

"Please stop," said Mira, but the words never made it from her mouth. After an interval, a second segment and two encores, the concert finally ceased, and a shadow loomed over her. "Did you get what you wanted?" the shadow asked.

"I did." She cringed, waiting for the death blow, but Jett continued standing there like a black hole in the fabric of hope. "Did you get what *you* wanted?" she asked back. It seemed the polite thing to do.

"Not yet," Jett said, and was gone.

Mira rolled into a sitting position, limber and alive, her body pulsing with new energy, Glow energy. It was normal to sleep after a large fix, let the body stew in its own regenerative juices while she took a mental rest, a reward for her procurement.

As the funk of sleep faded, she stared at her fingers, now long, carbon-black spider legs, her body a web of power and strength. She blinked, and fingers were just fingers again. Her body just a skinny woman drenched in piss, bile and half-digested soup.

She sat, remembering what she'd seen. Corrine Medlow. An unfathomable weight descended on her soul, grinding out the juice of joy, leaving just skin and bones held together by grief and survival instinct.

She breathed, and the burden slid from her shoulders. She saw memories and emotions but no longer felt them. *Corrine is dead and buried, and I dug up Mira, same material, different arrangement. The world turns. Walk it off.*

Fragments of office desk piled in the middle of the room blocked her view of the window. She stared at the huge footprint in a pool of blood by the door. Dried blood and metal splinters rimmed a circular hole in the floor. Other holes punched through walls into neighboring rooms. Flies were everywhere. She snorted like a horse, blowing a cloud of the black insects from her nostrils.

Her head felt clear, as if Jett had ripped away all her mental bandages, scars and all, bleeding out her memories, letting them run together and scab over into something new: a new, parallel Mira, one that existed only in Glow now.

I see the network and the network sees me.

She picked up the Glow dispenser cylinder, noting the gauge on the side – half full, better than half empty. Five doses left. *I'm back. I survived, but how do I get off this shit?*

She expected pops and cracks and pain, but instead stood with fluid ease, springing upright and almost tripping over the computer on the floor facing the empty window frame. A string of digits filled its screen in an extra-large font: a bank account, a very healthy bank account.

Something else hung by the window, dangling from a hook formed from a bent steel pole, jammed into an overhead concrete beam. The pole's hook-end had snared what looked like a ghastly yellow fish. Its single unblinking eye stared wide and oily as blue fluid leaked down and dripped onto the floor.

"Yellow?" His name caught in her throat. Limbless and missing an eye, his body was covered with tiny holes cauterized into black dots. The hook looped through his lower jaw and up into his gaping mouth. Jett had decided his lower jaw couldn't support the body weight, so he pushed the hook tip up and into Yellow's skull, securing him like a gutted fish in a market stall.

"Yellow…" she muttered again, torn between hatred, vengeance and sympathy.

She moved closer looking into the watery eyeball. "Yellow?" He blinked, and she jumped backward tripping over the computer and landing on her backside. "God damn it, Yellow." She picked herself up, looking again at the screen. "I bet you know your way around this account, don't you?" He showed no sign of hearing. "Is that your money? The money you were promised?"

He blinked franticly, the eyeball flicking back and forth between her face and the screen, which she now realized was carefully positioned right in his line of sight.

"Thorne's money?"

He blinked twice, more carefully this time.

"Money from people like me?"

His gaze froze on her face.

She sat carefully down, taking her time to adjust the screen and arrange herself so she and the screen were both visible to Yellow. She felt the barbs of anger lancing into the back of her head as she pulled up the keyboard, stroked the keys with a touch of sensual curiosity. "Let's see what we can do."

It was okay to look now, to remember her past. Handy-Person Services, their own little home business, doing anything to earn a buck from cleaning, fixing, digging gardens, cat-sitting, baby-sitting, errands. Michel did most of the heavy stuff, Corrine was accounts, networking, advertising. All skills of which she still possessed, somewhere deep inside. She even remembered their bank account number, although no money had existed in that account for years. The money transfer was grindingly slow over the primitive phone linkage, not like the distant days of Internet connectivity, but Jett had made it all easy for her with routing numbers, accounts and forged signature blocks laid out across the screen. *He left this for me. Why?*

The large monetary number was now in her account, and the balance on the screen read a big, fat zero. She nudged the computer closer to Yellow and stood to look him right in the eye. His face had lost the ability to form expressions, but she knew he was pleading with her: just let me down, help me or put me out of my misery. She moved close, breath reflecting off his eyeball. It blinked, angry, frustrated; furious blinks, raging on to resignation, and finally – defeat.

"Vengeance is a bitch, ain't it, Yell," she said, spitting a little soup-laden vomit-venom into his eye.

She turned and left, kicking the computer hard with the point of her toe, breaking it against the wall. She swept through the halls of the dead, cyborgs and military men, workers and soldiers, all just guts, components and flies.

Outside, the militia had strung a cordon around the entire street while they figured out what had happened. No one noticed Mira stepping from the elevator and striding toward the security tape with an air of unchallengeable confidence.

"You can't go in there, miss," a young militiaman said, confused about where she had appeared from.

"I know," she said, and kept walking away.

CHAPTER 38

Enter the Darkness

Ellayna didn't know where to go. Her apartment felt freakishly scary, memories of Trabian's attack inside a virtual copy made it hard to return there. Now she thought about it, she hadn't been home in ages. *How long exactly?* Stalking corridors, using bathrooms and rest places that hadn't seen people in years. *When was the last time I ate?*

Martin's last message sat like a wound in her inbox. "Ellayna, Taunau is calling an emergency meeting. Claims to have found a clause in the constitution that revokes your power. Something about fitness for leadership? He's calling a vote on it."

She found herself back at the medical wing, same guards looking at her as if she were crazy. *Must have come full circle.* She slumped back onto her medical cot, sweat from her earlier encounters still cold and clammy on the sheets.

No... no... no... no meetings, no clauses. "Martin?" He appeared in her vision, face tense but sad. "Denied!" she yelled. "Under the War Powers Act I can deny him the power to call a vote until after immediate danger has passed. And we are in *immediate* danger, Martin. Delay him, mess with his comms if you need to. I just need a few more hours to resolve these conflicts."

Taunau's anger stemmed from her earlier veto of a pre-emptive strike on Coriolis. Kill the plague, destroy Glow and whoever was making it. Protect the GFC's secrets, stymie the Alliance for just a few days more. *He'd really start a war and kill millions just for that?*

No, the GFC was finished, a rotten shell, so chewed and mauled, that its fibers barely held their shape anymore. She turned Utopia over in her mind, just unfurl that simulation one more time. Ambassador Hmech would probably meet her there in person, welcome her, plan to pick her off of the wreckage as Cloud9 disintegrated under the fire of either Gale's exploding ship or incoming Alliance missiles.

Sister-Zero's image remained frozen in a different corner of her vision. The machine had confessed everything: how Del persuaded the hidden Convolver sect within their Sisterhood to take Felix Siger, one of the misguided do-gooders behind the Nova-Insanity, as a volunteer to host Del's mind and the Star-River. This hybrid-being now called itself Rex, *after a fucking dog!* And was supposedly some path to the Future-Lord. Other paths included repurposing dead and used Simmorta into Glow. A process they followed but had no idea how it worked. Claiming divine intervention from the future had led them to the formula. And now Ursurper Gale's clone was chasing down this Rex, hellbent on killing him and taking the Star-River. *What have you done, Del? Do I really have to come down there and save you again?*

She snatched at the Utopia simulation, dropping herself inside, senses swept away and replaced by–

The echoingly large hallway. She stood, staring out massive windows across the gushing river that flanked her property. Mountains towered behind, swathed in pine trees and soft, white clouds. *So good, it must be real.*

"I'm here, Hmech," she yelled at the empty room. "Let's talk."

Such quiet. Such peace. "Hmech?"

Gale's collision-timer ticked down another ten minutes, ninety minutes to impact. She paced the room, swept up the stairs and into one of the many bedrooms, another fantastic view. A giant four-poster would work well in here. "Running out of time, Hmech. You want me, you'd better come negotiate."

Eighty minutes.

Through a giant walk-in wardrobe, out into sitting areas with river views. An upstairs kitchen? Guest wing... *yeah, for all those friends and family I don't have.*

She slumped into a corner: the view suddenly poison that made her sick. *They don't want me. They don't need me.* If she'd had anything in her stomach, she would have puked it up.

Her vision jolted into a buzz of noise and reformed back into the blank-walled medical booth. "What was that, Martin?"

"Cyber-attacks. Highest volume ever. They're coming from all around. Even those harmless looking satellites full of kids experiments are pumping out jamming signals and infiltration code." His face appeared in her mind, eyes spinning wildly. "I can't hang on much longer, Ellayna. They're in my head. Everywhere. Like worms in the rot." As if to emphasize his point, his image shattered into clusters of dots before becoming Martin again.

"Martin, hold it together." Her vision glitched again. "Just a bit longer, please."

"Fuck you, Hmech!" She hit the exit icon and was fully back in the medical booth. A shadow flicked past the door. From the corner of her eye it seemed to pause and bend into the room, just a void-dark head and shoulders that vanished when she looked directly at it.

"Guards!" she yelled. The pair of guards blundered into each other as they raced for her door. Neither of them saw any ghosts. "Stay close. Stay alert."

"Martin, how close are our Coriolis assets to the Sisters' hostel?"

Martin's eyes swam back from whatever dark waters they inhabited. "They're in a safehouse in Welkin. The city is on high alert, so it's hard to move them unnoticed."

"Talk with this Sister-Zero again. See if there's a backdoor into the hostel."

"Why?" Clearly frustrated by the pointlessness of this or any other request.

"I want our troops to grab this Rex before Gale's clone does. Then move him to a safehouse."

The wheels churned in Martin's mind, playing out in the creases on his forehead. "You... you want to be with Del? Again?"

"He will be a useful asset to the future GFC." The lie sounded terrible, but it might make it past Martin's befuddled mind.

"Of course, Ellayna." His face disappeared and then returned alongside some footage of an Alliance launch.

"That's big," Ellayna said. "For us?"

"Embassy craft, a hopper. Judging by its flight angle, it's the Coriolis invasion force."

"How long?"

"Fifty minutes. Yes, news feeds lighting up. The Alliance claims an historic victory on Coriolis, overwhelming voter support for their takeover of governance."

She cut Martin's feed and pinged Jesh Nameeb. "How long to remove Simmorta completely from my body, Jesh?"

"I can put the drug into shutdown-transport mode, force it to return to your bloodstream, and then pump and filter. About twenty minutes?"

She eyed her collision timer, sixty-five minutes. "Have the machinery ready. I'll be right there."

Act dead!

Rex slumped into an abandoned shop doorway. The side of the Sisters' cathedral lay far down the same street, looming like an apocalyptic storm cloud.

He'd wrenched himself away from his beloved dogs before dawn, stood to stare at the door to Mrs O's silent house before deciding that she was gone, nothing to see here. Volunteers would come. The dogs would survive, and he had to do the same and keep surviving. In the end, he did what he often did and let his feet decide. And, for once, he agreed with his feet's decision. It really felt like the only thing he could do.

Early morning people passed by, their eyes staring far away, minds still firmly inside their beds. The buzz from their muted conversations was of invasion: the Alliance, coming to save them, coming to kill them, coming to give them everything they needed, coming to take it all away.

Rex didn't care.

Act crazy!

Words tumbled from his mouth, a negotiation with himself. *How crazy is that!*

"If I believe you and your visions, then I should pull the cord, kill the dog, free the Prisoner."

But maybe you're just another liar. One of Mira's malignant glowworms trying to deceive me out of my body.

"It's the human thing to do. The responsible thing to do. Probably the only responsible thing I've ever done in my life."

But Sister-Eleven said "not yet". That I was a survivor and that's how I can help. By surviving!

"And you trust anything one of those despicable machines says?"

She wasn't a real Sister. She was something else. A Convolver, whatever the heck that is.

"Same difference, all just cold deceitful algorithms. He showed you that. Him with the name we can't speak anymore."

Who else do I trust? I have no one. A bunch of freaking dead people in my head?

"You've seen the assassin. You think even the Sisters can stop it? It wants me, you, us… whatever. I die in the end."

Who does this assassin even work for? I must be important. Is it death, the Grim Reaper, sent from the future to make sure humans fail?

"Fucking Christ, Rex. You're just some delusional, homeless guy with glowworms falling out your ass–"

Shut up! It's true. Look. If this, this Prisoner, really has the answers then this assassin wants him to fail, wants humanity to die.

"Or it's just an uber-lich looking for its Glow–"

No lich can take on a whole army, a whole nation–

"Are you ok, sir?"

Rex jolted alert and looked up at a small girl, a candy clutched in her hand.

"What?"

"You look kind of sad."

"Kind of. Yes, I guess I am." Rex struggled to sit. Blood ran down his face from where he'd torn a chunk of his scalp free with his fingernails.

"Mommy says it will be okay soon. The big ship's coming, and everything will be better." The glee on her face was real enough to be infectious.

A hand from around the door grabbed the girl and yanked her away and mommy stormed off down the road scolding her child for talking to strangers. The girl glanced back, waved her lollipop, grinned and began singing a nursery rhyme.

The words entered Rex's head: *The big ship sails on the ally-ally-oh!* And he remembered the alley, dead Xell, the voting machine. Yes, he'd voted for the Alliance. Sure, it was under duress, but he'd made a decision and contributed to this happening. But the voices had been different then. That huge voice was the Future-Lord, and the others just yammering demons.

The Alliance is coming.

"Maybe they can protect me."

No! They probably sent the assassin!

"Why would they want to destroy the world? They live on it too."

Not the world. Just me, a filthy parasite. I am the plague. He even said so!

"We sure are good at this crazy part." He lurched out the doorway and headed down the street toward the dark cloud of stone and dead-eyed windows. Were the Sisters watching? Their cameras all over the hostel exterior, sweeping the city with mechanical eyes. Surely, they knew he was coming. Why else would there be all these militia and hired guns patrolling the streets?

He ducked his head and shuffled drunkenly along, stumbling and stopping, prodding clods of goo and wrappers on the pavement before taking a few more steps. He edged down a side street, sidling along the length of the cathedral toward the front, one corner, one more, into another doorway.

And there it was, opposite: the entrance, like a giant downturned mouth. Rex felt its chill breath drafting from across the street.

He knew that entrance well, felt his steps and hops as he came back from work and carved another X on his room wall. He wondered how many Xs he'd missed. Had the Sisters scrubbed them away, erasing his tiny history, or did they still linger there awaiting his return.

Fifty paces and thirty-four steps away, an eternity for a sniper, even longer for an assassin with inhuman reactions and senses.

He'd never make it.

Men with guns patrolled the cathedral tower walkways. Checkpoints divided the street into fields-of-fire. A figure emerged from the cathedral's entrance, black habit, white face – one of the Sisters. She stood on the top step and scanned the street. Her head stopped tracking, facing straight at his doorway.

Fifty paces and thirty-four steps.

Run like hell!

He kicked back hard against the brick wall and launched out across the road zigzagging around pedestrians and the single car tracking down the center. On all-fours, then back on two, he felt two heartbeats, maybe three, pounding in overlapping rhythms. "Fucking yeah, Rex!" He heard Mira's voice. "Make sure it's the right heaven."

Bangs and shouts.

His face twisted into a grimace, anticipating bullets ripping through his chest, those long, skeletal fingers grabbing his neck. The Sister's head swiveled, locking onto him as he leapt the road barrier. She raised a hand, a signal to the militiamen. Rex hoped it was the right signal.

The right signal. The right heaven!

He hit the steps, bounding upward, five or six at a time. The

Sister came down, bending forward to grab his hand. "Rex." Her voice was soft and welcoming. "You're back."

"Sister-Zee. I have so much to tell you." His words tumbled over each other. He wasn't even sure they were words. "An assassin is after me but not one of those inside my head, it's real. It killed Sister-Eleven and there's a river of stars in my brain and a Prisoner who wants to escape and save the world but that means me dying and–"

"It's okay, Rex. Sister-Eleven confessed the Convolvers' sins."

"You're all I have left, Sister-Zee." He frantically scanned the building fronts across the street, feet twitching to keep running, keep moving. Standing still was a trap, a mistake.

His eyes roamed farther, past the shop fronts, up the curving hillside with its parallel lines of streets. Off into the distance across traffic signals and crosswalks. He couldn't see it, but he knew it was out there.

Sister-Zero eased him backwards up the steps, as his eyes remained fixated on an inconceivably tall building, the tallest in the city, the Parallax Tower. Leaning out over the Welkin, its glassy front was ten thousand eyes, and somewhere in there were two extra eyes, eyes that hadn't seen him. Yet.

The Sister talked, explaining the Convolution, their betrayal, and the Sisters' new plans to make things right by researching Glow eradication and rehabilitation.

Her voice faded to noise.

Two thirds of the way up the Parallax Tower one of the windows fell away. A dark mind stared out, its gaze compressing the space and time that separated it from Rex into a single, significant instant of meaning: *I see you.*

"It's there," Rex whispered.

Sister-Zero fell silent. Her sketchbook eyes followed his gaze. "It comes," she said, sadness in her voice. Something fell from the window, a black speck, tumbling fast then catching the wind like a glider. "It comes for us all. Inside, Rex, now!"

Her iron grip seized his arm and flung him through the doorway. Looking back, he saw the black dot sink below the rooftops. Alarms screamed from the building tops. A bright star burned through the cloud layers as the Alliance's huge embassy craft turned on its landing rockets over Coriolis City. Tracer bullets and bright-orange missile trails leapt up to meet it from militia rooftop emplacements.

The cathedral's gaping mouth swallowed him, and the massive doors drew closed. A blast-shutter dropped down from the roof. A gleam of sunlight pierced the door crack before it sealed shut. He wondered if he would ever see the sun again.

"The Sun will always be there," said the Prisoner, deep from inside his soul. "But is anything truly there if nothing conscious exists to perceive it?"

Jett didn't mean to kill his only friend.

He just needed to talk. To understand. The voices. The apparent hijacking of his AI-tagger. Distractions. Dog names popping up every time he saw a person or a tree or–

"What can I tell you, man?" Juggler had said. "You fucked with Glow, now it's fucking with you. Should've stuck to the good stuff like old Juggler told you to." He struck a forlorn pose in the middle of his floor, the remnants of yet another new door off to the side. "You could have just knocked, man," he said, the smatters of his chocolate drink dripping from the ceiling where it'd landed after his door surged towards him on the end of Jett's foot.

Jett heard nothing the little man said. Frustration was now a physical pain. Decisions so hard to make. And when his tagger flashed: *Rex!* over Juggler's face, he'd just reacted, a small slap, like that time he'd hit the technician.

He'd checked for pulse, breath, heat readings. He dredged through countless memories of people reviving other people, of pounding chests, blowing air through noses and mouths, jump-starting hearts with electric shocks and even grappling organs out of the body to massage them back into life.

But like Mira molding her child's face back together, none of those things worked.

He stood at the very edge of Juggler's tilted room, gazing through a window, across Coriolis City as meteor trails from TwoLunar slashed the blue overhead.

Are we winning, Ursurper?

The Alliance ship came in slowly over the cityscape, massive engines lighting the wisps of cloud as it gently barrel-rolled, orienting itself for landing. A monstrous craft, the GFC would never allow such a thing into orbit. But, clinging to the upper atmosphere, the super-hopper embassy class ship burned enough fuel to power a dozen cities as it coiled up from its distant launch pad, circled half the world and dropped back down to land.

Nothing shot at it from orbit. The GFC was either distracted, finished or had formed some pact with their mortal enemies. The only resistance came from the ground, flashes of missiles and laser fire from militia groups, arrows at a battleship.

No, the Alliance was here. They came for Jett, his Star-River, Glow and... Rex? Did they know about the annoying man who held a treasure trove inside his head? Were the Sisters going to trade him?

He mentally reached for AI-Gale, desperate for guidance, but stopped. Last time he'd tried it, Gale's skull-face had been replaced by a pixelated version of Rex that made woofing noises instead of speech.

He considered breaking radio silence. A final cry for help, but with the Alliance only kilometers away, scanning and jamming every communication for miles, it was a longshot, and one that would certainly betray his position.

The mission.

His focus returned to the cathedral. He'd watched their preparations from a distance, calling in hundreds of militiamen to rig the building with traps and kill-zones. If Rex was already in there, then why did their front entryway gape open?

He twitched with the need to fight, to storm the castle, to tear the place apart and find Rex, finish the mission, win! But couldn't. Something held him back. Self-doubt? Unfinished healing? Too many distracting voices yammering inside his head? *Mira!*

A Sister emerged onto the steps, scanning the surrounding buildings. Jett zoomed his gaze, mentally thrusting aside all the tags and thought distractions Mira's overactive mental imprint threw at him.

A man leapt the road barrier, running straight at the Sister.

Rex! The tag tried to hide itself, but he saw it. *Rex.*

The figure bounded up the steps, eyes all around, low and stealthy, up to where the Sister stood.

Definitely Rex.

No! No! No! Mira screamed, plastering tags across his vision. He smashed his head into a wall, punching through concrete and rebar. "Get out of my head!"

This ends now!

He kicked out a window, tripped over the sill and tumbled out. Plummeting like a meteor, his fingers spread wide, webs of fiber bridging the gaps like bat wings curling him up and out into a steep glide.

He sailed over two dozen streets before dropping below roof level, then flipped in midair, folding wings back into arms and heavy, spring-loaded legs. He hit the street, compressed, and sprang forward over another building down into the next street.

Mimicking Rex, Jett ran and then bounded, four legs, six, eight, tearing up the paving with fullerene claws ripping traction from the ground, propelling him forward through his own bow wave of sound, past cars and buses and out onto the main road to the cathedral.

Arrow-straight, he blazed a path through Welkin, through commuter buses and cars, leaving bodies and debris spinning in tornadic clouds. His mind was a roar of protest, a sea of tags and confusion. *Rex. Rex. Rex–*

He didn't notice the important tags through the haze:

Incoming.

Evade!

Evad–

The round smashed into his forehead, just left of center, and for the first time Jett became the darkness that he had always believed himself to be.

CHAPTER 39

And the Network Sees Me

Rex stared at the inside of the cathedral door. Latches and crossbeams clanked and growled, sealing the doors shut. Lights flickered as power switched from the militia-run generation grid to the Sisters' own, internal, sources.

Fucking Christ, Rex, you back in this cage?

"Mira?" He whirled on the spot expecting to see her standing behind him, but it was just more Sisters, their faces blank, devoid of any human features. Only Sister-Zero maintained a distinctive personality.

"Mira is not here, Rex."

"Mira's dead," he said, looking hard at the door, wondering if there was still some way to squeeze out.

A cheer rang out from the food hall where hundreds of residents milled around news screens, watching developments outside of the building. Sister-Zero turned back to Rex, her face now a more positive arrangement of features. "An auto-gun shot the assassin on the way to the hostel, Rex. The danger has passed."

"No, no. No, you don't understand, Sister, it doesn't just die. Shooting it just makes it angry."

The tone in the food hall changed as a deep guttural rumble spread through the building. "The Alliance ship is landing," Sister-Zero announced. "The militia resistance is futile, and they will take control of the Island. We have to get you to safety, Rex, before they arrive." Her grip was firm, the direction she swept him in non-negotiable.

They passed through a security cordon manned by fearsome, faceless Sisters with guns instead of hands. Through a door Rex had never noticed before and into an area of military cleanliness, shining metal, heavy locks and doors. Only Sisters occupied this area.

Doors slammed shut as they passed through, partitioning areas into defensible spaces. Sisters strung wires and welded metal bars across corridors. On through an ancient nave where a blank, stone wall resolved into a cunningly offset series of barricades that led to yet another hidden section of the building.

"Where are we going?" Rex asked.

"We have new allies, Rex. They will be in charge of your safety from now on."

"Who?" he said, feeling a sudden chill. The Sister didn't answer and that could mean only one thing: they were hiding something from him... again.

Like a beached squid, Jett's body took off across the pavement dragging its fractured head like a rock in a seaweed bag. It spun at a wall, thrashing through cement and rebar into an inside cavity, through the gap between floors, and on up the towering office building. Its nascent, survival-oriented mind sought darkness, confined spaces and altitude, avoiding warm bodies and noise.

Outside, militia flooded the streets, lively and confident at having seen their foe fall so easily. Puzzled by its apparent disappearance as if hauled offstage like a limp curtain.

Like Jett's body, his mind wove back together from strands. Not fullerene fibers but strands of awareness. Motes of who and where he might be that coiled together becoming more conscious. The feeling of gentle motion, of being carried, cared for... loved.

The glowworm voices were gone but some memories remained. Those ground and punished into him through training and repetition: his experiences. In that moment, he realized the lie of his existence. That he had never really existed before the mission. All those training exercises, voidian combat drills, battles across the Moon and Mars, through the vacuum of space... None of those happened, they were just simulations. Virtual beings jousting with machines and duplicates of themselves, copied and pasted into some base memory layer like the operating system of an old-fashioned computer. Jett saw all those layers: the innate survival memory buried under training simulations, all buried under those voices, the mass of additional memories he acquired through learning on mission. That part was still offline, and it needed to stay offline if he were to function as a warrior.

He was a fleeing rat: find a hole and hide, keep moving, avoid detection, find other rats. But all his kind of rats were up in space, fighting their way out of Cloud9 as his creator and mentor, Ursurper Gale, stormed the orbital.

And here I am–

His inner voice sounded calm and alone, not the AI-tagger, not his memory, not the annoying woman who'd contaminated his thoughts to distract him from his mission.

The mission.

His standard bipedal form gelled out of the ooze of fibers. His head twitched and rotated, arranging itself back on a coil of thick neck and shoulder cables. He extruded an extra-long arm and reached up to the high ceiling of the empty ballroom he found himself in. Grasping overhead beams, he hauled his body up and through another layer of structure. Up, rising through the floor into a living room, to pause like a smoldering stack of coal radiating the heat of combat exertion.

An old man sat in a chair watching a TV screen. He glanced at Jett, took a desperate swig of his drink and returned to the screen. Jett touched his head where the bullet had struck, a fist-sized section of skull had broken away. His finger probed the space inside: circuit modules, rolls of flexible silicon memory substrate, a separate module was probably his Inner-I. Another was the AI-tagger or some other add-on Gale had stuffed inside his crystal skull to enhance his functionality.

He withdrew the finger and a wad of fullerene crawled up his cheek and formed a plug for the hole. He was lucky to be alive. The bullet had ricocheted away, taking the skull fragment with it but not entering and shattering the precious circuits inside.

I'm just circuits. A machine, and yet I feel alive. I remember. I see. I feel.

The man in his chair completed a slow blink. His eyes opened onto an empty room with a smoldering hole in the floor and a man-sized break in his wall leading to the next apartment.

Think, Jett. Think and plan while you still can.

AI-Gale? He mentally activated the function, but no skull-face flashed into his vision.

He kept moving, cautiously taking back control of his body from his autonomous response systems. Damage warnings: major head trauma, impossible to heal. Some auxiliary memory modules missing, destroyed, but a reconstruction process had begun from backup arrays. A blinking bar across the bottom of his vision informed him of the time left until the reformat completed and the voices and memories he'd gathered from the Glow victims rushed back into his head.

He snatched clothes from wardrobes, draped himself in disguises, exited and entered new buildings working his way closer to the cathedral. His green arrow was back, blinking the direction he needed to go. He loved this silence, this clarity of thought, dreaded the voices. Was this how a Glow addict felt after a fix?

The cathedral loomed in the next street and the Alliance embassy craft angled in over the rooftops toward Welkin park. Landing was imminent, and Jett knew that whatever issued forth was of a severely higher military grade than anything he'd yet fought.

He found his mark, a long corridor in what was once a hotel. A window at the end looked out across one last street to the sheer side of the cathedral. The gray tiles of its roof started about ten meters above.

Jett stoked his micro-cellular-fusion reactors, bringing everything online, sucking air through microscopic pores, cracking hydrogen, fusing it and venting the exhaust helium through tiny ducts.

His consciousness tuned to maximum throughput and his world slowed, cars eased to a halt, people froze mid-step. Fluttering flags gelled rigid; their colors dimmed to grayscale. Sounds grew louder, faraway events moved closer, detail sprang from blandness. The inside of his mind grew larger, like the void of space.

Plan, reconfigure, fight, and win.

He eyed the length of the corridor, people poised mid-flight. Their heels and elbows motionless as they dived for escape doors and side rooms. Eyes wild with fear at the monster at the end, steam and heat rising from its furnace-red body.

Jett's core shrank, no point wasting material on a body. He became a mass of legs, arms, and appendages connected by webs. Two, slim, snakelike necks articulated his head.

I am Jett. Voidian. The ultimate warrior.

He touched his headwound like a salute. The external rumble of ship engines ceased. The real enemy was here. He imagined the voices of his voidian kindred cheering. "Burn brightly, Jett. For the voidian!"

I am a machine with one, singular purpose.

His sonic boom shattered all glass in the building as he roared down the corridor, fragmenting the immobile humans in his way. Jett exited the window, up and outward, massive back legs thrusting him into the air, shattering the concrete windowsill from which he leapt.

He sailed out into the air on toward the battle he remembered training for, the battle he imagined he'd wanted the whole of his short life. In his mind's eye, she watched as he blasted away into space, a pioneer. He who would change the world and create a galactic civilization. Nothing would ever be the same. He saw it in her eyes and felt it in his chest: *Pride.*

CHAPTER 40

Incoming

Ellayna clawed her way through the now very familiar corridors between the medical wing and Jesh's lab. Her coordination was way-off. Flashes of Inner-I noise threw her vision into pixelated color-scapes. Sounds came and went like alarm gongs sounding right in her ears. Tiny, yellow worms crawled the periphery of her vision as if chewing reality away from the edges. *Inner-I glitches or is something really eating me alive?*

She dipped a mental toe back into Utopia, hoping Hmech was waiting, then sidled out and back to Ben Nevis in case Del was there. *Screw you all.* She collided with a wall and crunched to a painful halt.

"You okay, Director Kalishar?" She spun around to confront the voice behind. Just one of her guards. She'd forgotten they were following.

Tomas's message icon blinked on. "Are you there, Ellayna?"

"Tomas, tell me you haven't done anything stupid yet?"

A low-bandwidth monochrome of his face prickled into vision. He looked better, more upright, as if he'd made decisions that he felt good about. "I'm waiting for you."

She threw all caution to the wind. What did it matter if Taunau, Martin, or anyone else decoded her intentions. "I tried reaching Hmech, but he refused contact."

"They're already here, Ellayna. Ghosts."

"If that were true, we'd all be–"

"Dead? I saw a ghost and hit myself with a low-power stun bolt from my finger gun. Knocked the Inner-I offline and there he was, plain as day. Would probably have gutted me too with his knife, but I was lucky, and some guards were just around the corner."

"Did the guards see this... ghost?"

"Of course not, our Inner-Is are hiding them. It's the opposite to augmented reality, artificial blindsight, and we, Ellayna, are so very, very blind."

She turned a corner and glanced back. The corridor behind was empty. "Tomas, my guards have gone."

"Come straight to my escape pod. Strapped inside, we can't hurt ourselves anymore. Once outside GFC control any contact and hacks through the GFC servers should be impossible."

"I'm meeting Jesh to remove my Simmorta. It's compromised, spying on us, Tomas."

"Figures." Tomas's shoulders slumped. "I turned mine back on. Increases my odds of making it through open space, surviving reentry, and remaining functional long enough to appreciate my escape."

She reached a junction. Her mental arrow showed Jesh's lab to the left, escape pod storage to the right. "Don't go anywhere yet, Tomas." She hung up his connection and pinged Martin. "Martin, my guards have vanished."

She heard Martin's breathing, a stressful sucking sound. "Martin?"

"Ellayna..." She almost gasped in relief. "Your guards are right behind you."

She stared into the light, willing a shadow, anything to betray a hidden presence. Martin's voice made her jump. "They're not responding to my pings. Must be coms failure or–" He vanished into a haze of static.

She ran toward Jesh, only thirty seconds away, gripping her finger gun, rotating the bezel to full power. "There are no guards, Martin."

There was something in front. A perverse inversion of reality like someone invisible crawling along the floor while their shadow walked through the air above. She startled to a halt and the shadow vanished. She turned sideways... *There! In peripheral vision.*

"For god's sake Martin, I need guards, support." Static gurgled back from Martin's feed.

She turned and jumped, kicking her feet off the walls and rolling into a side-on barrel roll, deliberately confusing her visual systems. If Tomas was correct and her Inner-I hid reality, then overloading it might throw off the hack. She grabbed at sims and news feeds, peering through the fakery. There! Closer now, moving steady and confident toward her, a hint of human shape in stop-motion.

She slapped her thigh, triggering the kill-switch. Her ARG went offline taking with it all her coms and information displays, clearing her vision. Nothing, no ghosts, no shadows.

Made sense. They'd infiltrated her Inner-I, not the ARG. She grabbed her finger gun and twisted the bezel back to its lowest setting and touched the ring to her temple.

"No!" yelled a voice out of nowhere as she pressed the fire button.

The electric jolt knocked her senseless. She convulsed, hanging in midair, legs curled under, dropping slowly to the floor.

Her eyes perceived the orbital without the benefit of augmented reality. *We really do live in a shit hole!* Filth clung to the walls and ceiling. She focused down the corridor and saw the ghost, now just a man dressed head-to-toe in light, pastel green, running toward her, knife in hand.

Jett shot from the hotel window across the road, spreading wide like a net to clamp onto the cathedral wall. A moment of sublime peace and purity of purpose. The red bar showed three minutes until his auxiliary memory reconfigured and swamped his thoughts. Enough time to find Rex, rip the Star-River from his skull and exit to safety.

With a single jolting bound, he was up and rolling across the roof tiles, microseconds ahead of bullet trails that dissolved the granite slabs into heat and shrapnel.

Sparks flew from Jett's fingers as he tore up the slates to the roof's peak. A laser grazed his shoulder, its energy dispersed along translucent fibers. He vectored sideways faster than the targeting system, and hurdled the roof peak to land on the other face looking out in the opposite direction. A second to pause, take images, plan, all his foes on this side of the building were off-guard, guns pointing the wrong way.

The Alliance embassy ship was down in Welkin Park, enveloped in a mist of incoming fire. Mobile gun platforms scurried across its surface seeking optimal firing positions. They clamped down like limpets and strafed the surrounding buildings, returning any incoming fire with deadly machine precision.

That battle was over. The militiamen were throwing their guns and fleeing. Their loyalty to their drug bosses and commanders suddenly and dramatically diminished.

Focusing downward, Jett swam through tiles and roofing material, down through layers of insulation, wooden joists and steel mesh. He dropped into the attic, landing at full run, his green arrow picking a logical direction and sending him barreling through work benches, washing machines, and ranks of drying sheets and towels.

Randomized search pattern.

Facial recognition prioritized: Find Rex.

The cathedral roof vault was six-stories of utility rooms, storage, and staff quarters. A wonderful three-dimensional combat zone where Jett had full range of motion leaving his cumbersome enemies shooting at shadows.

He cleaned out swathes of rooms like a hurricane through a paper city, avoiding doors and straight lines, spiraling along corridors, dropping through floors, popping up through roofs. People stood frozen in panic as he passed, those with weapons toppled into bloody heaps as Jett became a scything mesh cutting through flesh and stone, then rolled into a quadruped with huge thighs and battering-ram arms that bludgeoned its way through walls and barricades, leaving limbs and disembodied heads whirling through the mist behind.

His AI-tagger tracked targets: hundreds of heat signatures, some fading as bodies cooled into death. Snapping faces and running comparisons... *not Rex... not Rex...*

Reinforced doors loomed ahead. Goshguns forward. Panic preceded him like a shockwave. Heat signatures behind the doors milled and churned in terror. Even the Sisters had a little heat glow.

He struck the wall next to the door. High-speed debris killed most of the defenders. He flattened a survivor before his finger squeezed his gun trigger. Appendages like whips cleaved a half-dozen militarized Sisters into segments. White plastic heads spun and dropped as he left.

Not Rex... not Rex...

Next room. He didn't even see the people die: automatic combat. He left the room through the back wall one-fifth of a second after entering, firing both goshguns back over his shoulders, vaporizing survivors. The recoil propelled him through the wall into the next room, leaving an unholy mess behind for someone to clean up.

Not Rex...

Not Rex...

Two minutes to reboot.

As Sister-Zero robot-handled Rex through the cathedral's underground, a clatter of tiles on the distant roof roused alarms into full voice. Gunshots clanged through the echoing building. Something exploded with a muffled thump.

"I told you," Rex said, watching the Sister through narrowed eyes. He toyed with Cyc's destruction meme, while thinking circles around the Prisoner's actual name. *No, fuck it. Del, that's your name. You caused this. It's you it's after, not me. I don't even exist.*

The Prisoner stirred, shaking off its bonds and slowly cohering into Del, a fully formed, wholly actualized persona, pinned to the Star-River, encircled by Rex's dog-centric firewall.

Del tried to shrug off his bonds, but Rex held him tight.

"It's in the roof," Sister-Zero said, through the sound of another tile avalanche. The gunfire ceased and only the rumble of the Alliance ship's engines broke the eerie silence of the crypt.

Militarized Sisters closed in behind, following them up a stairway into a domed rotunda. Rex's feet clattered across an elaborate floor mosaic. Rings of pillars climbed and divided like tree branches to support the ceiling where they meshed into a sprawling stonework canopy. Militiamen clung to the rotunda's perimeter, using the pillars as cover.

They looked relaxed, carefree, just hanging with cigarettes in their mouths, guns pointing lazily at the ground. *Dead meat.* He stared at all the Sisters, *shattered machines.*

Five troopers emerged from a side door, led by a blank-faced Sister. Covered head-to-toe in body armor, only their mouths showed through transparent windows at the bottom of their helmets.

As they drew closer, Rex noticed iridescent bubbles covering their bodies. The bubbles glistened and jiggled confusing the light and his vision. They smelled like freshly sprayed paint.

The lead trooper's mouth moved, but no sound came out. Sister-Zero stood facing him, conversing through some technological interface. At some unheard signal they raised their visors exposing young, attentive faces and their voices spilled into the rotunda. "It's moving around up there." One of the troopers tracked the barrel of his gun across the ceiling following the trail of chaotic noise. "Moving real fast. Probably scoping the place, mapping defenses."

Rex thought their weapons looked too small; pencil-thin barrels that merged with their wrists. Cables looped away to ports on their amour.

"What are we fighting?" Sister-Zero asked.

The oldest looking trooper answered: "The boss calls it a prototype space exploration and colonization unit. Some fancy artificial biology makes it bad-ass." He slapped the shoulders of his fellow troopers. "Orders are to either kill it and return its bits to the GFC or destroy it completely in an incinerator."

Fear shot through Rex, but it was fear coming from Del. *He recognizes these troopers!*

"In the short term," the trooper continued, taking an ominous grip of Rex's shoulder. "We need to get this one to a safe house so the boss can figure out how we can arrest the treasonous son-of-a-bitch inside his head."

Arrest? Treasonous? Rex felt Del squirm, could anyone feel more trapped at this moment?

The sudden realization hit Rex and he grabbed a handful of Sister-Zero's clothing. "You can't just hand me over to them. What happened to me being important? Some kind of prophet?"

"Falsehoods perpetuated by the felon residing inside you, Rex. He duped the Sister-Eleven and the Convolver sect into helping him escape the GFC." Her mechanical fingers pried Rex's grip free and he stared at his hand as she turned and glided away.

"We should fight it here, in the open," said a trooper. "In close quarters it's killing the militia, look at the security feeds. They can't track it. It moves too fast."

"I'll stay and set an ambush," said the youngest looking trooper. "You move out."

They bundled Rex out of the rotunda and into a connecting corridor. A metal blast door creaked closed. *Cages within cages, minds within minds.* Mechanical bolts cranked shut, partitioning him off from everything behind. Ahead stretched what was left of his life, imprisonment for Del's treason, death at the hands of the assassin, or damnation: an eternity of hell buried inside other minds.

He took a firm mental grip of Cyc's destruction meme. When the time came, he would end it as best he could. *You ready, Del?*

he asked, but the Prisoner couldn't answer, still a mist of disparate thoughts, pinned apart like a science project inside his head.

When the end comes, I'll make sure that you see it, that you face it. You'll get to see what you've done to us both.

CHAPTER 41

Blind Sight

... Not Rex...

Jett cleaned out the habitation modules dangling from the roof of the cathedral's nave. His mental model of the building's interior grew, filling the blanks, mapping the Sisters' kill zones, crossfire lines, barracks. The emerging model suggested something important hidden behind a heavily defended cordon in an unmapped area that blinked red warnings in his mind.

Not Rex...

Not Rex...

He felt the frustration, time ticking by. Surely the Alliance troops were knocking down the cathedral door?

One minute to reboot. Voices stirred in his mind as his auxiliary memory self-tested. Jett tried to ignore them. *Why wasn't there an off switch?* But then why would there be? Why would a rational being switch off its own memory?

Down through the triforium, there were fewer defenders. Most had retreated to the transepts, grouped in clusters, their weapons pointing at the roof where they thought Jett still hunted. Seconds later he sprang down into the upper gallery, deserted.

Not Rex...

Not Rex...

Rex!

There, his tagger flagged a ninety-eight percent certainty, crossing the security cordon into the unmapped part of the cathedral, escorted by one of the Sisters and a string of militiamen.

His tagger plotted alternative routes. The guidance arrow pointed to an external stairwell on the nave's periphery. He broke through a wall, dropped down the full height of the building, ignoring the spiraling steps and passed through a storage room full of chairs and folded tables. His vision flashed red: *Warning! Unknown area beyond the wall.*

Forty-five seconds to reboot!

The voices stirred, Mira's voice. Traces of her thoughts began seeping into his mind like a slow poison. He hurled himself at the wall, busting through into a mosaiced rotunda.

A trooper, a gun, bullets shattered wall bricks behind his head. Jett curved up the wall, now a flattened net of loosely connected limbs. A hail of explosions tracked inches behind as the guided hyper-velocity munitions ripped the air, unable to correct course fast enough as stone pillars and Jett's random vectoring confused the missiles. The trooper tracked slowly in his stiff amour. Off-balance, surprised, he leaned away from his gun-arm, hoping its fire-control would save him.

Centrifugal force glued Jett to the wall until he snapped his limbs into a cone, flinging his body at a target pillar. In midair, he rolled nets back into solid cores, two massive arms extruding lance-like fingers that grabbed the pillar, sinking anchor-points into the stone, swinging him around to fire the goshgun at point-blank range into the trooper's chest. The gel bubbles over the armor dispersed the impact, but the colossal momentum of the hyper-compressed gas explosion smashed the trooper back into the wall. Fissures ruptured across the stone as he struck.

Not Rex.

Jett finished the trooper with a backhand swipe and exited through the door on the side opposite the Sisters' cordon before the body hit the ground.

Forty seconds to reboot.

A corridor, another blast door. Bipedal again, huge legs, battering-ram arms with clubbed fists. The uproar in his head grew louder, babbles now coherent voices.

Not yet!

He punched his head, tearing away the fullerene scab and exposing his headwound. He wanted to jab a finger through that hole and rummage around until the voices stopped.

Find Rex.

Find the Star-River.

He smacked the flap of skin back over his head. Noisy troops and the near-silent mechanical Sisters raced toward him from the security cordon. He ripped the blast door off its hinges and entered a long, straight tunnel. Echoes of footfalls came back to him along the corridor. *Rex is right here.*

He heaved the door back into its frame and tore it to shreds with his fingers, molding and bending metal into the surrounding stone, sealing it shut against the humans and their weak machines.

As a fullerene octopus, he blazed down the arrow-straight tunnel spitting granite cobbles and wall tiles behind.

Twenty seconds until reboot.

Another blast door ahead. He hunkered low, extruded more legs, bunching arm muscles into corded pillars, and hit the door like a supersonic wrecking ball.

The door went ahead of him, spinning and crashing along the tunnel as he exploded into a tentacled mesh, clawing along the walls, guiding the door ahead like a gigantic rolling shield.

Ten seconds.

There was definitely blood on that knife.

As if to emphasize the point, the man carefully wiped it clean on a cloth that he rolled and hid in the pocket of his sickly green jacket.

Ellayna could only stare as she bounced gently off the ground. Her shoes' magnetic field secured her feet in place while her head drifted like a balloon in a soft breeze. Her neurons crackled with the energy of her own stun-blast, struggling to reconnect with nerves and limbs. Her Inner-I remained offline. A flashing icon counted down the seconds until reboot.

The man moved closer, crossing her eyeline. "Ellayna, Ellayna," he said, shaking his head in disappointment. "What am I going to do with you?" He looked different from what she expected, older, face stressed and lined more like an old man than the near teenager that he was. His eyes held a deep sadness, signs of things he knew and had seen, had done. *Whose blood was on that knife?*

As he bent closer, reaching a hand to stabilize her wagging head, she knew him but couldn't form words, just a grunt and some drool that may have sounded like his name. "Trabian." He eased her up into a sitting position as another bubbling approximation of the words issued from her mouth. "How... you get... to Cloud9?"

"I've been here a while, Ellayna, doing covert work for the Alliance."

She wanted to scream at him, grab at his eyes. Instead she sank back into his arms. If he'd wanted her dead, then she'd be dead. As for his treason, well, he'd just done what she was doing, only he'd done it sooner.

"We pretty much run this place now." He glanced up at the ceiling where surveillance systems should have been alerting Martin and summoning help. "I can move and reassign guards, confuse cameras, hide from people's senses while in plain sight. The Alliance owns the GFC, Ellayna, and they own you."

"Bastard!" she said but didn't really mean it. Her Inner-I was back, low-resolution video feeds swam into focus showing conflicts breaking out around Cloud9 security zones.

Trabian chuckled and rolled back onto his haunches. "The GFC has been finished for a long time, you know that. I'm just helping it along and making sure the right people are in the right places when it all ends." He eased to his feet, gripped her under her arms and hauled her up next to him. "Now, since you've been such an influential figure in my life, I am going to go against my master's orders and help you. Tomas is prepping his escape pod, and nobody cares. Not the GFC, not the Alliance, not the dreaded Ursurper Gale coming to destroy us all and liberate the voidian hordes. Nobody cares if you defect." He looked behind toward a bustle of anxious voices and footsteps heading their way. "Time for me to leave. Go join your friend."

She noticed that Trabian was already gone. Her Inner-I now filtered him into the background, using his clothing like an old-fashioned movie green-screen but instead of adding special effects, it rendered him invisible. Not perfect, but good enough to deceive distracted humans whose minds were always looking inward. She felt his hands release. Her weight settled onto numb legs and an invisible hand guided hers to a handhold on the wall.

His voice continued out of the air before her face. "That assassination, that really was the Alliance hacking my feed. We had a falling out about that, but they forgave me, and they are willing to let you live." His voice moved away. "Goodbye, Ellayna." The Alliance hack of her systems was amazing, terrifying and clever, it even masked the sound of him walking away into total silence.

As she propped her weight against the wall, the shadow appeared at the end of the corridor, a head and shoulders shape looking back at her around the corner. "Goodbye, Trabian."

She hung on the wall awaiting the return of her strength, tears flowing out of control. *I'm sorry, Trabian, sorry for everything I did.* He'd saved her from the Alliance, negotiated her freedom. Maybe he was a traitor to the GFC, but his love for her was clear.

Even after eight years, she could still hear Taunau yelling like a madman as she shook the sleep-fog from her brain and dipped into the VR operations room. "We are all dead. All of us!" His hand waved at the virtual displays. "They've stolen a space truck transporter. Defectors. Traitors! Loaded it with picoforms. If they reach Earth, then our biomech monopoly is shattered and we starve and rot out here with nothing to trade."

The truck curved away from Cloud9, a rectangular hulk with a giant heatshield and four engines, used to ferry supplies up from Earth in exchange for the kilo or so of Simmorta that the remaining GFC picoforms outputted. Video images showed men and women, some who she recognized, Lyn Folley, Max Horton, Arraben Bose, many of Del's friends and compatriots, ones Taunau denigrated as liberal enemies of the GFC. The ones that wanted technology to be free and available to all… *exactly what caused the Nova-Insanity.*

Somebody had off-lined security while they stormed the truck and loaded their possessions and stolen machinery. This was a coup, a rebellion, a great defection.

"I've exploited a security flaw in the truck's AI. Sending a worm over now." Weimin, one of Taunau's hackers sat at a computer console. She shunned virtual interfaces preferring a keyboard and lightning fast fingers to trawl code. She was the only real person in the room. The rest were just holograms in virtual vision.

"Can we force them back?" Ellayna asked, hope filling her voice.

"No," Taunau punched the table. "There's only fuel for maneuvering and a landing parachute."

"My worm's inside," Weimin added. "Scanning for vulnerabilities."

"Where's Del?" Ellayna demanded. "He must know how to stop this."

"I'm battling Del," Weimin flashed her a look of contempt. "He's stayed on Cloud9 to coordinate this attack."

Del's not fleeing! Suddenly things didn't seem so bad. Sure, she knew he was planning something. Del always was. Those thinly veiled hypotheticals about what she'd do if she went back to Earth, how they could survive. They'd stripped Del of his founding status only days earlier, a consequence of his outspoken opposition to GFC policies, but this? *Treason?*

"Got something," Weimin's screen grew huge as she zoomed on lines of code. "I can blow the entry portal lock, emergency evac protocol. Vent everything into space."

"What? No–" Ellayna nearly choked.

Martin Haller's voice interrupted. "Hull breach!" A warning siren flared through Cloud9. A camera feed showed debris spinning off into space as something black and bipedal ruptured through the orbital's skin and into the void. "It's Gale. He's broken free of Del's lab and escaped."

"External gunnery!" Taunau yelled.

"All pointing the wrong way." Martin's tactical screens showed Gale vectoring off at an angle toward TwoLunar using a compressed gas cylinder for propulsion.

"We'll chase him down later. "Taunau's face was a deep shade of red, even in VR. "The truck will be out of our range soon. If we shoot it, we'll be murderers in the eyes of the world and the GFC. This way, it's a horrible accident and nobody but us need know the truth."

She watched the tiny blip on her screen moving away from Cloud9. "Only a few seconds of range left." Weimin eyed Ellayna. Her face had that sly smile that said: *You decide. You're so fucking important.*

"If it escapes, then we are finished." Taunau was right in her face. "They have to pay for this atrocity. We make examples of them and this never happens again." His eyes pleaded. She saw through him to the frightened little homunculus inside. Loyalty to the GFC was a front, a convenient security blanket over his cowardice.

Weimin began the countdown. "Ten, nine…"

"We can't just murder them–" Ellayna's voice rose to a near scream.

"Six, five…"

"They die or we die!"

"Two–"

"Do it!" yelled Ellayna. Back on her bed, she folded into a knot of horror. constricting her stomach until it wrung the vomit from her guts. Images of those people flashed through her mind, bursting and rupturing, their screams frozen in their throats.

What have you done to us, Del? What have I done?

CHAPTER 42

Adversarial Networks

"That was easy," chuckled one of the troopers casually lifting his helmet visor and grinning at Rex. It was not a friendly grin. "Thought the Sisters would give us shit for stealing their precious dog."

"Nah!" another said, "GFC's got them by the balls."

"Robots don't have balls, 'specially nun-robots."

"You in there, Del?" The older trooper rapped a knuckle on Rex's forehead as they paused in one of the many side rooms that lined the irrationally long corridor. "Martin thinks you are." He shrugged at Rex's lack of response. "Wouldn't like to be you, traitor."

A voice blared from the trooper's helmet speaker. Rex couldn't hear the words, but the tone was angry. "Yes, sir," they all responded, snapping to attention. Their faces now somber. "Scotty didn't make it. Move out!"

A sound like a massive bell resonated along the tunnel, followed by crashing, rolling thunder. "Fuck! It took out the blast door." They ran, Rex hoisted off the ground by a trooper on each side, passing through another door, securing it and searing the lock with a quick laser blast. A hundred very rapid paces down the corridor the tunnel bent ninety degrees.

"I'll stay," a trooper crouched at the corner, gun-hand sweeping back toward their pursuer. "Fucker's not getting past me without eating a hyper-wad."

The three remaining troopers grabbed Rex and raced for the next door. Pushing it closed, they left it unlocked so their rear guard could follow, if he survived.

Halfway down the next run, the bell tolled again. The thump-thump of a hyper-rifle snuffed into silence before the peal finished its second echo.

"Man down." They kept moving. Rex smelled their fear even through their armor.

"Stay," the lead trooper yelled at his two companions. "Lay down cover fire as you back away."

The two troopers dropped into a firing stance and peppered the previous door with shots.

Rex hit a ninety-degree bend as the bell rang again. The door fled its hinges and cartwheeled along the tunnel ripping away wall and floor chunks in a haze of shrapnel. A shadow bounded behind the door, its multiple limbs tearing up the floor, walls, and ceiling, as it accelerated toward them in an insane spiral maneuver shrugging off any incoming fire that snuck past the whirling door. Rex heard their screams. The battle-numbed shrieks of those whose time was over.

"Shit! Run! Go! Go! Get the fuck out of here!" The last trooper kicked Rex through another doorway. He stumbled onto all-fours and bounded on, sensing a shift in the air. A sniff of hope ahead. The promise of daylight one last time. Del was alert now, confused, but fully formed like a newly awakened astronaut floundering around the inside of a distressed reentry capsule. *You see this, Del? You see what's come for us?*

Behind, the trooper struggled to slam the door while pumping fire through the narrowing crack. A shockwave blew out Rex's hearing and swept his feet away, tossing him into a rolling ball that somehow regained balance and kept running. The door came at him like a piston in a bore, smearing the old trooper across a wall. Rex lunged at the corridor bend, hurling himself sideways as the door plowed on through the wall inches behind him.

We're never making it! Never going to make it!

Heart pumping, bounding, slipping, skidding on all fours then back on two. "Free me!" Del yelled, now a madman pressed to the glass of his prison cell. "I know this foe. I created it."

But Rex had no mind, no sense of reality. He just ran, pounding straight for the waft of air ahead. He burst into a room, throwing the door shut behind. Light, like the hand of the Future-Lord, reached down from a trapdoor above, welcoming him to Haven. He pounced at the staircase, hands grabbing at the light rays.

The door behind shattered. Rex screamed, a single wailing exhalation of terror as his front foot mounted the stairs.

A hand like a granite wall smashed him to a halt. He struggled in its grip, teeth and feet and fingers clawing at the grotesque face as it rose up on a sea of carbon-black limbs that folded and twisted back into human-like body parts.

Another hand with freakish long fingers encircled his head, fingertips clawing into Rex's eyes and ears and into his mouth, thumb poised on his temple ready to pry open his skull and root the prize from its contents.

He closed his eyes and focused on Cyc's baby. *The right heaven, the right heaven.* Imagining the string of connections that held together the tenuous mental threads that made him real, he pulled.

His world imploded.

"Got you," said Jett.

Take it. It's yours. And Rex was Rex no more.

CHAPTER 43

Convolution

"Martin? Are you out there?" Ellayna massaged the feeling back into her legs while stumbling toward Tomas's escape pod. *No time to remove my Simmorta. Maybe that's for the best.*

"Ellayna, thank the stars, thought we'd lost you. I'm losing feeds, people are dropping offline. It's – it's like they're here."

"They *are* here, Martin."

"How?"

"They hacked Simmorta, and used that to infiltrate our Inner-I software. We can't see or hear them. I know because I just talked to one of their agents, Trabian. He's turned, others have probably turned as well." She considered her next words as Martin seemed to sob quietly to himself. "I'm leaving now, Martin. You should do the same."

The sobs grew louder "Well, that's just fucking wonderful."

"I'm heading for the escape pods. I'll risk going full-immersion once inside and do whatever I can to help you."

"Fucking, fucking wonderful."

"Come on, Martin. I need you focused."

He sighed, "Sure, Ellayna." His feed vanished.

She shrugged off Martin's apathy and ran along the row of escape pod chambers. Some doors were open, a person inside frantically checking and prepping their pod. Others remained shut and locked. Her Inner-I identified Tomas's unit. "Tomas, I'm outside. Let me in."

The door opened and she stepped through into the prep room, tapping the door shut behind. The escape pod sat up on its maintenance cradle, hydraulic lifts clamped it in place next to the feed tube that would vent the contraption into space.

She touched the pod's door opener. It hissed and swung upward revealing a desperately cramped interior: twin padded coffins, face-to-face, only a nose distance apart. Webbed into the bottom casket lay Tomas's corpulent, naked body, so pale as to be almost translucent. Tubes and wires splayed out from him vanishing inside the curving wall of machinery to his sides.

Prepped to leave, Tomas breathed slow and shallow. Eyes closed, he could have been dead. "Tomas?" He didn't stir. She brushed fingers across his forehead, and he snorted. *Sedated?*

She flung off her clothes, paused naked next to the pod, fighting the claustrophobia. *Just a few hours... I can do this.* Simmorta could sedate her if necessary. She bundled her clothes into a tiny locker at the foot of the coffin and pressed a button that rolled the whole contraption in the hydraulic arms bringing the empty chamber down next to her with Tomas hanging above in his restraints. The chamber's side dropped open allowing her the space to shimmy inside. It felt slick, as if Tomas's sweat had dripped down onto her cot. "Don't you ever clean this thing?"

"Ellayna?"

"Martin?" His voice shook, an image screen opened, and she looked out of Martin's computer terminal into his mortified face. The lines, the tears, the pain. "What's happened?"

"Taking a lot of hits. They've got lasers on Earth and on satellites: x-ray, microwave, all kinds. We're shuffling shields and deflectors but they're coming from so many angles. Soon they'll start focusing, catching us in crossbeams, picking off their targets. They snagged me with a few glancing blows, got some minor burns. Don't think they want to kill me, just maim and incapacitate."

Sick and hopeless, she struggled for an answer, anything to tell the man. "Martin, just get out, go to your escape pod and take a chance–"

"No," Martin shook his head. "It's over. Some Protectionists broke into security's gun store. They all died, just ruptured, like – like balloons. The Alliance can take us anytime, anytime they want. They're letting you go, Ellayna, but not me." Martin sounded drunk. His head flopped back and forth as if struggling to keep his heavy skull upright. "I've signed over security protocols to you. The defense of Cloud9 is now in your hands."

She spoke through tears. "Martin, it's been an honor working with–"

"Yeah, whatever, it's been a real blast."

"No–" she screamed, as he flipped the tiny pill from his ring into his mouth and swallowed. "I'm sorry, Martin." She wept as foam boiled from his lips, dissolving his flesh and brains, making sure nothing remained to be copied, reanimated or used by the Alliance. With the last of his cognition and strength he pushed the finger gun under his chin and–

She cut the feed. "Oh god... Martin–" The sides of the cot hugged tighter, squeezing, as if she slid slowly down a serpent's gullet. Lights and screens flicked alive and the pod connected with her Inner-I.

"Pre-launch sequence initiated," said the calm, female voice of the pod AI.

Support webbing snagged her arms and legs. She gasped as the fluid recycling sheath wrapped around her body, sprouting bladders and smart tubes that squirmed like snakes as they located their assigned orifices. Tentacles grabbed at her chest and neck, inflating and gurgling as they ratcheted tighter. Unseen needles pinched and pricked at her skin, inserting monitors and nutritional tubes. *Is this the end? Assassination software in the pod's AI? No. Trabian said they'd let me live.*

The pod's lid closed, hissing tight; lights blinked through the darkness illuminating her body's entombment within the machine's digestive tract. She screamed a silent cry into Tomas's sagging face. Here, on Cloud9's remote rim there was just enough induced gravity to ease the drip of saliva from Tomas's lip off and down where it webbed to her nose.

"Come on, Tomas, wake up!" She pumped out messages in brightest, urgent red.

Silence.

She checked Tomas's flight-plan, not much of a plan really, just launch and drop. A few diagonal thrusts to line up on Tomas's European Utopia and then pray the landing rockets fired. Pray the Alliance or the Protectionists or Gale or someone she hadn't even thought of, didn't blow them into the void or fry their brains with energy beams.

She accessed Martin's security protocols, pulling up his tactical displays and plans, a whole different world of control and combat. She saw Gale's incoming ship, troop clashes across Cloud9, gun battery status, Tow Truck just hanging in space next to Cloud9. In another panel, five GFC troopers fled through a tunnel under the Sisters of Salvitor's cathedral on Coriolis Island and Alliance launches filled three full screens with estimates of military capacity, arrival times, defensive options.

A timer next to Gale's incoming ship read eight minutes to impact. "Hell, Martin, why aren't we firing at him?"

Empowered by her Inner-I information, she arranged the views into a single holographic pantheon like stacked glass, adjusting their focus points to grok everything simultaneously. Melding mind and information, she became Cloud9, a conscious machine.

Gunnery control: the bulk of GFC defenses pointed at Gale as his clock ticked closer to zero. All live, all tracking, all hers. In her mind she gripped the virtual triggers like the tail gunner on a fighter plane. "At least I'll take you with me, fucker!"

She gripped the mental trigger, poised to unleash the maelstrom, to watch Gale and his delusions disintegrate into micro-meteors. But as her mind focused on the moment, on that fragment of Del residing inside that electronic mind, her fingers eased, and slipped away, replaced by the simple question: *Why?*

Del Krondeck dropped into reality like a shrieking newborn, as the wave function of disparate thoughts collapsed into a singular being and dumped him into hard reality. From being just an abstraction inside a virtual world, he now sucked air through real lungs, focused actual eyes, and coordinated limbs and muscles, all while fighting a tsunami of pain from cuts and fractures and strained, torn muscles.

He dangled in the searing hot grip of a voidian, something that just shouldn't be part of any reality. He choked out words through his newly discovered vocal cords, "Ursurper Gale?" and felt the carbon-black fingers lock. The thing that might have been an arm jolted, and the ragged features covering the translucent crystal skull shifted into what might have been surprise.

The diamond hard claw pressed into his temple easing through bone like soft cheese. Del screamed and struggled, but the grip was impossible. "Ursurper Gale, please… it's me, Del Krondeck, your creator."

The face drew close, oily fluid seethed across the damaged features, swarms of wormlike fibers writhed, seeking out ends and anchors and raw fullerene nutrients as they bonded into temporary flesh, sealing over new wounds.

The realization hit him. "You're not Ursurper Gale." He expected to die in that instant, but instead, the grip eased, and the deadly finger pulled back from the edge of his brain.

Zero seconds. Memory reboot and configuration complete.

"No!" Mira's voice wailed inside Jett's head so loud it caused his fibrous muscles to spasm. His hand lashed out, snatching the fleeing man from the steps of the cathedral tunnel. His other hand crashed down to smash the skull open. It was there, the Star-

River, a nub of cold blue inside the red heat map of Rex's brain. A malignant growth that must be torn free.

"Stop!" The memory clone of Mira's thoughts grabbed control of Jett's body, holding him rigid, fingers circling the skull, but Jett eased back control. *Not so hard, don't damage the Star-River.*

Tags flashed in his face: *Not Rex. Not Rex... Not fucking Rex!*
Lies!

Rex hung limp, eyes rolled up so only the whites showed. But as Jett watched, they rolled back down, swimming through confusion before locking on to his gaze. Wide with recognition, they didn't hold the horror Jett was hoping for at that precious moment when he won and snuffed out his miserable life. Instead, he heard the name of his creator, and stranger still: the name of his creator's creator, a name that sparked many memories, feelings of warmth, loyalty and even fear.

Fear spread across the dangling human's face as a sudden truth seemed to dawn.

"You're not Ursurper Gale."

Jett fought his own body and Mira's banshee wailing inside his mind. He pulled the squirming man's face closer. "And you are not Del Krondeck."

"I know you're not Gale, but you are voidian. I created the voidian. I created Ursurper Gale. I *am* Del Krondeck!" The tiny human twisted with pain as Jett's fingers singed the flesh on his neck and scalp. "Tell me your name," Del gasped.

"I am Jett," he said, shocked that he'd felt compelled to answer. He struggled through layers of memory trying to recall what Del Krondeck looked like. *Why can't I remember ever seeing him?* A few fragments came to mind. "Lies. Del is imprisoned on Cloud9." Jett's hand twitched again as the urge to destroy, claim the Star-River and move-on grew strong. But Mira's yell and the man's absurd claim stayed his hand.

The man now calling himself Del continued talking. "Did Gale copy himself?" He reached out a hand and touched Jett's face, finger tracing the wound in his skull. "You're damaged."

"You're not Del," Jett hissed. "I know Del, his face is here in my mind."

"Sure, not the real Del, maybe a copy, like you, or I migrated my mind into a drug substrate. It's hard to tell at this moment what I am."

Jett shook off the induced calm. He needed that boiling rage to finish his task. "We'll see." His monofilament tendrils extruded from his fingers. Del squirmed and screeched as they found his nerve endings.

At first, he didn't see Del, just the usual mass of dormant, fragile personas stuck in the somanetic web. He saw Rex, now just a glowworm, dead and silent, awaiting some trigger to kindle him back to life. There were others, but they had shrunk too, their memories absorbed into Rex's more stable structure, leaving just the two beings, with a hint of a third that Jett couldn't quite see. It possessed few actual memories, but many connections to the host's brain, almost like somanetic maintenance patches for missing brain functions.

Del was his own massive web anchored to the Star-River but connected to Rex through a fragile cable of linked nodes, like the mythical astral cable that bound a mortal body to its soul.

Jett plunged into Del's life, witnessing the creation of his own creator shuffling around a lab like a robot, connected to machines and monitors. He saw Del's treason, freeing Gale, rebellion against the GFC. Incarceration. He saw the plot to escape by migrating his mind into a machine substrate. The painstaking years of working in VR building copies of everything he truly was. He saw Del's fear: the somanetic plague sequestering all life, leading to the algorithmic death of the universe. Cold, unconscious, ruthlessly efficient.

"Help me, Jett." Del's voice became an all-encompassing whisper. "A plague like nothing ever imagined is coming. I must be inside it, guiding its development. Losing means there's no humanity, no biology, and no voidian. Is that what you think Gale really wants?"

Jett hit the AI-Gale, and the skull flashed into vison. "This man claims to be a copy of Del Krondeck. Here on Earth with the Star-River. What should I do?"

AI-Gale remained silent. Then it winked out of existence replaced by a message tag: *Do it, break radio silence.*

Jett frantically messaged Gale, aware of the treacherous radio signature whipping out into air and space, alerting the antennas and tracking systems of the Breakout Alliance only a few hundred meters away.

Nothing returned. Just white noise.

He tried again, upping the signal, surely Gale was there, not dead and destroyed with the fragments of TwoLunar? He knew what he had to do: crush the skull, destroy this – this imposter. *Kill my own creator?* Seize the Star-River. *But why? If Gale and the voidian were all dead–*

Gale's image sprang into his Inner-I. "Ursurper?" Jett gasped in relief. "I am at the Sisters' cathedral and I have the Star-River." An icon blinked in Jett's vision as Gale synchronized with the AI version of himself, snapshotting Jett's experiences and data stores down the secured link.

Gale's voice oozed into Jett's mind. "This is a most unexpected development. The real Del is on Cloud9 and will soon be destroyed, but this – this other Del could be a valuable ally. If he truly has the Star-River, then he can get the device to safety and–"

"I can do that," Jett blurted aloud. "I can fight us out of here, evade the Alliance and GFC–"

"Jett, no. Your mission here is complete. We must trust Del's insight and set him free. I have another mission for you."

"But this weak human – this Rex. How can we entrust the Star-River–"

"The body Del chose proved worthy. It survived the streets of Coriolis, it even evaded you, Jett, for more time than our mission could afford."

Jett's fingers snapped open and the man calling himself Del dropped to the ground. He staggered to his feet and looked up at Jett, now a frozen monolith lost inside his own world.

"Go!" Jett roared.

Del stared at him a second longer, as if about to question his decision. Coming to his senses, he leapt up the stairs toward the glimmer of light.

"I am minutes away from dealing our enemy a mortal blow," Gale said. "Victory is ours."

"But I have failed you, Ursurper, I have no Glow, no Star-River, no insights into its creation."

"You have uncovered important connections between Glow and the Sisters. The Star-River is no longer with our enemies and now, Jett, you are right where I need you to be." A crash echoed along the tunnel from the cathedral as the enemy blasted through Jett's makeshift barricade. "Fight your way to the top of the cathedral tower. You have four minutes. If you make it in time, I will be there for you."

"There? How–" But Gale vanished, leaving Jett staring as Del scampered up the last steps and lurched out to freedom.

Jett powered back through tunnels past the remains of troopers and blast doors. Militarized Sisters and terrified militiamen met him halfway. He folded a metal blast door in two, wrapping it around his arm like a giant gauntlet. Compressing his own soundwaves ahead of him, Jett leaned into the oncoming fire and churned forward like a heatshield through dense atmosphere.

The voices were quiet at last, lost in his violence, stunned that he'd let Del or Rex go free. He looked for Her, needing that companionship, and there she was, radiant, red-haired, beaming at him as she held out a picture of them both together. The man she was with looked nothing like the human wreckage he'd held in his hand, but looking into his eyes had felt strangely like looking into a mirror.

CHAPTER 44

Head For the Light

The escape pod heaved and rotated, hydraulic rams hissed and groaned, shunting Ellayna nearer to Cloud9's exit port. The overly calm voice of the pod's AI spoke directly into her mind. "Escape pod ready to launch. Please confirm flight plan and initiate a ten second countdown."

Her webbing squeezed tighter prepping for acceleration. The lighting dimmed, and an ominous hum rose from the electromagnetic catapult that would fling her free of the doomed orbital.

"Flight plan confirmed," she said. "Hold at ten second countdown." She twitched as more saliva dripped down from Tomas poised only inches above her. She wanted to reach out and wipe his face, but her arms were pinned by webbing.

She focused on Gale's ship, four minutes to impact, close enough to see details. He'd deployed the vehicle's frontal debris scoop, gathering a small ball of rocky fragments onto the ship's nose. A little extra destructive momentum but scant protection against the GFC's defensive fire.

She reached out and pinged Gale. Instantly, he popped into her mind, carbon-black knots and twists sculpted into a weird asymmetric face. The beady black eyes seemed to reach across the shrinking void into her soul. "Ellayna," he said, mouth unmoving. "I'm glad to see you are still alive."

"Your clone did well down on Coriolis." She eyed the flatlined life indicators next to the GFC trooper screens.

"Jett captured Del and uncovered his audacious escape plan. Are you pleased, Ellayna?"

She struggled to keep her voice from shaking. "This... Jett... it killed him?"

"Jett crushed him to pulp and incinerated the remains."

Ellayna choked back the tears, reengaged her Cloud9 fire controls. "You sick bastard. I–"

"Couldn't let such a valuable mind fall into Alliance hands now, could I, Elly?"

Her fingers slipped again, mind swimming back to reality, staring up at Tomas as more drool plopped onto her face. *Elly?*

Between drips she managed a sad laugh. "You know there aren't any voidian people on Cloud9. This whole, 'save my people riff,' is false memory planted by Del to keep you attacking us."

Gale emitted a rasping noise, possibly an attempt at laughter. "Ellayna, please..." his face filled her Inner-I space, intimate and close like a lover's. "I think you have a deep misunderstanding of who my people are."

"The voi–" Suddenly her words seemed weirdly out of touch with reality.

"The voidian people are an idea. Plans hidden; blueprints sown in minds and technology caches. Who watches this conflict, Ellayna? The whole world watches. It's wondering who flies that suicidal mission into the crown jewel of the GFC hegemony. Who frees them from oppression, from addiction? One day they'll know who.

"The GFC is the pressure-vessel containing the pent-up echoes of the Nova-Insanity. I am punching a hole, Ellayna, letting that pressure explode free, propelling humanity to the stars and toward us. The idea. The voidian."

The timer ticked over to one minute. Gale's face twisted into a parody of a smirk. "It's been fun, Ellayna, but I must go and make my peace. I hope you choose not to shoot me down. My sacrifice will deny a great treasure to the Alliance and in that field of chaos and debris, just maybe an escape capsule can slip through."

His feed went dead. She sighed, mental fingers still twitching to fire but knowing that she couldn't. "May you find allies in unexpected places," Del had said. That was proving to be startlingly true.

"Time's up, Tomas, let's go." She hit the countdown.

"Sequence commencing, launch in ten seconds. Nine..."

"New flight plan approved. Seven..."

"What new flight plan? I didn't approve any new–"

Tomas convulsed, a vast, wracking heave, his face blooming red as blood vessels ruptured and a stream of acidic vomit splattered her face.

"Tomas?" she gagged. "What flight plan–" She fumbled through her control icons that fled her mental grasp as if deleted by a hacker's nimble fingers.

"Three..."

Tomas's tongue flopped out of his limp, dead jaw, almost reaching her face as the pod lurched sideways into the launch tube.

"Two..."

"Hello Ellayna." The voice was the only thing left inside her head, all controls had vanished, vomit burned her eyes and mouth.

She knew the voice. It scalded her heart the way Tomas's death bile seared her face.

"One..."

"Trabian? What have you done?"

"Zero."

Del Krondeck clawed his way up the steps as if wolves were dragging him down through the gates of hell. A smattering of daylight greeted him as he fell over the top stair and onto a sprawl of rough-hewn granite tiles.

A fearful glance back down into the tunnel confirmed that Jett really had let him go and had gone back down the Sisters' tunnel toward the cathedral building.

Freedom! He couldn't quite believe he'd escaped, not just from Jett, but from Rex's mental prison, and from years of confinement on Cloud9. He let that thought seep into his soul, through the clouds of glowworm memories to Rex, huddled and dormant, the light of freedom, like the gates of Heaven opening and shining through: *the right Heaven!*

The greatest jailbreak in history! Some day the world would know of this, but not now. Now, he had to lie low, escape to safety and plan the next stage of his infiltration into the spreading somanetic plague that he'd studied inside a Star-River simulation.

He rolled to his feet and ran. A real body, spindly, thin, malnourished, but sinuous and strong. "Thank you, Felix." He silently thanked Rex too, a temporary construct whose survival instincts and experiences had allowed him to continue existing while the glitches and faults of his great plan had worked themselves out.

He fled along a stone tunnel lined with the names of the dead. Light beams lanced through slits in the roof. The air was stale and old, not the air he expected on Coriolis Island. *A sarcophagus – a damned tomb. Ironic.*

He ran easily, sucking in the air, ignoring pain, and reveling in the feeling of actual motion. He skipped through a tiny door into a sparse, stone chapel. In the center, sat an old car with bars for windows and solid hand-carved tires. Cans and tools lay scattered. A guard-post blocked the only exit.

Standing half seen inside the guard building was a fierce looking robotic Sister. Her goshgun pointing right at him. "Shit." He slowly raised his hands as a sinking feeling of defeat dropped through his stomach. "Come on–" But the click of other guns prompted his silence. A dozen militiamen hid around the garage, their eyes filled with fear. Del noticed all their guns pointed behind him. Of course, they were expecting Jett.

"It's just me," he said, feigning confidence and control.

"Where's the infiltrator?" demanded one of the militiamen.

"I scared him away. Don't fuck with the dog-man." Del laughed nervously. A long silence followed as everyone chewed over this unexpected outcome.

A loud mechanical voice blared from the militarized Sister. "Sister-Zero confirms the infiltrator is back inside the cathedral." She paused as if examining data feeds on her internal communication net. "Detain Rex and move him to a secure location."

"Do you know who I really am?" Del shook his head, feigning disappointment in the Sisters and the militia, while carefully stepping forward, just a little closer to the outside world and true freedom.

"Yeah, we know exactly who you are," a rough voice said, as the cold barrel of a pistol jammed into the back of his neck. The rest of the motley militia found their courage and crept out from hiding.

"Secure him," the Sister said.

"That thing's coming back. If I were you, I'd get out of here." Del considered the look-behind-you-gag but doubted it would work.

The man with the gun spoke into his ear. "You can walk nicely, or we can start breaking things."

"Ten seconds of freedom. Thanks a lot." Del hung his head as men muscled him outside past the Sister and into the chapel's graveyard. The sky was clear and hot sun shone down on Coriolis Island. A streak of meteoric fire burned from horizon to horizon with a soft, whistling song.

"Wow!" One of the militiamen said, as they all gaped at the sky. "That one's going to hurt."

A trail of military aircraft swarmed the now distant cathedral tower like flies around rotten fruit. "The Alliance?" Del asked.

The militiamen nodded somberly. "We're all out of a job real soon."

Del sucked in the warm air and shuffled his feet through the alien environment of dirt and grass. "The world is changing," he said. "I hope you're ready for all this."

* * *

Jett's mind became mercifully detached from the heinous destruction his enemies inflicted upon his body. He reciprocated. Like a force-magnifier, the more they fought, the harder he killed back. Moving and acting with smooth speed and inhuman precision, without thought or compassion.

He became unsure who or what actually did the fighting. As a spectator watching through a sensory portal, he drifted farther away, ignoring the close-in imagery: the death, the chaos, the mounting toll of damage tags that striped his vision red. As his semi-autonomous body, cued by the overriding mental layers of training and planning, whirled him through a cathedral of enemies toward Ursurper Gale's newly defined destination: the peak of the cathedral tower. *"If you make it in time, I will be there for you"*.

Left eye: Destroyed.

Fiber damage thirty percent.

Head fractures. Head traumas. Damaged memory modules.

Inner-I damaged: configuring backup module.

The green arrow guided him completely now, an algorithm for fighting. He fired at everything and everyone, grabbing new weapons from corpses, emptying them into the next row of routing attackers, picking up more weapons, ignoring the damage, so much damage...

Alliance troopers stormed the cathedral, gunning down the militarized Sisters and their hapless militia allies. For crucial seconds they fought on the same side until it was just Jett and the new enemy. They didn't have the deadly hyper-rifles of the GFC troopers, but they had high-powered weaponry, explosives, missiles, and each hit chiseled another fragment of Jett away, sculpting him into nothing and tipping his body ever closer to its inevitable entropic death.

He crashed out onto the cathedral roof. The air buzzed with Alliance combat craft and their guns were all trained on him now. The force of fire thrust him through the tower door into a moment of beatific relief. He stopped and stood facing a wall, barely able to remember how to walk let alone climb, but his legs were already climbing, icepick fingers snatching handholds from the stone walls.

Something attacked him as he fell out of the stairwell into the bell tower. Mechanical hands grabbed at his head, twisting, pulling, trying to rip away his skull. The sagely Sister made her last stand amongst her books and servers until Jett threw a coiled fiber around her and yanked upward, spaghettifying her into a stream of plastic and metal fragments that jingled back to the floor.

One of the giant bookcases stood open like a secret door, and behind, Jett saw computers and micro-manufacturing machinery: the Glow factory, hidden right in the midst of the Sisters' cathedral. The place he'd glimpsed through the detached Scylla head. He thrust fibers into the machines, twitching carelessly into processors and memory substrates seeking the data he so urgently needed. With no mind to process the results, he routed them straight to AI-Gale and dropped into a heap in the middle of the room.

"I'm here, Ursurper." He fought to expel the words. His jaw was gone along with his rudimentary voice-box. No spare material remained under his control to form a speaker. He visualized the words curling out into space, seeking Ursurper Gale's distant antenna.

Damage critical. Repair nodes at overload.

Inner-I at baseline functionality.

He drifted for a while, just dreaming, thoughts of times and places he had never really known, training missions, fellow voidian warriors… All lies, fabricated memories designed to yield a specific personality, a warrior, a being with nothing to lose and a cause to champion.

A noise on the stairwell jolted him alert and he stuttered to life, snapping his appendages back from the Sisters' machinery to hurl chunks of stone wall back down the narrow shaft. The sounds stopped but he could hear machines gathering, lasers burning through rubble, real troops checking real guns. He wished he was in better shape. This battle would have been glorious.

He focused his gaze out the small, slit window. Something out there–

Sniper! Incoming!

A crack on the skull sprawled him across the room. A missile tracking behind the bullet lodged in what was left of his chest cavity and exploded. In that instant, Jett's body died. The nascent mind that held it together fragmented, and his fullerene tendrils fell limp, unwinding like the threads of an old blanket. Jett spread outward like a melting sculpture, settling into a mound of fabric with a shattered skull on top.

He saw his three-layer mind again, oddly inverted with the primitive, somanetic part dead, gist-memories shattered, but the higher consciousness functions still struggling on. He saw another level, something hidden until now, below even the primitive mind, like tiny emergency beacons winking to life using radio signals to seek out their kin. Not a mind, more of an algorithm. As he stared inward, it ground alive shunting dead fibers back together: *A recovery mode! There is still hope.*

"I'm here, Ursurper. Awaiting your arrival."

Both eyes were gone. Jett was a mental construct that failed to connect with any physical sensation. He wallowed in emptiness, a hollow, cavernous sadness. Something he'd seen in the eyes of so many humans as his hands snapped their lives away.

"Jett?" Gale's voice jolted him back into consciousness.

"Ursurper. Have you come for me?" He imagined Gale towering over his torn corpse, lifting him into a ship. *Like She did that time, lifting his bullied, teenage body into her arms.* But the voice was just an Inner-I voice, and the signal delay told him Gale was far, far away.

"Jett, I can't be there. The final battle has gone well, but I must see it through to the end."

"I understand," Jett felt Gale synchronize with his AI version once again and for an instant he was that youth, lying crushed and beaten on the pavement as the thugs scattered. She stood over him, face all concern and sadness. She balanced onto a single leg and put her shoe back on, and then bent down and heaved him up and into her arms. "I can't always be here for you, Del."

"I know," he said, as she struggled holding him up while walking him slowly back home.

Through the hazy memory, he heard his real voice talking. "I found the Glow factory, Ursurper. Right here in the Sisters' cathedral."

"You have done well, Jett." He felt the pause as Gale examined the data.

"How do they make Glow, Ursurper. How did they break the GFC's code?"

"They didn't. They followed instructions sent to them over a secured link. The Sisters never possessed such knowledge."

"Then I have failed, Ursurper."

"No, Jett. You are exactly where I need you to be."

Of course, Jett understood now. He was a tool, a distraction. The enemy assumed he had the Star-River and they wanted that and the Glow factory. Let them think they had it all in one place, as the real Star-River scampered to safety inside the body of a frail, odd human.

"I can still fight, Ursurper. I feel the recovery algorithm kicking alive inside me."

"Rest, Jett. There is nothing left for you to do. In the future, humans and voidian will thank you for your sacrifice. As long as one of us still exists then a little of us all remains."

Jett felt the algorithm finish, grappling together as many of his microcellular fusion nodes as it could into one single, ringed configuration.

"I understand, Ursurper." The warmth grew stronger, swelling his imaginary chest with pride. Jett tried to speak but the heat burst from his core like love, smothering his words and thoughts and any feeling of existence.

For a fraction of a second, Jett blazed like the sun's core, a nova of heat and light so bright it shone through solid stone.

The cathedral became shimmering glass, a transparent outline suspended in midair that collapsed into an expanding lake of plasma. The buildings of Welkin toppled inward before blasting back out. Dust and debris rolled across Coriolis Island riding the leading edge of a shockwave, like the aftermath of a meteor strike.

CHAPTER 45

The Right Hell

"A lot of good men died because of you," said a thick-set militiaman, whom Del had christened Oik. He prodded Del in the back as they walked along a street away from the city center. Swathes of militia lined the rooftops, looking down on them as they passed. Oik commanded a silent respect from the others.

"Yeah," said the moon-faced man with the piglet eyes. "What does he know that's so important that the GFC got involved?"

Del guessed Oik was an important figure in this militia faction. Moments earlier, he'd led a coup against the Sisterhood, leaning into the goshgun blast that blew the militarized Sister into fragments while the others cheered and chanted, pounding the sky with bullets and cursing the GFC.

Del gazed up to the narrow strip of daylight above the alley as contrails from meteoric fragments drew bars across the sky. In the distance an old-fashioned air-raid siren bawled out its desperate cry.

"Dunno, might be worth something though," Oik said.

"Fuck the Sisters," Moon-Pig said. "We can sell him to the Alliance."

Del focused on the bigger picture: he was the virus within the virus, the autodestruct inside the plague. Here at the beginning of an endgame that so many prophecies foresaw, he was exactly where he needed to be. Apart from these goons selling him to the Alliance, something that might well be worse than returning to the GFC. If there was even a GFC left.

"We should find out what he knows before selling him." Oik grabbed his shoulder and pushed him to the ground.

Not again, he thought, feeling Rex's street memories stir, curling into a ball waiting for the attacker to punch himself out or get bored. *Act dead, act crazy, run like hell... fight!* He laughed at the simplicity of the chant, and reminded himself that Rex was never real, the fragments, the leftovers – maybe the best parts – of other minds, glued together by a simple unshakable belief. Fascinating. An emergent Glow-based somanetic organism, a conscious being, born inside a drug-substrate. The idea was so intriguing. Perhaps form dictated function, the body needed to survive so the somanet spawned a complex survival meme, a persona dedicated to simply surviving that–

A chubby fist smacked into his cheek. He winced but felt nothing. This body was old and numb beyond its years, beaten, burned, tortured, surgically altered, drugged and mangled. It had surprisingly little in the way of nerves left.

He rolled back into a kneeling position, ready for the next blow, carefully angling his feet on the ground, ready to spring and *run like hell!* He wouldn't get far, too many angry men with too many fists. He wasn't a survivor like Rex. If it wasn't for Jett, then he'd still be buried inside that purpose-built survival construct. *Perhaps that's my best chance.* He focused on the Star-River and tried to fall back into nothingness. He knew Rex had used a destruction meme, a mental thread that he pulled to topple his own tower of awareness, but Del had nothing like that to cling to.

His view down the street ended at a warehouse, rows of increasingly taller factories and blocks lined up behind. In the distance, he saw the tower of the cathedral. Somewhere inside, Jett fought on. He wondered how that battle went: the anachronistic versus the futuristic.

For an instant, the world was quiet, birds stopped singing, people ceased moving, everything froze in a singular moment of hyper-awareness.

A leaf seemed to stick in the air just in front of his nose—

Oik's fist touched his cheek, lining up for another strike—

And then everything became light.

His assailants shrieked, the top halves of their bodies melting into flame. Del felt the laser focus of heat-blast singeing the top of his head. His survival construct kicked-in rolling him into the road gutter, a familiar place of water, shit, and oil, with a sturdy concrete curb to shield from attacks.

The electromagnetic pulse intensified, and the somanet that was Del Krondeck fizzed in and out of coherence, fighting with all the tenacity of a space-born radiation resistant biomech.

Through the disruption another mind surfaced, unaffected by an EMP; the buried, tattered, shreds of biological brain flickered to life. Each of the mind's disparate components perceived its own reality, but the image of a cathedral dissolving inside the heat of a nova bomb slammed those fragments back together, searing new connections, cleansing away the atrophy.

"No!" Felix wailed, stumbling to his feet, trying to fry his own pathetic brain in the fading heatwave. "Not again!" He leaned into the wind, heat scorching his face. This was how he deserved to die, in the furnace of his own creation. How he should have gone years ago, but the heat flash faded too soon and still, he lived.

The rush of debris and wind came at him like a brick wall as he fought the dog for control of his body. The dog didn't understand, it knew nothing of bombs and explosions, but it knew fear. Even as Felix tried to stay in the path of the deadly storm, his legs twitched, thrusting him sideways out of the street and into a doorway. An instant later a freight train of wind-born debris ripped past, gutting buildings down to stumps and rubble piles, turning cars and people into shrapnel.

The dog faded, content to hide and whimper in a corner. Felix also had no will to move, laying still in the choking darkness. The howling wind stopped, and airborne wreckage crashed back to the ground leaving the stout shop doorway and a jagged chunk of wall standing like a monument to the dead.

Zero...

Ellayna screamed as acceleration tried to ram her brain out the back of her skull. Vomit spewed from her mouth only to slap back into her face. She blinked away the filth, unable to tear her gaze from Tomas's dead face just inches away.

"Trabian," she gasped. "What have you done?"

Trabian's face appeared on her Inner-I surrounded by the webs and wiring of an escape capsule interior. He smiled, a sad, resigned smile. "Have a look, Ellayna. Your empire, your creation, your baby. Watch it die." A portal in her mind showed space, Cloud9, the tiny dot of Gale's ship moving so fast. It raced at the orbital's side and vanished, no fire or drama, fragments emerged from the other side of the orbital almost instantly as the hypersonic projectile ripped through. She saw the internal explosions billowing jets of gas and fluid. As she stared, Cloud9 seemed to rupture down the middle, one half imploding, the other curling lazily away, gouts of smoldering wreckage leaking from the open wound.

All dead, all gone. But that didn't matter. "You changed my course, Trabian. Where are you taking me?" Terror crushed her chest. *He* had control. *He* could send her plunging to Earth or into the heart of the sun, and there was nothing she could do.

"Nowhere, Ellayna. I'm sending you absolutely nowhere. A nice long tour of the solar system, very erratic orbit, maybe you'll be back in a few years' time."

"You bastard! Why?" She stared at Tomas, imagining the rot spreading, the fluids leaking from his head, bugs erupting and filling the tiny space... and all the while tubes and needles force-fed her and her treacherous Simmorta kept her alive and breathing.

"I'm fulfilling a promise I made to myself after the Alliance revealed to me what you did to my mother, Ellayna."

Her tears seemed to freeze upon her face. "No... Trabian... you don't understand. Times were different, we made decisions... bad deci–"

"I could have just killed you, Ellayna, maybe tortured you for a while, but that wasn't nearly enough. I wanted to send you to hell, but not being a believer in such things, I decided to make one all of my own."

"Please... please, Trabian, find a way to forgive me."

"I've loaded the pod with nutritional resources for a couple of years. Your Simmorta should keep you fully awake, vitally alive, even as things decay into something truly horrible. I'll give you a few years, Ellayna, maybe I'll forgive you then."

"You utter fuck!" she screamed.

Trabian's voice grew loud and reverent. "This is for my mother, and my father who forgot who he was after you murdered the love of his life. This is for me and all those others you've oppressed and ruined over the years. I'm heading to Earth now, Ellayna. The Alliance has a lovely mansion set in the Canadian mountains waiting for me."

"No... please no–"

The pod's heater clicked on, ramping the temperature up to the limit of human endurance. She shrieked at Trabian's image as it faded. Her throat bled as she tore her voice box into silence. Ellayna struggled, squirmed and twisted in the tiny margin of space available to her... not even enough to reach a hand to her face, if she could even free a hand from the fullerene snares. Maybe she could sever an artery or induce a stroke, but the tiny machines inside were hard at work sealing wounds, nourishing, making her young and perfect again. And again. And again.

Her Inner-I went dead, blank and empty. For the first time in her adult life she was truly without it, no VR, no escape, nothing. *Soloing.*

The lights in the pod faded. Only the red system LEDs blinked through the darkness illuminating the dead face only inches from hers. Like tiny flames burning through eternity, the distant fires growing closer as she approached and passed through the gates and entered Trabian's hell.

CHAPTER 46

All Things Must End

Mira left her hired bodyguard at the foothills and climbed the last hundred paces onto Transit Mountain's base plateau. She saw the craft waiting for her. It didn't look like an airplane, more like a helicopter with two side-by-side rotors humming like giant fans.

The Sister stood next to the vehicle, waving as she walked across to meet her. News feeds cluttered her new Inner-I: casualty reports, riots, war raged across the world and through the Earth Halo. She touched the scar on her temple where the surgeon had made the incision. She was a rarity now, a Glow addict with an Inner-I. The Sisters had found her online very quickly, offering help for her addiction.

"It is good to meet you, Mira," the Sister said.

Mira shook her hand, soft and plasticky, but with an unnerving feeling of strength. "What do I call you?" she asked.

"Sister-Eleven." She stepped up to the ladder leading to the pilot cockpit.

"Why Eleven?" Mira asked, mounting the separate ladder that led into the rear compartment.

"How many fingers do you have?" Sister-Eleven replied.

"Ten," Mira said, unsure what this meant.

"And what comes next?"

Mira assumed it was one of those nebulous Future-Lord sayings and climbed into the back seat. She looked out over distant Welkin. Fires still burned; smoke shrouded the city. The cathedral was gone, along with most of the surrounding skyscrapers. Somehow the giant Parallax tower remained standing, although it leaned more than ever. The gigantic pyramid of the Alliance's Embassy craft quietly smoldered. The nova blast had stripped away the buildings, leaving it standing alone next to the newly formed fusion-glass lake. The blast had thwarted the Alliance's takeover of Coriolis Island. Some said it was a massive suicide bomb and that the Sisters were responsible. Others claimed the GFC was involved. For the moment, the various militias could rejoice: Coriolis remained free, if that was the right term. The Alliance would undoubtedly be back.

Mira slammed the door behind her and settled back in the seat. It wasn't as plush as she'd imagined: hard, plastic bars across the windows and a heavy mesh separating her from the pilot cockpit. "Where are we going?" she asked.

"New Galapagos," Sister-Eleven replied, her head turning to face Mira, swiveling like a tank turret with her body pointing straight ahead.

"I didn't think anyone lived there," Mira said.

"They don't." Sister-Eleven stared at her as the craft trundled along the short runway and became immediately airborne.

"I wonder if Rex made it," Mira said, almost to herself.

"If he survived, then we will find him for you," Sister-Eleven said. "We have teams out searching."

Coriolis vanished into a bluish haze and open ocean stretched before them. Mira felt oddly relaxed, strangely happy, despite the horrors she'd been through. Meeting with the Convolvers over their Glow addiction program felt like a good decision.

"Tell me about your confrontation with Jett," the Sister said.

Mira registered a tug of surprise that she knew about that encounter. She felt something stir in her mind as if vestiges of the monstrous being remained. She shook the feeling off. Jett was gone, life was going to be okay. She eased back, feeling the fibers of her body relax and unwind. The fresh ocean air taking control of her mind, coasting her into a pleasant sleep. In her dream she carried Rex, light and fragile in her arms. "I can't always be here for you, Rex."

"I know," he said, smiling up at her.

"But I will when I can."

Felix staggered through choking dust, across fields of shattered concrete and rebar, past gutted, smoldering buildings.

A glint caught his eye... a gun?

He grabbed up the weapon and spun the old six-shooter barrel. One bullet. Enough. "Why am I here, Del? I'm supposed to be watching from the background as you fix this mess." But Del didn't answer. He was the Prisoner again, a dream state of ideas glued to the Star-River.

Felix put the gun to his head, finger trembling on the trigger. His brain would finally die, blown out across this hellscape. Maybe someone would gather up the nanotech scraps and piece them back together inside a new body. Perhaps Del would carry on and save humanity. Would any part of Felix still exist as witness?

He adjusted the gun barrel, a different angle, into his eye-socket, under his chin, down from above on the top of his head. He shoved it in his mouth and spun around trying to distract his thoughts enough to just let his finger do the work. That twitch, that miniscule contraction that *he wouldn't even know about. It would just end.*

Just end!

He threw the gun down, "Fuck!" He picked it up again. He'd done this many times in the past, back when he roamed Coriolis, homeless, lost, crushed by his own guilt. He'd never had the courage then, why did he think he had it now? Drugs worked, drugs and booze and the pain of physical dereliction.

He stumbled on, drunk on angst, pointing the gun at random people, hoping someone would shoot back. He even clicked the trigger once or twice, hoping that last bullet would fire, and he could throw the gun away.

His feet carried him along, or maybe it was his nose. The smells of destruction faded as he followed the flow of refugees out of Welkin to the Caelum district.

Dirt smelled different here, good soil for growing things, not the filth of drains and machinery. After hours of trudging, he came upon a village. Small, smart rows of houses were separated by lawns and trees. This was the type of place people came to die when their life clocks expired. Ancient faces watched through twitching curtains as he grumbled through.

One house caught his interest, small and mildly neglected with a large, well-manicured garden. Like all the others in the row, but with a fortress of vines and flowering bushes defending its perimeter.

He stumbled along the side, peering over the fence into the rear garden. An elderly couple sat in rockers on the patio, reading and snoozing. The old man stood and walked over to his vegetable plot. He poked at the dirt with his shovel, thrust a hand into the small of his back and went to sit down.

Felix hopped the fence into a clump of prickle bushes and crept out the far side toward the garden's rear. A tall hedge separated the back half from the vegetable plot; a rose arch joined the two different worlds. He wandered through, smelling the roses, admiring the colors, brushing against the thorns. The arch led to a secret garden, a small plot of flowers and grasses. A fence marked the garden's end. Beyond lay rolling hills and cattle fields, and a small lake, close enough to fish without leaving the garden. Far away, distant Coriolis City boiled in smoke.

His feet seemed to halt of their own volition. "Here?" he asked them. "This is where you want me to do it?"

He pulled out the gun and snuck a look at the chamber. The bullet was next in line. No chance escapes this time. Unfair, he decided, and looked away. He spun the chamber and put the gun to his temple, aware that if it fired there would be no oops-moment, no ouch, no regret, no sense of failure or loss.

"Last chance, Del. You want back?"

Silence. Just birds.

He squeezed.

The gun clicked, the barrel rolled, and his hand dropped back to his side. "Best out of three I guess." He lifted the gun again, but his foot caught on a rock and he looked down onto a simple grave of rocks and flowers. Two sticks formed a cross, the old type of orthogonal cross, not one of those diagonal Future-Lord crosses.

He stuffed the gun into his back pocket, knelt and read the wooden plaque at the base:

Here lies Rex.
Our friend forever.
He died and so we live.

He touched the rock pile, expecting a jolt of energy, but there was nothing – just peace.

"Can I help you?" The voice came from behind.

He looked up and saw the old man standing in the arch looking nervously down at him. From the standing stance he'd been just an old man, a shine of baldness crossed by wrinkles and sun-damaged scars, but from low on the ground, he looked so different so–

The colors of his world changed, full of powerful, immediate smells and vibrant sounds. A sense of awe and love swept away the despair. He recognized this man. He knew him with every sense, with every emotion. His friend, life companion, love, leader... his – his master?

"You look kind of familiar." The old man strained his aging eyes to get a better focus. "Do I know you?"

"Maybe," said Felix, but he didn't feel like Felix anymore. Felix was falling away like a fading smile, back to nothing, back to fragmented motes that watched and cared, but wanted no part of this world.

Instead of Felix, Rex eased up from the ground, feeling the prickle of the gun in his back pocket.

"You look kind of beat up," the Master said. "Better come inside. Millie used to be a nurse. She'll fix you up." He turned and ambled back through the rose arch, stroking the blooms with careful hands.

Rex pulled out the gun, eyed it thoughtfully, and then with a swing of his arm hurled it over the fence where it plopped into the lake and was gone. He raced after the old man on all-fours, rising back onto two.

"Do you like jazz?" the old man asked.

"I think I do," Rex said, barely able to contain his elation at being alive, at being free. At being here with his master. *The right heaven!*

"That's good, jazz is important. A great man once said, 'life is jazz'. I never understood what that meant until I was crusty and old."

Rex's mind wandered off to Cyc's destruction meme. He saw the baby, but those dominoes had fallen, and new forces held his mind together now. The voices were gone, but were still part of him on some different level. And Del? He was back with his Star-River, immersed and lost.

But Rex? Rex was complete, something new, not a brain or a human, but a chimera, a mind born on a somanetic substrate infecting the hijacked body of a brain-damaged man.

I am the very definition of Del's plague. An image of Mira jumped to his mind, her green, pain-addled eyes staring up from the greasy burger plate on route to Transit Mountain. "How come the Glow doesn't hurt you?" He didn't have the answer back then, but it was obvious now.

Mira, I am Glow! *And I choose not to harm myself.*

All things must end, and when the time came to save the world, Del would surely find a way to take back control. But not yet. Not here.

"I have a story to tell," Rex said.

"Well that's great. I like a good story."

He caught the old man up and skipped on ahead, eager to see the Mistress again and the underneath of their dining table. "It's kind of a long story."

"Well, that's fine," his Master said. "I don't have much time, but I've got all day."

ACKNOWLEDGMENTS

I'll start by thanking the robot army, the boots on the ground, the folks at Angry Robot Books. Many thanks to Etan Ilfeld and Eleanor Teasdale for choosing Glow out of countless manuscripts and taking the leap of faith in nurturing a new author through this daunting process. With special shoutouts to Angry Robot's editors: Gemma Creffield, Paul Simpson, Sam McQueen, and Rob Lowry. I have learned so much from your insights, comments and sheer patience. Big thanks to Glen Wilkins whose creative magic conjured this most succinct representation of Glow: The creature stepping through the O, the portal that divides the real world from the Glow-world.

Thanks to Sam Morgan, my agent, for acting as a smart, always-encouraging backdrop of wisdom and guidance for this project.

Thanks to my friends and family for all your support and for believing in this and all my crazy visions. Especially to Mum and Dad for giving it all in raising four boys. I think we all came out amazing and that's all on you.

And biggest thanks of all to my wife, Joanna, who is there every step of the way, in life and in authorship. Without your love I could never find the inner strength to do this.